Sierra,
Dreams do co
true even
they seem imp-
Thanks
Phil 4:13

The
Forest
of Arrows

Book 1: The Prince of Old Vynterra

V.F. SHARP

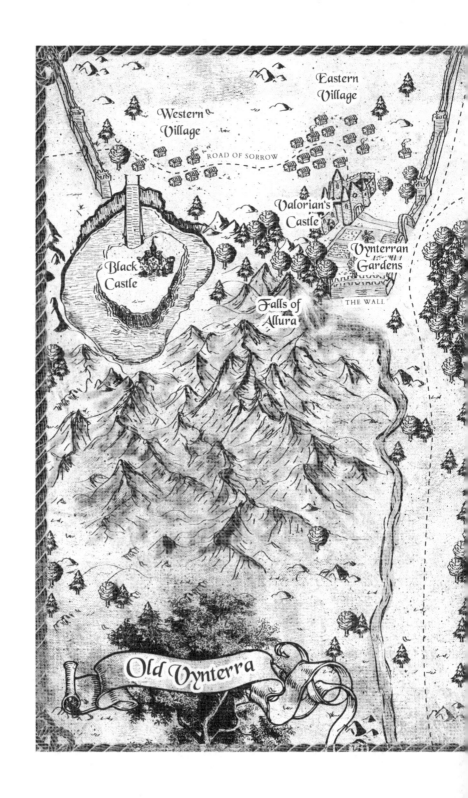

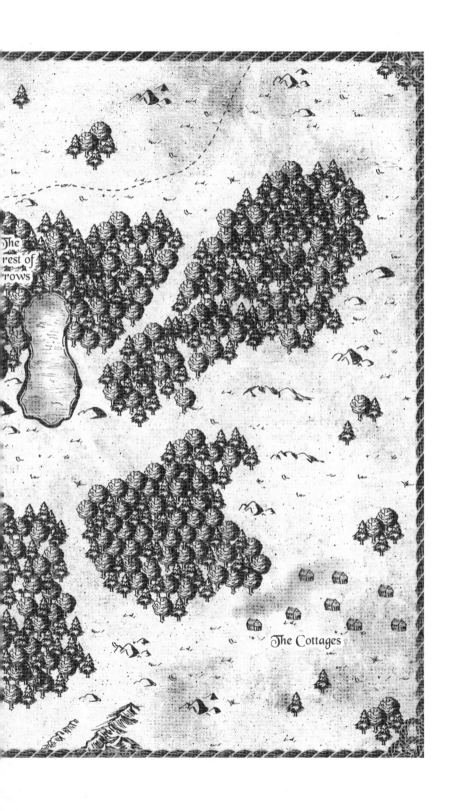

The
rest of
rows

The Cottages

ACKNOWLEDGMENTS

I would like to thank my fantastic editor, J.B. Manas, for not only doing an amazing job editing my book, but also taking me under his wing to teach and mentor me. The time he invested in me will not be forgotten, and I know that what I learned from his insights will shine in every novel I write. J.B., thank you for putting so much tender, loving care, into this story!

I'd like to thank my cover artist, Fran/rabBIT, for doing an incredible job on my cover and map and for being such a pleasure to work with!

Thank you to all my test readers, and especially, Azariah, my momma, and Lindsey. Your insights to the novel were crucial and helped me transform the areas that needed a bit more icing on the cake. Thank you Linds, for your brilliant proofreading, valuable suggestions, and tireless dedication. It assured the novel will be of the highest quality possible!

I'd like to thank DesNDave Photography for taking beautiful headshots! We all know that getting me to take them was like pulling teeth! Thank you for encouraging me to take them.

Thank you to my sister Des for sacrificing your time and using your resources to help me make some amazing bookmarks. They were gorgeous and exactly my style!

Thank you to my best friend, Crystle with an 'e'. Thank you for always being available to hear me cry and always being there to encourage me through the hard times and to celebrate with me during the exciting times. Love you!

Thank you to all my siblings for the encouragement and continuous love and help during this journey. Thank you, Dave and Des, Jesse and Lindsey and Tynisha and Maverick. And thank you Jesse, for letting me pick your brain on the story! Love you all!

And of course, thank you to my momma and daddy. Words couldn't fully express how important you are in my life. I love you both so much. Thank you for praying, pushing and encouraging me, *all* my life!

And mostly, thank you to my husband and to my babies who I will always call my babies! Thank you for your encouragement, excitement, patience, love, cooking, cleaning, and care during this busy time. I love you all more than my life.

Above all, thank you to my Lord and Savior Jesus Christ, who had given me an amazing dream one night, then gave me the courage to write the story and placing some very talented people in my path to make this new writing endeavor come true. Writing this book has drawn me closer and closer to You and may every book I write do the same.

Thank you to all my friends, social media friends, and supporters! Thank you for joining my journey, encouraging me, pushing me, rooting for me, caring for me, praying for me, supporting me, and being so awesome during this writing path. It truly means a lot to me.

The Forest of Arrows: The Prince of Old Vynterra

V.F. Sharp

For my handsome and amazing husband,
who supports *all* my endeavors and dreams.
I love you so much!
As your barista sidekick;
I love you a latte, more than I can fully espresso…

CHAPTER ONE

Ezstasia was ready, her fists clenched with determination as adrenaline pumped through her blood. She gripped the reins tightly as she sat mounted on Tia. As far as giant, long-eared rabbits went, Tia was one of the strongest, her soft brown fur covering a deceptively muscular frame. Ezstasia swallowed as she felt her long, loosely braided, brown hair blowing from side to side with the shifting breeze, tugging gently at the back of her head. She glanced down to make sure the tip of the braid didn't get caught on Tia's saddle. She remained still as she waited for Fin to draw his nine-arrow bow, launching the pointed weapons into the sky. Even after all these times playing *Arrows*, this part of the game still gave her a thrill—the calm before the storm.

There were nine riders playing, all friends who had known one another since childhood. They were all lined up, mounted on their bear-sized rabbits. Like her, they were all getting ready for the moment when they'd hear the loud call, "Arrows!"—the single word that would begin the game.

"Are you sure you checked this place out?" she said to Fin, without turning her eyes from the forest ahead.

"I'm telling you, it's perfect," he said. "There's no way anyone will see us here. We're hours away from the Cottages.

1

Or anything else, for that matter."

She turned to him and noticed he was delicately smearing the light blue powder on the nine arrows.

"What!?" she said, loosening her grip on the reins. "You're just putting the powder on *now*?"

"We can't play without it," said Fin.

She watched in disbelief as he applied the powder to the arrows with a small brush, like the great painters from the northern kingdoms.

"I can't believe you brought that whole bag of powder," she said. "You were supposed to apply it back at the Cottages. What if someone saw you with it?"

"Trust me, they didn't. Besides, this is the weakest kind of magic there is."

"It's still forbidden," she said, glancing around the perimeter for signs of prying eyes.

"Hey, I'm an artist," he said, smirking. "And I felt like working in the fresh air."

"Since when are you an artist?"

"Since today."

She shook her head and rubbed Tia's soft fur. It was sad to think the giant, beautiful rabbits were the last remnants of a bygone age, as was the ancient game of *Arrows*—a game Fin had discovered while reading the old scrolls. She would've loved to have lived during the days of magic and magical beings. Even at nineteen, it was still one of her greatest desires.

"Do you think the Magiclands are real?" she said to Fin.

"Of course, they're real," he said, continuing to paint.

"How do you know? Nobody's been there in ages."

"Can you see the wind?" he said.

"Of course not. Nobody can."

"Then how do you know it's real?" He laughed.

"That's stupid," she said. "I can at least feel the wind."

Just then, she felt an odd breeze, alternating between warm and cold air.

"Did you feel that?" she said.

Fin's forehead crinkled. "Feel what?"

"The wind. It was coming from straight ahead, where that big forest is. It was cool. But warm at the same time."

"Just like me," he said, grinning. "Cool, but warm."

"That's the cheesiest line you've ever served me. No, I'm serious, you didn't feel it?"

He looked up from his arrow and tapped his head. "The power of suggestion," he said. "You didn't know I had magical powers, did you? All I had to do was mention the wind, and then you felt it."

"Okay, great magic one, then I guess you don't need to be putting that powder on the arrows. You should be able to make them fly on your own, right?"

Fin laughed and bowed to her, as if to acknowledge his defeat. "You win the debate, my lady," he said, jokingly. After a brief pause, he turned to her again.

"But *I'll* win the game," he added, grinning.

"We'll see about that, Mr. Magic," she said. "Seriously, nobody's winning this game until you get those arrows done."

She watched as he returned to his 'painting.'

"Seriously," he said, "the wind is nothing to get mystified about. It happens every day in these parts."

"Not this kind of wind," she said quietly to herself.

Ezstasia once again glanced at her surroundings. The field ahead was just as Fin had described: a massive green pasture in the shape of an hourglass. Behind her to the south lied the green, rolling hills that led back to the farmlands of the Cottages.

She returned her gaze to the dense, unknown forest ahead, and noticed some unusually tall trees. Though still far in the distance, an odd beam of light could be seen escaping through the foliage, illuminating the mysterious forest with a soft glow. Intertwining vines wound their way from the treetops down to the trunks of the massive trees. She wondered what manner of ancient secrets hid within its thick brush.

"Ladies and gentlemen!" yelled Fin, shaking her out of her daydreams. "We're ready!" There was a smattering of cheers from the other riders.

Ezstasia resumed her grip on the reins, remaining still and ready as Fin slowly brought up his bow, aiming it directly toward the sky. She could hear nothing but the slight whisper of the wind as he slowly drew back the bowstring, adding the stretching sound of the wood to the wind's natural symphony. She followed his line of sight to a small crack in the clouds up above. There was complete silence. Then she heard the loud whisk of the bowstring as he released his fingers, sending the nine arrows speeding toward the small crevice in the sky.

The arrows traveled higher and higher into the air—a glistening rainbow mist trailing behind each one like a tail.

"Arrows!" Fin shouted. He quickly mounted his rabbit, and she and the entire group of friends instantly rode off in different directions; each rider going as fast as their rabbit could go. Ezstasia raced straight for the forest, hoping that when the arrows eventually came back down, at least one would travel in her direction. She noticed a few other riders heading in the same direction as her, including Fin.

As she held on tight to Tia and darted forward, she looked up into the clouds. At first, she couldn't find the arrows. Then she spotted the faint lines of the weapons high up in the sky, soaring upward until they were nearly out of sight. She returned her focus to the forest ahead and then glanced up again just in time to watch as the arrows ran out of momentum and turned, diving back down toward the earth.

The arrows plummeted, their speed accelerating and the magic colors streaming from their tail, growing brighter and brighter. Just as they were about to hit the ground where Fin had released them, all nine arrows changed direction. They began flying horizontally, parallel with the earth and toward different locations, as if they were following the various riders.

If all went as planned, each rider would have an arrow of their own to chase. Sure enough, a few of the arrows were headed in Ezstasia's direction as she headed toward the forest.

Now the game was on! She frantically squeezed her legs together to drive Tia forward. She glanced back to see the leftmost arrow headed her way.

"Come on, Tia," she said, leaning forward for maximum speed. "It'll be caught up in no time."

The rabbit raced forward at lightning speed as the wind blew against Ezstasia's face, making her gasp for air.

The arrows were faster than the rabbits, passing some of the riders overhead, and some passing beside them. Fin's arrow was about to pass him. She noticed Meldon to Fin's right, the sun reflecting off of his oversized glasses. A third arrow was flying just above him. Knowing Meldon's meticulous tendencies, he was probably calculating his arrow's weight and exact rate of velocity. He was the oldest of the group by a couple years, but he acted like he was eighty-five.

Ezstasia glanced back to see an arrow quickly gaining ground from behind her. She readied herself to lock in, just as she knew the other riders were doing with the other eight arrows. The chase for the first one to grab their respective arrow had begun. She wasn't sure how many riders were headed toward the forest with her, but she had noticed that a few of the others had headed the opposite way toward the hills.

All she knew was that she, Fin, and Meldon were about to be engulfed by trees as they rapidly approached the end of the open, green pasture, heading full speed into the thick, mysterious forest brush—each in pursuit of their own arrow.

Just as Ezstasia entered the forest, her left ear buzzed when an arrow whizzed past her.

"There it is, Tia!" she shouted. "Come on, you can do it. Let's win this game."

Tia sprinted faster and faster, disturbing leaves and dodging branches. One brushed Ezstasia on the cheek, leaving a small cut.

She maneuvered Tia as quickly as possible through the forest, avoiding anything that could slow down their speed.

"C'mon Tia! Stay focused on the arrow's tail." She gave Tia a light tap with her foot.

Just as Tia sped up, the arrow did the same. Its magical tail grew further and further away and made a quick turn to the right, disappearing into an especially dense part of the forest. Ezstasia tugged the reins and turned her rabbit in that direction, but the arrow was nowhere in sight.

"Oh no, we lost it!"

ℝ ℞ ℝ ℞

Fin was determined. One way or another, he was going to catch his arrow. After all, he had a reputation to uphold.

"Come on, Zon, there it is!" Zon, was the largest of all their rabbits. He was missing an eye, but it didn't slow him down. He was fast.

Zon was right on the arrow's tail, the magical colors glistening almost within reach. Fin could feel his heart racing,

6

but his focus was unrelenting. He knew he couldn't allow one obstacle to slow him down.

He shifted from side to side with Zon as he dodged trees. He had to duck occasionally as the branches were barely passing above his head. Fin was so intent on catching the arrow that he paid no attention to the scratches he knew were accumulating on his face and arms.

Fin realized they were drawing near to the speeding arrow. Carefully, he released one of his hands from the reins and reached to grab the arrow as Zon's speed brought him closer and closer to it. The tips of Fin's fingers were only a few feet away from the arrow's tail. He stayed in that position as they continued at high speed, dodging one tree after the other. His fingers were getting closer to the arrow, but then the arrow inched ahead.

"I am not... losing... this... game!"

As he steered Zon through the brush, damaging everything in their path, he could hear the crackling of branches breaking as falling leaves rained down upon him. Just then, a large leaf flew from out of nowhere and stuck to his face, obscuring his vision.

"Ah!" he yelled out, brushing it aside.

He reached back out. His fingers were just inches away from the arrow.

"Go Zon! Go!" he yelled.

With one final push from Zon, Fin grabbed the arrow with his right hand, closing his fist tightly around it.

As soon as he touched the arrow, he knew just what to expect. Within seconds, a huge flash of bright, colorful magic permeated the entire forest. Hues of sparkling greens, blues, purples, and reds showered down around him. He knew at that moment that all of the other arrows would be falling to the ground, as the game had been won.

"We won, Zon! You did it!" Fin always liked to give Zon

7

credit for the win. He was convinced it made Zon perform better.

He began to slow the tired rabbit down and raised the arrow over his head as if the trees would cheer him on.

"Yay, us," he said quietly to his imaginary cheering section.

"I knew we had this," he said, bringing Zon to a stop. "You get extra carrots today. Good job, buddy!"

Fin dismounted and let Zon eat some of the greenery off the ground cover, along with some berries that were in a nearby bush. It's amazing how many berries a five-foot tall rabbit can eat.

He grabbed the dented, faded tin canister that was tied to the saddle, and after taking a few large gulps, shared some with Zon.

"Okay Zon, let's head back to show them who won this game… again," he said, as he laughed and pet the rabbit's head.

Fin tied the canister back to the saddle, got on his rabbit, and headed to the open pasture where the game had begun.

ഭ ൞ ഭ ൞

Ezstasia had been so close to finally grabbing her arrow when it suddenly dropped like an anchor into a bush. Instantly, a huge flash of light appeared through the trees. She knew what that meant the moment it happened. Someone else had won. They had beaten her by a split second.

"Oh Tia, we were so close!"

Ezstasia began to gently run her hand across the top of Tia's head, as if the rabbit had any sense at all of what had just happened. Tia was still raring to go.

"It's okay girl, time to slow down. We'll get it next time."

As Tia slowed to a gentle hop, Ezstasia began looking around for the arrow.

"Where did it fall?" she said aloud, as if Tia would answer.

Ezstasia saw a tuft of powdered magic twinkle in a bush, just long enough for her to spot it before the colors faded away in an instant.

"Oh, there it is," she said. "It fell in that really thick bush over there." She winced as she saw the immense size of the thorny shrub. "Of course it did." She wondered why it couldn't have fallen in a place where she could've just easily grabbed it.

She dismounted when she got to the bush and allowed Tia to feed on the grass.

It was at this moment when Ezstasia noticed *how* mysterious this forest was. Nothing looked normal. Its beauty was breathtaking, and yet parts of it looked oddly out of place—and certainly not natural. Just then, a soft breeze in the distance whistled quietly and eerily. She could feel the fine hairs on her arms standing up.

"Why does this place seem so creepy now?" she said to Tia.

Tia began to shimmy a little further away toward a small bush brimming with purple berries. Ezstasia had barely noticed her, as she had been mesmerized by the forest. The bright flowers and berries seemed oddly out of place in the midst of the endless, winding vines and the giant tree trunks that spread out into ghostly formations. There were areas of shadowy darkness that were oddly punctuated by brighter patches, with lush green foliage that formed natural archways in different directions. Dark turned into light and light turned into dark, as if death and life were intertwined.

"I can't decide if this place looks enchanted or haunted." Indeed, it resembled her most beautiful dreams and her darkest nightmares.

Ezstasia stood still, slowly gazing around at the forest that now surrounded her. The ground below her feet was dark and slightly damp, and she noticed a soft, thin mist of steam delicately and slowly rising from it. Had it been there the whole time? She wasn't sure.

She walked under a vined archway until she came to a moss-covered area surrounded by a variety of bushes and trees with no commonality whatsoever. Many of the trees looked dead, but next to them were trees which were lush and full of leaves. She noticed some of the bushes were scraggly and full of thorns, while others were green and thick, with small, bell-shaped red and purple berries.

Her curiosity piqued, she proceeded to another clearing that was much larger and her mouth dropped. There were endless shades of green all around her. The moss that covered most of the ground was a bright green—the brightest she had ever seen—punctuated by the darker grass that grew in large tufts throughout.

As she looked closer at some of the surrounding trees, she marveled at the sheer size of some of the trunks, many which ran together, forming a thick base. As they rose higher, they resembled snakes, twisting around one another all the way to the top. It looked like each one was trying to be higher than the previous one.

She noticed three other trees that looked like giant arms were coming out of the ground. The top of each tree was shaped like a hand with the palm facing upward. Each palm had several finger-like branches that seemed to extend out in different directions as if to grab the nearest prey. The trees had no leaves at all and appeared dead except for the odd patches of moss that traveled up the trunk and on each 'finger.'

She walked further and came upon a couple of the largest trees yet. They stood majestically, as if they were the grandfathers of all trees. They were the width of several cottages and extended up so high they seemed to reach the clouds. She felt so small, she half expected one of them to just step out of its roots and crush her. These trees, too, had snake-like roots twisting from the ground all the way up the trunk, as far as she could see. The climbing roots clung to the tree like parasites that had no fear of anything or anyone, *for they knew who they grew on.* Indeed, these majestic trees, beautiful yet imposing, were to be revered and respected. The roots knew it, and she knew it, too.

She turned briefly to look for Tia and noticed something else she hadn't seen before—a misty blue fog off in the distance. As she looked around, she could see between the trees that it surrounded the forest in all directions. She couldn't tell whether her eyes were playing tricks or if the blue mist had actually created shapes that looked like thousands upon thousands of dancing silhouettes around her. As she walked, she noticed the silhouettes always kept the same distance from her.

Between the strange trees, the blue mist, and the visions of dancing figures—as beautiful as it was, this perplexing forest had begun to flood her senses. She was beginning to feel nervous and anxious. Besides, she had to get back to the open field. The others must be waiting for her by now.

"Tia! Tia, where are you?"

She was so wrapped up in the forest that she had nearly forgotten about her rabbit. Worse yet, she wasn't even sure what direction she was facing now. Just as she started experiencing a feeling of panic inside her chest, she heard a rustling of leaves behind her. She turned around quickly and looked through another moss-covered archway of vines. She could make out a familiar figure up ahead.

"Tia, there you are!"

She walked through the archway, and that's when her

heart nearly stopped. She saw a handful of trees that simply gave her chills. The trees were almost completely black, and looked like the harbinger of death itself—or worse yet, the thing that you send to scare the harbinger of death. Almost immediately, she felt a solitary, cool wind blow right through her, which made the hairs on the back of her neck stand up. She felt as if these particular trees were sucking the life out of her just by looking at them. She was frozen. They were big, for sure, though not like the majestic ones. No, these trees were intimidating in an entirely different way. They had a dark presence about them, even more so than any of the other trees she'd seen.

Though Ezstasia wanted to back away, she remained still as a rock, studying the trees in more detail. The different sized roots came up from random spots in the ground, without design or formation. They were all entangled, almost as if they were lost or rebellious, refusing to grow how they were designed to.

Some roots grabbed onto others, as if fighting to kill, fighting for breath, fighting for power, as they climbed over one another all the way up the tree. Others remained separate and alone, each one standing straight up from the ground with a perfectly vertical posture and a point like a dagger. The branches that grew atop the trees also came to a sharp point, as if each tree had an assortment of knives and swords at its disposal to ward off any visitors. And it must have worked, because there wasn't a single sign of green life—or any color for that matter—growing on it or near it. Even the grass kept its distance. Maybe she should, too.

Indeed, these trees instilled a fear that was different than what the majestic ones conjured. There was a sense of the darkest of forces being entwined and harbored in these trees. Ezstasia felt in the depths of her soul as if nothing but pure evil lived there.

A shuffling sound nearby brought her out of her stupor. She turned to see Tia's reins dragging on the ground as the oblivious rabbit stopped at each bush to graze for berries. Ezstasia picked up the reins and climbed up onto Tia.

"It's time to go, girl. This place is starting to freak me out. We need to leave. Now."

Heading back, as she passed one of the bushes, she spotted a small sparkle of colored, twinkling magic—no doubt from her arrow.

"The arrow! How could I forget that? If anyone found that arrow, we'd be in serious trouble." She briefly thought about the danger of anyone finding the arrow with the residue of forbidden magic, and the consequences that would follow for her and her friends.

She jumped off of Tia and ran toward the bush, not wanting to spend another moment in this forest. Just as she was about to kneel down and reach into the thick brush for it, she saw something moving out of the corner of her eye. As she turned toward it, she could have sworn that she saw one of the black, dagger-shaped roots move. It was pointed right toward her and was connected to one of the largest of the black trees. She was positive that it hadn't been facing in her direction before.

Ezstasia felt her heart pounding in her throat. The chills that ran down her spine before were now permeating her entire body. She felt paralyzed with fear. Unable to move, she stood there like a statue, listening to the sounds around her—her senses now elevated. She could hear the slight breeze whistling in her ear, the gentle rustling of the leaves, the songs the long grass made as it gently swayed—and then she heard something chewing close by. She turned to see Tia up ahead, chewing on more berries.

Tia looked up at her, tufts of greens hanging out the sides of her mouth. She stopped chewing as she stared at Ezstasia, almost as if *she* was confused by Ezstasia's mannerisms and could sense her fear. Then she resumed her normal rabbit duties and continued chewing as she searched for more berries.

Just then, Ezstasia heard a branch crack from behind her. She didn't even look to see what it was. She bolted toward Tia as fast as she could.

"Forget that arrow! We're getting out of here now!"

She leapt onto Tia. She wasn't about to waste another second in this place.

"Let's go! Hurry!"

She was about to grab the reins when Tia darted forward. She could have sworn something grabbed her foot at the same time, but it all happened too fast. As the rabbit sped off, she tumbled backward. The next thing she knew, her head hit the ground really hard. A sharp pain enveloped her head and began to throb. She thought she heard Tia's footsteps racing off into the distance, and then everything became foggy. She heard branches cracking nearby, and then her vision slowly faded to black.

CHAPTER TWO

Fin couldn't wait to see everyone's reactions when they would come to find out that he was the first to grab his arrow. His friends were always amazed that he managed to pull off victory after victory, no matter how challenging it seemed. He loved the praise. It made the cuts and scars he had received while playing all worth it. Truth be told, he even impressed himself, and he was a hard one to impress. He kept replaying the picture of his winning grab over and over again in his mind as he began to slowly ride Zon back through the dense forest.

He saw the bright sunlight through the cracks of the trees, and caught a glimpse of the familiar field up ahead, its green grass glistening. He felt the proudness rise within him as he realized he was almost at the pasture. Fin dismounted and decided to give Zon a well-deserved rest. He held Zon's reins as he walked beside him.

"I can't wait to see their faces, Zon! It's been a while, my friend." He lifted the arrow up in victory again. "Just remember, today is *our* day, you and me. When we're together, nobody can—"

He stopped mid-sentence. He noticed a weird movement at the top of one of the trees up ahead. Two small vines that climbed up the tree seemed to extend out in a quick jolt, twisting around one another.

"Did you see that?"

He pulled the reins for Zon to stop as he gazed up at the tree. Nothing up in the tree was moving now. Not only that, but he couldn't even find the twisted vine he had seen, no matter which angle that he looked from.

"I could've sworn I just saw vines or a branch moving," he said aloud to himself. "Strange."

He stared at the vines and branches for a moment and then glanced over at Zon, who was standing there looking like he was waiting for a treat—a rabbit's priorities, as it were. With no treat forthcoming, Zon began searching for something to munch on in the nearby greenery.

"You know, Zon—I really wish you could talk." The rabbit looked up at him again, as if he knew he was being addressed.

"Hey don't look at me like that. I'm already seeing things, so why not a talking giant, one-eyed bunny?"

He took one last gaze up at the tree and then shrugged his shoulders.

"Ha! I'm definitely seeing things. Let's go Zon. It was probably a squirrel." Fin mounted back up onto Zon and steered him toward the sunlit, open green pasture.

He was halfway toward the middle of the field where the game had started when he looked around and saw the other riders emerging. Some had their arrows on their backs, some had them in their hands, and some had them tied to their rabbit's saddle. He couldn't stop grinning as he held up his arrow to show everyone. He felt like one of the great knights from the scrolls.

When he got to the center of the pasture, he stopped, dismounted and waited for the others to catch up. He was mentally preparing his victory speech when he noticed that two riders were missing.

One by one, he looked at each of his friends' faces as they got closer. Everyone was there except for Ezstasia and Meldon. Knowing Meldon, he was probably still somewhere calculating exactly how he lost. But Ezstasia should have been back by now. He'd seen her enter the forest just before he did. Besides, her rabbit, Tia, was one of the fastest. Oh well, they would turn up sooner or later.

෮   ෬   ෮   ෭

Meldon couldn't find the arrow he was chasing, even *with* his new wide-view glasses, which he had specifically constructed for this game. He thought he saw it land in a section of the tall grass. In fact, he was sure of it. But now that he was looking there, it was nowhere to be found.

He scanned the area but to no avail. The fact that the arrow wasn't exactly where he was sure to have seen it land, was defying logic, and this made him extremely nervous and frustrated. He was an over-analyzer by nature, and he always liked to consider every possibility. As usual, he had tried to warn everyone about the risks of playing Arrows.

Some people liked adventure, but to Meldon, if there wasn't adequate planning, it meant foolishly taking risks. Well, this was the last time he would do that. Of course, he's said that at least three times before, but this time, he meant it.

After looking a few more minutes, he decided to dismount his rabbit, Mr. Feet, a name he'd chosen because of the bunny's extra-large feet—appendages that were massive even by giant rabbit standards. He wrapped Mr. Feet's reins around a branch from one of the tall bushes. Reaching into the bag on the rabbit's saddle, he pulled out the can that had the word *water* etched onto the side of it. He had marked the canister to differentiate it from the can of lime root and hydrated calendula flowers he'd concocted, just in case anyone got hurt. Scanning the ground, he spotted a perfect piece of fallen bark that could be used as a water saucer. The sides from the bark were slightly lifted, so it no doubt came from a knot in the tree's trunk. He brushed all the dirt and leaves out of it with his hand and placed it on the ground, filling it with some of the water from his can.

"Drink up while I find that arrow, Mr. Feet."

He reached in the bag again and pulled out two carrots with the greens still attached, just as he and Mr. Feet liked. Everyone had always teased Meldon for how well he organized his bag, but that's just how he preferred to operate. Each time, he would take pleasure in telling them, "I only know one way to do something. The right way. And that means proper planning." Fin would then roll his eyes, but, as strong and heroic as he was, he'd still listen. Even Fin had to give him some credit. He was usually right.

Content with his organizational skills, Meldon held the two carrots next to one another and examined them.

"Here, you can have the bigger one," he said. "You rode well. But we can't always win, can we? No, we can't. I always tell you that. But we would sure beat them all in Kingsman's Chess now, wouldn't we?"

He placed Mr. Feet's carrot right by his saucer of water and kept the smaller one for himself. Munching the carrot, he began to look around for his arrow. He examined the surrounding bushes, looked on the sides of some nearby fallen trees, and trudged through all the tall grass in the area. There was still no sign of the arrow.

One thing he hadn't noticed before, though, was just how unusually beautiful this forest was. A tremendous variety of plants, with varying levels of intense greens and bursting with flowers of every shape and color, were scattered as far as he could see. The colors were more vibrant than any he had ever seen, even more than in Mr. Codsworth's garden—which, incidentally, everyone paid good money to see. As he looked up, several thick vines cascaded down and looked as if they were hanging from the sky, ready to be swung on.

"Sweet carrot sticks, will you look at all this! I am actually glad that I haven't found the arrow, Mr. Feet. Otherwise, I might never have had the chance to see such beauty. It's exquisite! And a child's dream, I might add. Those vines would be a delight to swing on. Well, not by me. By someone else of course. And I don't mind saying, without some sort of stability check, whoever that someone is would be asking to hit the ground like a melon. Ew. No, thanks."

Just as he was contently devouring the last piece of his carrot, something caught his eye. A blue mist rose in the distance. When he squinted his eyes, it appeared to contain dancing shadows of something—or someone.

"Astounding! That fog looks like human silhouettes."

He stared at the mist more intently, trying to make out what it could be.

"You know, Mr. Feet. If I hadn't been privy to the ancient stories of powerful magic—especially the... well, you know which I speak of, I dare not even say it. But if I didn't know about all of that magic having been seized many years ago, I'd say this place may have had some very strong magic placed upon it."

He stood there a few moments longer, staring at the distant fog. It was mesmerizing to watch the smoky silhouettes slowly dancing, swaying from side to side—each one vanishing to make room for another to appear. This was one beautiful, ghostly dance.

"There must be hundreds, or possibly thousands, of silhouettes all around us. It's strange, they keep disappearing and reappearing every second. It's like we're surrounded by a massive army of... fog soldiers."

That made him think of something.

"You know what this reminds me of? It makes me think of cumulonimbus clouds which continuously form a shape, and then another, as—"

He realized Mr. Feet was paying no attention, he was too busy munching on the remaining piece of his carrot.

"I guess it doesn't matter what it reminds me of, does it, Mr. Feet? If we don't hurry and get back, everyone's going to be pretty concerned!"

He took one last look around, analyzing whether the risk of losing the arrow was less than the risk of staying too late in the forest trying to find it.

Just then he noticed a glimmering sparkle in the tall grass.

"What?! There's no way it's there. That was the first place I looked."

He made his way toward the tall grass.

"Maybe it's some kind of sparkly insect." In truth he couldn't think of any insect that sparkled like that.

As he approached the area, lo and behold, the arrow was sitting right on top, creating a large dent of the same shape in the grass. It wasn't even hidden and would've been impossible to miss. He stood there staring down at it in disbelief.

"I know I looked here. I specifically made a point of methodically looking section by section in this very spot. I looked here, Mr. Feet. I know I looked here."

He could feel his face getting red. Now he wasn't just confused; he was angry. Clearly, something was amiss here.

He picked up the arrow and stomped back to Mr. Feet, hurriedly grabbing the reins from the bush. He tied the arrow securely to his saddle using one of the loose ropes that was hanging from it. As he mounted Mr. Feet, he slowly took one last look at the forest around him and shook his head.

"I'm no fool," he said, studying the trees once more to reassure himself he wasn't crazy. Frustrated, he rode off.

Meldon didn't like having his mind played with. If there was one thing he could count on in this world, it was being able to count on things that could be counted on. And now he couldn't even count on that.

As he rode back toward the pasture, he went over the situation in his head. He began to question his initial search: *Maybe I didn't look there. Was it another piece of grass that I thought was that one? I could've sworn...*

He remembered, he had specifically mapped out the sections as he'd searched. No, there was nothing wrong with him. It was this forest.

Finally, he saw the light of the open green grass pasture ahead and sped up to exit the forest. His friends were just ahead on their rabbits. They looked like they were arguing about something. Then someone pointed his way and they all yelled his name, rushing toward him on their rabbits.

"Meldon, what took you so long?" Fin yelled as he approached. "Are you okay?"

"Yes," said Meldon. "I was just enjoying the beauty of the forest. Was I gone that long?"

"Yes you were," said Fin. "Do you have the arrow?"

"Yes, of course I have it," said Meldon. "You know I'd never—"

"Is Ezstasia with you?" said Lanzzie, trotting up behind Fin.

"Your sister isn't back yet?"

"No," said Lanzzie, "she hasn't come out of the forest."

Meldon found himself distracted and mesmerized by Lanzzie's beauty. She was one of the most stunning girls he had ever seen. She always wore ribbons in her long, dark hair, with dainty trinkets placed at perfect intervals. Her hair was always styled beautifully, and he couldn't help but to admire her precision and perfectionism. As she stared at him with a quizzical look, he couldn't avoid noticing her wide, hazel-green eyes.

"Meldon!" said Lanzzie, snapping him out of his trance. "Did you see Ezstasia in there?"

Lanzzie dismounted her rabbit and began walking past him toward the forest.

"I didn't see her," he said. "But she may still be exploring. That's a pretty crazy forest."

"Crazy how?" said Fin.

"Well… uh… beautiful crazy," he said. "There's a lot to see." He didn't want to get into too much detail or they would have thought him mad. And he especially didn't want *Lanzzie* to think he was bonkers.

"I'm going to ride along the tree line and call her," said Lanzzie.

Meldon watched as she climbed back up onto her rabbit, Jewel, the whitest and fluffiest of all the rabbits. Everyone knew Lanzzie always cared for Jewel like it was her own child.

He stood silently as Lanzzie grabbed Jewel's white reins, which were fittingly embroidered with different colored jewels. She rode off calling Ezstasia's name as she rode along the tree line.

"I'm gonna join her," said Fin as he mounted Zon. "It's getting dark soon and it'll be harder for Ezstasia to find her way out."

"Yes," said Meldon, "calling her name may help if she's confused about which direction she's facing." He steered Mr. Feet beside Fin to join him.

"Let's split up," said Fin. "We can all ride along the tree line, but don't go back into the forest unless you see her. We don't need to lose anyone else."

"You don't have to tell me twice," said Meldon. He knew

all too well what kind of weird things were happening in that forest and especially didn't want to be in that place after dark.

He followed Fin and the rest of the group, as they split into different sections along the forest line.

As they rode back and forth along the tree line shouting out Ezstasia's name, Meldon began to grow worried as he mapped out what could've happened to her. There could've been so many reasons why she wasn't back yet, compounded with the possibility that there might be magic in that forest. He gazed at the others along the forest line as they each waved a hand horizontally to indicate they hadn't seen any sign of her yet.

Time passed and there was still no sign of her. She definitely should've been out by now. Meldon felt a gnawing in the pit of his stomach as he began to get the disheartening sense that something was truly wrong. The skies were growing darker, and his outlook along with it. Always one to contemplate the risks, he began planning for the worst. If they had to go back into the forest, what approach should they take so that they didn't all get lost? And what if they still didn't find her? How could they possibly return to the Cottages without her? And what would they even tell the townspeople? After all, they had been playing with magic, which presented its own set of problems. Even with weak magic, they could all be thrown into the dungeons.

He was terrified for Ezstasia. She was such a kind girl, just like her sister, but more curious, almost naïve in a way. He sure hoped her curiosity didn't get her into trouble in that forest. But Ezstasia was resourceful. That girl didn't give up. He truly believed she would turn up eventually.

After what seemed like hours, and with the sun quickly setting, there still wasn't any sign of Ezstasia. He watched helplessly as Fin rode up and down the forest line, telling everyone to meet back in the center of the pasture. It was time to make some decisions.

€ &#x2; € &#x2;

Fin was nearly at the center of the pasture when he saw Lanzzie rushing toward him looking as if she were about to cry or hurt someone—or both.

"Fin!" she yelled as she approached. "We're running out of sunlight. We have no time for this. We need to get back out there now and keep looking. Every minute counts."

He knew she'd be upset. Of course she was, it was her sister.

"Lanzzie—"

"We can't leave her there, Fin!" said Lanzzie in desperation. "Not in that dark forest. There's nothing to discuss."

"Lanz, please calm down. We can't fall apart right now. We have to be strong."

"I'm not leaving without my sister."

Before he could reply, she turned her rabbit around toward the forest and began heading away.

"I'm going," she yelled back at them, "no matter what you all decide to do."

"She's right, Fin," said a female voice from behind him. It was Jezreel. "I'm going with her." No surprise there. Jezreel was about as compassionate as they come. Everyone always tagged her as meek and dainty—someone who needed looking after. But the truth was, she was always caring for everyone else.

Jezreel steered her rabbit around toward Lanzzie. "Come on, Buttons," she said. The grey rabbit, like her, was the runt of the litter.

Fin heard someone else moving behind him, too. It was Ithron.

"You're going, too?" said Fin.

"If I must," said Ithron, who sounded completely indifferent, though his concern for Jezreel wasn't hard to miss. Actions spoke louder than words. She was about the only thing he seemed to care about, though he'd likely never admit it.

"Will everyone please stop for a minute?" said Fin.

Fin gazed out at Lanzzie, who was still riding away.

"Wait!" he yelled, loud enough for her to hear.

Lanzzie halted her rabbit and turned to face him.

"I have an idea!" he yelled. He motioned for her to come back, but she put her hands on her hips in protest.

"Just hear me out," he shouted. "That's all I ask."

He watched as patiently as he could as Lanzzie raced back.

"You better hurry," she said as she approached. "The sun's setting. I don't have much time."

"Everyone gather around," he said. "You all need to hear this."

He looked at Meldon as others approached. "Is everyone here?"

"I count seven of us," said Meldon.

Fin glanced around. Lanzzie, who looked ready to dart away any second, Jezreel, and Meldon all stood around him. Ithron was just outside of their small circle, only half paying attention as he sharpened a stick with his dagger. The twins, Zander and Randin had just arrived as well.

"We seem to be missing somebody," said Meldon.

Pallu, pudgy and red-faced as always, came meandering into the circle, holding a giant loaf of bread.

"Do you ever stop eating?" said Zander.

"Why would I?" said Pallu. The way he crinkled his brow made it seem as if Zander had asked him if he ever stopped breathing.

"Guys!" said Lanzzie. "I'm leaving here in two seconds.

25

Start talking."

Fin gave one last look to make sure he had everyone's attention and took a deep breath.

"Okay," he said. "I don't have to tell you all, but just as a reminder, if the people from the Cottages find out we were playing with magic, we'll be locked up—or worse."

"Locked up?" said Zander. "We could be beheaded!"

"Zander," said Randin, "beheadings are just for dark magic. We'd be hung at worst."

"What's the difference?" said Zander.

"Gentlemen," said Meldon. "The treaty clearly states that frivolous, harmless magic—which this is—warrants a minimum of ten years in the dungeons. The laws haven't changed in hundreds of years. You should read it sometime."

"But is it?" said Ithron.

"Is it what?" said Meldon.

"Is the magic harmless? We just lost someone while using it. That *is* why we're standing here discussing it, right?"

"He's right," said Zander. "She could be missing her arms and legs for all we know. And—"

"Not helping, Zander," said Randin, always the calmer of the two.

"That's it!" said Lanzzie. "I'm leaving."

"Wait, Lanz," said Fin. "Can we all agree that being locked up in the dungeons would not be a good thing? And that if we *are* locked up, then we can't be out here looking for Ezstasia?"

"What's your point?" said Lanzzie.

"My point is, that if we go back into that forest, everyone will realize by nightfall that we're all missing. Especially when we don't check in our rabbits. They'll come looking for us. And then what'll we tell them?"

"How about that we're on a camping trip?" said Pallu. "I brought plenty of food for all of us. They may even believe it. I always pack lots of—"

"That won't work," said Fin. "We have to report any camping trips to the stable keepers way ahead of time."

"He's right," said Meldon. "You know the rules, Pallu. We have to have the rabbits checked in by nightfall and overnight trips must be reported in advance to get approval."

"Exactly," said Fin.

"So, if we can't go into the forest," said Meldon, "what *is* your plan?"

"We go back to the Cottages now, and—"

"Without my sister?" said Lanzzie. "You brought me back here for *this*?"

"Hear me out," he said. "We need to show our faces back there so that there isn't any attention drawn to us. We check in our rabbits and we meet in the morning at the stables and come back here first thing. Ezstasia's a strong girl. You know that better than anyone."

"That's not a plan!" said Lanzzie.

"Listen, Pallu still lives with his parents. What do you think will happen if he doesn't come home?"

"He's right, you know," said Pallu. "They'll have a search party out here in no time."

"And trust me, that search party will make sure we're all accounted for," said Fin. "But if we all go back and check in our rabbits, and people see most of us, they'll assume we're all back. Plus, it'll give us a chance to hide these arrows and the magic I brought. It's the safest plan. It's the *only* plan at this point."

"I still can't believe you brought the magic," said Lanzzie. "And did it ever occur to you that the search party can help us look for her?"

"Lanz," said Fin, "they can't catch us with these arrows, or even worse—this!" He held up the bag of magic powder. "I'm sorry I brought it. But think hard and listen to what I'm saying."

"What about Tia?" said Meldon. "If we go back now, that might draw attention toward Ezstasia if her rabbit's missing."

Fin thought for a moment. Meldon had a point. Leave it to him to think of every possibility.

"I have an idea," said Jezreel. Everyone looked at her. She wasn't usually one to speak up. "What if we say that Ezstasia felt like sleeping with her rabbit tonight?"

Zander threw up his hands. "Yeah, sure, they'll believe that," he said, not even attempting to hide his sarcasm.

"No, she's right," said Meldon. "It's better than having nine rabbits missing. At least they'll have eight checked in and a report of where the last one is. And she's done it once before."

"There you have it," said Fin. "If it's good enough for Meldon, it's good enough for me."

"Won't she get in trouble?" said Randin. "I mean, for not checking in her rabbit?"

"Yes, but she isn't here to get in trouble," said Fin. "And when we find her, we can deal with it then. At least we won't all be in dungeons for using magic."

"Always a good thing," said Ithron.

"I like this plan!" said Pallu.

Lanzzie cleared her throat.

"What about the part where my sister spends the night alone in the forest? Are you all forgetting that part?"

Fin put a hand on her shoulder to comfort her and spoke softly. "Lanzzie, it's hard for all of us to have to leave her. You're her sister, but we all care about her. Can't you see that we have no other choice? If we get caught, then none of us can help her. You understand that, right?"

"You're overcomplicating this," she said. "Why can't we just go find her and if they come looking for us, we'll just tell them we were exploring and lost her?"

"You're forgetting about the arrows," he said. "We can't ditch them. It's nighttime, and the powder doesn't completely wear off, they glisten. You've seen it yourself, it can take days. And what about this entire bag of magic?"

Lanzzie paused for a moment and took a deep breath, apparently trying to calm herself.

"Okay," she said, "then what if we go back, check in the rabbits, and come right back here?"

"On foot? It would take forever. By the time we got here it would be the middle of the night. It'll be dark and we'd never see a thing. *And* we'd be on foot. Better to come in morning with our rabbits. At least we'd be prepared and better able to do a proper search. I'm sorry, but that's a bad idea Lanz."

Lanzzie held her head down. It looked like she was finally getting it. He felt bad for her though. He couldn't imagine what she was going through.

He leaned in.

"Remember," he said. "We always pack plenty of food and water for ourselves and the rabbits, so she at least has food for the evening. We'll come first thing in the morning. I promise we'll find her."

"Some of us," said Zander, patting Pallu on the belly, "pack excessive amounts of food."

"The smart ones do," said Pallu. "You just never know when your stomach will scream out that it's hungry." Pallu was about to take another bite from his loaf of bread, when he stopped and looked at Lanzzie.

"Lanz," he said. "Fin's right. She'll be fine. You know how many crazy adventures Ezstasia has gone on alone?"

"Yes, but why hasn't she come out by now?" Lanzzie looked back at the forest. "She's tough. She would have found a way."

"Even if she got lost," said Pallu, "she's smart and maybe

decided it was safer to camp out for the night. We shouldn't assume something bad. I'm just saying—"

Pallu paused to take one last bite from his loaf of bread before tucking it back into his food bag. Unlike the others, he always brought three saddle bags—two just for food and one for supplies. Fin thought Pallu was clumsy and forgetful, but that curly-haired, freckle-faced, roly-poly bear had a heart of gold.

Speaking of forgetful, Fin noticed something seemed to be missing from Pallu's saddle bag.

"Hey, Pallu?" said Fin.

Pallu looked up with the face of innocence.

"You do have your arrow, right?"

"Oh, my arrow," said Pallu. "Um, yeah... so... about that."

"You don't have it?"

"Pallu!" said Lanzzie. "You're kidding me, right? Please say you're kidding. We don't have time to deal with this."

"It's okay," said Pallu. "I—"

"This isn't happening," said Lanzzie. "This really isn't happening."

"Why didn't you say anything?" said Fin.

"Hold on, well, wait," said Pallu, "I was going to, and then all the talk about Ezstasia made me forget."

Fin shook his head.

Pallu opened his saddle bag again and took a piece of bread out, probably out of subconscious stress.

"You probably lost it when you stopped to eat," said Lanzzie, smacking the bread out of his hand. "Do you and your fat rabbit always have to be eating?"

Startled, Pallu quickly pet his rabbit as if to comfort him. "She didn't mean it, Thumps. She's just upset."

Though Thumps had fat, round cheeks and an ever-growing double chin, he was really cute. And, like the other rabbits, he was completely oblivious to what was going on.

"Ugh!" said Lanzzie, as she turned her rabbit around and headed toward the large rolling hills that led back to the Cottages.

"So… you're okay with going back?" Fin said, relieved. He knew he was annoying her.

"We don't have a choice, remember!" she shouted without turning around.

Fin watched as Lanzzie and Jewel rode off. Most of the others began to do the same. He shrugged and turned to Pallu, who was always the last to leave—or arrive—or to do anything for that matter.

"What were you thinking?" he said. "You know how—"

"Fin, I didn't lose my arrow."

"You what?! You didn't?"

He watched as Pallu walked to where the bread fell, picked it up and looked at it for a few seconds. He gently brushed it along his shirt a couple times to shake off the grass and dirt and took another bite.

"No, I know where it is. It got tangled in some bushes on the hillside," said Pallu, as he attempted to mount his rabbit, which took a few tries. "I just needed help crawling in there and cutting it loose. My… uh… 'manly' size limited my ability to get it."

Fin laughed and rustled up Pallu's auburn hair. "Well, you manly-sized, curly-haired beast, let's go get it. Lead the way."

He followed Pallu as the others made their way toward the Cottages.

"You know what I'm thinking?" said Pallu.

"Is this about dinner?" Fin said, smiling. It felt good to smile amidst all this worry. Pallu often had that effect. He could make anyone smile even on their worst day.

"Dinner?" said Pallu. "No, of course not. I'll just munch on my way back."

"I figured you would," said Fin.

"It's about breakfast. I can make us a hearty and delicious breakfast tomorrow so that we'll have lots of energy for the road."

Fin grinned and shook his head.

"Hey," said Pallu.

Fin looked at him and raised his eyebrows.

"We're going to find her, Fin. She's my best friend. I can't, and won't, live without her."

"I hope we do," said Fin. He gazed ahead and nodded toward Lanzzie in the distance. "Especially for her sake."

CHAPTER THREE

As soon as the sunlight hit her face through the eastern window, Lanzzie jumped out of bed. She'd slept in her clothes so that she'd be ready to go as soon as she opened her eyes. She'd already packed a bag full of food and supplies that would help her survive for a handful of days.

Though she had agreed last night to return to the Cottages if they hadn't found Ezstasia by sunset, she'd stay until she found her. She wouldn't allow any negotiations today. There was no way she was coming back without her sister.

She grabbed the arrow from under her mattress and examined it for a second as it twinkled. For a moment, she wondered if she should take it. After all, if her quest to find Ezstasia took days, someone might investigate her disappearance and search her cottage. She started to put it into her orange, canvas sack, and then paused. She remembered Fin's concern the previous night, if someone searched her sack for whatever reason, they might notice the sparkles instantly.

"Stop being stupid," she said out loud to herself.

She pulled the arrow back out and placed it back underneath her mattress. Ready to go, she walked out of her bedroom and into her small kitchen. She grabbed two water

cans that were on the round, walnut table and tied one of
them to the wooden stick of items she was taking with her,
placing the other in her orange sack. Finally, she headed to
the front door to leave. Just as she opened the door, she
turned and took one last melancholy look at her cozy home,
wondering if things would ever be the same again. She shook
the thoughts from her head, then stepped outside, closed the
door and slowly turned the key to lock it.

"You're up early, Lanzzie," said a cheerful, squeaky voice,
though it made her nearly jump out of her skin. She turned
to see her neighbor, Miss Ponzo, standing a few yards away,
holding a braided wicker basket full of vegetables and bread.
She had a white napkin gently placed over the food. Her six-
year old boy was next to her with tangled hair falling into his
eyes. He tugged on her long, worn-out dress which was so
faded that it was hard to see the floral design that had been
originally printed on it.

"Good morning to you."

Miss Ponzo was a heavy woman, and very sweet. The
white bonnet she wore on her head made her face look more
red than it was, and the matching apron she was wearing
didn't help.

"Um, good morning, Miss Ponzo," Lanzzie said, as she
tried to quickly walk away.

"Lanzzie, wait. I have a question for you."

Lanzzie stopped, worried for a moment. "Yes, Miss
Ponzo?" she said, as she slowly turned around.

"I'm sorry, I couldn't help but notice, it looks like you're
packed for quite a journey. Are you planning to be gone for a
few days?"

Though the jovial woman smiled, Lanzzie wondered what
she was getting at.

"I'm not sure, but I may be. I'm visiting some friends in
the lower Cottages."

"Oh, where at? I have cousins there."

Lanzzie thought for a moment. "I'm not quite sure exactly," she said.

"Oh," said Miss Ponzo, looking like she was contemplating the situation. "Well, would you like me to look after your place? I'd be happy to."

Now what? If she didn't take her up on the offer, she might grow suspicious on why she'd refused or what she was up to. She may even question if she was hiding something in her home. Or maybe Lanzzie was just being paranoid. Either way, now Miss Ponzo was fully aware that she'd be gone and would be observing the length of her journey.

Realizing she was taking too long to respond, she finally blurted it out.

"Actually, that would be wonderful. Are you sure it's not too much trouble?"

"Not at all," said Miss Ponzo.

"Thanks. I owe you."

Lanzzie quickly turned to walk away and then heard Miss Ponzo clearing her throat, no doubt trying to get her attention. Lanzzie was so anxious to get to her rabbit that she pretended she didn't hear.

"Lanzzie? Aren't you forgetting something?" Lanzzie turned around.

"I need a key, silly," Miss Ponzo said with a sweet smile as she approached her.

"A key?" said Lanzzie, realizing her dilemma was bigger than before. "I... umm... I thought maybe you would just keep an eye on it and make sure that thieves didn't break in, or anything like that."

"Yes dear, of course! And I'll also tidy up the place and water your plants. You don't want your plants to die, I'm sure. Everyone forgets about their poor plants."

Lanzzie felt the sweat forming on her palms. "Of course, I

don't… yes… okay… I'm sorry, I didn't get a lot of sleep last night." She handed her key to Miss Ponzo, trying to steady her trembling fingers.

"Oh, Lanzzie," she said, glancing visibly at her fingers. "You look hungry. How about you take some of these fresh fruits and vegetables, too? We just got them from the market. I like to shop early so I can pick the freshest and plumpest ones. Edgar used to love that. God bless his soul."

The more Lanzzie tried to tell herself to act calm and normal, the more she felt like she was acting strangely. She forced a smile.

"That's so sweet of you, thank you, but I couldn't."

"Please, I insist." Miss Ponzo held some apples over Lanzzie's orange sack, waiting for her to open it. Lanzzie undid the rope and held the bag open, grateful that she didn't have the arrow with her. But she did still have an assortment of supplies that could raise questions.

Miss Ponzo dropped the apples in, and threw in a few pears, turnips, and carrots for good measure. Just as Lanzzie was about to tie the bag closed, Miss Ponzo yelled, "Wait a minute, young lady! Don't close that bag so quickly."

"Is there something wrong?"

"Of course there is! Open your bag back up."

Lanzzie slowly opened the bag, while she felt the sweat on her brow and wondered what Miss Ponzo had seen.

"You can't leave without a piece of this freshly baked bread," said Miss Ponzo. "The baker knows I'm always there to get it hot, right out of the oven. Here, I insist." She broke it in half, steam slowly rising from the inside.

Lanzzie took the large piece and quickly put it in her sack and tied it.

"I can't thank you enough," she said. "It smells wonderful. And I've never seen such bright, colorful vegetables. Now I know the secret, early shopping in the market."

"Shhh," said Miss Ponzo. "Don't be giving away my secrets now." She gave a slight, sweet giggle. "Us neighbors have to keep one another's—"

"Oh, you don't have to tell me," said Lanzzie, forcing another smile as she turned to leave. That was the understatement of the century.

Finally, she was off to head for the stables. She felt her feet against the crisp, dry grass. Ordinarily, she'd feel a sense of oneness with nature. But though the weather was perfect, her mood was anything but. All she wanted to do was get back to that forest and find her sister.

"You're going in the wrong direction!" yelled Miss Ponzo.

Lanzzie sighed. "I know," she yelled back. "I—I have to go get my rabbit first."

She looked back and saw that Miss Ponzo was about to yell something else, but she pretended she didn't see her and kept moving. She only hoped that it hadn't been a mistake to give her a key.

ಬಿ ಞ ಬಿ ಞ

As Lanzzie approached the stables, she was glad to see Fin walking his rabbit out.

"There you are," said Fin. "I would've expected you here a little—"

"Don't say it. Don't even go there. Let's just say I had neighbor trouble. Did the stable master ask you anything about Tia going missing?"

"No, but I'm not Ezstasia's sister. He'll probably ask you. Have you thought about what to say?"

"I did. But now I don't."

"Huh?"

"All the terrible delays this morning took me out of warrior mode."

"Warrior mode? So you went to bed as Lanzzie and you woke up as a warrior? I would've liked to have seen that."

She could see him smirking.

"Shut up, Fin," she said, pushing her way past him, toward the entrance of the stables.

"Was that push from the warrior or you?" he said, as she made her way through the huge double doors to sign her rabbit out.

She walked through the entrance, and on the right side of the large, U-shaped, multi-level barn, she almost tripped over the remains of a broken wooden ladder. It was one of many, used for reaching the animals' food on the upper level. This ladder had seen better days and seemed ready to become firewood. The only light crept in through the doorway and through the cracks between the uneven boards that made up the walls and ceiling. Hay was strewn out all across the floor and the intense smell of the animals permeated the air.

Finally, she saw a line of people ahead, waiting to check their rabbits out. As she approached, she spotted the twins, Randin and Zander. Both wore their typical baggy trousers and colorful suspenders. The two always matched like little boys—maybe out of habit from their younger years or maybe simply because Zander looked up to his slightly older twin brother.

"Yellow today?" she said, looking at both of their suspenders.

"No, red," said Zander, with a perfectly straight face. He was being facetious. Their suspenders were as yellow as a canary.

"So, are you boys checking out your rabbits? Ready for our big adventure?" she said, intentionally loud. She wanted the stable workers to think they were doing something normal.

Randin looked at her like she had two heads.

"Why yes, Lanz!" said Zander, a bit too chipper, and even more obvious than she was. "Just like we always do every morning."

Randin kicked him.

"Why do you wear suspenders all the time, anyway?" she said, trying to direct the subject toward a more normal conversation. One that wouldn't draw any attention to them.

"To keep our moonshines safe, of course," said Zander, in a sing-songy voice.

So much for a normal conversation. She turned to Randin. "What is he even talking about? Is he serious?"

"Umm… I'm afraid he is," said Randin, his face turning red as he gave his brother the eye. "It's… well—moonshine refers to our butt cheeks. At least that's what our mum called them."

"Okay, well that's a little—"

"Only our future misses get to see our moonshines, though," said Zander. "Isn't that right, Randin?"

"Can we please talk about something else?" said Randin, his forehead crinkling.

"So, are you both in line to sign out Bun and Nee?" said Lanzzie, following Randin's lead.

The twins immediately started laughing. "I told you Randin," said Zander. "We gave our rabbits the best names ever. We should get a reward for that." Then he whispered, loud enough for her to hear, "And didn't she already ask us that?"

"Shhh," said Randin, as he finally got to the front of the line.

"Morning, sir," he said to the old man at the table. "We came for Bun and Nee."

It wasn't the regular morning stable master. Of all days, Mr. Pudge must've taken ill.

"Bun and Nee," repeated the man, whose face was so

worn and wrinkled he must've spent his life on a sailing vessel. "Think yer funny, do ya? Well it's a little funny, I'll give ya that."

Zander was still chuckling like a schoolchild.

"I trust ya got yer identification, lads."

Randin held up his necklace with the pendant, and Zander did the same. Lanzzie watched as the man squinted to make sure the marking on the pendants matched their rabbits' feet markings, which were imprinted on his parchment. Mr. Pudge knew each rabbit's owners, so he never even checked, but this man was new.

Next it was Lanzzie's turn.

"I'm here to check out Jewel," she said, her voice cracking.

"Yer identification, miss?"

She quickly fished through her orange sack looking for it, when Miss Ponzo's apples and pears started to tumble out, along with a few carrots and turnips.

Flustered, she quickly grabbed her pendant and tossed it on the table. Then she began to pick up the vegetables and fruit.

"Just how long are ye plannin' on takin' yer rabbit?" said the man, marveling at all the fruits and vegetables.

"Oh, just for the day," she said. "The fruit's for my whole group. I'm not much for apples myself. Would you like one?"

"I think not," said the man. "Unless ya have apricots. Them I like." He smiled, which was when she noticed his crooked yellow teeth. He had a piece of straw hanging out the side of his mouth, one he chewed on at random intervals, making him look oddly like Jewel.

"I'm so sorry, no apricots," she said.

He studied her pendant, then looked down at his parchment.

"Aye, yer just the lassy I was lookin' for."

"Me?" This was exactly what she was afraid of.

"And you've a sister named Ezstasia, is that not correct?"

"Yes, it is."

"Well, yer sister has a rabbit. Goes by the name of Tia, who happens to be missin'."

"Oh yes," she said. "I remember now. She said something about taking Tia to her cottage last night."

"To her cottage, Miss..., Miss..." he scanned his parchment to look up her name, "Lanzzie, is it?"

"Yes, sir."

"Well, Miss Lanzzie, I'm sure ye and all yer friends are well familiar with the rules regardin' these delicate giants. They're all that remains from the days of magic, bred for hundreds of years. They must be watched and cared for at all times. Aye, but what would ye know 'bout magic?"

"Nothing at all, sir," said Lanzzie. "I don't know a thing."

"Of course ya don't. 'Twas a hypothetical question." He leaned forward.

"Just ye remember, while ye and yers sleep soundly at night, we have lads here who stay awake like gravediggers, tendin' to the every need of those rabbits. It's not safe to take these beauties home. They're not pets, and they're not hounds nor horses."

The man stared at her and squinted his eyes, as if he were looking right through her lies.

"I know," she said, "it's just that—"

"It's just that nothin'," said the man, banging his fist on the table. "We need that rabbit back."

She could tell that he took his job very seriously.

"I'm sorry, I'll get it back from my sister. She was just sad and needed someone to cuddle with. What happened to our parents still haunts her, and—"

"What exactly happened to yer elders, lassy?" His tone seemed to instantly warm up a bit.

41

"If it's all the same, I'd rather not talk about it. It was a long time ago, and—"

The man held up his hand to stop her. "Say no more," he said. "However…"

He examined his parchment more closely. "I do see here that yer sister has done this before. This *will* be the last time."

"Thank you, sir. I mean, yes, sir."

"And if she needs *cuddlin'*," he pronounced the word as if he'd never heard it before, "have her nuzzle a goat or somethin'."

"Will you please hurry up!" yelled a man in the back of the line. "I have somewhere I need to be!"

"And you'll be walkin' there if ya don't have patience," said the old man loudly. He then turned to one of his stable keepers. "Retrieve the rabbit named Jewel for this young lady. Number fifty-two." He looked at Lanzzie and winked. "On ye go, lassy. And don't ye forget what I said. We need yer sister's rabbit back today or it'll be no more rabbits for the lot of ya."

"Thank you, sir. I'll find my sister. You'll have both back by tonight."

"I only need her rabbit."

"Oh, right," she said. "I know. I mean… I meant both rabbits, mine and hers." That wasn't at all what she meant, but she was glad to have recovered quickly.

She took a deep sigh, then stepped to the side and gazed down the long stable hall, waiting for Jewel to be brought to her. Finally, she could see the young stable keeper coming, holding the giant, fluffy white rabbit by the reins. It never failed to put a smile on Lanzzie's face when she saw Jewel's beauty.

She smiled at the stable keeper, then grabbed the reins and walked Jewel outside to where her friends were all gathered. They were packing their saddles and getting ready for the day's journey. She was about to say something when she heard a loud yell to her left and turned her head.

It was Pallu. Of course.

"Wait," he yelled. "Guys, hold up!" She watched as he ran toward them with several oversized canvas sacks in his hands. He moved like an overweight duck.

"Here, hold this," he said as he dumped one of his bags in Lanzzie's arms. "And you hold this," he said to Zander as he dumped the other against his chest. "I'll be back. I just have to get Thumps."

"You're just now getting here?!" Lanzzie said. She could feel her face getting red, thinking about what Ezstasia might be going through in this very moment. "Pallu, I'm not holding all of your stuff, nor is anyone else," she said, letting the bag fall to the ground. She turned to Zander.

"Drop that... junk."

Zander looked back at her with a blank expression and opened his arms, letting the giant bag fall to the ground as the sounds of clinking metal echoed through the field.

"Mom's famous stew is *not* junk, Lanz!" said Pallu as he was walking to the stables. "I'll remember that when you want to eat some."

"It's famous?" said Zander. "Funny, I've never heard of it."

Pallu jogged away toward the stables and turned toward them to yell, "And I guess you don't want my mom's famous gooey bread?!"

Zander looked at Lanzzie and shrugged. "I've never heard of that either," he said, loudly enough for Pallu to hear. She could tell by his grin that he was teasing Pallu as usual. In reality, everyone in the Cottages knew about Pallu's mom's cooking. She made sure of that, generously doling out richly-scented savory platters and sweet pastries to the villagers.

Lanzzie approached Fin, who was loading up his rabbit.

"He's too much," she said.

"Who?"

"Pallu, who else? Why are we even taking him? He'll just slow us down."

Fin kept packing his supplies. "Lanzzie, Lanzzie, Lanzzie," he said without turning around. "Pallu can be—well, Pallu. But he's part of the group and he's our friend. And getting angry won't get us there any faster. Plus, he's Ezstasia's best friend, let's not forget that. And one other thing…" He turned to face her as he gave Zon a friendly pat on the side.

"What's that?"

"His mom's stew," he said, grinning. "Need I say more? I'd carry Pallu around on my back for days just for a few bites of that."

She couldn't help but smile at the thought of that. She really did like Pallu. It was just hard to deal with these delays when Ezstasia's life might be at stake. "I'm sorry," she said, suddenly feeling guilty. "I just want to find my sister."

"We all do," said Fin. "You know that."

She nodded. "How about I head to the pasture with the twins while you and the others wait for Pallu? This way, I can at least be there in case she comes out looking for us."

"Fair enough," he said.

She motioned to Randin and Zander.

"Time to go, boys," she said.

She and the twins hurriedly finished tying their equipment to their rabbits' saddles, and rode off in the direction of the pasture.

𝕤𝕠 𝕔𝕤 𝕤𝕠 𝕔𝕤

Fin tied the last sack to Zon's saddle and headed over to Meldon, who'd just finished loading up his own rabbit, Mr. Feet. They stood, leaning back on Mr. Feet's saddle, as they waited for Pallu.

Fin noticed Ithron tying his supplies to the black saddle on his rabbit, Strike, who was also black, aside from a few small white spots.

"Ithron is quite the loner, isn't he?" said Meldon.

"That he is," said Fin. "If everyone says go right, he'll go left."

"He's unpredictable," said Meldon.

"Predictably," said Fin.

"I like that," said Meldon as he laughed. "Predictably unpredictable."

Ithron took a drink from his water tin, tied it up and mounted his rabbit. He rode right up to them.

"I'm heading out to meet Lanzzie and the twins in the valley. See you both there."

Just then, Fin noticed Pallu emerge from the stables with Thumps, though he was still pretty far back.

"Why don't you just wait?" he said to Ithron. "Here comes Pallu now."

"Well then, I guess you chaps won't be far behind."

"Predictably unpredictable," whispered Meldon to Fin.

Ithron turned toward Jezreel, who was climbing onto her rabbit. "Are you coming with me, Jez?"

Jezreel paused, with a tentative expression on her face. "Um, I better not. Fin said to wait for Pallu."

"Suit yourself," said Ithron as he rode off.

"He's definitely smitten with that one," said Meldon who was looking toward Jezreel.

"Yeah," said Fin. "Not even his bad boy self can hide those feelings. He has a funny way of showing them though."

"Maybe he doesn't know how."

"Meldon, my lad. I think that's about as good as it gets for Ithron."

They watched Ithron ride off.

"Hey guys," said Pallu, just arriving and nearly out of breath. "Thanks for waiting. What are you guys staring at?"

"Ithron," said Meldon.

"Ithron? Please do tell! Me and Thumps are all ears."

"Thumps and I," said Meldon.

"Okay, all of us then," said Pallu.

"Nope, times up," Fin said, smiling. "We need to go, buddy."

"Okay, maybe later? Maybe for tea time. I brought the best tea for a great story, so maybe—"

"Pallu, please. Get your stuff loaded onto Thumps. I'll help you. The others are waiting." Fin started picking up Pallu's things and handed them to him.

"Fin," said Pallu, looking more serious. "I know everyone's anxious to get there, and I am too. But Ezstasia's a strong girl. One time, we were camping out in some forest. We set up our tents and I made us a great dinner on the fire we started—uh, well, *she* started. Actually, and—well, due to, uh certain circumstances—well, anyway, she ended up camping alone, because I had to run home. And she did just fine."

"We know this story, Pallu," said Meldon, his head buried in a map. "You chickened out like a chicken and went home."

"What? No! That's *not* how it happened."

Fin handed him one of the supply bags, which he quickly grabbed to tie to Thumps.

"I guess it depends whose side of the story we are listening to," said Meldon, looking up from his map.

"Well, I'm telling the story at the moment," said Pallu, "and I went home because of a stomach ache."

"Whatever you say," said Meldon, climbing onto Mr. Feet's saddle.

"We need to go," said Fin.

"I'm ready," said Pallu, trying to get onto Thumps. It took him a couple jumps until he finally mounted the chubby rabbit.

As they headed off toward the pasture, Pallu rode between them, continuing his explanation. Jezreel followed behind.

"It was a really bad stomach ache," he said. "My stomach was full of air bubbles. It was horrible. I don't think you want more details, but I can tell you, if you saw my under—"

"Don't tell us," said Fin. "Please."

Meldon leaned into Mr. Feet's ear. "Is Pallu still talking? What's that? You say he's a chicken?"

"Yes, I'm still talking," said Pallu. "And I'm not a chicken. I'm more like a cuddly bear. But Ezstasia? She's a lion. She's tough. She's strong. And I know she's okay. She's the bravest person I know. And I'll tell you another story—"

That's when Fin and Meldon looked over at one another and sped their rabbits ahead of Pallu. Jezreel caught up to them and Pallu lagged slightly behind, still jabbering the whole way.

₨ ℛ ₨ ℛ

After traveling for what seemed like forever, they finally arrived at the large, hourglass-shaped pasture. Fin spotted the twins up ahead, staring at the tree line of the forest.

"There's Zander and Randin," he said, pointing to them. "Let's go!" He gave Zon a slight kick and shook the reins to get him to pick up speed. Meldon, Jezreel, and Pallu followed close behind.

As they sprinted toward the twins, the tree line grew closer and closer. In an odd way, it almost seemed like it was waiting for and beckoning them as the branches gently swayed. Eerily, there wasn't even the slightest breeze.

"Where are Lanz and Ithron?" he said as he approached them.

"Lanz is riding the tree line," said Randin. "She had us stay here to wait for you, and—"

"Ithron's riding the tree line too," said Zander, "but on the other side. He's over there." He pointed to the right.

"Do you two always finish each other's sentences?" said Fin.

"Not always," said Zander.

"But sometimes," said Randin.

Fin shook his head. "Okay. I take it nobody has seen any signs of Ezstasia?"

"No, but this place is creepy," said Zander, riding Nee a little closer to Randin.

"It's just a forest," said Fin. "All forests can look creepy."

It was time to round up the troops. Fin put two fingers in his mouth and whistled loudly, a trick his father taught him as a child. It was so loud, everyone turned to face him.

Ithron, off in the distance, turned toward him and began heading back to the pasture.

"There's Lanzzie," said Meldon.

Fin turned to see Lanzzie approaching from the other direction.

"Any sign of Ezstasia?" he yelled to her.

"None," yelled Lanzzie.

He watched as she and Ithron trotted over to meet him from opposite directions.

"This forest is already frustrating me," said Lanzzie. "I feel like it changes every time I go back over the tree line. The trees move or change themselves into something else. It never seems to be the same, like it has a mind of its own."

"Maybe your worries about your sister are making you see things," said Fin.

"No, I know what I saw. I was just telling Ithron about

this. Can you see that giant tree trunk over there? The extra wide one?"

Fin glanced over to where she was pointing. "Yes, what about it?"

"Well, I'm pretty sure it wasn't there before."

"What are you talking about Lanz? Tree trunks don't just appear. Maybe you were mixed up and in a different area."

"You know," said Meldon," I felt similarly to that when we were playing Arrows yesterday. I saw my arrow land in a patch of grass and when I went to grab it, it wasn't there anymore. It was just gone. Then, after searching around, when I came back, there it was. It was in that exact spot that I had already looked."

"I think you're all just stressed out," said Fin. "My arrow went pretty far into those trees yesterday and I didn't see anything like that."

Just then he remembered that he had seen a vine twist, which he'd later convinced himself was just a squirrel. "Wait, there was this one vine," he said. "I could have sw—"

"Guys, you're really starting to make me nervous for Ezstasia," said Jezreel. "I thought it was the most beautiful forest I'd ever seen. Now you're making it sound dreadful."

"You weren't even in the forest," said Meldon.

"Yes I was," she said. "I was going toward the hills when my arrow turned and went into the trees. As soon as I crossed the tree line, I was overwhelmed by the beauty. It was unreal. Everywhere I looked, there were flowers of every color."

Ithron cleared his throat loudly. Fin and the group looked toward him.

"My arrow flew just outside of the forest," said Ithron. "Over there." He pointed back toward the pasture. "Not much flowers there. Or trees. Or anything else, for that matter."

"Okay, so you saw nothing," said Meldon. "Anyway, Fin, did you notice anything peculiar?"

"No. I'm sure if there was anything I thought I saw, it was just animals." Fin wasn't exactly sure what he had seen, but the last thing he wanted to do was get everyone all worked up.

"Well, I definitely know something happened to me in that forest," said Meldon, pushing his eyeglasses back up on the bridge of his nose. "I'm positive. I'm not one to make things up. And you know what I think? I'll tell you. I think someone's been dabbling with magic."

"Yeah, us," said Ithron.

"Someone other than us," said Meldon.

"There hasn't been magic in centuries," said Fin. "I mean besides the occasional hidden stash of light magic. Nobody would dare use the strong stuff, even if they could get it."

"Well, there *are* those who are still capable of the kind of magic we're talking about," said Meldon. "They live in the Magiclands."

"Well, we're not in the Magiclands, are we?" said Fin. "For all we know, they don't exist anymore. Not to mention the Magiclands are on the other side of the world—an ocean away."

"Enough already!" said Lanzzie. "I'm sorry I even brought it up. Let's just get on with this. We need to find my sister, so what's the plan? Should we split up?"

"Did anyone see where she entered the forest?" said Fin. He was glad to be able to help Lanzzie refocus everyone on the task at hand.

"Well, I was heading toward the pasture," said Zander. "But I thought I saw her going that way." He pointed toward the left side of the tree line.

"I know she was to my left," said Fin. "But I don't know exactly where *I* was. I was too focused on catching that arrow."

"You were to my left," said Meldon. "And I calculate that I was precisely about 35 degrees from where I am right now, judging by the distance of those trees to my right."

"So, you're saying we should search for her to the left?" said Fin.

"Some of us should. But if we want to do this the smart way, we should split into three groups to cover more ground."

Fin thought for a moment while looking at the tree line. "Okay, here's the plan," he said. "Randin, Zander and Pallu, you guys go in straight ahead. You'll be the right flank. Ithron, Meldon, and Jezreel, head toward that big tree to the left. You'll be the center group. Lanzzie and I will be the left flank. This way we'll have wide coverage. Let's be sure to meet back here before nightfall, no matter what. Questions?"

"What about food?" said Pallu, his forehead crinkling.

"Are you kidding me?" said Zander.

"No, seriously. Should we meet back here for lunch? We have to time these things."

Fin held up his hand. "Plan to eat wherever you are, whenever you want," he said. "This isn't your mom's house where meals are served at certain times. Any other questions? Important ones?"

"That *is* important," said Pallu. "At least for those of us who appreciate living."

Zander rolled his eyes.

"Okay, when we call for Ezstasia," Fin said, once again addressing the group, "we need to make sure to make noise. Sing, whistle, yell her name—whatever. Anything so she can hear you. And make sure you listen for her, in case she—"

Fin saw the nervousness in Lanzzie's face. "—in case she's stuck in a tree or something and needs help getting down."

"I can do that," said Pallu.

Fin could see that some of them looked apprehensive, especially Jezreel. He took her hand and squeezed it, looking around at everyone.

"We can do this," he said. "Remember when we lost Pallu and Thumps for half a day, only to find him having a picnic with himself near a stream?"

The twins and Jezreel laughed. Even Ithron almost smiled, which was a rarity indeed.

"When you're lost, just eat," said Zander. "That's his motto."

"Hey, I wasn't lost," said Pallu. "I just went to take a drink from the stream and Thumps looked hungry, so I made him food and then joined him."

"Pallu, I've never seen your rabbit look hungry," said Randin. "He always looks like he's full. Overly full if you ask me."

"Busting out of its cheeks full," Zander added.

"Can we get on with this?!" yelled Lanzzie. The red on her face became more saturated by the second. She turned to Fin. "I'll be in our section to begin searching, while you and everyone else continue to discuss this nonsense."

"Lanz is right," he said. "We can't waste any more time. I know we're unsure about this forest. But we're here, we're prepared and our friend is counting on us. There's strength in numbers. None of us are going in alone. If things get really weird, we can simply come out. Are you all ready?"

He looked around, and most of them nodded their heads in agreement. The rest were silent.

"Good," he said. "Now let's go save our friend."

CHAPTER FOUR

Zander proceeded cautiously into the mysterious forest with his brother and Pallu. In spite of Pallu having to go with them, he was relieved that Fin had grouped him with his brother. He still felt uneasy, but it gave him a little bit of security to have Randin by his side. He may have been a jokester on the outside, but on the inside he was still that scared little kid who grew up in the Cottages and relied on his brother for protection.

"It's a hot day," said Pallu, wiping his forehead.

"Hot?" said Zander. "It's not even warm."

"I think maybe I'm just—"

"Don't say it. I know. You're hungry. Well, it's not lunch time yet, so you and Lumps will have to wait. We just started."

"I was going to say thirsty. But now that you mention it, we do need to make sure our energy stays up. And, Zander, his name is *Thumps*."

Zander shook Nee's reins and the rabbit rode forward. "I have lots of energy!"

Randin caught up with him but Pallu lagged behind.

"Keep up, Pallu," yelled Randin.

"I'm perfectly fine," said Pallu. "I'm keeping watch for

us."

They made their way further into the forest, while Zander listened for any sounds. All he could hear were the rabbits' footsteps and the thumping of his own heartbeat.

"Notice something strange?" said Randin.

"Just this whole forest," said Zander.

"I mean the flowers. We haven't had rain in ages, so why all the perfectly colorful flowers?"

"Maybe they're like Mr. Codsworth's flowers," said Zander. "Doesn't he have flowers year round?"

"Yeah, but Mr. Codsworth is there to water them."

"Maybe someone comes here," said Pallu.

"Oh right. It's not like it would be hard to water an entire forest," said Randin.

"That reminds me of a song," said Zander.

"We should save our song voices for a little bit later," said Randin.

"No, I think now is the perfect time," said Zander. What he really meant, but refused to say aloud, was that it would distract him from the panic he was beginning to feel.

Zander began singing the old folk song that has been sung in the Cottage pubs for ages.

We I say we,
Need a day of sunshine,
Come to us
In the days of all this rain time,
Where we have had
Not one (Not One!)

Randin and Pallu had joined in. Their voices brought Zander a sense of calm as they continued singing with him.

Now we wonder,

Where is all the rain time,
Come to us
In the days of all this sunshine,
Where we have had
Not one (Not One!)

We I say we,
Need a day of rain time
Bring us crops
From the drought of all this sunshine,
For we have had
Not one (Not One!)

"One more round!" said Pallu.

They laughed and sang it once more until everyone became abruptly quiet, as if they all realized at once that they were getting pretty deep into the dark forest.

"We should listen for Ezstasia," said Randin.

"Yeah, singing isn't the same without a pint of cider, anyway," said Zander.

"Do you think she's okay?" said Randin.

"Guys, trust me," said Pallu. "I know Ezstasia and I'm sure she's safe, wherever she is. It's just a forest."

"You must not be seeing the same forest I am," said Zander.

"I think it looks like every other forest we've been to," said Pallu. "Maybe. Well, it's a little different. Maybe a little spookier."

As they continued riding, Zander could see Pallu marveling at the gargantuan, creepy-looking trees that seemed to have existed since the dawn of man.

"Yeah, now that I think about it," said Pallu, "it's completely different. Way different."

"I don't know," said Randin. "It looks kind of...

beautifully mysterious to me."

Zander looked at him. "Beautifully? Really? To me, creepy isn't beautiful, it's just... creepy."

They continued further, listening for any sign of movement or noise. Then, without warning, Pallu stopped his rabbit and began looking around frantically.

"Do you hear something?" said Zander.

Pallu didn't answer. It was as if he was in a daze as his head darted from tree to tree.

"Pallu, what are you doing? We need to keep going."

"The trees," said Pallu, still transfixed by something.

"What about the trees?" said Randin, who'd just turned his rabbit around when everyone had stopped.

Zander looked around at the trees and didn't see anything particularly strange. Pallu had gone silent. He looked at Randin, who just shrugged his shoulders.

"Hey, Pallu," said Randin, winking at Zander. "If we get moving, we can have lunch soon."

"Lunch," said Pallu, snapping out of whatever spell he was under.

Zander watched, confused, while Pallu kicked Thumps's side and the overweight young man on his overweight rabbit went hopping past him. Randin took the lead and Pallu followed. Zander rode last, just to make sure Pallu was between them, focused and on track.

"Ezstasia!" yelled Zander, hoping she was in the area and could hear him.

Pallu yelled even louder. The three of them took turns calling her name to no avail. Sometimes, they'd all yell at once for maximum effect.

They continued further until they passed through some vines that were hanging from above.

"Strange," said Randin, slowing his rabbit down. "Look at those vines."

"Yeah, you usually only find those in the jungles," said Pallu. "That mist seems strange and out of place, too."

Zander looked at him. "What mi—"

Just then, he spotted it. As his eyes traveled around to the abundance of blue and yellow flowers that ran from the trees to the ground, there was a misty, white steam rising from the soft dirt. It continued all along the path up ahead.

"I noticed it a while ago," said Pallu.

"Why didn't you tell me?" said Zander.

"You didn't ask me."

"How would I know to—oh, never mind," said Zander, realizing this conversation wouldn't go anywhere.

They proceeded carefully through the misty path when they came to a huge, fallen tree that blocked their way. Even as it lay on its side, it was taller than they were. As he looked around, Zander could see several smaller trees that had fallen, half-hidden in the unusually tall grass.

"What could've caused these trees to fall?" said Randin.

"They look alive, but dead," said Zander.

Pallu turned to him. "All trees are alive," he said, "unless they're dead."

"That was dumb," said Zander. "And not even an ounce of funny."

"Ezstasia!" Randin called out. His brow crinkled as he looked at Zander. He yelled out again and then looked even more confused. "Well, that was strange."

"What was?" said Zander.

Randin yelled out again. "My voice isn't carrying at all," he said. "It's like the sound hits an invisible wall. I don't think it's even getting past those trees."

"I didn't notice it," said Pallu, "but I bet if Meldon were here he could explain it."

"I'll try it again," said Randin, this time cupping his hands to his mouth. "Ezs—"

In mid-yell, he stopped his rabbit and stared.

Zander pulled the reins to stop Nee and looked ahead in the same direction that his brother was staring. He squinted his eyes to be sure of what he was actually seeing. There was some sort of blue fog in the distance.

Pallu's mouth dropped, as he halted Thumps. "What in the Magiclands is that?"

"The outlines look human," said Randin, still mesmerized.

"They look like they're moving or swaying," said Pallu. "What are they doing?"

"Who cares what they're doing!" said Zander. "We see blue fog people and you're concerned about what they're doing? How about what we should be doing? Getting out of here!"

"But we can't," said Pallu. "We have to find Ezstasia."

"Are you kidding me?" said Zander. "I have a general line I don't cross and when it comes to blue fog people, that's my limit."

Pallu took a deep breath. "Why don't we eat something and then decide."

"How can you think about eating right now?" said Zander.

"No, Pallu is right, Zander," said Randin. "I think we need to take a break and eat. Then we can make a rational decision. Besides, the rabbits will need food even if we decide to go back."

"For once, a man of reason," said Pallu. "And I saw the perfect spot for us to stop."

Zander and his brother followed Pallu and Thumps to a nearby clearing under a huge tree with a massive trunk. Several small roots stuck out from the ground and were formed perfectly into loops for back support. He noticed the roots traveled along the ground to the base of the trunk, where they began to attach themselves, taking refuge on the towering tree.

The ground in front of the tree was flat, with soft moss that provided a bit of padding for walking or sitting.

"Now, isn't this a perfect spot?" said Pallu, beaming, as he dismounted Thumps and tied him to a nearby bush loaded with berries.

Zander began taking carrots out of his sack for Nee to chew on. He glanced down at the ground, relieved to see there wasn't any mist in the area. He sat on the soft moss and leaned against one of the raised roots. He was about to open his food sack when he heard a crackling nearby.

"Ezstasia?" he said.

"Where?" said Pallu.

"Do you see her?" said Randin.

Zander was too focused to answer. He stood up and listened. He heard the noise again. It was coming from somewhere close. He spotted a tall tree a short distance away and wondered if that's where the noise had come from. Maybe she was hiding up in the branches.

"Zander?" Pallu said. "What is it?"

He walked toward the enormous tree to get a better look, gazing up to see where the noise was coming from. Then he heard more crackling from above. He proceeded closer until he was at the foot of the tree. It was coming from the other side, so he walked around the massive trunk, stepping over some roots that were protruding out from the ground.

"Ezstasia!" he called out, hoping she was up there.

"Did you hear her?" yelled Randin from the picnic area.

"No," Zander called back. "I just thought I heard something. Must've been the branches or maybe some small animals."

He kept focusing on the tree and realized that it was quite dead—a pale grey color, with well-worn grooves in the wood and several dark knots surrounded by fading white rings. The decaying bark was peppered with deep scars of black while countless dead roots clung to the base of the tree.

He ran his hands along the bark and several pieces crumbled off, spewing dust in the air. Crackling echoed from above and it startled him. His eyes traveled up the trunk of the tree again, toward the sound. He stumbled backward in utter shock as two of the larger knots high above him opened up like giant eyelids, each one the size of his head. He rubbed his eyes, thinking he was seeing things, and looked up again. To his dismay, the two large, black eyes were still there and were very, very real.

He saw more movement as three smaller knots beside the left eye opened widely, and then three more beside the right eye. Zander wasn't about to wait around to see anything else. He slowly crept backward just as one of the long roots at the base of the tree cracked loudly, startling him breathless. Before his eyes, the root broke free from the ground and soared up the trunk until it clung to the right eye like a large appendage. Before he could yell for the others, the sound of thundering branches from above made him freeze in his tracks. Then, more roots broke free and catapulted up to attach themselves to the left side of the trunk.

In that instant, the partially formed face in the tree jutted out from the rest of the trunk, as if some invisible force had pulled it loose. Sharp pieces of debris shot out and fell to the ground in front of him. He ducked to prevent one from hitting him. He jumped back, and a tremendous flurry of crackling permeated his ears, as roots began flying up to the top of the trunk to join the other newly formed appendages. Debris and a large cloud of dust filled the air around him. He hesitated, but finally mustered the strength to look up. His mouth dropped in sheer horror. He wanted to scream, but nothing came out. Fully separated from the massive trunk and now resting against it, was a dreadfully recognizable, eight-legged figure.

Zander didn't want to believe it, but it was as real as his very breath. On each leg, pieces of the root began poking out like little hairs and splintered throughout the creature's entire body. An abdomen began to take shape, as the eight menacing eyes pierced through him. His chest pounded when he saw exactly what he knew had been coming: two long, sharp fangs protruding from the beast's mouth.

He felt a lump in his throat. He hesitatingly stared up at what was clearly an enormous, wooden, grey and black tarantula the size of his entire cottage. It peered down at him, ready to attack.

Zander turned to run and immediately tripped over something on the ground. His body twisted awkwardly and he fell backward onto his behind. He felt like he couldn't breathe. The level of fear in his body was greater than he had ever known. Ezstasia briefly flashed through his mind as he remembered that she was in this horrifying forest—*alone*.

The giant wooden arachnid jerked its ugly head in his direction as it pulled its newborn legs loose from the tree. He frantically tried to get to his feet just as the eight-legged beast let out a loud hiss and scuttled down the tree trunk, jumping to the ground and running right in his direction. Zander catapulted himself off the ground and screamed in horror, running toward Randin and Pallu.

"Untie the rabbits!" he yelled. "Untie the rabbits!"

Zander could hear the shuffling and cracking of wood, knowing the creature was close behind him. Pallu and Randin had untied their rabbits while he desperately tried to untie Nee. His hands fumbled with Nee's rope as he felt the shadow of the enormous creature fall upon him. With the rope finally loose, he jumped on Nee and kicked the rabbit hard to get him to run.

"Go, go, go!" he yelled, as the spider hissed and opened its mouth, showing its two large fangs and hundreds of miniature sharp teeth. He didn't even have time to see what his friends were doing. He raced through the forest as fast as Nee could go. He heard branches moving behind him, but he couldn't decipher whether it was Randin, Pallu, or the massive spider. Finally, he saw Randin to his left, riding parallel to him. Pallu was on Randin's other side. Zander breathed a huge sigh of relief, but they looked as panicked as he had been. They were brushing aside low-hanging branches from their path as they sped through the forest.

That's when Zander realized that; if they were to his side, then the spider was the one behind him. A sense of dread filled his entire body; there wasn't any way that they would be making it out alive.

"Keep going, Nee!" he yelled, shaking the reins. "Faster!"

Zander glanced back and saw the spider scurrying closer as it cut through the thick branches and hissed ferociously at him. The beast's black eyes now had glowing red centers, gazing right at him. He turned his attention forward again and lowered his head to gain speed as Nee ran faster than Zander had ever felt him run before.

Randin and Pallu were ahead of him now, back on his same path. He noticed they kept turning around and looking back toward him, possibly keeping an eye on the spider behind him. He watched as they jumped over a fallen tree at full speed and he prepared Nee to do the same. As soon as he made the jump, he looked back again, hoping the fallen tree would slow the creature down. Zander's fear intensified as he watched the spider use the tree as a catapult, leaping forward with its front legs and long fangs extended.

It was above him now.

Only seconds away from the spider landing on him, Zander darted to the left, forcing his way through a dense thorn bush that punctured his arms and Nee's fur. He heard a loud hiss and raced forward again on the new path, looking behind him for signs of the beast. As he gazed back at the thorn bush, he spotted the glowing red eyes through the foliage. He turned forward again just in time to get rammed in the head by a low hanging branch, knocking him off of his rabbit.

He hit the ground hard. The world began spinning as he drifted off to the faint sound of leaves shuffling behind his head—and the thundering of branches.

৪০ ෬ ৪০ ෬

Zander was half-conscious. He hadn't even opened his eyes yet, but he felt something pressing against his forehead. His head was pounding. Something began pulling him backwards. Then he remembered: the spider! He was afraid to look and made the potentially regrettable decision to keep his eyes shut. Maybe he was better off playing dead. Or maybe he would wait for an opportunity to run. That is, if he even had the ability to do so. He could barely feel his legs.

"Zander," said a voice. He was still groggy, and he honestly wasn't sure if he had imagined the whole thing.

"Zander!" yelled a voice, snapping him out of it.

He forced his eyes open a little, though it was hard to see with the sunlight glaring in them. He could see a silhouette of a person staring down at him.

"Do you know who I am?" said the voice coming from the silhouette. He instantly realized it was his brother, Randin.

"Yes," said Zander. "Of course I do. Where are we?"

"Don't worry," said Randin. "We're out of the woods—literally."

"We're safe?! I didn't think we'd get out of there alive."

"I think we are. We're in some open field. We pulled you out when you ran into a branch. You went down hard, brother."

Zander felt a tear form in his eye. He couldn't believe he survived that ordeal. They all did. At least he hoped they all did.

"Pallu?" he said to his brother. "Where is he? Did he—"

"I'm right here, my friend," said Pallu, peeking out from behind Randin.

Zander forced himself to sit up. He shook the debris off of him and looked around. Randin helped him to his feet.

As soon as he rose, wobbly legs and all, he hugged Randin with all his might.

"It's alright, Zan," said Randin.

"Don't I get one too?" said Pallu.

Zander turned and hugged Pallu.

"Where's Nee?" said Zander, just realizing he didn't know what had become of his rabbit.

"Over there," said Randin, pointing to a group of bushes in the distance. "Pallu patched him up. He had quite a few thorns in his fur."

Though he was glad to be alive, he realized his hands were still shaking from the experience. He knew one thing: he was never going in that forest again. Then it dawned on him: Ezstasia! His friend was still in that forest. He hoped with every ounce of his being, that whatever that creature was, it didn't get to her. He felt like the biggest coward in the world, and helplessly unable to do anything for her. He walked toward his rabbit with a feeling of utter defeat.

"It's going to be okay," said Pallu, appearing to have read his mind.

"After seeing that... thing, I'm really worried about Ezstasia." He dreaded to think of what has become of her.

"Zander," said Randin, interrupting his thoughts. "I hate to bring this up, because I know how scared you were, and you just woke up and all that... but... uh..." Randin paused and scrunched his face, as if he was afraid to say whatever it was that he was about to say.

"Don't even think about going back in there," said Zander looking back and forth between Pallu and Randin. "You two wouldn't seriously consider that after what we just saw, would you?"

"Well, that's the thing," said Randin. "Pallu and I aren't really sure what you saw."

"What *I* saw? What do you mean? I don't understand," said Zander. "Neither one of you saw that monster chasing us?"

"No Zander," said Pallu. "We didn't see anything."

Zander was dumbfounded.

"It was as big as a cottage, hard to miss," said Zander in utter disbelief.

Randin shook his head.

"Not a thing," said Pallu.

"This is some kind of joke, right?" said Zander indignantly.

"We're really not kidding," said Pallu. "We didn't see anything in there."

"Then what were you running from!?"

"I don't know," said Pallu. "We were running because you were. You looked mortified, which terrified *us*, or *me* anyway. So I got out of there as fast as I could and your brother did the same."

"I saw a spider," said Zander. "A huge spider. I know I did. I'm not going crazy."

"Spider?" said Randin. "That's what we were running from, a spider?"

"What!? I hate spiders," said Pallu.

"Well you would've really hated this one!" screamed Zander, now starting to panic. "Am I going crazy? I saw it birthed right from the tree. It was enormous and made of roots and branches, with giant eyes and…" He felt a tear run down his cheek. Had the forest made him lose his mind?

"Zander," said Randin, "we didn't see it, but I believe you."

"How can you believe me? I probably wouldn't even believe me if I were you. But it was horrible and very real. And it ran so fast."

"Why didn't you just step on it?" said Pallu.

"Step on it!? It was the size of a cottage! The fangs alone were taller than me. How could you guys have not seen that?"

Just by looking at Randin, he could tell that his brother didn't know what to think. Zander began to feel weak, so he knelt down on both of his knees.

Pallu grabbed his shoulder.

"C'mon, Zan," said Pallu. "Let's go relax on the blanket I set up for us. The rabbits are finally eating."

Zander was in a daze, but he rose up and followed Pallu and Randin.

"I don't get it," he said. "Why did it only come after me? And why couldn't you guys see it? Am I cursed?"

"You're not cursed," said Pallu as they walked side by side toward the blanket. "It was probably just because you were the closest one to it. If I'm starving, or even just hungry, I'm gonna eat the chicken closest to me. Especially if there were a whole bunch of chickens and they were all about to run away, I'd grab the closest chicken. Not that I'm saying you're a chicken… or that you *were being* a chicken." Pallu's face was turning red. "I mean, it would be the same if it was jelly or cheese. Oh wait, they don't run. Let me think of something that runs but is definitely *not* a chicken. And, well, never mind."

Zander looked at him and saw beads of sweat forming on Pallu's forehead. Randin's face was turning red from trying to hold in his laughter. Zander tried to keep a straight face, but he couldn't hold back any longer and burst out into a combination of laughter and tears as Randin joined him. Leave it to Pallu to make them laugh even in the midst of a nightmare. Pallu looked greatly relieved and wrinkled his brow and smiled.

The rabbits, left over by the bushes, had raised their ears, startled by the new, gleeful noise that filled the air.

As he joined Randin and Pallu on the blanket, Zander looked up at the sky. The sun was beginning to set, and a few bright stars were making themselves known in advance of the rising moon.

"It would come in handy to be a star right now," said Randin. "They can see everything from up there, including Ezstasia. I wonder if anyone has found her yet."

"I think she's okay," said Pallu. "I choose to believe that."

"How I hope you're right," said Zander. "I do know one thing, though."

"What's that?" said Randin.

"I know why our ancestors tried to hide their magic away for safekeeping. I think they wanted to prepare themselves for something like this, just in case they had to protect their families. I know it makes *me* want magic, and I don't mean the weak powder kind."

Zander stood and gazed back at the forest where his worst nightmare had just taken place. As he pondered on how the others were doing and whether Ezstasia was truly okay, he was sure that he had heard a faint scream coming from a place deep within the forest.

CHAPTER FIVE

Meldon tagged behind Jezreel and Ithron as they rode their rabbits through the forest, looking for Ezstasia. He enjoyed watching the two of them interact because they were as opposite as could be. On one hand, Ithron seemed to favor her presence, and on the other, he remained as aloof and awkwardly sarcastic as always. Jezreel seemed even more nervous than usual around him. Judging by Ithron's casual mannerisms as he waved his trusty knife around while talking to Jezreel, Meldon wasn't sure if Ithron even noticed her nerves.

"Ohhhh!" shouted Jezreel, startling Meldon.

He shook Mr. Feet's reins to catch up to her.

"What? Did you get hurt?" he said as he approached. She was staring off into the forest and pointing at a clearing between the trees.

"Look at those flowers!" she said. "I could live in this forest."

"Please don't yell out like that," he said. "Yes, I see them. Very nice." He did spot some flowers scattered about, but he didn't see them as anything extraordinary. They were quite colorful though, a mix of violet and white.

"Nice?" she said. "This place is beautiful! Just stunning!"

"You have a strange idea of beauty," said Ithron, riding behind them.

"Ezstasia must've been so mesmerized she decided to stay," said Jezreel.

"Stay? Here?" said Ithron, snickering. "All I see is ugly rocks and moss."

"Look," said Jezreel, pointing to her right.

Meldon looked where she was pointing and saw a group of large, moss-covered rocks with small yellow and pink flowers sprouting up from the cracks.

"Ugly rocks again," said Ithron. "That's about it. Now why don't we call out for your friend? That's why we're here, isn't it?"

"She's your friend, too," said Meldon.

"If you say so."

Meldon and his friends had speculated about Ithron's aloof personality many times. Although Ithron had been part of their group of friends since childhood, and all by his own choice, he would usually drift off into his own world and offer sarcastic, jaded responses to just about any question. Sometimes he was downright mean. Though nobody wanted to ask him outright, they'd all agreed it was a mystery as to what had happened to him in his past that may have contributed to him being that way. Meldon figured if anyone could get him to open up, it would be Jezreel.

"Ezstasia!" yelled Jezreel. "Where are you!?"

Meldon joined in the calls for Ezstasia, until their hollering was drowned out by an agonizing yell from behind them.

He turned to see Ithron lying on his back on the ground, waving his knife around at something. His rabbit, Strike, was chewing leaves off of a nearby bush.

Meldon turned Mr. Feet around. "What happened?" he said, approaching Ithron.

As he climbed down from Mr. Feet, Jezreel, who had

already dismounted Buttons, came running up.

"Are you okay?" she said, crouching down to help Ithron get into a sitting position. "You're bleeding."

"Something came at me, and I don't know what it was," said Ithron. He looked dazed.

Meldon noticed the blood on his elbow, and quickly reached in his saddle bag for supplies. He was trying not to look at Ithron, as he could already feel himself getting queasy. If there was one thing he couldn't handle, it was blood.

"What did it look like?" he said to Ithron, without looking toward him.

"I just said I don't know," said Ithron, annoyed. "Some stupid black thing flew across the path and knocked me over."

"Hurry, Meldon," said Jezreel. "It's getting worse. It's starting to—"

"Don't... say another word," said Meldon, shielding his eyes with his arm. "I do *not* want to hear any details regarding blood, thank you."

He pulled out the bandages and supplies and closed his eyes as he handed them to Jezreel.

"You must have fallen on the sharp rock and cut yourself," she said, taking the supplies, "because it's all over—"

"A-a-nd there goes my stomach," said Meldon, as he got to his knees and felt his guts rising into his throat.

"Take a deep breath, Meldon," said Jezreel, now playing nurse for the two of them.

Meldon did as she said, counting as he inhaled and exhaled.

He began to feel better. He rose to his feet, feeling a minor sense of victory. He still couldn't look at Ithron, though.

"You said a black thing," said Jezreel to Ithron. "What kind of black thing? Hold still, I'm trying to wrap this."

"You're cleaning the wound first, right?" said Meldon. "I gave you a little jar of—"

"Yes, I already did that," she said. "And you can look now, it's pretty much wrapped."

Meldon turned to see Ithron looking up at her as she finished wrapping his elbow. It was an inquisitive look; he was studying her face.

"So, are you going to tell me?" she said to Ithron. "What kind of black thing flew at you?"

"It looked like a snake or an arm or something. Maybe a branch. Look, if I knew, I would tell you," said Ithron, more civilly this time.

Jezreel helped Ithron to his feet and Meldon took hold of his other arm. She seemed to have a knack for soothing him in a way that nobody could.

"It was probably a black snake," said Meldon. "We should check for bites."

Meldon started to lift Ithron's light, wispy hair, but Ithron grabbed his wrist and pulled it away.

"I didn't... get... bitten," he said through his teeth. "And besides, snakes don't fly."

"Neither do arms," said Meldon.

"Boys, please!" said Jezreel, in a surprisingly bold voice for such an innately calm girl. "We can't argue. We need to find Ezstasia. Now, if you're okay, Ithron, let's get back on our rabbits."

Meldon glanced over at Ithron, who glared back at him, as they both followed Jezreel's lead and climbed back onto their rabbits.

⚘ ⚘ ⚘ ⚘

Time had passed as they proceeded deeper into the forest. They had called for Ezstasia a number of times, but there still hadn't been any sign of her. They continued down another path. Meldon was distracted by thoughts of Ezstasia and her safety as he played through all the possible scenarios in his mind. He was startled from his daze when he noticed a familiar blue fog in the distance—the same he had seen the day before. The silhouettes were swaying back and forth, continuously appearing and disappearing, except they seemed to be slightly larger than what he had remembered.

"Tell me you see that fog," he said to the other two, as he was halting Mr. Feet.

"What is that!?" said Jezreel. She and Ithron stopped beside him.

"I saw it yesterday," said Meldon. "When I was looking for my arrow. It always stays the same distance away, no matter where you ride. Like a rainbow does. Now that I think about it, did you know a rainbow is—"

"I don't care about rainbows," said Ithron. "What *are* those things?" He pointed to the fog.

"It looks like enchanted people," said Jezreel. "They look beautiful."

"Like I said," said Ithron, "you have a strange idea of beauty."

"I've loved flowers ever since I was a little girl. And they're everywhere here! How could I not be fascinated?"

"What are you talking about? I haven't seen a single flower. Not one."

"But you see the blue fog?" said Meldon.

"Of course, I see it. How can you miss it?"

"How can you miss the flowers?" said Jezreel, with a hint of teasing sarcasm in her voice.

Without saying a word, Ithron climbed off of his rabbit and he began to walk toward a bush while pointing to it.

Midway, he stopped, and his face grew pale. His arms fell to his sides and he froze.

"Ithron," said Meldon. "Do you hear something?"

Ithron remained silent.

"Ithron, what's wrong?" said Jezreel, looking concerned. "Ithron!"

He didn't respond. He didn't even move a muscle.

Jezreel dismounted her rabbit and walked toward him. She placed her hand gently on his shoulder and Ithron jerked his knife up into the air, making her jump.

"Whoa!" said Meldon as he sprang off his rabbit and darted toward them. He carefully grabbed the knife from Ithron's hand.

"Jezreel!" said Ithron, turning toward her. "I'm so sorry, I thought that you were—"

"You thought I was… what?"

"The black smoke. I saw it slither across the ground and thought it was a snake." He turned and pointed to the ground ahead of him, breathless from fear. "It was there, gliding right toward me. But the black smoke rose from the ground and grew larger. It hovered over me and took a different shape. It formed an outline of a ghost with shredded clothes and disgusting rotting bones. It had no eyes and long fingers that inched toward me. It was like it was trying to capture my soul or something."

"You're scaring me," said Jezreel.

"I'm not trying to scare you, Jez," said Ithron. "But it happened. I must be seeing things. I know it sounds crazy. It's impossible. This is all impossible."

"Well, where is it now?" said Meldon, curiously.

Ithron took a step back and frantically turned his head in all directions, looking for whatever it was he saw. Jezreel began looking around too.

Meldon glanced toward the trees and bushes that were

nearby and even scanned the ground, but he didn't see anything resembling smoke.

Ithron abruptly stopped moving and stared toward a rocky hill beside the trail up ahead.

"What do you see?" said Meldon. He looked in the same direction and couldn't see anything out of place. A squirrel ran up a trunk and a bird landed on a branch. But there was no other movement, and there definitely wasn't any black smoke.

"Where is it, Ithron?" he said, spotting a look of pure horror on Ithron's face.

"It's coming right for us!" said Ithron, with a panic Meldon had never heard from him. "The hill!" he said, pointing toward the same direction he was looking at before. "It's coming from over there!"

Meldon could see a rocky hill along the trail up ahead, but there was no sign of smoke.

"Where on the hill?" said Meldon.

"There's an ocean of smoke rolling right down toward us!"

Meldon saw nothing of the sort, but he witnessed the urgency in Ithron's facial expression.

"Ithron, get back on your rabbit!" yelled Meldon. "If something's coming, we have to get out of here."

Meldon and Jezreel quickly climbed onto their rabbits and were ready to go. They waited for Ithron to mount Strike. Meldon could feel the hairs on his arms stand up as he continued to look around for whatever might be coming. It was an eerie feeling to know that something dangerous was approaching, but yet have no ability to see it. He was baffled. He looked at Ithron to see what was taking him so long, and watched him creep backward toward his rabbit as he continued to face the direction of the hill.

"Hurry up, Ithron!" yelled Jezreel. "Turn around and get

on your rabbit!"

At that moment, Ithron let out a bloodcurdling scream that made Meldon's stomach churn.

Meldon watched as Ithron gazed higher and higher, as if this invisible force was growing to huge proportions right in front of him.

Ithron stopped and stood frozen in place.

"What do I do!?" said Ithron, as he started to slowly back up again. "Give me my knife, Meldon! Quick!"

Meldon and Jezreel looked at one another in fear and confusion.

"He can't see the flowers," said Meldon, "and we can't see that."

Ithron let out another horrific scream and fell backward.

Meldon and Jezreel jumped off their rabbits again and rushed toward him.

Ithron was lying on his back, his eyes wide open.

"He's... dead!" screamed Jezreel. "He's dead!"

Meldon leaned down with urgency and grabbed Ithron's wrist. He let out a huge sigh of relief. "He's not dead, Jez. Don't worry. He's just in shock."

"Ithron, what's wrong!?" said Jezreel, grabbing his shoulders and shaking him. "Talk to us," she said, her voice cracking with emotion.

Meldon gazed around at the surrounding trees and didn't see anything out of the ordinary.

"I'm thinking that maybe at some point during the time we've been in this forest, he was poisoned by something he touched. It has to be poison."

Jezreel examined Ithron's skin.

"I don't see any redness on his skin," she said.

"Neither do I," said Meldon. He was stumped. "There has to be a logical explanation," he said, waving his hands in front of Ithron's eyes, to no avail.

Jezreel was crying.

"It's okay," he said. "We'll figure all of this out."

He looked down at Ithron and slapped his face slightly, to try to wake him. Then, in desperation, he slapped him harder.

"You're going to hurt him," said Jezreel.

"I'm trying to help him." He had to admit, part of him was enjoying the opportunity to slap Ithron around a little. But still, he didn't want any harm to come to him.

"Wake up!" he yelled. He could hear his voice echoing. "Come on, you're making Jezreel cry. You don't want that, do you?"

It dawned on him that Ezstasia might be sprawled out somewhere in the exact same state that Ithron was in.

He took a deep breath, pushed his eyeglasses higher on the bridge of his nose, and yelled at the top of his lungs as he shook Ithron by the shoulders. "W-a-k-e… U-u-u-p!"

"Ithron, it's Jez," said Jezreel, softly. "Please wake up."

Ithron let out a long gasp, reaching for his knife instinctually.

Jezreel grabbed Ithron's wrist and held it. "It's okay, she said. "You're okay."

Ithron looked around half-dazed and terrified. Jezreel gently rubbed his arm to calm him.

"It was horrible," he said.

"What was it?" said Meldon. "Jez and I couldn't see it."

"How could you not see it? It was taller than the trees!"

Jezreel brought her hand up to Ithron's shoulder, where she rested it. "Can you tell us what you saw?"

Ithron closed his eyes as if he was envisioning the whole scene. Jezreel sure had a calming effect on him. She was about the only one who did.

"It started out low to the ground. A thick, black smoke. Then it came rolling down the hill—right toward me—and after stopping only meters away, it rose up until it was practically right on top of me." His voice trailed off as he remembered it.

"Then what?" said Meldon. "Tell us."

Ithron cleared his throat.

"The smoke... it formed into the shape of a giant figure, but it was different than the last time. The shape kept shifting every time it moved, so it was hard to make out at first. But it was definitely a figure, like a black skeleton, except with a giant, oversized skull. It looked like it took up the whole forest! The whole thing was made of black smoke—and it smelled just like the sulfur pits back home. The skull kept coming toward me, as if it was separate from its body. I could see it grinning, like it was mocking me. Every time I looked at it, I felt it sucking the life and joy out of me."

Ithron's voice was cracking, so Jezreel ran her fingers through his hair to relax him. Meldon saw a single tear running down his face.

"You should have seen its eyes," said Ithron. "Giant, dark sockets, full of emptiness and evil, staring right down at me. Then it..."

Ithron paused, as if he was afraid to speak aloud the horrors he had seen.

"What?" said Jezreel into his ear. "It's okay. You can tell us. What did it do?"

Ithron had a pained look on his face and tightly closed his eyes.

"It swooped its head down toward me," he said. "Roaring and screaming like nothing I've ever heard in my life. It pierced my ears and I could feel its horrible scream rush right through me. I could feel its darkness creep all the way into my bones, and it hurt. It was like ice and fire were entering my body, burning, freezing and destroying it, one limb at a time. Then I fell backward, and… well, I don't remember any more."

He began to shiver, and Jezreel put her arm around his shoulder.

"It's over Ithron," said Jezreel. "I'm glad you're okay."

"Jez," said Ithron as he looked down at the ground. "I remember something else."

Ithron glanced up at Jezreel and then at Meldon for a second, but he quickly looked down again as his face grew flush. It was the first time Meldon had ever seen Ithron act shyly. After a few seconds, Ithron looked up at Jezreel.

"I heard Meldon saying your name, Jez. And I heard your voice. I heard you speaking, and that's what I focused on. That's how I got out of that nightmare."

There was an uncomfortable silence and even Meldon wasn't sure how to formulate a response at this moment. He noticed the embarrassed look on both of their faces and he suddenly felt out of place.

"Uh… okay, Ithron," said Meldon, taking hold of Ithron's arm. "Let's get you up."

Jezreel grabbed the other arm and they both helped him to his feet.

"We need to get out of here," said Ithron, his head darting around like a raven as he looked around for the smoke creature.

"I think Ithron's right," said Meldon. "Even if this was just in his head—"

"It's not in my head!" said Ithron.

"Well, it *is* possible that you may have touched a poison plant or that you were bitten by something. Either way, I agree, we need to get out of this forest."

"I feel so bad for Ezstasia," said Jezreel. "What if the same thing happened to her?"

"For her sake, let's hope it didn't," said Ithron.

"Well, the good news," said Meldon, "is that it seems you can recover from it. Maybe the others found her."

They made their way to their rabbits, who were fortunately still where they had left them.

"Before we go," said Meldon, "I need to go behind that tree, just really quick." He pointed to a tree a few feet away from their rabbits.

"No, we need to go now," said Ithron, scowling at him.

"What do you think you'll find back there?" said Jezreel.

"Nothing, I hope," said Meldon. "I need to... well, I drank a lot of water earlier and... I'm sorry, I really cannot wait."

Jezreel's face turned bright red. "Okay, go do your... thing," she said. "We'll be right here."

"Hurry," said Ithron, as he took out a carrot from the side of his saddle bag and ripped off the greens, throwing them onto the ground.

₧ ℂ ₧ ℅

Meldon quickly finished his business behind the tree and walked back to the others. But when he returned to the spot, his friends weren't there. He looked around the clearing, but there was no sign of anyone, not even the rabbits.

He checked for footprints, but only saw his own against the soft dirt. Even the carrot greens that Ithron threw to the ground weren't there.

"Guys?!" he yelled. "Jez?! Ithron?!"

He wouldn't put it past Ithron to leave him there, but he knew Jezreel would never do that. Even if they were playing a quick joke on him for some awful reason, he didn't think that they would have taken his rabbit *and* the carrot stems.

"Guys, seriously. If this is a joke..." His heart started to quicken as he realized that he was alone in this forest, and without Mr. Feet.

"Guys!" he yelled in desperation one more time. Now panic began to set in. He frantically ran around the area, but nothing looked familiar. Now he couldn't even find the tree that he 'went' behind. Had he lost his path? Or did they wander off? Could something have happened to them? He began to feel dizzy when he heard the faint sound of laughter coming from behind him.

He immediately ran toward it and finally recognized the clearing. But where before there was no one to be found, now he saw Jezreel and Ithron laughing and surrounded by their rabbits.

"Is this some kind of joke!?" said Meldon, startling them.

"Why did you come out from over *there*?" said Jezreel, with a perplexed look on her face.

"Took you long enough," said Ithron.

"Enough with the jokes already," said Meldon angrily.

"Meldon, what happened?" said Jezreel. "Why are you so upset?"

"Did things not run smoothly?" said Ithron, smirking.

"Like you both didn't know that I was over there," said Meldon, pointing back to where he had just come from. "I came right back, and you guys weren't here. And neither were the rabbits. Not funny, with everything we're going through right now."

Jezreel and Ithron looked at each other. Meldon recognized that look. It was the same look he and Jezreel gave each other when Ithron had his encounter.

"Meldon," said Jezreel. "We never left this spot. We would never joke around like that."

Meldon's mind was racing. He knew for sure he had checked this very spot, which reminded him of this same situation that had happened the previous day with his arrow.

His eyes scanned the area and he spotted the carrot greens

that Ithron had thrown to the ground in the same spot. He knew for a fact that it wasn't in his head. It was this forest; he was now completely sure of it. He was sure of something else, too. Now that they were all together, they needed to stay together until they were out of this creepy place.

"Hey look," said Ithron, interrupting his thoughts. He watched as Ithron picked a yellow flower off a bush and handed it to Jezreel. "They really do have flowers here."

"Wait a minute," said Meldon. "*You* saw a flower?"

"Don't you see it?" said Ithron.

"Yes, of course. But is this the first one you've seen?"

"Yes," said Ithron.

"Interesting. This means something," said Meldon.

"What are you talking about?" said Jezreel.

"I'm not sure yet, but I know it seems—"

He stopped when he noticed Ithron staring at something and backing up.

"Oh please tell me you can see this," said Ithron, horrified.

"Oh, no, not again," said Meldon.

"Ithron," said Jezreel. "Stay with us. Don't give it any attention."

"It's not real," said Ithron, closing his eyes, his legs trembling. "It's not real." He kept repeating it, but his face was growing paler by the second. Meldon tried grabbing his arm to pull him toward the rabbits, but without warning, Ithron began gasping for air. As soon as his hands went to his throat, he fell backward, slipping out of Meldon's grasp and hitting the ground hard.

Jezreel screamed and her eyes flooded with tears. Meldon rushed to help Ithron, who was sprawled out on his back with his arms to his sides.

He knelt down and checked Ithron's pulse.

"He's alive," he said. A minute later, he could see Ithron's skin turning a pale grey, his lips drying up and cracking before his very eyes.

"What's happening?!" screamed Jezreel. "What can we do?!"

"I don't know." He ran to his saddle bag and started rooting through it.

"Hurry!" she yelled.

"I'm trying, I'm trying. I don't know what he needs. I don't know what's wrong with him."

Meldon realized there was nothing in his saddle bag that could help, but he did recall that some plants he had studied about did have healing properties. He searched his mind trying to recall which plants were the correct ones and began pulling leaves from certain bushes and trees. He realized that it was a desperate move that probably wouldn't work.

He heard shouts coming from behind him. He turned just in time to see Fin and Lanzzie galloping toward them on their rabbits.

"Lanz!" yelled Jezreel. "You have to help us. It's Ithron!"

As they got closer, Fin and Lanzzie jumped off their rabbits before they had even come to a halt and rushed toward the fallen Ithron.

"I think it's possible that it's a toxin from a plant or insect," said Meldon. "So I took these leaves and figured—" He noticed they were both bruised and bloody. "Are you guys okay?"

"It's no toxin," said Fin. He lifted up Ithron's shirt.

Meldon gasped.

Ithron's chest under his shirt was grey and cracked, with portions of his skin completely burnt and black. As Meldon stared in disbelief, he saw something so faint that he wasn't sure if his eyes were playing tricks on him. On Ithron's ribs, the cracks in his skin had formed the faint outline of a skull. Horrified, he closed his eyes, shook his head and opened them again. He watched in confusion as the skull slowly faded away. The cracks began to intensify and spread throughout Ithron's entire body.

Jezreel jumped back and hid behind Lanzzie.

"Take those leaves and mix them with water," said Fin.

Meldon looked at him. "But if it's not a toxin, what good will they do?"

"Just do it!" said Fin. "I'll explain later."

Meldon ran to his saddle bag and grabbed a stone bowl. He filled it with water from his canister and mixed the leaves in.

"Hurry," yelled Fin. Meldon quickly brought the mixture to Fin and watched as Fin laid one wet leaf at a time along Ithron's mouth.

"The key is familiarity," said Fin. "Anything that can bring his mind back to us and away from what he saw. Awakening his senses can help him fight it."

"How can you possibly know that?" said Jezreel.

"Long story," said Fin. "No time to explain."

"If you're trying to alert his senses," said Meldon, "then put these dry leaves under his nose. We taste more through smell than we do through our taste buds."

Fin looked up at him. "That doesn't sound—"

"Just do it!" said Lanzzie.

Fin quickly put a leaf under Ithron's nose, while leaving the others on his mouth.

After what felt like forever, Ithron still wasn't responding.

"It's not working," said Jezreel.

Fin shook his head. "We need to get him out of the forest now." He looked up at Meldon. "Help me lift him onto Zon."

Fin grabbed Ithron under the shoulders while Meldon took hold of his feet.

As he helped Fin position Ithron across Zon's back, Meldon checked his surroundings. He was anxious to get out of the forest before anything else happened.

🐓 ⤊ 🐓 ⤊

Meldon rode alongside Fin, holding Strike's reins as the rabbit rode close behind him. Lanzzie and Jezreel lagged slightly behind. Finally, he could see the sunset over the open field just ahead. They quickened their pace until they emerged out of the forest's brush. He breathed a sigh of relief as he gazed out at the expanse of the field. He was overjoyed to finally be out of the forest, though he was still worried for Ezstasia and Ithron.

"Let's get him down," said Fin.

They all dismounted their rabbits. Meldon and Lanzzie assisted him in delicately lifting Ithron off of Zon and onto the soft grass. Jezreel was anxiously observing. Meldon suspected she was growing quite fond of Ithron, though she was a caregiver at heart, regardless.

Lanzzie and Fin crouched down by Ithron, who still looked grey. "You need to fight this!" yelled Lanzzie to Ithron.

"Come on, wake up!" shouted Fin.

Meldon checked Ithron's pulse once more. His heart was still beating, though it didn't seem as strong as before. He was about to start slapping him again when he heard shouts coming from the other end of the field. He looked up to see Randin, Zander, and Pallu galloping toward them on their rabbits.

"Look," yelled Pallu. "They have Ezstasia!"

Meldon could hear their voices echoing across the entire field.

"No we don't!" Meldon yelled back. "It's Ithron!"

Meldon glanced over at Lanzzie, who was visibly heartbroken to see they didn't have Ezstasia. The hopelessness in her eyes was palpable and the frown forming on her quivering lips spoke volumes.

Jezreel knelt down behind Ithron and began whispering to him when Zander, Randin and Pallu arrived, clumsily climbing off their rabbits.

"What happened?" said Pallu.

"A giant, black fog skeleton attacked him," said Meldon, suddenly realizing how ridiculous that sounded.

"Oh," said Pallu. "Zander's was a spider."

Meldon looked at Zander. "A spider?"

"A really big one," said Zander.

As Meldon joined the others in trying to revive Ithron, Pallu hovered overhead.

"Come on, buddy," said Pallu. "You need to snap out of it. And besides, grey is so not your color."

Zander elbowed Pallu. "He looks like a dead fish and you're making jokes? This is serious."

"No, it's fine," said Fin, glancing up. "He needs positive encouragement, and anything familiar." He focused his gaze on Ithron again. "Come on, lad, we're all here with you. Fight this! I know you can hear me."

"I know what he needs," said Pallu. "And I'm going to go get it. Ithron, don't go anywhere." He ran toward his rabbit.

"Meldon," said Fin, "do you still have those leaves?"

Just as Meldon was about to hand him the bowl, Pallu returned, carrying a large jug with an oversized wooden spoon.

"Is that what I think it is?" said Meldon.

"None other than my mom's stew."

Meldon shook his head. He felt like they were all wasting their time with silly ideas.

"Pallu!" yelled Zander. "Are you serious with that?"

"Why not try it?"

"I think we need to get him back to the Cottages and have

the elders look at him," said Meldon. "They can at least consult the old scripts."

"I doubt the old scripts can do anything about this," Fin said, as Pallu knelt over Ithron.

"And *I* doubt the old scripts have my mom's stew recipe," said Pallu, dipping the large spoon into the jug.

"Please Ithron," said Jezreel. "Please come back to us. I know you can fight it."

Meldon wasn't sure if he was just seeing things, which he seemed to be doing a lot of lately, but it looked like Ithron's skin began to lighten every time Jezreel spoke.

"Nobody can resist my mom's stew," said Pallu, holding the spoon under Ithron's nose. "Nobody."

Meldon watched intently. He could've sworn Ithron's skin was lightening even more. Pallu put the jug next to Ithron's head and fanned the fumes toward his face.

After a few moments of that, along with Jezreel's words of encouragement, Ithron made a slight move.

"He blinked!" yelled Fin.

Then his fingers began to twitch.

"I think it's working," said Meldon. "Pallu, keep it up. Come on, Ithron, fight this!"

Pallu continued to fan the fumes toward Ithron as Jezreel leaned over Ithron's face.

"Wake up, Ithron," she said, softly, touching his forehead. "It's Jez. We're all here for you."

Ithron took a sudden deep breath and his eyes opened. He looked up at Jezreel and the color began to return to his face. Slowly, he lifted his shaky, weak right hand and touched her cheek. It was the most sincere gesture Meldon had ever seen him make—another first for Ithron during this journey.

"*You,*" said Ithron, longingly, as he gazed up at Jezreel's beaming face.

A tear formed in his eye. Even Meldon was getting choked

up, and he wasn't one to be sentimental.

"Her!?" said Pallu, breaking the moment. "Hey buddy, let's not give her all the glory. My mom's famous stew deserves a *you*."

After a slight delayed reaction, everyone began to laugh at once, while Jezreel continued to gaze down at Ithron.

Pallu was trying to help Ithron sit up, when Ithron grabbed Jezreel's face and planted a long, passionate kiss on her lips. Nobody was expecting that, especially Jezreel. It didn't look like she minded it, though. It was obvious that she very much enjoyed it.

The awkward moment seemed to go on forever. Everyone looked at one another uncomfortably.

"Well, that's one way to get a bride," said Pallu, breaking the silence. Meldon burst out laughing along with everyone else. Jezreel's face turned bright red, while Ithron looked at her with a big smile.

"Meldon, help me figure this out," said Pallu. "How do I get myself to turn grey so I can wake up kissing *my* bride? Should I eat a grey, poisonous mushroom? Or maybe I should let a giant grey bug sting me? Because I'll be happy to do either one of those."

Zander put his arm around Pallu. "It won't help," he said.

Meldon noticed that Lanzzie wasn't laughing, and he knew that she had a good reason. He approached her and put his arm around her.

"I don't think I'll ever see her again," she said, sobbing.

"You don't know that, Lanz," he said. "I'm sure she's hiding somewhere safe. We have to believe that."

"But we don't know that," she said. "Ithron was lucky we pulled him out of that forest so quickly. My sister's been in there for two days now."

Meldon had to admit she had a point, but he wasn't about to tell her that.

Fin approached and saved Meldon from offering up an awkward response.

"We're not giving up yet," said Fin. "We'll need to get back to the Cottages before dark, but if we have to risk telling others, then that's what we'll do. We just have to figure out a plan."

"Lanz, don't give up," said Jezreel.

Lanzzie seemed too defeated and exhausted to answer. She simply nodded.

"Everyone, listen," said Fin, walking to the center of the group to address them. "Let's meet at my cottage after we check in the rabbits and unload. Bring food to snack on. It'll help keep us awake. We may have a long night of planning, so you might as well bring blankets, pillows, and whatever else you need, just in case. It's time we make some important decisions."

Meldon patted Lanzzie on the back gently to show support. He watched a tear roll down her face, but he didn't know what to say. He couldn't even fathom how helpless she must've felt.

"Whatever you do, you can't lose hope," said Fin. "I've seen how determined you can be. You're just like your sister. She'll need that from you now. She's out there alive somewhere, you have to believe that. We're not giving up."

She looked at him and gave a slight smile that Meldon could tell wasn't entirely sincere. "Let's go Lanz," said Fin.

CHAPTER SIX

Prince Alazar sat at his ornate wooden desk—a desk that once bore witness to the fabled glory days of Old Vynterra in this very spot. He contemplated the gravity of his position, especially now, with rumors of forbidden magic running rampant.

As he thought about what he was going to write, he held two white, feather quills side by side and examined them. He placed the shorter of the two into a well-polished wooden box that contained the full set. He sighed and observed the ancient desk, with its magnificent three-headed dragon carved into the front panel and one on each of the curved legs. He opened the bottom drawer and placed the box of remaining quills inside. Ready to begin, he lifted his chosen quill and nodded to his archminister, Eliezer.

With a slight look of concern, Eliezer, who was advanced in years, placed the scroll on the desk and unraveled it, his wrinkled hands shaking as he spread the material out. Prince Alazar dipped the quill and began to write on his parchment while Eliezer tended to other matters around the chamber.

The prince paused occasionally to ensure that every word was written with wisdom and heart. He truly felt the burden and weight of each sentence that he wrote, and knew all too well that his words would one day become etched into the annals of history, alongside the scrolls of long ago. Indeed, he was documenting the actions he'd soon have to take to protect the kingdom—the kind of actions that brought nothing but death to his beloved, legendary ancestor—Prince Valorian. But the potential risks in that forest were simply too great to ignore.

He stopped to stare once again at the intricately crafted three-headed dragon on the desk.

"Tell me," he said to the wooden dragon. "Do I act with honor?" He thought of the Great War and how the kings of old must have felt before signing the treaty that changed the world forever—a treaty that separated all magic from the human world, and one he'd sworn an oath to protect.

"The dragon won't tell you that," said Eliezer, gazing at him from across the room, "any more than the blessed stars advised your ancestors."

"So, you heard me," said the prince as he let out a slight chuckle.

Eliezer smiled. "I may be old, but my ears still work sometimes—*and* my eyes. You ask if you act with honor. Pardon me for saying, sire, but it seems to me you confuse honor with wisdom."

"How so?"

"You have a keen sense of duty," said Eliezer, approaching. "Of that, I have no doubt. But what you really want to know is whether you act with wisdom."

"And do I?"

"Even wisdom has its limits in times of uncertainty, my lord. And these are uncertain times indeed."

He noticed Eliezer was holding an old copper balance scale, which the old man placed on the desk.

"You must act," said Eliezer. "But act with prudence.

With caution. Prepare for the risks. Once you have done that—"

He paused and lifted a shaky hand to place a small gold coin on the left side of the scale. The scale teetered until the left side eventually lowered to the desk.

"The rest," said the old man, "will fall as it may."

The prince nodded. He always respected Eliezer's advice, which, over the years, has shaped who he's become today.

Eliezer exited Prince Alazar's study and the prince returned his attention to his scroll. Hearing someone enter, he looked back up and saw that Sir Borak, one of his more hard-headed knights, had entered the room.

"Forgive me, my lord," said Borak, "but we have the criminal prepared to be hanged."

"And which criminal are we speaking of?" said the prince.

"The thief—who stole from one of the nobles."

Prince Alazar shook his head. "How has it gotten this far?" he said. "I ordered that he should receive a just punishment. Do you consider this just?"

"If you please, my lord, justice should be swift and harsh."

"Justice should be fair. That is the very meaning of just. I will not have a man hanged for stealing baubles from royalty."

"I believe it was more than that, sire. It was—"

"Whatever it was, was it worth more than his life?"

"I... I don't know."

"Do you know *why* he stole?"

The knight remained silent.

"I thought as much. You don't know whether this man was desperate or simply a glutton. In any case, hanging is quite extreme, don't you agree?"

"Yes, my lord."

"The justice I decree is that he will be imprisoned in the dungeons for as long a time as it took for the owners to earn the items he stole. Then he shall be freed. Is that understood?"

"It is, sire. But the owners… they're nobles. They didn't necessarily *earn* what he stole."

"Then it's a simple matter of determining their average monthly profits from land rentals, farming, and bank interest and dividing it by the value of what was stolen. Have I made myself clear?"

"Yes, sire."

"Let it be known that I give equal favor to all people, whether they're royalty or not, just as my ancestors did within the very walls of this castle. You would do well to read the scrolls."

The knight knelt and bowed his head.

"You may go, Sir Borak."

After Sir Borak exited, the prince heard a gentle knock at the open door.

Eliezer showed two noblemen in, whom the prince immediately recognized as Zebulun and Hiram. They were hard to miss. Hiram was as wide as Zebulun was tall. They were already arguing with one another, which was no surprise. Despite being best of friends since childhood, they rarely agreed on anything.

Both men immediately bowed.

"You summoned us, my lord?" said Zebulun, whose hawkish face and pronounced cheekbones projected a certain air of intelligence.

"Yes," said the prince. "It concerns the forest. I'm sure you're aware of the rumors."

"Most certainly, sire," said Zebulun. "It's getting considerably worse, I must say."

"Children's tales, if you ask me," said Hiram, his portly face turning red. "Gossipers, all of them."

"Hardly," said Zebulun. "There were three sightings this

week alone. Seven in a fortnight. I know that I don't need to tell you what the villagers are saying, Your Highness."

"And what *are* they saying?" said the prince.

Zebulun smirked. "Some say the dark forces of old have returned from the Magiclands."

"And others?"

"They say another kingdom may be involved."

"Terrible theories, both of them," said Hiram. "No kingdom would dare. And the Magiclands are across the sea."

"But, my dear Hiram," said Zebulun, "I haven't even told *you* the worst rumor."

"Of course you haven't," said Hiram. "And I suppose you won't hold your wretched tongue in telling it now, will you?" Hiram grumbled under his breath.

Zebulun leaned in toward the prince. "If you don't mind me saying, my lord, there's talk about the woman who was just found. The one who died in that forest. They think she was someone from our villages. Some say she was the one responsible for the strange happenings in the forest, and they're becoming increasingly vocal about it."

"Good," said Hiram. "Maybe it'll stop all the confounded children from running to that dreadful place just to gather up a fright. It's terrible what—"

"Gentlemen," said the prince, rising from his desk. "The woman we found in the forest was not from our villages, nor do we believe she came from any of the nearby Cottage farms. We suspect she's a highborn lady, but from where, we're unsure."

"Highborn?" said Hiram. "Why were we not told of this?"

"I'm telling you now."

"But how will we know what kingdom to notify of her passing?"

"I must agree with my well-fed friend, my lord," said

Zebulun. "We must do what we can to find out where she is from. Her poor family has a right to know of her death."

"I plan to find out," said the prince. "As soon as she awakens."

"Awakens?" said Zebulun, his eyes as wide as dinner plates. "What manner of woman is this who awakens from the dead? Is she a ghost, sire?"

The prince laughed and walked around his desk toward the nobles and placed his hands atop Zebulun's shoulders. "Not a ghost, dear Zebulun. The woman we found in the forest is very much alive."

"Alive? And a highborn?" said Zebulun. "Then the villagers are right! Another kingdom *is* behind this. Why else would a highborn woman from another kingdom be in that forest, so close to the Vynterran border?"

"That's the very question I've been pondering myself," said the prince as he walked back to his chair and sat down. "At any rate, I'd caution you not to make any assumptions or hold judgment of the lady until I've had a chance to speak with her."

"It does seem to be an awful coincidence," said Zebulun, "does it not? Her appearance at such a time?"

"I make it a habit to never speculate without the facts," said the prince. "Meanwhile, I called you both in here for a reason."

"Of course, my lord," said Zebulun.

"We're at your service," added Hiram, puffing his chest up with pride.

Prince Alazar leaned back against his chair. "We've all seen the recent evidence that there may be something in that forest after all. I won't deny that. But, until we know more, I'm not going to guess what's behind it. I don't want anyone else to do so, either. I need you both to put the twin villages at ease."

"But how?" said Hiram. "Especially the Western villagers. You know how they are, my lord."

"Inform them that we're investigating the situation and that they should continue to observe my decree and remain within the Vynterran territory, by order of the prince. They are commanded to stay out of the forest. Inform them we have an injured woman, not a dead one. Speak ambiguously of her because we don't know the facts. And report to *me* if anything escalates. Do I have your word?"

"Of course, my lord," said Zebulun.

Hiram nodded. "You do, sire."

"Good," said the prince. "If this woman is in any way involved, or if there is a threat to our kingdom, I'll call a meeting of the council, and we will then discuss how and when to raise the alert. For now, my work calls to me." He rubbed his hands together. "Good day, gentlemen."

The two men bid their farewells and exited the room as Eliezer came to collect them.

Prince Alazar picked up his quill and continued to write. The words were flowing more smoothly now. He had become more clearheaded about how he wanted to frame his position on the matters at hand.

As soon as he completed the final sentence, he carefully rolled up the parchment and tied it with a loose ribbon. He stood and walked to the bookcase, pulling out the fourth book from the left on the upper shelf. The faded, unmarked book was hollow, like several other books which had been left there for ages. He placed the scroll inside the book and returned it to the shelf.

He turned around and there was a knock on the door, startling him.

"Eliezer, no more visit—"

He looked up to see that it wasn't Eliezer. It was his head housekeeper, Miss Tee.

"Beg your pardon, my lord," she said, "but you did say to come to you once the Lady from the forest has awoken."

"She's awake?" he said.

"Wide awake, my lord. She even spoke to me."

"Good, good. What did she say?"

"Well, for one, m'lord, she said she isn't a Lady at all."

"That's odd. She said her name was Lady Ar—" He paused and wondered for a moment if there was more to this strange woman than meets the eye. He gathered himself, then looked at Miss Tee, calmly.

"Did she say who she is?" he said.

"Why yes, she gave her name. Oh dear, what was it?" she said, scratching her head. "Oh yes, it's… Ezstasia."

CHAPTER SEVEN

Still too exhausted to rise, Ezstasia held the cream, silk covers against her face. They were made of the softest, smoothest material she'd ever touched, and the delicate fabric felt soothing against her skin. The bed she was in was fit for a king or queen, with a plush, burgundy, draped canopy supported by four wooden posts, each with an intricately-carved serpentine swirl design. Wherever she was, the family must've been well-to-do.

A brief knock at the large double wooden doors startled her. She lifted her head slightly and watched the doors slowly open, the old hinges creaking loudly.

The same woman who she had seen earlier entered the room. She was a pleasant enough woman, jolly and plump. Ezstasia's head felt heavy, and she felt herself drifting in and out of sleep.

"How are you feeling?" said the woman. "I see you didn't touch your food tray. Poor thing, I suppose you don't have an appetite."

Ezstasia could barely utter a syllable, but she managed to let out a slight groan. Then her head fell back against the soft pillow and she shut her eyes.

"I'm sorry, Miss Ezstasia," said the woman. "You've had quite the fall."

Too tired to open her eyes again, she heard the woman's footsteps move closer to the bed.

"Where am I?" said Ezstasia, still with her eyes shut.

"Don't worry, dear, you're in good hands. In case you've forgotten, I'm Miss Tee. I'm the head housekeeper here. I've been caring for you."

"Housekeeper... Miss Tee," she repeated, half asleep. "How did I get here?"

She felt the throbbing pain intensify on the side of her head. She tried to remember what had happened, but she couldn't recall a thing. She opened her eyes again and focused on a faded, silver, ancient tree that was stitched into the red canopy above her.

"Never you mind about that now. Are you feeling well enough to take a warm bath? That always helps me when I've taken ill."

"I don't know," she said.

She forced herself to sit up slightly, as she watched Miss Tee walk past the foot of her bed and toward a set of rickety, wooden window shutters on the far right wall. The shutters were already slightly open, and, after her vision cleared, she could see why. A vine had grown right through the center of the shutters from the outside in, winding up the wall and across the ceiling, continuing halfway across the room. She moved the canopy drape aside and saw that the vine was twisted around an old, wrought iron chandelier which was mottled with hints of faded gold plating. Miss Tee opened the shutters wider, bringing more light into the room, revealing the dust particles in the air and the peeling frescoes on the wall by the door.

"Pardon our appearance, dear. This chamber hasn't been occupied since—well, come to think of it, I'm not sure if it ever was occupied."

Ezstasia lifted her hand and felt her head where the intense pain was coming from. She felt heavy bandages wrapped all the way around her head.

"Oh no. Don't do that, dear. Our physician tended to your wound and patched it up quite carefully. You probably don't even remember taking the Betony Milk. It's also why you're lightheaded. The warm bath should help clear your head."

Ezstasia watched as Miss Tee grabbed the silver food tray on the small wooden table by her bed and placed it at the foot of the bed. She was surprised Miss Tee could even lift it. The shiny tray was loaded with bread, cheese, grapes, dried meats, and a silver water pitcher accompanied by a small dainty cup.

"I think I'd like that bath," she said, "if it isn't too much trouble."

"No, no, no dear," said Miss Tee. "Not at all, I insist."

As Miss Tee helped her sit up, Ezstasia gazed around the room. It was magnificent with its high ceiling, beautiful tapestries, and an enormous chandelier. However, it did look as if it were from the days of antiquity and hadn't been used or cleaned since then.

As she stared beyond the foot of her bed, she could see a dusty, stocked bookshelf on one side of the far wall. Along the rest of the wall, empty picture frames of all sizes were arranged haphazardly, though a few of the larger ones had glorious paintings of flora and fauna. Between many of the frames stood random wooden shelves of varying designs, each displaying unusually-shaped pottery and other objects. Ezstasia shifted her focus to an old desk that stood alone against a wall, with a drapery of clear canopy netting falling gracefully around it from the ceiling.

She glanced over at the fancy food tray on her bed and began picking at the food. The grapes were sweeter than any she had ever tasted, and the assortment of cheeses were exquisite. She hadn't realized just how hungry she was.

"I'll fetch the servants to prepare a nice hot bath with lavender and lemon oils," said Miss Tee.

"Servants!?" said Ezstasia. She was sincerely concerned about not knowing where she was or what happened to her, but she was grateful that they were treating her with such care and kindness. She wondered who these people were that had such riches.

Miss Tee exited, shutting the large heavy door behind her while Ezstasia reached for the snack tray and grabbed a few more grapes. She noticed that the thick, silk blanket which had been keeping her warm had a large, ancient golden tree stitched into it, with a border of golden tree roots outlining the edges.

She pushed the blanket aside and brought her legs to the floor. She felt sore and weak. She wondered what had happened to her and where her sister and friends could be.

She rose and slowly pushed the thick canopy drapes aside, proceeding to the small desk area. She parted the netting that surrounded the desk and entered. Approaching the desk, she spotted three small wooden boxes on the desktop, just beside a pewter inkwell. Feeling a bit dizzy, she pulled out the dainty wooden chair and sat down. She picked up one of the boxes and placed it in front of her. She slowly, opened it up and looked inside. There was a small silver-lined mirror with a diamond-studded handle. She took it out carefully and looked at her reflection. She looked awful! No wonder Miss Tee wanted her to bathe.

Just as she was about to open one of the other boxes, a knock on the door startled her. She stood just as Miss Tee entered.

"Your bath is ready, dear."

Ezstasia followed her out of the room and down a long

corridor. It was like entering another world, with frescoes painted on the left wall with overlapping swirls of varying shades of red. The wall to her right had been painted in vertical stripes of dark blue and light blue. She followed Miss Tee past several wooden doors on both sides, each adorned with intricately detailed tree carvings. With each door she passed, she wondered what was behind them.

One thing was for sure: whoever owned this place was infatuated with trees.

Finally, Miss Tee stopped in front of two beautifully designed double doors, pristinely coated in gold, with silver tree branches for knobs. She pushed the doors open and Ezstasia followed her inside.

"Your bathing room," said Miss Tee, as two servant girls bowed.

Ezstasia couldn't get over how opulent the room was. In the center lay a beautiful wooden tub, with pearl inlays and elaborate swirls carved into its base. Just beyond the foot of the tub was a small, marble fireplace. The walls were covered in shiny, golden mosaics with pearls and other gems sprinkled throughout. Even the cathedral ceiling had been covered in an intricate, gold design. Thick steam filled the air and the satisfying smell of a sweet lavender and lemon citrus wafted up from the tub. She looked around at the welcoming candles sitting on iron wall sconces and saw a chorus of small flames dancing and flickering through the mist. The whole space was mesmerizing.

"I feel like I'm in a dream," she said.

"The water will clear your head, dear," said Miss Tee, apparently taking her statement literally.

As Miss Tee left the room, one of the servant girls approached and held up a warm robe, which was her signal to undress. Still in a daze, she slowly removed her garments and stepped into the plush robe.

"There are towels next to the grand mirror, Miss," said the girl. "And you'll find rose and mint soaps on the glass table by the bath. If you need anything, my name is Elyse. You can just call for me."

Ezstasia was far too entranced by the room to respond.

"If there isn't anything else, I will leave you to your bath, Miss," said Elyse, as she and the other servant girl left quietly.

Ezstasia looked up and noticed a small open window high above her, letting a singular ray of light shine into the candlelit room.

She removed her robe and placed it on the marble vanity by the gold-lined, grand mirror. Carefully, she pulled the back and sides of her hair loose, without disturbing the bandage, untying the braid and letting her hair fall down to the small of her back. She slowly stepped into the tub; the marble fireplace flickered only a few feet in front of her. As soon as she lowered her body into the tub and leaned back, she could feel the warmth envelop her body, the scent of lavender and just a hint of lemon intoxicating her. She rested her head on the back of the tub and gazed up, noticing a delicate chandelier dangling right above her. Each arm of the fixture was shaped like a pearl-covered branch with hundreds of thin, dainty leaves dangling down from each of them. The chandelier gently swayed with the soft breeze that emanated from the small window overhead. It gave the impression of a living tree as each leaf moved in its own fashion.

As she began to wash, her mind drifted. She thought of her sister and her friends, and exactly what had occurred to lead her to arrive at this magical palace. She was anxious to find out, but for now she was too tired to think about anything else. Between the candles, the warmth, and the lavender, it wasn't long before she found herself losing the fight to stay awake.

ഇ ഌ ഇ ഌ

Ezstasia didn't know where she was. She felt numb and surrounded by darkness. She heard someone calling to her from a great distance, but she couldn't discern who it was. It was a female voice yelling and calling her name. She couldn't answer. She tried to move her lips, but she felt paralyzed. She felt two hands grasp her arms and begin to gently shake her. Then a loud yell near her ear jarred her.

"Miss!"

She opened her eyes. That's when she realized she was still in the tub. The servant girl, Elyse, was above her looking down. She must've fallen asleep.

"We were worried about you," said Elyse. "You did not answer when we called, and with your head… well, anyway, how do you feel?"

Ezstasia waited a few seconds to fully awaken.

"I think I'm, ok. I'm—I'm freezing." She looked at her quivering, wrinkled hands.

"You were in here for a long time."

As Elyse held up the robe, she rose out of the tub and slipped into it as she tried to keep her quivering body still. It actually felt really warm. Elyse must've warmed it by the fireplace.

"I'll show you back to your room, Miss," said Elyse.

She followed Elyse back to the room, where she noticed Miss Tee had laid out a variety of fancy gowns that looked like something a princess would wear.

"Miss Tee will return shortly," said Elyse as she exited, shutting the door behind her.

Ezstasia examined the gowns and selected one that was long and flowy. It was forest-green with a braided gold rope that tied around the waist. She laid the gown out on the bed and admired it. Careful not to tear the delicate material, she tried it on. She became slightly giddy when she realized that it fit perfectly. She picked up a small, silver hairbrush and meandered back to the desk area to grab the hand mirror. She gently combed through her hair, avoiding the bandage around her head, and styled a loose fishtail braid in the back.

Just as she finished tying the gown's golden rope, Miss Tee knocked lightly on the door and entered.

"Oh dear," said Miss Tee. "You look absolutely stunning. And dare I say refreshed."

"Miss Tee," said Ezstasia, "you've been quite gracious, but my sister and friends must be worried sick about me. I've got to get back, and I really must find out what happened to me."

"Of course, dear, we have every intention of helping you. I'll take you to my lord now, and he'll explain everything."

"Your lord? Is that how I shall address him?"

"Oh he's not picky, but you can call him my lord, Your Grace, Your Highness, sire, Your—"

"Wait a minute. Are you saying I'm—"

"I'll let my lord tell you where you are," she said. "He insisted on being the one to tell you everything. Oh dear, I've probably said too much already."

Miss Tee walked past her toward the desk area and passed through the clear netting. "Come now," she said. "Through here."

"Through where? I only see a desk and a wall."

"You'll soon learn that nothing is as it appears to be here."

Confused, Ezstasia followed her through the canopy netting as Miss Tee walked to the right of the desk and moved some of the netting to the side.

"Do you see those protruding roots on the wall?" said Miss Tee, pointing up at the wall by the desk. "The ones between the dragon sculpture and the rabbit painting?"

"Um… I do. They're beautiful," said Ezstasia, unsure what Miss Tee was getting at.

"Push the one that's directly aligned with the inkwell on the desk. The third one from the left. Go ahead, try it."

Ezstasia walked to the right of the desk and spotted the oddly shaped root. Hesitatingly, she pressed it, noticing that it pushed into the wall quite easily.

Immediately, she heard a loud rumbling, a deep thundering which shook the floor in front of her. A section of the wall, resembling a door, began to open away from them, revealing the entranceway to another room.

Ezstasia could sense that the expression on her face was one of bewilderment.

Miss Tee smiled at her reaction. "The builder was quite inventive, as you see. Go ahead. It's quite a cozy haven. I'm quite sure you will love it."

Ezstasia walked toward the doorway, eager to see what was inside. Part of her wondered why Miss Tee didn't seem concerned about keeping this secret chamber a secret.

She entered through the doorway and pressed a hand to her chest in amazement as she gazed around the surprisingly large, cavernous circular gallery. She looked up and saw a high cathedral ceiling. The room was well-lit, with sunlight coming in from large stained-glass windows. Huge candles in giant sconces surrounded the entire area, offering additional lighting.

She was enthralled by the wall-to-wall bookshelves, replete with thousands of books. Each wall hosted a rolling track ladder, used to reach the highest shelves. Above them, an upper loft wrapped halfway around the room with a wide, spiral staircase leading up to it. The iron railings on the staircase were magnificent in themselves, with serpentine swirls going all the way up.

"Miss Tee, this is just—"

She turned to see Miss Tee had gone.

Ezstasia returned her gaze to the magnificent gallery, and then spotted something that took her breath away. It was the most magnificent thing she had ever laid eyes on.

Directly in the center of the great chamber stood a massive tree—a real tree—lush and alive, with branches, green leaves, and pink flowers. A circular area of soil surrounded the tree, though the roots had extended out below the black and white checkered floor tiles, breaking through and pushing many of the tiles up.

"How is this even possible?" she said aloud.

She walked to the right side of the tree and noticed a plush, red bench with an exquisitely swirled gold frame and lavishly designed legs. She took a seat on the soft fabric and realized that she was facing a giant fireplace with a stone mantel. The stone had been carved into a face of a dragon. As the dancing orange and red flames flickered, some of the smoke that rose from the fire appeared to be escaping through the nostrils of the massive dragon. Ezstasia was in awe at the brilliance of the design.

Hanging just above it was an enormous painting of a garden that overlooked the distant ocean. A large, white, fur rug was laid out in front of her, and to her right was a small round table with a single, old book resting on top of it.

"What a wonderful place for reading," she said aloud to herself. She envisioned waking up in the morning and walking in to sit on the soft bench under the welcoming tree, while warming up by a cozy fire. As a pink flower fell upon her lap, her mind wandered. She thought back to the fables from the old scrolls about Valorian's Castle, with its secret chambers and magical rooms. She pretended she was back in mythical times in that legendary fortress. She determined that whoever's castle this was took some inspiration from the great fables.

She wasn't sure exactly what she was waiting for, but she glanced once again at the old book to her right and decided to pick it up. Brushing off the dust, she opened it and leafed through the fading pages.

Ezstasia couldn't understand the writing in the book; it had been written in a text that she had never seen before. Maybe it was the old tongue, similar to what had been written on the original parchments of the ancient scrolls. There were a number of delicately painted pictures in the book, many of which she recognized as scenes from the old stories. As she turned the pages, she saw pictures of rabbits, both large and small. She also saw the fabled Tree Lords with their magnificently built mansions high up in the trees, and the tiny Mushrim folk, who lived in mushroom-shaped dwellings. There were pictures of all species together, living in harmony.

She flipped the pages to the back of the book and cringed at the sight of a much more horrific picture. She'd learnt about the terrible event depicted in the scene—an episode during what was known as the Great War—but it was gut-wrenching for her to see such a detailed rendering of it. Men, women and children floated limply in a large river of blood. Those whom were among the dead were innocent villagers and nobility alike, as well as benevolent magical beings including the Tree Lords, Mushrims, giant rabbits, and many others. They were attacked by a variety of terrifying giant creatures that she had never seen or heard of before. Some looked like serpents and rose from the sea. Others had arms and legs like a human, yet appeared to be formed from the fiery depths of Earth itself. She saw the vicious diamondwolves hiding in the dark shadows of the surrounding trees, their eyes glowing as they waited patiently for their prey. She had heard the stories about these wolves—they were nearly the size of horses, with beautiful, glistening white coats, piercing, multi-faceted, diamond-like eyes, and razor-sharp teeth. She was glad she wasn't alive in that time. It was that very war that led to the treaty which now defined her magicless world.

She gazed at the illustration and spotted a giant rabbit in the water that looked just like Tia. Tia! Despite everything going on, how could she have forgotten about Tia!? She tried to think of the moment when she had last seen Tia. She had a fleeting memory of riding with her in a forest. But that's all that she could remember. She needed to find her. She needed to find her sister and her friends.

"Lady Arrow," said a male voice behind her, startling her.

She slammed the book shut and turned around toward the voice. Standing with Miss Tee at the entrance to the gallery was a tall, slender man with handsome chiseled features, impeccably dressed in royal clothing. She dropped the book on the bench and rose.

"My apologies," he said, offering a slight smile. "I meant to say… Miss Ezstasia."

His piercing blue eyes met hers with a combination of kindness and suspicion. Yet, he seemed pleasantly surprised by her cleaned-up appearance in the beautiful, flowing, gown.

"How's your head?" he said, approaching her, as Miss Tee left the room.

"It hurts," she said, tensing up. "I can hardly remember anything. May I ask how I got here and what happened to me?"

As he came up to her, he lifted his hand to check the cloth on her wound. By instinct, she nervously pulled away.

"I'm just checking to see how it's healing," he said, ignoring her request for information.

She slowly brought her head forward as she felt him gently peeling the cloth open.

"It looks much better," he said as he returned the bandage

to its spot. "But I'm afraid you are in no condition to leave, quite yet. If you'd like, I can send a horseman to alert your kin to let them know where you are. And that you're under my care."

"And where is it that I am, Your... um... I mean, my lord?" She wasn't quite sure what to call him, nor was she doing particularly well at hiding her discomfort.

"Oh yes," he said, "I apologize. I'm Prince Alazar."

"Prince!? As in—a real prince?"

"Real?" he said, with a slight chuckle. "The last time I checked I believe I was real, though some people may dispute that."

"I'm sorry, my lord, I meant you no disrespect."

"Well, now that we've both said our apologies..." He smiled again—a warm smile, which put her at ease. "Welcome to Old Vynterra."

"Old Vynterra!? I thought it was in ruins." She had heard countless tales of the legendary kingdom as a child.

"I'm restoring it." His eyes almost twinkled as he said that.

Now that he mentioned it, she remembered hearing about a prince restoring the old ruins a few years ago. She found it odd that she could remember things from years ago, yet she had very little recollection of where she had been for the last few days.

"You're the son of King Izhar," she said, "I've heard of you. Well, I think everyone has." She couldn't believe she was talking to an actual prince, let alone the very son of Izhar the Great.

"Indeed I am. Upon my request, my father bequeathed this kingdom to me while he sits on the throne at Rhyceton. I've chosen to restore it to its former glory. You've seen a very small part of it, such as this gallery. But I assure you there's much more to be seen. Valorian had quite a keen inventor's mind."

"Wait a minute," she said, feeling her heart fluttering. "*Valorian?* Prince Valorian from the scrolls!? This isn't—"

"I assure you it is," he said. "You, Miss Ezstasia, are in Valorian's Castle."

বে ঙ বে ঙ

Ezstasia was beside herself. This castle was a piece of history every living soul had heard about. Her parents used to tell stories about the magnificence of Prince Valorian before she and Lanzzie fell asleep at night. But Prince Valorian of Vynterra was only known from the stories that had been passed down from generation to generation, and from the tales told in the ancient scrolls.

There were rumors about what remained of Old Vynterra. Some believed it to be haunted or cursed. Others claimed it to be a mystical place where magic once prospered. In any case, everyone agreed it was the seat of old magic, a living testament to the tales in the old scripts—prior to the Great War, after which humans and magic folk had split forever. And here she was, within its very walls while standing before the one and only son of King Izhar the Great.

While the Cottages were, by law, not part of any kingdom, everyone who lived there had heard of King Izhar of Rhyceton, the wisest ruler of all. He had been revered for his compassion and fairness. Rumor had it that his son was of the same disposition—noble and just. She felt faint in the surrealness of this moment.

"One thing intrigues me," said Prince Alazar, breaking her out of her trance. "If you're not a Lady, then where are you from? I haven't seen you around the villages, and I make it a point to know my people personally."

"I'm from the Cottages down south."

"The Cottages? I wouldn't have guessed. You don't look

it, you know."

"And why not?" She didn't know whether to be delighted or insulted.

"For one, your hands are unmarked. They're too clean. And two, the clothes you were wearing when we found you were much too elegant for a Cottage girl. Your shoes looked like they hadn't seen a day of labor."

"We're not all root farmers, you know."

His brow furrowed. "I suppose not. Still, you look more like a Lady than a Cottage girl. No offense, of course." He glanced once again at her gown with respectful admiration.

"Who could be offended at being called a Lady?" she said.

"Who indeed," he said, smiling.

She couldn't tell for sure, but there was a hint of suspicion in his voice. But now it was her turn to ask the questions.

"Your Grace," she said, "is there a reason you haven't told me what happened to me?"

He looked at her with both inquisitiveness and surprise.

"None at all. I was hoping that you'd be able to tell me."

"But how can I, if I don't remember anything?"

"Fair enough." He held out his hand. "Come. Fresh air will help. We'll go out on the terrace. I'll have Miss Tee bring us some freshly baked bread. It's the best in the kingdom."

On the way out of the gallery, he pulled a bell cord on the wall twice. She followed him back into the bedroom that she had awoken in.

She watched as he walked to the wall where the wooden shutters were. The wall was cluttered with paintings and wooden carvings. He grabbed two protruding vines and effortlessly spread them apart, pulling open two large doors that led outside to the terrace.

"Why would you ever need a secret terrace?" she said.

"Some rooms were hidden for sheer amusement, and some for other reasons. I think it's safe to say this was one of those 'sheer amusement' designs."

She wasn't sure what he meant by *other reasons*, but she followed him out onto the large terrace. Immediately, she was in awe at the beautiful landscape that stood before her. The sun was setting, and the sky was a blended hue of vibrant purples and oranges. She walked past the small wrought iron table and chairs and toward the iron railing that surrounded the terrace, where she could get a better view. To the far right was a magnificent, rocky mountain range with a giant waterfall cascading down the front of the tallest peak. A thick mist rose from the bottom of the waterfall, and she saw a slight rainbow within its moisture. The peak of the falls looked to be even higher than the castle, which, from what she could see, was high up on a hill.

She looked down and spotted the front courtyard, decorated with flowers of every color and a tremendous fountain in the center. Enormous stone statues of various historical figures surrounded the garden. To the right of the garden was a path leading to an impeccably manicured green maze.

"Quite impressive, isn't it?" said the prince, as he stood next to her, leaning on the terrace railing. "As long as I've been here, it still takes my breath away."

"Especially those waterfalls," she said, gazing once again at the staggering beauty of the falls.

"Those are not just waterfalls." He smiled. "Think back to your history."

Then it hit her.

"Are those the actual Falls of Allura?" she said. She felt the goosebumps forming on her arms.

"They are indeed. Valorian named them after his wife, the princess."

She was speechless. She gazed farther out, straight ahead, and noticed the imposing stone and iron gated entrance that led to a paved path toward the castle's front doors. She shifted her gaze to the left, where she saw another path that wound around behind the castle. She could just about make out the tail end of a village, with its thatched roof dwellings.

"That path leads to the twin villages," said the prince. "*The twins*, we call them. I find the term ironic."

"Why is that?"

"As east is opposite to west, the people of the Eastern and Western Villages are as different as could be from one another. Let's just say it makes governing a challenge."

She heard a shuffling from behind her and turned to see Miss Tee carrying a tray of bread and tea, with what looked like an assortment of creams and jams.

"Shall we sit?" said the prince.

He held out his hand toward the iron table, which she noticed had been designed after the roots of a tree. She sat in one of the matching chairs, and the prince took a seat opposite her. Ezstasia could see that the chairs were quite worn, with the cream-colored coating, having all but faded away. She wondered what marvelous pieces of history these chairs and table were privy to, all faded into the distant past, just like the decaying paint.

She also noticed that there were fallen leaves all over the terrace floor, and a few were scattered on the table. The prince brushed them off as Miss Tee placed the silver food tray down. How could all these leaves have traveled so high up? Even the strongest wind couldn't have blown them here from any of the trees that stood so far below.

"Where did all of these leaves come from?" she said, pulling one out from a crack in the table.

Miss Tee abruptly stopped pouring the tea into the saucer cups and glanced at the prince—a glance he returned with a smile.

"Thank you, Miss Tee," he said. "That will be all for

now."

Miss Tee placed the tea pot down and exited. Their odd behavior piqued Ezstasia's interest.

"I'm sorry," said Ezstasia, "I was just curious. I don't see any trees nearby."

The prince took a sip from his cup. "A little mystery now and again is good for the soul and wisens all men."

"Excuse me?"

He smiled. "It's an old saying. But I have a more important mystery I'm hoping you can solve for me. You say your name is Ezstasia, and that you're from the Cottages, correct?"

"Yes."

"Okay. So what I'm trying to figure out," he inquired, "is why you told me your name was Lady Arrow?"

"I told you that was my name?"

"Yes, when we found you."

He tore off two pieces of the bread and handed her one.

"I have no idea why I would've said that. I'm sorry, but there must be a misunderstanding. That's not my name."

She spread the sweet butter onto the warm bread, its aromatic heat rising to meet her senses. She took a large bite. It was delectable!

"You remember your scrolls history well enough. And you know exactly who you are and where you are from. You will have to excuse me if it sounds peculiar, but initially, you had told me you were Lady Arrow."

"I can't tell you why I would've said my name was Lady Arrow. I'm Ezstasia and I'm from the Cottages. I can tell you everything about the Cottages if you want." She felt herself growing frustrated with the line of questioning, but also with herself for not being able to remember.

"That won't be necessary," he said.

As he looked out at the open expanse, apparently

contemplating his next words, she couldn't help but think of how attractive his features were. He was fully in control, intimidating in a way, yet calm and pensive. She admired that about him.

He leaned back against his chair and smiled again.

"Okay, Lady Ar—" He paused to correct himself. "Miss Ezstasia. I'll tell you how we found you. But you must tell me any details that come to your mind as you remember them. Is that a deal?"

"Of course."

"Good." He leaned toward her and looked right at her with a sincere, but serious expression.

"A few days ago, I was alerted by several of my knights that they saw something peculiar in the direction of that forest. Quite a few villagers also reported it. It was the strangest thing. Small stars of colorful light fell from the sky overhead. Just about there," he said as he pointed to the sky directly above the forest.

"Stars?"

"Not quite stars, but something colorful—of that we have no question. We've received rumors over the last year or so about strange sightings in that forest, but this was the first one seen by the masses. Soon after those colors were seen falling from the sky, something even more interesting happened. A tremendous flash of light reached across the entire forest and it was gone in an instant. I took a few of my best horsemen with me to investigate."

Her eyes drifted as she tried to remember anything she could. Something about the colored lights sounded familiar. Noticing that the prince had stopped speaking, she looked back at him to find him staring at her even more intently. She knew he was cautiously analyzing her reactions in response to what he was saying.

"That does sound strange," she said, returning her

attention to him. "What did you find there?"

"You," he said.

"Me!?"

"Yes. When we went into the forest, we heard loud shuffling, so we rode toward it. We heard someone talking. It was a female voice—*your* voice. I was curious, so I dismounted my horse and attempted to move closer. And there you were. I couldn't quite tell what you were doing, but I must have startled you because you frantically and pretty abruptly attempted to leave. And while trying to do so, you took an unfortunate, dreadful fall off your rabbit."

"Tia!" she said. Suddenly it all started coming back to her. She was with Tia in that forest. They were playing Arrows. She wondered if that had anything to do with the name she had given him: Lady Arrow. But she didn't dare reveal that thought.

"Tia. Is that your rabbit's name?"

"Yes, it is. Is she—"

"She's fine," he said. "But let's stay focused."

"I do remember something. I was in the forest and I remember it being eerie. I remember hearing a noise behind me—a branch cracking—and I panicked."

He smiled. "That was likely me. That solves that mystery. But why did you say your name was Lady Arrow?"

She shook her head.

"You were barely conscious when I got to you. One of my horsemen said you appeared to be highborn. That led me to ask, 'Are you a lady?' You repeated *Lady* a few times. So I asked, 'Lady who?' Then, very slowly, you said *Arrow... Lady... Arrow.* Does that help you recall anything?"

"I really don't remember," she said.

"Do you remember why you were alone in the forest? A young woman from the Cottages just doesn't venture into a place like that on her own."

She hesitated and looked down.

The prince gently held her chin and lifted her face toward his. "Ezstasia, I want you to look at me and tell me honestly why you were there."

"I—we, my friends—oh, my friends! I was with my friends. They'll be so worried! I have to get back to them."

"So, you weren't alone? There wasn't anyone else around when we got to you. We would've seen them."

"They must've ventured off. I'm sure they were looking for me. That forest! That—"

"Why were you all in that forest to begin with?"

"We were just exploring. That's all. One of my friends discovered it so we all wanted to see it. It was a new place. Something different."

"It's different all right, I'll give you that. And the arrow?"

"What arrow?" Her heart sunk.

"The arrow you mentioned when you told me your name."

"Oh!" She breathed a sigh of relief. She had to think of something quickly. "I remember now. It's something my father called me," she said. "I forgot all about that."

"He called you Lady Arrow?"

"No, just Arrow. He called me Arrow because I was good at archery. I mean I still am." The latter part was true; she *was* particularly good at archery.

He leaned back and appeared to be digesting it all. He didn't look like he completely believed her story.

"Lady Arrow," he said, smiling. "It's a shame, I liked the sound of it."

"I do too," she said. "You can still call me that if you'd like. Or at least Miss Arrow. I mean, if it's not inappropriate."

"Lady Arrow it is," he said, returning his gaze to her. "I suppose you'll be wanting to get back to your friends when you're well. And your rabbit, of course."

"Very much," she said, relieved.

"Can you think of anything you may have left in that forest?" he said. "Besides your rabbit?"

She shook her head.

"No, Your Grace." She tried to keep her legs from trembling while thinking of the forbidden magic on the arrow that she'd never retrieved.

He stood and walked to the terrace railing to gaze out at the landscape. She wondered what he was thinking. The last thing she wanted was for him to associate her with the so-called 'stars' that everyone had seen. Or the bright flash that followed the win of their game.

"And you didn't see anything in that forest while you were exploring?" he said, still looking off of the terrace and out toward the forest.

"I don't know," she said. "Maybe if I had my clothing and belongings, I might remember something. Are they in my room? I didn't see them." She figured maybe he'd reveal what he found, if anything.

"Ah yes, I forgot about your clothes," he said. "I'll have Miss Tee set them out for you." He seemed preoccupied as he walked past her toward the terrace doors. She sensed that something was bothering him.

Her eyes followed him as he approached the terrace doors and turned around.

"It's a shame," he said.

"What is, Your Grace?"

"To waste all that bread. When you're done, I'll have Miss Tee collect whatever is left and distribute it to the poor."

She glanced at the two large loaves of bread that they had barely touched. When she turned around to reply to the prince, he was gone.

She rose and went back into the bedroom. Her mind

began to wander. Had he found her arrow? Or was he simply hoping that she would be able to shed light on the mysterious sparkles and flashes? Did he know the answers to some of his questions, but was testing her honesty? She wished she could ease his dilemma by revealing the truth, but she dared not. She could never put her friends at risk like that, or herself for that matter.

Ezstasia paced the room and occupied herself by testing all the wall fixtures for other possible secret chambers.

She was interrupted by a soft knock at the door that she recognized as Miss Tee's knock. As expected, Miss Tee entered, carrying a large sack.

"Miss Ezstasia, my lord has asked me to bring you your things and to lay them out for you, so you may see what was collected."

"Thank you, Miss Tee. Please, you can put them down on the bed."

Miss Tee did as she asked and took out her belongings and placed them in a neat pile on the bed. She wanted to ask her if she was free to leave, but she hesitated. She didn't want to appear over-anxious, or worse, guilty.

"Call for me if you need anything, dear," said Miss Tee as she left and shut the door behind her.

Ezstasia walked over to the bed and was relieved to see her silver necklace resting right on top of the pile. It had a special orb which was derived from tree resin and had belonged to her mother. It was an irreplaceable heirloom. After her parents had died, leaving Lanzzie to care for her, it was the only thing she had left from her.

Under her perfectly folded clothes, she saw her water can and Tia's tag chain wrapped around an arrowhead. They were both resting on top of her large, brown cloak. Slowly, she began to lift the cloak, wondering if perhaps her arrow might be underneath it. She wasn't sure if that would be a good thing or a bad thing, as it would likely still be sparkling. Of course, if it wasn't there, then someone could still find it in the forest—or had found it already—which was definitely a bad thing.

Tired of speculating, she decided to lift the cloak. She closed her eyes and felt her heart pounding. Then, with one swift movement she lifted the cloak up and tossed it aside.

She opened her eyes.

There was no arrow.

She felt panic rise within her heart and up to her throat, but she considered one more possibility, which she hoped for—maybe the arrow was with her friends. Wherever it was, she needed to return to the Cottages, and fast—injured or not. For all she knew, her sister and her friends could be hurt or in serious trouble.

She hurriedly threw her belongings back into the sack and threw it over her shoulder. Still wearing the gown, she quietly made her way out the bedroom door and into the corridor. As gracious as the prince was, it didn't sound like he was willing to let her leave right away, so she'd decided to make that decision on her own.

Glancing around for any signs of Miss Tee or the castle staff, she continued past the colorful frescoes and the seemingly endless intricately carved doors. There were quite a few wall carvings in sporadic places, and she wondered how many of them led to secret passageways or chambers. Eventually, she came to a large open doorway. She peeked into the dimly lit room, where she saw countless suits of armor and weapons hanging on the wall. This must've been the castle's armory, she thought to herself.

She continued past the armory and came to another opening. She felt a rush of air hit her as she peeked in and saw that it led to an inner courtyard. Ordinarily, she would've loved to look around, but there was no time now. She moved further down the corridor as quietly as she could. She noticed that the ceiling had begun to rise much higher—a glorious, towering, arched ceiling, parts of it coated in gold. The magnificent corridor wound around to the left. Just as she turned the corner, her mouth dropped. What stood in front of her was the largest set of wooden double doors she'd ever seen. She felt like an insect in comparison.

She gazed in awe at the detailed carvings of a giant tree that was outlined in gold and extended across the two doors. Both doors reached all the way up to the high ceiling. The same ancient writing she'd seen inside the old book in the hidden room was also carved in silver across the tree. She carefully grasped the two, vine-shaped golden handles, almost afraid to see what was on the other side. She hesitated for a moment and contemplated how she'd react if she ran into someone. She knew that she hadn't asked for permission to explore, nor to leave her room. As she prepared to pull the heavy doors open, a shuffling sound behind her made her jump.

"Valorian truly loved his trees," said a male voice that she knew all too well.

She turned to see Prince Alazar staring right at her.

CHAPTER EIGHT

"Your Grace," said Ezstasia. "I—I was—"

"You were leaving," he said, nonchalantly. "You wouldn't have gotten very far. Our gates are guarded day and night."

"So you're saying I'm a prisoner?"

"A prisoner? I just gave you tea and bread on the most beautiful terrace in the kingdom. I was headed to your room to invite you to dinner. I'd hardly call you a prisoner."

Now she felt guilty. She especially felt guilty lying to him, or at least not telling him the full truth. But she couldn't.

"I'm sorry, Your Grace. I didn't mean to be ungrateful. I just need to get back to my friends."

"If you recall, I told you I can get word to them of your whereabouts."

"It's not that, it's just—I'm afraid you don't understand."

"You're right. I don't understand. So enlighten me. Please."

"I just miss them, that's all. This castle is beautiful and you've been as gracious as can be, but I need to see my sister."

"And see her you shall. You have my word on that. But you still need your wound to heal. Surely, your friends *and* your sister would understand that?"

"But what if they're injured as well? You said yourself that strange things are happening in that forest. I need to make sure they're all okay."

The prince sighed and then nodded.

"Okay," he said. "I promise to send word first thing in the morning. If you're feeling well enough to leave the following morning, I'll have my horsemen take you home. Do we have an agreement?"

She thought about it and realized it was the best she was going to get.

She nodded. "We do."

"Good. Then without further ado, there's something I'd like to show you before dinner."

He turned and signaled to a servant who had entered the hallway behind him. The servant approached and held out a hand to Ezstasia, offering to carry her sack of belongings.

"Allow me," he said. He had an oversized mustache that was too large for his face.

She handed it to him and he hoisted it over his shoulders.

The prince headed toward a grand, descending staircase and motioned for her to come with him. She'd barely noticed it because she was so enamored by the huge doors straight ahead.

"What was behind those giant doors?" she said, walking with him down the elaborate staircase that wound around to the left. The servant followed a distance behind them.

"You ask a lot of questions," said the prince, smiling, though still not answering her question.

She followed the prince and descended the carpet-lined marble steps, holding tightly to the magnificent wrought iron railing. She looked down and saw an enormous dining hall. Waiters were running back and forth, preparing the long, wooden table for an extravagant meal. Enormous tapestries lined the walls, and the cathedral ceiling was covered in gold mosaic. Above the table hung a crystal chandelier that held more candles than she had ever seen one hold.

As she stared in wonder, the prince led her through several more corridors until they entered a section of the castle that had dark grey stone walls with torches and heavily barred doors on both sides.

It didn't take her long to realize that these were the dungeons. Her heart sank with the sudden thought that her sister and friends may be here if they had been caught. Is that why he was leading her here? Or was it for some *other* reason?

"Do you have any prisoners at the moment?" she said, realizing her tone was a bit too anxious. She slowed down her pace to get a glimpse of any prisoners inside the cells.

"Prisoners? As matter of fact, we just received one this morning. He's in another section of the cells. He was almost treated unjustly, but I put a stop to that. Justice must be served quickly, but fairly."

"What did he do? What kind of justice?" Her pulse quickened.

The prince must have been able to see that she felt nervous, because he glanced at her and smirked. But she couldn't determine if it was a reassuring smile or an ominous one, like he was leading a pig to slaughter.

"You do ask a lot of questions," he said.

Then finally, obviously seeing the level of her discomfort, he continued.

"He stole property from some of the nobles. We get prisoners on occasion, mostly for minor infractions. Obviously, a larger crime would warrant a much more severe punishment."

"Your Grace, if you brought me here to scare me into revealing something, I assure you I've shared as much as I remember."

He laughed. "Dearest lords, no! I brought you here because it's the quickest way out to the Eastern Village. What I want to show you is outside."

With still no hint of what he was planning to show her, she felt her stomach turn with anticipation. She couldn't wait until she was back home at the Cottages.

"Are you okay?" he said. "You look like you've just seen Izhar's ghost."

"I'm fine, really. Who was he anyway?"

"You're still concerned about that prisoner?"

"No, I meant the Izhar in 'Izhar's ghost.' Who was he?"

"Ah, he was my father's ancestor, and mine. Izhar the First. Valorian's father. They say his ghost travels the kingdom, endlessly mourning the loss of his son."

"Have you ever seen it?"

"I've seen a lot of things, but no, I have never seen a ghost."

The skies were dark now, and the village looked magical in the moonlight. She could see an endless array of homes, packed much more tightly together than the Cottages. Most were made of stone, with patios and thatched roofs. They turned and continued up a path, past a stone well. She heard loud footsteps behind them, and turned to see two rows of knights, fully dressed in armor.

"Are those knights following us?" she said.

"They're part of the Vynterran Guard. They give protection whenever I leave the castle. Although, I truly don't believe I need a guard in *this* kingdom."

Just as he said that, a group of villagers waved to him from their patio. The prince returned their hello with a smile and a wave.

"Pardon me for saying, Your Grace, but they don't seem astonished to see you walking about their village."

"Why would they be? I make it a point to be seen among

my people daily. I want to know their problems and hear their conversations. I learned that from my father."

"No wonder he's known as Izhar the Great."

They continued along the walkway past a series of stone houses with thatched roofs, and then proceeded through a field of wildflowers. She could see the moonlit mountains on her left, and, from here, the powerful rush of the waterfalls was louder than ever, though she could barely make them out from this angle.

Before long, they came to a tree-lined dirt road that looked almost as eerie as the forest. It seemed to go on forever.

"This is the Road of Sorrow," said the prince. "It's where Izhar the First was forced to watch his son Valorian being led to his death. It connects the Eastern and Western villages."

"This is the actual Road of Sorrow?" she said. Everyone had heard of it from the Old Scrolls. She never imagined that she would actually walk it.

"The very one."

They continued down a steep decline, which made the back of her thighs hurt. Eventually they emerged into an open pebble-covered path, which led past rows of homes on the right.

"Those are the Western Villages," said the prince.

Then she saw something ahead on her left that made her stop in her tracks.

"What is that!?" she said.

She gazed in awe at an imposing black castle that looked even bigger than Valorian's Castle, but with less extravagance. It had large, stone buttresses along its walls.

"It's the Black Castle," he said, smiling. "An obvious name, I know, but that's what Valorian called it. We use it for training. "It's only partially restored, but with the increasing rumors about the forest, we felt it—well, let's just say we want to be prepared for anything."

"What kind of training? Is that where the knights train?"

"So many questions, Lady Arrow," said the prince.

They resumed walking, and as they got closer, she could see a large moat surrounding the castle, with thick, iron gates along the perimeter. An enormous stone bridge led from the land to the castle's gates, with guards blocking the entrance to the castle grounds.

She gazed up and could've sworn she saw a man in a form-fitting black face mask staring out of one of the windows. Just then, the prince grabbed her arm, making her jump.

"Look to your right," he said. "That's what I wanted to show you."

As she looked to see where the prince was pointing, she became excited. It was a large, wooden stable, with a wooden sign above it that read, *The Cozy Barn*. She could hear the sounds of goats and horses awaiting their dinner.

"Tia!" she said.

"Go ahead," said the prince. "She'll be anxious to see you."

She didn't know what came over her, but she hugged the prince with a tight grip. He looked a bit surprised, but he seemed pleased with her gratitude.

As soon as she'd entered the barn, she saw Tia in a stable, munching on some carrots. She ran up to Tia, who, for a rabbit, looked genuinely excited to see her. At least she did for a moment, but then the rabbit returned to her carrots.

Ezstasia went into the stable and hugged the soft, giant rabbit. Even Tia's smell made her nostalgic for the Cottages.

"I figured you would be anxious to see her," said the prince from behind her. She turned to look at him and saw the large grin on his face.

"You have no idea. Can I take her home now?"

"Now? Do you have any idea how long the journey is from here to the Cottages?"

"Tia's strong. If you just pointed me in the direction of—"

"We already discussed this and came to an agreement. I'll send word to your friends in the morning, and you can take Tia home the next day if you'd like—with my guards escorting you of course. A head injury is not something to take lightly."

"But, I'm—"

"I'm asking you to stay," he said, his tone becoming more serious. "Please. If not for me, then for your own safety. I can't let you leave at night in good conscience, not even with an escort."

As anxious as she was to get home, she had to admit she felt a bit flattered by his persistence in her staying.

"I appreciate your concern," she said, "but I'm fine. Really."

He paused. Ezstasia jumped at the opportunity in his potential moment of weakness.

"I must warn you, Your Grace, I do win most arguments." She smiled.

He smiled back. "Well, I assure you, Lady Arrow, you won't win this one."

ಙ ಚ ಙ ಚ

Lanzzie couldn't stay still in the sitting room in Fin's cottage. It was getting late, and even though she was exhausted, she paced back and forth and fidgeted with her hands; her mind was racing in all directions. Ithron and Jezreel were curled up in the corner. The others were scattered around the room, sitting quietly and staring at her without any new ideas to suggest, though she was sure they were just as tired as she was. All she could think of was her sister. And now she had to worry about staying out of the dungeons long enough to find her. She usually appreciated the stable keepers, but in this situation, she was furious with them.

"Lanz, we'll figure something out," said Fin, sitting to the right of Randin and Zander on a large fur rug by the wall.

"When?" she said. "Did you see how that old stable master looked at us?"

"He didn't just look at us," said Zander. "He said he'll see us later."

Randin elbowed him.

"It's a bluff," said Meldon from a rocking chair that he couldn't stop rocking on. "He had to say that."

"I wish Mr. Pudge was back to run the stables," said Lanzzie. "At least he liked us. This one has the personality of a hedgehog."

"And the looks of one," said Zander. "Plus, he eats hay. At least he's always chewing on it. Maybe he really is in the hedgehog family?"

"Hedgehogs don't eat hay," said Meldon. "And the man was chewing on a straw, which is an entirely different thing and is used for—"

"Guys," said Pallu, glancing out the window into the darkness. "Shouldn't we be thinking about what to say if he finds us?"

"He won't find us here," said Fin.

"Don't be so sure," said Zander.

"He's coming," said Lanzzie. "I just know it. You know how determined he was. He kept reading the rules over and over to us. What do we tell him?"

"Let's offer him some food," said Pallu.

"Yeah, sure," said Zander, rolling his eyes. "Let's invite him to dinner. That'll solve everything."

Pallu shrugged. "It can't hurt to try and win people over."

"We already told him Ezstasia's coming with her rabbit,"

said Fin. "That may buy us some time."

Lanzzie threw her hands up. "We've been giving them excuses for two days now. We don't *have* any more time!"

"You're all panicking unnecessarily," said Meldon. "Let's calm down and focus. There are eight of us with eight different cottages in eight different directions. The chance of him coming to this one by tonight is small. Very small. *Infinitesimally* small."

Just then, there was a loud pound at the door.

"Okay. Maybe not that small," said Meldon.

"I knew it!" said Lanzzie. "Now what do we do?" She looked down at Fin, who was still sitting on the floor. "We should've just stayed in the forest!"

"Lanz, take it easy," said Fin. "We didn't break the rules, Ezstasia did. She's the one who'll have to answer and we can worry about that when we find her. And we *will* find her."

The pound at the door grew louder.

"Fin," said Meldon. "Where did you put that sack of magic powder?"

"Don't worry, it's safe. Besides, he's a stable master. He's looking for a giant rabbit."

Another loud pound on the wooden door gave every indication that it was about to be broken down.

"I know yer in there," said the unmistakable voice of the stable master through the door.

"I'm coming," said Fin, standing up.

Lanzzie watched nervously as Fin meandered to the door. She quickly looked around for possible emergency exits or hiding spots. She could almost hear the pounding heartbeats of everyone in the room as Fin pulled the door open.

The old man stood there grimacing, with the long straw between his yellow teeth.

"Mr. Stable Master," said Fin. "What a nice surprise!"

"Surprise, aye, but the pleasure's all yers I think. I'm here to collect a certain rabbit. And me name's Krimp. Archibald Krimp. Mr. Krimp to you, Fin Fennel."

"How do you know my surname?" said Fin.

"I know a lot of things about you, laddie."

As he stood in the open doorway, he looked inside at all the friends, blatantly suspicious. Nobody said a word.

"Ye all become mute and unable to answer doors?" he said, sarcastically. "Need I summon a medic?"

"No rabbits here, sir," said Zander.

"I'll be the judge of that."

"They're not hard to miss," said Randin.

Lanzzie cringed as the old man looked right at her and took a step forward.

"Where's yer sister, lassie?"

"I don't know," she said. "I'm sure she's—"

"Yer sure of nothin', that's what yer sure of! Yer little group has been fabricatin' excuses, but there'll be no more fabricatin' tonight."

"Have you checked her cottage?" said Fin.

"Are ye mocking me, boy? Of course I checked her cottage."

"I'm just trying to help," said Fin.

"Good," said Krimp. "Then to make sure ye all help as much as possible, I'm taking all yer ridin' privileges away until *her* sister," he pointed right at Lanzzie, "comes back with that rabbit."

"That won't be necessary," said a strong, female voice from outside. "You can leave now."

"What?" said Krimp, turning around. "Who, pray tell, are ye to give the likes of me orders?"

Lanzzie and Fin strained to see who it was behind Krimp. As the woman stepped closer into the moonlight, Lanzzie couldn't believe her eyes.

It was Ezstasia.

Her sister looked not only well, she was beaming and absolutely stunning. She was dressed up in the most exquisite, flowing emerald green gown she'd ever seen.

Lanzzie felt the pent up emotion of the last several days rise to her throat and her eyes filled with tears.

"Ezstasia!" she finally yelled, running outside toward her sister and hugging her for dear life. Everyone jumped up and ran toward them.

"Lanz," said Ezstasia, "I was so worried about you."

"Me!?" said Lanzzie, so choked up she could barely get the words out. "We thought you were dead! Where were you? And why are you dressed like that?"

"I have so much to tell you," said Ezstasia. "All of you."

"Well, ye can start with me," said Krimp. "We have rules here, and ye broke every one of them. But first, ye owe me a rabbit."

"You mean that rabbit?" said Zander, pointing behind Krimp.

"There's Tia," said Fin, as the beautiful, brown rabbit hopped toward them with a carrot in her mouth.

"I reckon that's the one," said Krimp, picking at the straw that was dangling from his mouth as he examined her. "Well, ye don't look any worse fer wear," he said, grabbing the rabbit's collar.

"So that means everything's okay now?" said Fin.

Krimp rose and looked at him sharply.

"No, it does not mean everythin's okay." The old man's eyes darted back and forth among the group. "Ye all conspired to do somethin' off kilter, and I aim to find out what. This creature was out who-knows-where without the proper care, and everyone in this room spoke false fer it. I want to know why." He looked at Ezstasia. "Starting with you, lassie, and how ye came to be here lookin' like ye flew out of a fairy tale."

132

"Miss Ezstasia!" called a man from the darkness, as a horse whinnied. "Is there any trouble?"

Lanzzie saw what looked to be two royal guards approaching into the moonlight on two beautiful, majestic, brown horses.

Ezstasia looked at the stable master. "I don't know, Mr. Krimp. Is there?"

Krimp grumbled.

"Sir," said one of the men to Krimp, "we must ask you to leave."

"Under whose authority?" said Krimp, looking up at them. "I'm the stable master. I have every right to be here."

One of the guards put his hand on a sword, a maneuver that Krimp obviously noticed as well, because he backed down immediately.

"*However*, I was leavin' anyway," said Krimp. "I have my rabbit." He looked at Lanzzie and the group. "Ye all know the rules fer the future. I expect ye to obey them."

Lanzzie stood dumbfounded as the stable master walked off with Tia. Ezstasia nodded to the royal guards, thanking them as they rode off.

"He was right about one thing," said Pallu to Ezstasia, as they all headed inside.

"What's that?" she said.

"You do look like you flew out of a fairy tale, except for the bandage. Are you okay? What happened? Who were those men?"

Ezstasia grinned, obviously overjoyed to be back.

"It's a long story."

ॐ ॐ ॐ ॐ

Lanzzie took Ezstasia's hand and led her into the sitting room, elated to have her sister back.

"Why is she dressed like that?" said Ithron from the back corner of the room. He was, of course, sitting with Jezreel. They hadn't left one another's side since their kiss.

Pallu approached Ezstasia with his arms out. "Now for a proper welcome," he said, giving her a bear hug. "Where have you been? We were out searching for you all day. And yesterday, too."

"I'm so sorry," said Ezstasia. "I'll explain everything. I was worried about all of you as well. I'm so glad you're okay."

"Okay!?" said Ithron in a tone of sheer frustration. "Is that what you call it?" Jezreel tried to hush him and gestured to Ezstasia that she shouldn't go there just yet.

"I'd say okay is relative," said Zander, who was sitting on a chair next to his brother.

"I'm sorry, I don't understand," said Ezstasia. "What happened? I assumed—"

"You know what I assume?" said Zander. "I assume by your gown that you didn't get captured by a giant spider. And that big hairy wooden creature didn't try to eat you."

"A giant what?" said Ezstasia, looking completely confused.

"It's a long story," said Pallu. "Zander had a little incident, which he's still a little traumatized by, as you can tell."

"A little incident!?" said Zander, upset.

"Why don't we let her explain what happened?" said Fin. "Then we'll tell her our stories. I think we may all need some ale for this."

He invited everyone to sit around the large rectangular table in the center of the dining room, where he poured ale into tin cups for everyone. The fireplace was burning in the corner, crackling in the sudden silence.

Once everyone had gathered around, Ezstasia opened her mouth to speak, but before she could get a word out, Lanzzie held a hand up.

"First," said Lanzzie, "I want to say how happy I am—how happy we *all* are—to have my sister back with us. I don't know what I would've done without her. No matter what happens from here, the important thing is that we're all together."

"Here, here!" yelled Fin, raising his tin cup and pounding it hard on the table, letting whatever liquid spill out that may. Messy as it was, the others followed suit, as was customary after a speech—the age old Cottage tradition called *splonking*.

"I can't thank you all enough," said Ezstasia. "I can only imagine what you went through to find me. I know a lot has happened since we saw each other, and—"

Lanzzie wondered why Ezstasia paused mid-sentence, but then she saw the reason. Ezstasia had noticed Ithron and Jezreel seated together at the far end of the table, cuddling and giggling. Everyone in the room was grinning.

"Yes, a *lot* has happened," said Pallu, as the others laughed.

"Okay," said Ezstasia, setting a more serious tone. "I'll tell my story, but then I must hear all yours."

Everyone nodded and she continued.

As Lanzzie listened intently, Ezstasia told her story of how she had awoken in a strange place with her head bandaged. She spoke in great detail about the castle, Prince Alazar, how he had found her, and how she had been made to stay despite desperately wanting to get back to her friends. Above all, she told of the prince's kindness and compassion—and of his awareness and concerns about the very forest they'd been in the day before. Then she sprung the question Lanzzie had forgotten all about.

"By the way," said Ezstasia, "did you guys happen to find my arrow?"

Lanzzie and Fin looked at one another.

"You don't have it?" said Meldon.

"I told you," she said, "I was unconscious when the prince found me. I didn't even—"

Ithron jumped up while Ezstasia was mid-sentence and headed for the door, slamming it behind him as he stormed out.

"What was that about?" said Fin.

"I'll go talk to him," said Jezreel, getting up and following him outside.

"I'll go to the kitchen," said Pallu, lifting himself off the chair with far less elegance. "I think we all need to eat."

"You were actually in Valorian's Castle?" said Zander.

Lanzzie noticed a tear falling down Ezstasia's cheek.

"This is all my fault," said Ezstasia. "I know he's upset because of me."

Lanzzie put an arm around her.

"It isn't your fault," said Fin. "I think it's safe to say we all experienced some craziness in that forest. Who knows what would've happened to you if that prince hadn't found you? You could be dead."

"He's right," said Zander. "I got chased by a giant tree spider the size of a cottage. Nobody else saw it, but I'm telling you it almost killed me."

Zander was known for telling white lies occasionally. Lanzzie noticed Ezstasia kept looking over at her with slight suspicion as he told some details of his story.

"That's quite an exaggeration, Zander," said Ezstasia. "How big was it really?"

"I'm *not* exaggerating," said Zander. "It was like twenty or thirty feet high. Or maybe even a little bigger, now that I think about it."

Zander continued to recount the details of his ordeal as Ezstasia listened with her mouth agape.

"Are you really sure that's what you saw?" she said.

"Pallu and I were with him," said Randin, "and we

couldn't see it."

"Don't tell me you don't believe me again, especially after what happened to Ithron!" said Zander.

"I told you we believed you," said Randin.

"Wait a minute. What happened to Ithron?" said Ezstasia, her voice cracking.

"Oh dear, that's not such a good story," said Meldon.

As if they heard and knew it was time to enter, the door opened and Ithron and Jezreel returned.

Ithron looked around uncomfortably without making any eye contact. Jezreel nudged him.

"I'm sorry," said Ithron, "I guess I got upset hearing about a prince and eating grapes and taking fancy baths while I almost died while we were trying to find you."

"I'm so sorry for what you went through for me," said Ezstasia.

"I can tell you what I went through if you want," he said, taking a deep breath.

"Yes. Please do," said Ezstasia, her heart broken with the thought of the pain he must have experienced.

All eyes were on Ithron as he stood at the edge of the table. His eyes and nose were red while he recounted the terrifying ordeal. Lanzzie heard audible gasps from Ezstasia as Ithron told of the multiple attacks and the excruciating pain that penetrated throughout his body.

"We saw the physical signs of it on Ithron's body," said Meldon. "He didn't just imagine it. His skin was grey and cracked, and his body was rigid. We thought he was dead."

"Until Jez brought him out of it," said Zander.

Jezreel put her arm around Ithron.

Ezstasia began sobbing uncontrollably. "I didn't know," she kept saying over and over. "I didn't know."

Just then, Pallu entered the room with a tray full of something that smelled amazing.

"How about a serving of my family's most famous recipe: Honey Sweet Muffin Flats? That'll cheer everyone up. You surprised me, Fin." he said as he looked toward him. "You actually had all of the ingredients."

"Don't be so surprised," said Fin. "They're your ingredients from the last time you were here."

Lanzzie grabbed one from the tray and handed it to Ezstasia. "What do you say we stop the storytelling for now and just celebrate the fact that we're all alive and well? Are you ready to celebrate?"

"Of course she's ready," said Pallu. "I mean, look at these. They're just like a muffin, but flat. I drizzle the honey on it at the perfect moment just before I flip it. The trick is to leave the top moist while the honey gets toasted to a crisp on the bottom."

Lanzzie grabbed one for herself. She had to admit, she would do anything for Honey Sweet Muffin Flats. Anyone would, to be honest. In the Cottages, Pallu's family was well known for this secret family recipe. Not even the best bakeries in town could make them so delightfully flavorful and perfectly moist, with that specific delicate crunch that came from the crystallized honey. It surely wasn't from a lack of effort, though.

"Lanz, I haven't heard your story yet," said Ezstasia, still looking concerned. "Or Fin's."

"You can hear our stories later," she said. "I think that's enough for one day."

Ezstasia nodded.

"See?" said Pallu, as he passed around the delectable muffins. "Delicious food is the answer to every woe."

"It's actually the answer to why you can't get out of your chair," said Zander, grinning.

"After hearing your stories," said Ezstasia, "I think this forest is even worse than the prince thought."

"It's one forest I'll never set foot in again, I'll tell you *that*," said Ithron.

Lanzzie thought hard about the mystifying forest and their unexplainable sightings and experiences. She stared into the flickering embers of the fireplace and her mind wandered to the fascinating tales of old—many delightful and some horrific.

"It's back," she said quietly, staring into the flames. She turned to the others, who were all staring at her in silence.

"It's back," she repeated louder.

"What's back?" said Randin.

Zander looked downright frightened.

"Magic," she said. "Someone has been using magic in that forest—dark magic."

"They could get thrown into the dungeons for that," said Pallu. "Why would they risk it?"

"Whoever *they* are," said Lanzzie, "they must not care about the consequences."

"We don't know that for sure," said Fin. "Let's think for a bit."

"I agree with Lanzzie," said Meldon. "Someone's using magic. It's the only logical explanation."

"So what do we do about it?" said Randin. "We need to warn someone about that forest."

"We can tell the Cottage Elders," said Pallu.

"Those old buzzards?" said Fin. "They nearly had a fit because of a missing rabbit. What do you think they'd do if they thought there was dark magic somewhere?"

"Even if they wanted to do something," said Meldon, adjusting his glasses, "they don't have weapons to prepare for something like that. Well, they could take out their billhooks and sickles, I suppose."

"Uh, yeah," said Zander, in a mocking tone. "If there's one thing dark magic users are afraid of, it's farmers with billhooks and sickles."

"Why do we need to tell anyone?" said Ithron, as he took out his carving knife and began to examine it. "It's nobody's business."

"You're wrong, Ithron," said Ezstasia, rising from her chair. "It's everyone's business. It could mean life or death to any one of us or to our entire village and kingdoms. There's something bad in that forest. I also saw it in the prince's eyes. He was gravely concerned."

Ezstasia began to pace around the room, fiddling with her hands—a habit Lanzzie knew all too well. They both did it whenever they were in deep thought.

After a few seconds, Ezstasia stopped and looked at everyone.

"When I was in that castle," she said, "Prince Alazar said there've been rumors about that forest for a while now, even before they saw the light from our game. He didn't know the light was from us, and I didn't tell him, but he was concerned enough to go and investigate it with his knights. He told me about his ongoing suspicions before I left. People have seen a lot of things in the last few weeks alone."

"So, they're already looking into it," said Ithron. "Good. Let them take care of it. They're more qualified anyway."

"That's not the point," said Ezstasia. "*We* are who the prince needs. All of you are the proof that something malevolent is happening in that forest! Nobody in his village has firsthand experience with the evil entities like you did. There've only been *rumors* of sightings. This forest is more dangerous than even they realize. They need to know what they're dealing with before something happens to someone else."

"What can they do?" said Meldon. "All the knights in all the kingdoms combined couldn't do anything to stop dark magic."

"The prince has access to every scroll imaginable," said Ezstasia. "Maybe something in those scrolls can help."

"Wait a minute," said Ithron. "Did it ever occur to you that maybe the prince is behind all of this himself?"

"That's ridiculous," said Ezstasia, appalled at the accusation.

"He has access to the old scrolls. He's living in Valorian's Castle, for crying out loud, the very man who died for hoarding magic. We could be walking right into a trap."

"He has a point," said Meldon.

"I don't believe that for a minute," said Ezstasia. "You weren't there. The prince is a fair man. I saw evidence of that on more than one occasion. And besides, he rescued me. Shouldn't that count for something?"

"If this is really true," said Pallu, "and magic is coming back, I don't think I'm ready for that. You know the old stories. People died horrible deaths. We need every form of protection we can get."

"Shouldn't we still tell the elders so they're able to prepare and protect themselves?" said Randin.

"If we do that," said Pallu, "who knows what that may unleash and then we may never get the chance to tell the prince. We can tell them afterward."

"Let's make a decision," said Fin. "Do we go to the castle or not? I say we do. He has the knowledge. He has the men. All those who agree to go to the castle, raise your hand and say 'aye.'"

Lanzzie considered the options; she trusted her sister's judgment. She raised her hand.

"Aye," she said, as she looked around the room.

Pallu and Fin were in favor. Ezstasia was as well, of course. But Zander, Randin, Ithron, and Meldon kept their hands down. Only Jezreel remained hesitant on giving a response. She would be the tiebreaker. Ithron was staring at her.

Just as Jezreel firmly put her hands in her lap, Zander changed his mind and raised his hand, saying, "Aye!"

Randin looked at him. "What are you doing!?"

"You didn't experience the terror I did with that spider," said Zander. "If there's any chance that the prince or anyone in that castle can figure this out, then I'm all for it."

"Then it's settled," said Fin. "We set out in the morning."

"You mean *you* set out," said Ithron. "I'm not going through that forest again."

"We don't need to go through the forest," said Ezstasia. "There's a road that goes through the hillside, west of the forest."

"I think we should join them," said Jezreel. "It's important we stick together."

"Besides," said Ezstasia, "yours is the most important story of all. The prince needs to hear it from you."

Ithron contemplated silently for a long moment, then finally nodded. Lanzzie assumed that he just didn't want to be apart from Jezreel. But no matter what his reasoning might have been, she was glad that he had agreed to join them.

Lanzzie knew she wouldn't be getting much sleep that night, because every possible scenario would be playing continuously through her mind. As of tomorrow, they would be bypassing the Cottage elders and going directly to a neighboring prince. They'd be in the former capitol of magic, Old Vynterra, in Valorian's Castle itself. She had to admit that she was quite excited about seeing the grand kingdom. But then she thought of a possible snag in their plan.

"How are we going to get the rabbits tomorrow?" she said. "That old, crotchety man didn't look like he wanted to ever see us again."

"It's too far to walk," said Ezstasia.

"Well then, let's all put our best happy faces on when we greet the old bugger tomorrow," said Fin. "For now, let's get some rest."

"I want it on record," said Meldon, "that I'm not in favor of going on this unplanned journey. There are already foreseeable risks at hand."

"Then you better start calculating and planning, Meldon," said Zander.

"I'll bring the muffins," said Pallu. "Just in case."

"Pallu," said Zander, "as good as they are, not every problem in life can be solved with muffins."

"As usual, I think you underestimate the power of delicious food. Especially mine."

"We'll see about that," said Zander.

CHAPTER NINE

As she stood on the dirt road outside the stables, observing the sunrise with the others, Ezstasia's mind was racing. On one hand, she was excited about the prospect of seeing the prince again as well as being thrilled that her friends would be able to experience the magnificence of the castle alongside her. On the other hand, she was nervous on how the prince would react to their news, or if her friends would be subject to intense questioning about the arrows. There was also the issue of getting the rabbits from the stables. She took a deep breath as she waited, then exhaled, her breath visible in the cool air. She could see Fin pacing back and forth, and the others were getting anxious, too.

"Do we really have to wait for him?" said Zander, as the first rays of the sun began shining through the clouds, providing some much needed warmth. "I don't understand why he couldn't just leave with the rest of us."

"He needed his beauty sleep," said Randin.

"Here he comes," said Fin.

Ezstasia looked up to see Pallu walking casually up the hill. She looked at his smiling face and the large sack he was carrying and immediately knew that he brought food for the whole group.

Pallu approached, grinning at everyone as if he hadn't a care in the world.

"Late again, are we?" Zander said to Pallu. "How is that even possible? We all slept in the same cottage."

"Correction, my friend. I may be last, but I'm not late. The sun just came up, so technically, I'm right on time. You, on the other hand, were early, wasting what could've been precious sleep time." He moseyed past Zander toward Fin. "It's all about energy conservation," he added.

"Since when does laziness equal energy conservation?" yelled Zander.

"Time to head in there," said Fin.

Ezstasia took Fin's signal and began walking toward the stables. The others followed her.

Just as she entered into the stable, she saw Krimp sitting at the registration table talking to one of the stablekeepers. Her nerves were already at their peak when she saw him. As they walked closer to the table, she watched as Mr. Krimp spotted them. He stared intently in their direction, so much so, that he seemed to be ignoring the words of the stable keeper next to him.

She let Fin go first, since he was typically the best conversationalist, and also the calmest.

"Morning, Mr. Krimp," said Fin, trying to be cheerful and nonchalant.

Krimp stood up, chewing on his piece of straw. A smile formed on the old man's face.

"It *is* a good mornin'!" said Krimp, much more animated than he was the night before. "Here to check out yer rabbits, are ya?"

"Yes, sir," said Fin.

"And you'll have them back before dark?"

"We will, sir."

The old man gazed at him for a moment, then nodded.

"Pendants, everyone," said Krimp to the group.

Ezstasia wondered why he was being so cordial. This seemed too easy.

Fin held up his pendant and Krimp checked the rabbit footprints on his parchment for a match.

"Get number forty-one," yelled Krimp to one of the stable keepers standing nearby. "The rabbit named Zon."

Lanzzie went next, then Meldon. Ezstasia let Ithron, Jezreel and Pallu go before her. Finally, the twins, Randin and Zander approached the table.

Now it was Ezstasia's turn. She walked to the table as she watched the others' rabbits being brought out to her friends one by one.

Krimp gave her the biggest grin of all as she lifted her pendant to show him.

"The lady of the hour," he said, his crooked yellow teeth showing.

"I won't have Tia out so long this time, I promise."

"Oh I know ya won't," he said. "Matter of fact, ya won't have 'er out at all."

"What do you mean? We're all going out together. I need her. I got her back safe and sound, you said so yourself."

"Correction, lassie. I said she appeared to be no worse fer wear. I won't know fer sure how sound she is until the waitin' period is over."

"What waiting period!? Who made that rule?" Now she could feel her face growing red.

He laid a parchment on the table and turned it around for her to see.

"Article seven, section three, line twenty-three. See fer yerself." He grinned and looked up at her, obviously enjoying this far too much.

"Any rabbit kept out overnight," he added, "must undergo a three day waitin' period to fully assess their health."

"Mr. Krimp, I can read," she said. She glanced over and saw Fin talking with Randin and Zander. The three of them kept looking over at her. Their rabbits were with the rest of the group, further back. Then Fin approached.

"Sir," said Fin, "first—I must say that's a nice straw."

"What're ya gettin' at, lad? Out with it."

Ezstasia was wondering herself what Fin was doing.

"I know rules are important and everything," said Fin. "I mean we all have rules to live by and all. And I understand that this rule was created to protect the rabbits because after all, they're delicate creatures. Aren't they so delicate? They're just beautiful crea—"

"That's it. Yer tryin' my patience now."

Ezstasia tried appealing to his sensitivity, if he even had any. "Look, sir," she said. "It's really important that I check out Tia so that I can ride with my friends. Otherwise, I'll be left completely alone for the entire day. I promise I'll take good care of her."

"I'll take good care of her, too," said Krimp. "And that starts with followin' these rules."

"I think what she's trying to say," said Fin, "is that it would mean so much to us if you could overlook this rule just this once?"

"Have ya gone mad?" said Krimp. "Let me tell ye somethin'."

He leaned forward.

"I had the highest of hopes," he said, "that ye might all come in today, just so I could exercise me duties to enforce this rule. Ye said yer peace. Now I'll say mine. After all the games ye ladies an' gents have been playin'? I don't think I'll be overlookin' anything this day. So me answer is no. You may not take out the rabbit in question."

"Sir," said Ezstasia, "I will not t—"

"What she means to say," said Fin, interrupting her, "is

that we will not trouble you any further with this. We understand."

Ezstasia stared daggers at him. "What do you mean we—"

"Ezstasia, let's be respectful of this gentleman here," said Fin. "Come on, let's head outside."

"But Fin—"

"We'll deal with it. He's just trying to do his stable master duties. Let's just go."

"A smart man," said Krimp. "Ye heard him. Run along."

Ezstasia wasn't ready to give up so easily, but Fin grabbed her arm and pulled her toward the exit. On her way out, she glared at Mr. Krimp, who returned the same look while chewing on his straw.

"What are you doing!?" she said to Fin. "We need my rabbit today. This is too important to wait on, just because some old crank refuses to break the rules."

"Give the guy a break," said Fin. "It's not his fault that he can't break the rules."

"Are you crazy!?" she said.

Fin smiled. "I said *he* couldn't break the rules. I didn't say *we* couldn't. Turn around."

Ezstasia turned around to see a smiling Zander, holding Tia by the collar. In the midst of all the distraction, somehow the twins had managed to sneak her out of the barn.

"Your steed, m'lady," said Zander.

"Let's get out of here before they notice," said Fin.

Just as he said that, two stable keepers came running out from the stables.

Ezstasia jumped on Tia and grabbed the reins, while Fin and Zander did the same with their rabbits.

"Follow them!" yelled Krimp, emerging from the stable doors.

Ezstasia kicked her legs to get Tia moving faster. "Run, girl!"

The stable keepers were almost upon them, but then the rabbits picked up speed. The rest of the group were already ahead on their rabbits.

"Keep moving," yelled Fin, up ahead.

Ezstasia could see Zander, Meldon and the others to Fin's right. The only one she didn't see was Pallu.

She looked back and saw the stable keepers throw their hands up in defeat as they turned around.

"We're clear!" she yelled to Fin and the others.

Once they were out in the open field, Ezstasia caught up and they all paused to give the rabbits a rest.

"Where's Pallu?" she said.

"Don't tell me he's still back there," said Fin.

Ezstasia called for Pallu. No answer. This was bad. They needed to get out of there before the stable keepers caught up. After all, the keepers may have gone to get their horses.

"It took you guys long enough," said Pallu, emerging with Thumps from a row of bushes.

"How did you get here?" said Zander.

"I left the stables as soon as I got Thumps. We came to our favorite spot to have a little snack. How did everything go?"

"Are you crazy?!" said Zander. "We all thought you didn't make it out."

"I told you," said Pallu. "Energy conservation."

৪০ ৫৪ ৪০ ৫৪

Once they were far enough from the stables and couldn't see any of the stable workers behind them, Ezstasia began to feel a little safer, though she still felt uneasy. After what they just did –it was likely that they'd never be allowed to take the rabbits out again. And who knows what kind of trouble they'd be in when they returned. But these were unusual times, and life itself was at stake—not only for them, but also for their neighbors and all the Cottage people. They would have to understand that. She determined that the outcome of this would greatly depend on the prince's reaction and how she and her cohorts were received in Old Vynterra.

"Worried?" said Lanzzie, coming up to ride beside her.

"Everything's changed so much in so little time," she said. "I feel like our whole lives are upside down."

"There's no going back now. But for what it's worth, I think we're doing the right thing."

"Of course, we're doing the right thing!" said Pallu, as he rode up beside them. "We're like brave warriors. We may even go down in history."

Lanzzie smiled.

"I'm serious," said Pallu. "Our journey will be in books one day. I can just picture a beautiful painting of me hanging over mantels of the rich, the poor and everyone in between. Can't you envision it? I can."

"Uh, right," said Zander from behind them. "In your mom's house maybe. And that's a maybe."

"Ye of little faith," said Pallu. "We might end up saving all of the Human Lands."

"I hope not," said Ezstasia. "I mean let's just hope that there's nothing they need saving from."

Pallu shrugged. "Well, if they do, they're lucky to have us. On another note, I think a few rounds of *By the Falls of Old Vynterra* are in order. Who's in? C'mon Zander, you like singing."

As they rode on, Pallu led the group in a rendition of the old folk song. Ezstasia thought of the song in a whole new light, now that she'd actually seen the falls. And soon enough, her sister and friends would also see its beauty.

ಬ ಜ ಬ ಜ

They continued riding north throughout the morning, making stops as planned. It wasn't until the early evening that Ezstasia started recognizing her surroundings. Soon, they came to the fork in the road that she had been waiting for.

"We take the left path," she said. "It's the back way into the kingdom, but it's the only way I know. The right path would take us through the forest."

"Left path," said Zander. "Definitely the left path."

They continued for a while along the path, which wasn't so easy for their rabbits because it was a gradual incline the entire way. Eventually, they came to a steep hill, and she knew the moment had arrived. They were approaching Old Vynterra at last.

"We're almost there," she said, beginning to wonder if this was a good idea.

As they reached the peak of the hill, she could see a tree-lined path up ahead, their upper branches connecting to form a natural tunnel. She remembered going through that path on her way back to the Cottages. Just beyond it lay Old Vynterra's Western Gate.

As they descended the hill and made their way through the tunnel of trees, everyone became silent. Even Ezstasia couldn't help but think back to the forest and its ancient trees. These looked just as old.

"This feels a bit creepy," said Pallu. "He's nice, right? The prince?"

"Of course," said Ezstasia. "Trust me."

"Just checking," said Pallu. "I keep thinking of the saying from the old tales, the one about never trusting a scary road to a castle—or something like that."

"They're just old tales," said Ezstasia, trying to reassure him.

"Somebody wrote them for a reason," said Zander.

They finally emerged through the tree-lined path. The road curved and the friends saw their first view of Old Vynterra's tremendous, imposing walls, with its ornate, iron and brass gate.

"I can't believe you actually got to stay here," said Lanzzie with an awestruck tone in her voice.

Ezstasia nodded, but she was a bit distracted. Things looked different. As they approached the walls and the gate, which was wide open, she could see knights walking around inside, and some riding their horses. They were scattered throughout the expansive field. Some were in groups speaking to one another while others seemed incredibly distracted.

"Are you sure we can just ride in there on our rabbits?" said Meldon.

"It'll be okay," said Ezstasia. "The guards should remember who I am."

"Lead the way," said Fin.

Ezstasia led the group through the gate, where they continued along the dirt road that led through the open field toward the stables. To the right, there was an inner wall being freshly constructed from large stones. Beyond the partial barrier, she saw the buttresses of the Black Castle peeking out up ahead. She wondered why all this new activity had suddenly begun.

"Was it like this when you were here?" said Meldon.

She shook her head. "No. It was much more peaceful when I was here. I wonder if something's wrong."

"What do you mean wrong?" said Fin.

"Well, they're still rebuilding the old village, but they seem to be on high alert. There weren't this many guards out when I was here."

"Maybe something happened," said Pallu.

"Wouldn't the gate be closed?" said Lanzzie. "We wouldn't be able to just wander in like this if something was wrong."

Before anyone could answer, she watched as a group of knights on horseback began to ride toward them.

"This can't be good," said Zander.

"Okay, now I'm scared," said Pallu. "Those are real knights. They even have swords and stuff."

"Relax, Pallu," said Fin. "They wouldn't be very good knights if they didn't carry swords."

Everyone stopped as the armored horsemen approached them.

"Don't worry," said Lanzzie. "Ezstasia's a friend of the prince."

"Do they know that?" said Zander.

"Will you all please be quiet?" said Ezstasia. She was nervous enough without all the bickering in front of the prince's men.

The horsemen approached the group. One of the men, whose chest armor was more decorated than the others, rode forward.

"What business do you have here?" he said, in a bellowing, deep voice.

Ezstasia's heart was pounding.

"Hi, I'm—uh, I was here yesterday and—well, I know Prince Alazar, and—"

"Everyone knows Prince Alazar."

"No, I mean, he knows me personally. I was here a few days ago."

"I will ask you again," said the leader, more sternly. "What is your business here?"

As Ezstasia struggled to find the right words, Fin rode forward.

"We have vital information to share with the prince

personally," said Fin. "We believe he'll want to hear it from us directly."

"What kind of vital information?" said the knight.

"It's about the forest," said Ezstasia. "The prince rescued me from there and I have more information for him. We all do."

"Lady Arrow!" called a voice from the rear of the knights. "You've returned!"

The knight who spoke rode around to the front. She didn't recognize him.

"I have," she said. "Forgive me, but have we met?"

"Lady Arrow?" said the lead knight, looking befuddled as he turned to the other knight. "Are you certain it's her?"

"Quite certain," said the knight. "I was with the prince when we found her in the forest. How is your injury, my lady?"

"Much better, thank you. Thanks to Prince Alazar."

The leader bowed his head to her. "Apologies, my lady," he said. "I didn't realize who you were. And whom have you brought with you on this day? Your servants?"

"What? No, they're my friends," she said, realizing they must not have been informed that she wasn't actually a *Lady*. "And this is my sister. We have urgent news for the prince."

The knight turned to address his guards.

"Make way for Lady Arrow and her friends," he said.

The knights parted, with three on each side, as the leader rode toward the villages that led to the castle.

Ezstasia followed him and Lanzzie rode beside her. The others followed behind.

"Lady Arrow?" said Lanzzie. "You forgot about mentioning that one small—or should I say giant—detail. This, I have to hear."

"Later," said Ezstasia. "It's a long story."

"You can tell us 'servants' later, too," said Fin from

behind, laughing.

As they rode past the horsemen and toward the village, the grandiose Black Castle, with its tall, black, iron gates, began to come into full view. Ezstasia could hear her friends behind her, whispering intently.

Soon they approached the Western Village, first passing the stables and the outdoor markets on the left. Shortly after, the Black Castle could be entirely seen on her right. Ezstasia could hear her sister and friends marveling at its commanding presence as they rode past.

"Who lives in there?" said Pallu. "That's one creepy castle!"

"As far as I know, nobody," said Ezstasia. "They use it for some kind of training."

She noticed the village was much more crowded than it had been previously. The villagers were outside of their homes. Most of them were busy running to and fro; transporting crates and pushing wheeled carts. They all seemed to be extremely focused and in a hurry. Between the knights and the villagers, it appeared that Old Vynterra was preparing for something big. But what?

They arrived at the steep ascent which led to the eerie tree-lined path that Ezstasia recognized from before—the one Prince Alazar had said was the famous Road of Sorrow. She made a mental note to herself to tell the others about this road, as well as the beautiful Falls of Allura, whose distant rumbling sounds she could hear coming from the mountains—as soon as they had some time alone.

They walked through the small dirt path in the field of beautiful wildflowers, then passed through the bustling Eastern Village. After what felt like an eternity, the prince's castle finally emerged up ahead. She felt butterflies in her stomach at the thought of seeing Prince Alazar again.

She took a certain pride as she saw the look on her sister's face at the sight of the majestic castle. She could hear all the gasping and whispering from her friends and turned to see their reactions. Even Ithron seemed to be in awe.

Before they reached the rear entrance, the horseman stopped.

"Please wait here, Lady Arrow. I'll have to announce your arrival to the prince."

Ezstasia watched the knight walk away and curiously turned to see what her friends were doing. She saw her sister and her friends were busy watching the villagers hurrying about. The townspeople hardly paid any attention to them, even with their giant rabbits. Either they were terribly preoccupied or they were simply accustomed to receiving visitors.

Meldon and Fin focused on the architecture of the castle, gawking at the exquisite stone statues and the intricate carvings.

"I still can't believe you got to stay here," said Lanzzie as she rode a few steps closer to Ezstasia.

"This is nothing," said Ezstasia. "Just wait until you see the inside. And the gardens."

"I'll bet it's—hey, what's Pallu doing?"

Ezstasia looked to see Pallu walking up to one of the village women who was holding a couple baskets of food.

"Pallu!" said Lanzzie, whispering as loudly as she could so as not to draw attention. "Where are you going? We're supposed to wait here."

Pallu ignored her, apparently too focused on his mission.

Ezstasia tried to hear what he was saying to the woman.

"Miss," said Pallu. "Please let me carry those for you. Those are much too heavy for a lovely lady like yourself to have to carry on her own."

The young, fair-haired woman seemed shy, but she handed him the braided baskets and led him to one of the corner homes with a white, wooden fence. In the front on the road stood a donkey-drawn, wooden wagon. Its two large wheels had sunk into the soft dirt that it was resting on.

The porcelain-skinned girl motioned to the wagon and Pallu loaded the baskets onto the back. They began talking about something, but Ezstasia couldn't quite hear their conversation. Based on the young woman's mannerisms and the way she held up the vegetables, it appeared as if they were discussing cooking. That wasn't much of a surprise to Ezstasia, knowing Pallu.

"What's Pallu doing?" said Randin.

Zander shook his head. "I guess his mission to get a bride continues. He's persistent, if nothing else."

The knight emerged from the castle and walked toward Ezstasia.

"Lady Arrow, the prince will see you and your friends now. Our guards will tend to your rabbits during your absence."

"Pallu, let's go!" yelled Zander.

Pallu finished a few last words with the young villager before kissing her hand and meandering back. He was halfway back when he turned to her and yelled, "We'll talk soon, Miss Ellie."

"We shall!" she yelled back, a beaming smile on her face.

"You're so lovely," he yelled. "And your peaches are wonderful!"

"Pallu!" yelled Zander, shaking his head.

As Pallu approached, Zander grabbed him by the shoulders.

"Your peaches are wonderful? Really? That's the best line you could come up with?"

"Well they were," said Pallu. "It's hard to get those this time of year. And—"

Lanzzie grabbed them both. "We need to go in *now*," she

said.

Ezstasia took a deep breath as she followed the knight, the others tagging closely behind her.

౪౨ ౧౮ ౪౨ ౧౮

Ezstasia couldn't believe she was about to see Prince Alazar again. The butterflies in her stomach were so powerful that, she thought they might flutter right out. On one hand, she was excited to see him. After all, everything paled in comparison to spending the day with a prince in a regal castle. She was reminded of that incomparable feeling as they entered through the intricately carved front doors into a sprawling, tapestry-lined breezeway. On the other hand, she had to remember that she was a cottage girl. She couldn't afford to get too enamored with a prince, of all people.

The knight led them down a familiar, well-appointed corridor and into the magnificent dining room.

"Please be seated," said the knight. "The prince shall arrive shortly."

Ezstasia took a seat on one of the long benches that lined the endless wooden dining table. Lanzzie and the others were still marveling at the elegant tree-themed frescoes and tapestries on the walls. And the imposing architecture with its carved statues and elaborate designs.

"They sure love trees here," said Pallu.

"You have no idea," said Ezstasia.

Just then, footsteps could be heard beyond the room. And like a bunch of schoolchildren who suddenly behaved when they were aware that the headmistress was coming, everyone rushed to the dining room table and took their seats in preparation for the prince.

Ezstasia could feel her heart pounding through her chest as the footsteps grew closer. Prince Alazar entered the room.

The prince gave her a quick, polite smile as he approached and stood at the head of the table.

"Lady Arrow," he said. "Or I suppose I should call you Miss Ezstasia, at least in front of your friends?"

Lanzzie elbowed her.

"Stop," whispered Ezstasia to her sister, "this is awkward enough."

"Either is fine, Your Grace," she said to the prince, composing herself.

His eyes scanned the group. "To what do I owe the pleasure?"

His voice seemed friendly, but more formal than it had been before.

"Thank you for receiving us." She tried to keep her voice as controlled and calm as possible, even though she felt like jumping out of her skin. She hadn't realized until now how strong her feelings truly were for the prince. "While Your Grace was tending to my injuries, my sister and my friends experienced some terrible things in the forest. I know you're concerned about the forest, so we thought you should be made aware of their stories."

The prince's face grew more serious.

"Go on," he said.

Ezstasia looked over at Fin and nodded.

"Your Grace," said Fin, "when Ezstasia was in your care, we searched the forest for days, not realizing that she was safe in your castle. Some of us had... I suppose I would call them... bad experiences. It could only be explained by one thing, really."

"Yes, yes, well what's the one thing?" said the prince, growing impatient.

"What he means to say," said Lanzzie, "is that we think someone is using forbidden magic in that forest, and not just forbidden, but, well... dark magic."

The prince raised an eyebrow.

Ezstasia tried to gauge the prince's reaction to their news, but his face was unreadable. She wondered if he was thinking of something else entirely. Then he glanced up at a portrait displayed above the fireplace mantel opposite him on the other end of the table.

"Prince Alazar," said Fin, "some of us experienced frightening things in that forest. And some of us didn't see or personally experience anything. We can tell you the stories. I think you'll find them quite peculiar."

"Perhaps later," said the prince, seeming only mildly interested.

"Later?" said Ezstasia, slightly annoyed at the prince's indifference, and more than a little surprised.

"Tell me," said the prince, "did any of you tell anyone else of these… stories?" He said the word *stories* as if he was searching for the right word.

They all shook their heads.

"Does anyone know about your journey here?"

Once again, they shook their heads, though Ezstasia could see the others were as confused as she was.

"But you're all witnesses to these events, by your own word?"

"We are, Your Grace," said Fin. The others nodded.

"Good," said the prince, glancing once more at the portrait. "You will all remain here in the castle until further notice. You'll be well cared for and Miss Tee will summon you for dinner. Meanwhile, I'll have my servants show you to your rooms. Your rabbits will do quite nicely in our stables."

The prince bowed his head to Ezstasia and smiled, then turned to leave.

"Prince Alazar?" said Ezstasia.

The prince turned around.

"Did you know something like this was happening in the

forest? You seem to have many more knights on alert, and—
"

"You'll be staying in the same room as you did last time. Miss Tee will attend to you and your friends shortly." He grimaced slightly.

"But what about—"

"There are plans afoot, Lady Arrow. That's all you need to know for now. As I've said, Miss Tee will make sure you're all taken care of. For now, my steward, Veterus, will have the servants show you to your rooms."

He spoke in a patronizing, faux-happy voice that didn't seem at all sincere. Then he left the room.

Within moments, a number of servants entered and stood at attention while the steward, Veterus, walked in to give direction.

"Our esteemed guests!" said Veterus, with a flamboyant tone. "Allow us to escort you to your rooms." He was a skinny man with prominent cheekbones. He stood tall, adorned in a plush, burgundy jacket that complemented his silver hair rather nicely. "Prince Alazar requests that you stay only in the areas of the castle that you've already seen. Exploring beyond those points is, shall we say, forbidden."

"Even the kitchen?" said Pallu.

"Especially the kitchen. The cooks are terrible gossips."

"Are we allowed outside?" said Pallu, no doubt anxious to meet his new girlfriend.

"Never again, I'm afraid," said the steward. "You shall be condemned to darkness for all the days of eternity."

Ezstasia couldn't believe what she heard, and Pallu looked mortified. Then Veterus offered a sly smile.

"Of course you can go outside," he said. "You're not prisoners here. The prince simply asks that you respect the boundaries of his home. And, of course, that you do not share your stories around the village. But I'm sure you already knew that. For now, the guards have been made aware of your status as our guests. If there are no further questions, the servants will take you to your rooms."

"Whoa, things get done rather quickly around here," whispered Zander to Pallu. "Maybe you can learn a thing or two."

"Shhh," said Ezstasia, unable to hold in her chuckle.

Ezstasia and the group followed two of the servants out of the dining room and up the large, spiral staircase.

"I think I could get used to this place," said Zander.

"Yeah, well don't," said Randin.

Halfway up the steps, Lanzzie grabbed Ezstasia's arm.

"I don't get it," said Lanzzie. "Why did the prince respond like that?"

"I'm wondering that myself." Actually, she was more than wondering. She was furious that the prince was so dismissive.

"It sure wasn't what I expected," said Lanzzie. "I mean, he didn't directly answer your question about the knights, and he didn't even seem to want to know exactly what happened to us. Why? Do you think he already knows something about the forest?"

Ezstasia shrugged. "Maybe. They do have an awful lot of knights outside. But either way, he should've told us *something*. He wasn't like that before. He was more... open."

She started thinking back to her last conversation with the prince before she'd left for the Cottages. She remembered him saying that there were strange sightings in the forest, but he hadn't mentioned any specific details.

"Maybe he's just being cautious," said Lanzzie, interrupting her thoughts.

As they reached the top of the stairs, Randin caught up beside them.

"You know what I think?" he said, apparently eavesdropping on their whispers. "I think he may be behind it all."

"Randin!" said Ezstasia in the loudest whisper she could muster. "Quiet!" She motioned toward the servants just ahead of them, hoping they didn't already hear him.

"We can all meet in my room after we check into our own rooms," said Lanzzie. "Randin, tell the others."

⁛ ⁜ ⁛ ⁜

Once Ezstasia got to her room, she saw that Miss Tee had left a tray with some pastries and a note that read, "*Welcome back, dear.*"

The others had already gone to their rooms. Exhausted, she fell back on the bed and began trying to make sense of everything that had happened. Why had the prince been so aloof? Why hadn't he wanted to hear the stories, or the many reasons that brought them here? He'd seemed far more forthcoming during her last visit. Now, in front of her friends, he'd made her look like a fool. She began to wonder if coming here was one huge mistake.

Her thoughts were interrupted by a knock on the door.

"Are you coming?" said Lanzzie, through the door. "We're all waiting for you."

Ezstasia took a deep breath and rose to go to the door. She was almost embarrassed to see her friends. After all, she had led them here into nothing but uncertainty. She opened the door and silently followed her sister up the long hallway. The next room on the left was Lanzzie's.

As she entered, she was surprised to see the size of the spacious, circular room. It was even larger than hers, though more sparsely decorated in natural wood and white linens. Everyone was sitting around on benches and chairs, the sun's ray's beaming down through large windows, high above them on the walls.

Ezstasia took a seat next to Lanzzie on one of the benches.

"We were just saying that the prince is probably responsible for all of the dark magic in the forest," said Zander.

"Well, we didn't say that exactly," said Fin. "But it does look suspicious."

"Yes, his response was a bit odd," said Randin. "That's why I brought it up."

"It's not the prince!" said Ezstasia. She didn't know why she was defending Prince Alazar, but she still didn't think he was the cause of the magic. It just didn't add up.

"Whoa, a little defensive, are we?" said Zander. "How do you know he isn't?"

"Because it wouldn't make sense if he were. Why would he bother to save me and care for me? And then let me go back to the Cottages? I just think maybe he knows something, but he doesn't want to share it right now."

"She has a point," said Pallu.

"You're all listening to the girl with a crush," said Ithron, sitting with his arm around Jezreel.

"You're one to talk," said Pallu.

"I do not have a crush, Ithron!" said Ezstasia. She could feel her face getting red, though she wasn't sure if it was from embarrassment or anger.

"Can we get back to the issue here?" said Meldon. "Let's talk about what we know so far. The prince has a lot of magical artifacts and history in this castle. That much is clear."

"That doesn't mean he's responsible for the magic," said Ezstasia.

"I didn't say he was," said Meldon. "But when you combine that with the fact that he knows we're all witnesses to the magic, that he specifically asked if we told anyone else about, and that he's holding us here, it sure seems like a possibility."

"You don't know that," said Ezstasia.

"That's why it's called a possibility," said Meldon.

"You haven't seen how he treats his people," she said. "They adore him."

"Well, who else anywhere, has that much access to magic?" said Zander. "He's not far from the forest. He's mysterious. He keeps everything to himself. It has to be him."

"Then why would he be training knights to get ready for whatever is in the forest? He told me himself that he was concerned about it."

"Pardon me," said Meldon, "but I have to raise a small concern with that."

"Which is?" she said, defensively.

Meldon pushed his glasses up on the bridge of his nose. "If you suspect magic, why would you train knights? No knight in the world can fight the things that I saw. Or shall I say—the things that I didn't see? That begs the question: What exactly is he training for?"

"I'll tell you what he's training for," said Zander. "He's training to fight humans. I bet he wants to take over all the Human Lands. And he's using magic and knights to do it."

"Yeah," said Ithron. "You could've brought us straight into a trap."

"Stop!" yelled Ezstasia, making Zander jump. "Just stop. I hear all your theories, but the fact is that you're all wrong. I told you already, he made a point of telling me he was concerned about the strange sightings in that forest. He didn't have to tell me that, but he did. Why would he do that if he was the one causing it? And aside from that, he was trying to get *me* to shed light on what was happening in there and wanted to know if I was the one behind it. It doesn't make sense that it would be him."

She wasn't sure if she was angrier with them or with the prince. She even began to doubt herself. Could Prince Alazar really be the cause of this? Why would he have rescued her? Was she an unintended victim and he simply felt guilty? Her mind began to wander back to the Black Castle. Something was going on inside of that castle. She just knew it. The prince said they were using the castle for training, but there must be something he wasn't telling her. She had to find out what was happening there, if only to ease her mind. And that's just what she was going to do—she was going to visit the Black Castle.

"Let's talk about this like the respectful young ladies and gents we all are," said Fin. "Nobody's jumping to any conclusions. We're only discussing possibilities."

Ezstasia stood up.

"You can all discuss it without me," she said. "I'm tired."

"Ezstasia, please don't do this," said Lanzzie.

"Do what?" she said. "I'm seriously tired."

"Since when do you go to sleep this early? We haven't even had dinner!" said Lanzzie. "Not to mention, you've always had more energy than all of us. This is important."

"Now she's acting like the prince," said Ithron. "Just walking away at the most crucial time. Yes, I'd say it's a crush all right."

"Maybe you all forgot I had a head injury," she said. "I'm going to my room to lie down. If you all want to continue discussing these things, be my guest."

She turned and left the room, fully aware that everyone was staring at her like she was crazy. But there was no choice. One way or another she was going to visit that castle and find out exactly what was hidden behind its walls.

ಋ ಇ ಋ ಇ

Lanzzie looked at Fin. "Something's not right," she said.

"That's the understatement of the year," said Ithron.

"There's no way she's going to sleep," said Zander.

"I have to say, I agree," said Fin. "It's not like her at all. She was acting a bit peculiar."

"A bit?" said Zander.

"Maybe she really is just tired," said Pallu. "We did have an awfully long walk. I'm tired myself. And I have to say, a little hungry."

Zander looked at him and rolled his eyes. "I think she's up to something."

"Well, I'm sure it's nothing bad," said Pallu, as he stood. "And there's nothing we can really do now anyway. Now if you'll all excuse me, my cooking skills are about to be sharpened with the help of a pretty little lady who has the same love for food as I do. And so, I bid you adieu." Pallu mockingly bowed and waltzed out of the room.

"Pallu, wait," said Ithron, who rose up and helped Jezreel stand to her feet. "We're going outside, too."

"I'm not sure we're quite ready for double dating," said Pallu.

"Don't flatter yourself," said Ithron. "We just want to explore the village. Maybe annoy the villagers a bit."

"I'm not sure that's a good idea," said Fin.

"Calm yourself. I was kidding. Mostly."

As the three of them left, Meldon stood. "Well, if we're done here, me, myself, and my mind are going to go map out the coordinates of this place. We may as well get familiar with our surroundings. Plus, the architecture here is superb. I wouldn't mind getting a better look."

As he left the room, Lanzzie thought more about Ezstasia and quickly made up her mind.

"I'm going to go check on my sister," she said, standing.

"I want to find out what she's really up to."

"Not without us, you're not," said Fin, jumping up.

Randin and Zander looked at each other as if they silently came to the same conclusion.

"We're joining you," said Randin, as they rose.

Lanzzie nodded and headed into the hallway, the others close behind her. When she got to Ezstasia's door, she knocked quietly.

Nobody answered.

"Ezstasia," she called.

They knocked several more times. No answer.

Lanzzie slowly turned the knob.

"You wait here," she said to Fin and the twins.

She slowly walked into Ezstasia's room. She didn't see anyone on the canopy bed. As she walked further into the room, she realized it was empty.

"She's not here," she said loudly enough for the others to hear.

Fin, Randin, and Zander entered.

"Wow, will you look at this place!" said Zander.

"I wonder if she would consider switching rooms," said Randin.

"I guess she wasn't tired after all," said Fin. "Wonder where she went."

Just as they stepped back out into the hall, Pallu came running back from down the corridor.

"What's wrong?" said Lanzzie.

"Nothing," said Pallu, out of breath. "I got halfway there and realized I forgot my cloak in case it gets chilly later. What are you guys up to?"

"Looking for Ezstasia," said Fin.

"I just saw her on the stairs. She was heading down while I was coming up."

"Did she say where she was going?" said Lanzzie.

"No, she just said she was thirsty. But I must say, she seemed to be in a big hurry for that water. Sorry to cut this short, but time is a tickin'. See you later."

"Are you thinking what I'm thinking?" said Fin to Lanzzie with a large grin.

"Yes," said Lanzzie. "Let's go follow her."

CHAPTER TEN

Once outside the castle, Ezstasia unfolded the long, hooded cloak Miss Tee had given her and draped it around her shoulders. She fastened it to cover her clothing, trying to inconspicuously make her way through the villages toward the Black Castle. It helped that the sun had set and brought upon her a cover of darkness. She didn't want to run into any more of her friends, who may have been out exploring the village. She was lucky it was Pallu that she'd encountered on the stairway; he was too wrapped up in his new love to care about anything else.

She could feel the gentle breeze blowing her braided hair as she made her way through the dirt road, the path illuminated by tall torches on both sides. She could see candles flickering in the windows of many of the homes, and human silhouettes moving about. Each home had lanterns mounted on their outside walls and on their porches. The cottages back home were more spread out, whereas this felt like a festival of lights.

Along the way, she could hear laughter and shouting coming from the homes. As she continued, rich aromas permeated the air. The heavenly smells of meats and vegetables, seasoned with the most delectable spices wafted past her, reminding her that dinner would soon be served at the castle. She still had an hour or so to get back. The last thing she needed was for her friends to try and wake her for dinner, or worse—for the prince to call for her before she had returned.

She passed one establishment that was particularly loud, with people pouring out onto the porch. They danced and drank to what sounded like an old pub song, though she hadn't heard it before. A wooden sign swayed in the gentle breeze above the porch that read, *The Crazy Root*. Then, just after passing the riotous pub, she spotted them.

Ithron and Jezreel were sitting alone at a small wooden table on a white porch. Even though dusk had fallen, the brightly lit village allowed Ezstasia to see the colorful flowers that hung from the porch's roof and overflowed from wooden pots mounted onto its balusters. They appeared to be in deep conversation. Ithron must have been telling a funny story because Jezreel laughed every time he gestured with his hands. As he spoke, she sipped from a dainty teacup and looked up at him with such awe and fascination. Ezstasia noticed the small sign that read *Flowered Tea 'n Honey* sticking out of the ground next to the white fence that marked the entrance. She couldn't believe how much Ithron had changed. She never thought she'd see him in any place that had the word 'flower' in it and she never expected to see him open up the way he had.

Ezstasia picked her hood up to block her face and continued walking, although, even if Ithron or Jezreel had spotted her, they probably wouldn't think it so unusual. Besides, they were too wrapped up in each other to care about anything she was doing.

She was about to pass one of the bakeries when she heard an unmistakable voice, quickly followed by a delicate female laugh. Out of the corner of her eye, she saw Pallu and his new girlfriend emerging from the bakery. If anyone deserved to be happy and in love, it was Pallu. She wondered how he got to the bakery so quickly from the castle; he was on his way upstairs when she ran into him earlier. But at least this proved that, with the proper motivation, Pallu could move pretty quickly.

She held her hood up and kept moving.

Ezstasia left the Eastern Village and made her way through the field of wildflowers which she remembered seeing earlier. The mountains were visible to the left, as were the majestic Falls of Allura. Before long, she came to the Road of Sorrow.

The tree-lined dirt road was even scarier in the dark, but she walked quickly through the eerie path and emerged. She had reached the steep decline which led to the Western Village. She made her way down the hill and up to the pebble path that led through the quieter village and could finally see the imposing Black Castle on her left. Its tremendous stone buttresses pierced the night sky. She continued toward the castle and saw the long bridge that led to its massive doors. The bridge extended over the large moat surrounding the castle and led to the guarded gate. She thought it odd that this castle had a moat and Valorian's Castle didn't. Why did this castle go through such great lengths to have protection?

Her heart pounded as she approached the bridge, not only because of her trepidation about the guards, but also from her fear of heights. She stepped onto the bridge and continued slowly, daring to look down into the moat only once. As beautiful as the moonlight was on the flowing current below, she immediately regretted looking. It made her realize just how high up she was. Glancing ahead at the castle's entry gate, she could see the guards questioning two figures dressed in black, head-to-toe uniforms. She realized they were also trying to enter. Their faces were covered with form-fitting black cloth with narrow eyeholes, just like the man she had spotted in the castle window the day before. After some questioning, the guards let them pass. That's when she noticed several similarly-dressed, masked men coming in and out of the castle. The uniforms must have been a form of protective gear. But protection from what?

As curious as she was, her bigger issue at the moment was to determine exactly how she would get inside the castle. She could lie and say Prince Alazar gave her access or had sent her for training, but the guards would no doubt question her. Or maybe she could cause a distraction and lure the guards away, but that, too had risks.

She took a deep breath and made her way toward the guards. The closer she got, the more she wanted to turn around, but she was determined to try. She needed to find out what was in that castle.

As she approached, the guards stared intently at her. She immediately realized she still had her hood over her head, which must've looked awfully suspicious. She lowered her hood and kept moving toward the guards, her long cloak dragging along the ground. One guard stepped forward.

"Entry is off limits," he said in a strong, firm voice. "You should know that."

"I'm sorry. I'm a guest of Prince Alazar."

He turned back to the other guards, then back toward her.

"Guest or no guest, you need orders to enter. Do you have orders?"

"Orders?"

"If the prince sent you here, he'd have sent you with written orders. A parchment. Do you have it?"

"No, I'm afraid I—"

"Then you'll need to turn around."

She pointed to the men dressed in black behind the gate.

"I didn't see any of *them* with a parchment," she said.

"They're with the Valorian Order. They're authorized to be here. Now turn around."

"What's the Val—"

"Enough questions. Now move."

She turned to leave, but then the guard yelled out from behind her.

"You! Miss!"

She spun around to face him.

"What's your name?" he said.

"My name?"

"Yes. You say you're a guest of the prince."

From the skeptical tone of his voice, Ezstasia assumed that he probably wanted to confirm her identity with the prince, which is the last thing she wanted.

As she stood there contemplating whether to give him her real name or a false name, a bloodcurdling scream rang out from the castle doors.

A man ran out of the castle. He was on fire from head to toe. Ezstasia froze and found herself staring in complete shock. Other men, wearing the same black outfits and masks, came running out after him as the guards rushed toward him.

"Get the water buckets and pumps!" yelled one of the masked men to the guards. "Now!"

Ezstasia watched in horror as the men tried to keep the screaming victim from running rampant. She wanted to help but she didn't know what to do. Then she remembered her cloak. She quickly unfastened it and removed it as she ran through the now unguarded, gated entrance.

"Use this," she yelled to one of the masked men. The man grabbed it and threw it over the screaming worker in an attempt to smother the fire. The guards returned with two water buckets and a hand pump.

In the midst of the chaos, people ran up and down the bridge, horsemen began to arrive and people yelled at one another from every direction.

Ezstasia got pushed back toward the castle over and over again by the growing crowd, until she couldn't see what was going on. During a break in the crowd of people, she got a glimpse of the man's badly charred face as the guards doused the flames. She covered her eyes at the sight, unsure if he was alive or not. As the smoke-filled air penetrated her nostrils, she slowly removed her hands from over her eyes. She watched as the guards carried the man on a wooden board, covered in her cloak. They loaded him onto a carriage and began dispersing the crowd. Thinking fast, she covered her mouth and ran to an arched breezeway just inside the castle gates.

Lost in all of the mayhem, only now did Ezstasia realize that she'd somehow, through a bizarre twist of fate, achieved her goal. She was inside the castle gates.

She saw what must have been a hidden stone door on the side of the castle. It was cracked open. She hid behind a pillar and saw one of the men in black emerge from the hidden door. As he removed the black mask that covered his face, he knelt to the ground and stared at the dirt. He began to sob. After a moment, he stood, pulled himself together, and headed back inside the door as he put his mask back on.

Ezstasia waited a few moments and quietly stepped forward from behind the pillar. Just as she began to head toward the hidden door, a hand grabbed her arm.

ಐ ಐ ಐ ಐ

"Fin!" said Ezstasia, relieved to see that it was him, but also embarrassed that she was caught. "You scared me half to death! What are you doing here?"

"Me!? What're *you* doing here? We were trying to figure out where you were going, so we followed you here."

"We? Who's we?"

Just then, Lanzzie, Randin, and Zander stepped out from behind a corner of the castle.

"Do you know how much trouble you can get in?" said Lanzzie. "Let's all get out of here now."

"You go," said Ezstasia. "I can't. There's something I need to find out."

"Find out!?" said Zander. "We just saw a man come out of there on fire. What could you possibly want to find out?"

"I wanted to prove to you all that the prince is preparing for something, just like he said." In truth, she wanted to prove to herself that he wasn't guilty of putting the magic in the forest to begin with. But now she wasn't sure of that either.

"Ezstasia," said Fin, "for all we know, the prince could be responsible for whatever set that man on fire. It's too dangerous to be here."

Ezstasia hesitated. As she considered how she should proceed, a tremendous rumbling came from inside the castle. She glanced up and thought she saw smoke bellowing from one of the windows. Another loud sound shook right through her bones, this one resembled a roaring furnace, and it caused the stone walls to vibrate.

"What was that?" said Randin.

"I don't know, nor do I want to know," said Zander. "Is that smoke coming from the cracks?"

Ezstasia watched as they looked toward the smoke. In that short moment, she had made up her mind.

While her friends were distracted, she ran toward the hidden side door and entered.

Just as she slipped through the doorway, she heard the deafening noise again. She made her way into the side corridor which led to a stone foyer. She could feel a burst of heat enveloping her face, making it difficult to breathe. No wonder those men wear masks over their faces, Ezstasia thought to herself. But how could they handle wearing the black outfits in this sweltering place? And what were they even doing in here that required so much heat?

After passing through the large foyer, she walked to an opening that led into a long hall, dimly lit by torches mounted high above. She slowly walked into the long hall, and as her eyes met the torches, she realized the walls didn't even reach the ceiling. In fact, the castle didn't seem to have multiple floors.

She felt her spine tingle with the thought that someone may catch her and there'd be nowhere to hide. But still, she made her way forward, convincing herself that she would just get a glimpse of what was going on. Then, with any luck, she could leave unnoticed.

The intense, rumbling commotion startled her again and she held onto the wall for balance. She was much closer to the source of the noise now and she felt another burst of scorching heat come her way. She could hear metal chains dragging along the hard, stone floor in the distance.

She realized that the hall was about to come to an end as she quietly and slowly approached the end of it. She peeked into the adjoining room that it led to. It was a massive area with a towering ceiling. As she looked around, she could see stone steps built into the walls that looked like they led to exterior rooms.

She spotted a few of the men in black. They were approaching a row of giant, black vertical bars that appeared to be made of iron. Each bar was at least three or four times her body's width. She leaned her head in quietly to get a better look and, could see that these bars were actually part of an enormous cage.

Taking care not to be seen, she stepped softly into the room and ducked behind a pillar, where she could hopefully get a better look.

Just as she got behind the stone column, she heard the sound of a heavy chain moving again, followed by a dull rumbling. It was coming from the cage. She peeked her head out from behind the pillar and her mouth dropped. She felt like she couldn't breathe. She had never seen such an enormous creature.

She couldn't believe her eyes as she looked at this giant, heavy behemoth with scales. Just as she had decided that she was going to leave this castle, it slowly picked up its neck and she saw the beast's enormous head, scales jutting out the sides of its face and under its chin.

She blinked several times to make sure she wasn't dreaming. But there wasn't any doubt. From the giant scaly body to the long, spiked tail and the glowing yellow eyes, she realized that she was staring at a real, live dragon.

Ezstasia was face-to-face with a creature that she thought no longer existed, at least not anywhere outside of the Magiclands.

The beast began moving again, dragging the heavy chains with it. She looked over to see that the men in black were outside the cage arguing with one another over something she couldn't quite make out. They were in the heat of the debate when Ezstasia turned back toward the cage and almost fell backward in shock. She watched another head slowly pick itself up inside the cage. It had two large horns on the top of its head. Then another head came out of the shadows, with a long horn protruding downward from underneath its chin. She felt her breath quicken as she tried to comprehend what she was seeing.

The other two giant heads came forward and small bursts of yellow and orange flames began to illuminate the belly of the terrifying beast. Her mouth dropped when she realized exactly what she was seeing—an ancient creature she'd only read about in books. The three heads belonged to a single, monstrous beast. She was staring face-to-face with a three-headed dragon!

"Back up!" yelled one of the men to the others.

She could see the men slowly stepping backward, nearly tripping over the large chains that extended out from the cage along the ground.

A loud horn blasted from an outer room and startled her. She could hear footsteps and loud voices in the distance, coming from all directions, including the hall she'd just come from. Whoever it was, they were running.

She froze in place as the men in black all sprang into action, each grabbing a chain that hung from the towering ceiling next to a large curtain. They all pulled the chains as two layers of large, heavy black canvas dropped over the dragon's cage. She certainly couldn't emerge from behind the pillar, and now she couldn't leave through the hall either.

The footsteps were getting closer.

Just then, two guards emerged from a large doorway across the room. One was more decorated than the other and stepped forward, as the men in black that she was observing came toward them.

One of the men in black lifted his face mask, revealing chiseled features and a scar down the side of his face.

"Sir Aldus," said the decorated castle guard, "we have a breach."

"What kind of breach?"

"A group of spies were caught inside the castle. Three men and a woman."

"So you actually caught them, then?" said Sir Aldus. He turned to his colleagues in black. "These castle guards are getting better," he said, smiling.

"Maybe not all of them," said the guard. "I'm told there was a woman trying to enter the castle earlier. We don't know if she made it in or not, but we can't afford prying eyes, so we've engaged our breach protocol."

"You've secured the full perimeter?"

"We have. No one can get in or out without being checked. I've already alerted all the guards."

More guards entered from all directions and walked toward Sir Aldus and the other men.

"Good," said Sir Aldus. "We'll search in here and secure Trycernius. Have your men check their assigned sectors."

The head guard motioned to the others and they all followed him out of the room. Sir Aldus nodded to the men in black, and they responded by checking the surrounding area.

Ezstasia's heart was pounding through her chest. As Sir Aldus and his men began searching the room, she looked around for a place to hide. There was nowhere to go, and she couldn't make it to the corridor without being seen.

This was all her fault. Now her friends were likely in the dungeons—or worse. She contemplated whether to give herself up, but if the prince was indeed behind the return of magic, then she'd just be trapped along with her friends. She would be unable to help them—or anyone—for that matter.

The men searched behind the pillars opposite her. They'd be upon her soon. She had to think fast.

She looked behind her, desperately trying to find a hiding place. Then she spotted it. Hidden in the shadows was a large crack toward the bottom of the thick stone wall. She tried to focus on the inside of the crack and thought the hollowed area in the wall may be just large enough for her to fit her entire body inside. But could she fit through the slit of the crack? There was only one way to find out, though she risked being seen.

She quietly moved from behind the pillar toward the dark crevice in the shadows. One of the men turned in her direction but didn't appear to have seen her. She knelt down to peer inside the opening. Instantly she felt the hairs on her arms rise. Inside she could see what appeared to be hundreds of silk webs covering the wall. They glistened in the soft lighting that poured in from an unknown place. She could make out several enormous, vicious looking spiders waiting to catch their prey. She thought to herself that the men in black were doing the exact same thing with her. Ezstasia was overcome with dread. There was no way she was going in there.

She looked over at the men in black who were thoroughly searching the far corners of the room, but they were getting closer and closer to her. She peeked back into the hole and stared at the spiders. They seemed to be staring back at her, just waiting for her to enter their home. Ezstasia's palms began to sweat.

"We didn't check over there yet," Ezstasia overheard one of the men say. She looked up and saw that he was pointing in her direction.

"Go look, then," said Sir Aldus.

He began to move quickly toward her, she took a deep breath and stuck her foot into the crack, feeling the cobwebs crack and pop as she pushed the rest of her body inside.

She nestled deeper into the web-filled darkness and tried not to make a sound. She watched the man in black approach the pillar she had just been hiding behind. He looked carefully around it and then slowly turned his head in her direction.

She felt one of the webs beside her face begin to vibrate. She shifted her eyes toward it and saw a giant, furry spider menacingly inching its way down the web. She gasped loud enough for the man to have heard her. Much to her dismay, he jerked his head toward her and immediately began to walk in her direction. Fear pulsed through her body as she felt one of the spiders gently lower itself onto her shoulder. She threw her hand over her mouth as she felt the weight of its body against her skin. She tried to remain still, though she wanted nothing more than to scream and shake every spider off her trembling body.

The man knelt and squinted into the shadows that surrounded her as she tried to control the shaking in her breath.

The spider was on her neck now, tapping its hairy legs against her skin.

She glanced down and saw more spiders at her feet. Ezstasia felt as if she might faint at any moment. She had to remind herself over and over to keep breathing and to not focus on the furry eight-legged creatures that surrounded her.

To her immense relief, the man stood and turned to walk away, just as a group of knights entered, carrying swords in one hand and torches in the other.

"Find anything?" said Sir Aldus.

"Nothing here," said the man in black. "I thought I heard something, but it seems to be clear."

"Let's keep searching. If you heard a noise, the woman could be nearby. You check near the west hall."

As the man left, Sir Aldus held the torch just in front of the wall that she was hiding in. The flames illuminated the floor in front of her. He began to stoop down to get a better look, just as the spider crawled to the other side of her neck and then into her hair. She clutched her fists and squeezed her eyes tightly shut, feeling the sting of tears behind her eyelids. She felt the eight-legged arachnid creep up the left side of her head. The knight stooped down even lower.

She would give anything in this moment just to be back at the cottages with her friends and to put this entire forest and kingdom behind her.

"I was sent to help," yelled one of the castle guards from

across the room, whom had apparently just entered. "Should I put on a suit?"

Sir Aldus walked away toward him. Ezstasia wiggled her head to try to shake the spiders loose, to no avail. The castle guard was holding one of the black suits up, which he'd pulled out from a wooden box which lay across the room.

"I think not," said Sir Aldus. "We're just about done in this area. You'll be out of here soon."

Just then, a soft rumble grew louder and turned into a deafening roar.

"Not soon enough!" yelled the castle guard.

"We should probably get out of here for your sake," said Sir Aldus, seemingly impervious to fear. "Trycernius isn't in the best of moods today."

The two men left the room while smoke and heat filled the cavernous space.

Ezstasia had never been so thankful to have a raging three-headed dragon in the same room as her. She burst out of the crevice, frantically rustling her hair and shaking her legs to get rid of the spiders. She could still feel one in her hair, so she clenched her teeth together and swatted the menacing creature off her head. She didn't dare look; she couldn't bear to see the size of it once it hit the floor. She ran toward the wooden box, her body still twitching. She saw from her peripherals as it scurried off.

Ezstasia opened the box and grabbed one of the black suits, putting it on just as the dragon roared again, flames shooting out the side of the canvas that covered its cage.

She quickly grabbed one of the accompanying black masks from the box and slipped it over her head and ran past the dragon's cage. The thick smoke made it hard for her to breathe. She ran through the large, open room and down the long hall to the exit, hoping nobody would stop her.

She felt the sensation of spiders crawling up her legs and

slapped at them every few feet. But that was the least of her problems now. She moved quickly, constantly looking around for anyone that would be searching for her. Meanwhile, she realized that she was taking a huge risk in trying to brazenly walk out of the castle, even if she *did* have a disguise.

She approached the castle's entrance and saw several knights and guards grouped together in conversation. She braced herself and ran right toward them, yelling in as deep of a voice as she could muster.

"In there!" Ezstasia yelled. She pointed back toward the hall from where she had just run out.

The guards looked confused, but they listened and ran toward the direction that she had pointed. Just as she attempted to pass the guards that stood at the castle gates, one of them grabbed her arm.

"Sir, with respect, we have our rules," he said. "No masks past this gate."

She kept pointing at the castle, trying to distract him.

"Are you okay, sir?" said the guard.

Ezstasia's frantic pointing at the castle didn't seem to be working. She watched as more guards approached them.

"Sir, what's your name?" said one of the new guards.

"We need you to remove your mask," said the first guard.

Ezstasia took a deep breath and began pulling up the mask, starting near her left jaw. Before she was about to reveal her eyes, she was startled by a loud horn. It was the same sound she'd heard earlier, the one that had alerted the knights about the breach.

"We found evidence of the breach!" yelled a guard from the entrance. "The woman's in here. All hands inside the castle!"

The guards left her and ran toward the castle. Unsure of what was happening or what kind of evidence they found, she took the opportunity to run across the bridge, quickly ducking behind a large boxwood shrub on the other side. Once her breathing had calmed, she pulled off her mask and uniform and pushed it deep underneath the shrub.

She knelt beside the bush as she glanced around. Once she felt it was safe, she stood up and moved as nonchalantly as she could toward the prince's castle. Going to the prince was her only option. Even though she was unsure about his exact role in everything, she had to beg him to let her friends out of the dungeons. She knew without a shadow of a doubt, that it was her fault that they were in there in the first place. She also wanted to confront him alone. She felt that something about him trusted her, or possibly even liked her. Regardless, she needed to find him and speak with him quickly.

Just as she emerged from the Road of Sorrow, she saw two knights standing guard along the right. Ezstasia tried to appear completely aloof. She walked forward and looked to the left to prevent them from seeing her face.

She held her breath as she walked past, and didn't look back. She walked as cautiously as she could, all the way back to the castle.

Before long, she was nearing the castle's entrance. Two knights stood by, appearing to observe everyone that approached the area.

She spotted two horses tied up by the trees straight ahead. They belonged to the knights. She picked up a medium-sized rock and threw it at the trees. Spooked, the horses both jumped up and began whinnying.

As the knights ran to the horses, she darted into the castle.

Once inside, a young servant saw her. He had been carrying a tray with a silver pitcher on it, but he immediately dropped the tray and ran away. His reaction told her all she needed to know. They were looking for her.

She ran up a few flights of stairs toward the prince's study when she heard footsteps behind her. She turned but didn't see anyone, so she ducked behind a large suit of armor on display in the large hallway.

She heard a knock coming from a nearby door, followed by the creaks of the door opening.

"Lady Arrow is back," said a male voice. "Inside the castle, I hear."

"Okay, please alert the prince," said another man. "Is she the last of them?"

"Well, there are four in the dungeon and four still in the village, but yes. They are all accounted for." Even though Ezstasia had already confirmed in her mind that her friends had been locked up, hearing those words made her blood boil, knowing the prince was allowing them to be put away.

Ezstasia waited a moment and then peeked out from behind the armor as the footsteps grew further away. She removed her shoes to carry them and ran quietly to follow the man who had just divulged that horrific information.

She remained at a careful distance, hiding as best she could. Once she descended the stairs, she thought she had lost him, but then spotted him walking up one of the adjoining halls. She followed him through a number of corridors until the man had approached three large, ornate doors, side by side. He knocked on the middle door and a servant opened it from inside.

Ezstasia hid along a recession in the wall.

"Sire," said the man, "I'm sorry to interrupt, but Lady Arrow has returned and has been seen inside the castle."

The prince appeared at the door.

"I thought my knights had instructions to bring her to me as soon as she returned."

"We believe she snuck in, sire."

"Snuck in?"

"I'll have everyone search the castle immediately for her. And as a precaution, we shall have your door guarded, just to be—"

"That won't be necessary," said the prince, chuckling. "Just bring her to me when you find her."

"Yes, sire."

Just as the man was closing the door, Ezstasia saw his face grow pale as he noticed her step out from her hiding spot. For a brief second, he made no movement whatsoever, but then gently knocked back on the prince's door. He continued staring at Ezstasia and didn't blink an eye. The door slowly creaked open.

"Yes?"

"So sorry to interrupt—again, sire," said the man, still staring at her, "but the woman, is here. Lady Arrow is, uh… well, she's right here, my lord."

The prince stepped out of the room and gazed at her, seemingly at a loss for words. He made a hand gesture for Ezstasia to enter the room.

This was it. She had a chance to get her friends out and one way or another, she'd find out just whose side the prince was on. It wasn't lost on her that her fate—and that of her friends—hung in the balance.

CHAPTER ELEVEN

Ezstasia entered the prince's library which was a different room from his study. She gazed up at the huge bookshelves. There must've been hundreds of books in there. She was almost afraid to look at him.

"You're quite the busy bee," said the prince, breaking the awkward silence. He stood by a massive armchair in front of a fire place while he stared at her intently. It made her extremely nervous. She felt her courage and anger become quickly replaced with anxiousness.

"I'd like to know what you're up to," she blurted out. She couldn't believe those words came out of her mouth.

"What am I up to? I believe I should be asking you that. I assume you somehow snuck your way into the Black Castle with your friends."

"Are they in the dungeons?"

"They're unharmed. Why did you go to the Black Castle? You were specifically told that private places were off limits."

"What we were told was to respect the boundaries of this castle, which we did."

"So you *were* there. You all knew the Black Castle was off limits. The only way to get in is to sneak in. What were you looking for?"

As she contemplated her response, a knock on the door caused her to jump back.

"Can this wait?" yelled the prince. The door creaked open slightly. "I'm in the middle of a—"

"I apologize, sire," said a servant's voice outside the door. "This cannot wait. It's quite urgent and will only take but a moment."

"Come in," said the prince.

The door opened and the servant introduced a castle guard, who came walking in with a sense of purpose. Ezstasia didn't recognize him.

The guard bowed and then handed something to the prince. She couldn't see what it was.

"We found this near Trycernius," said the guard. "The woman hasn't been found, but this proves she was there." The guard looked at Ezstasia, apparently confused as to whether or not she was the one they were looking for.

"You can call off the search," said the prince. He nodded toward Ezstasia. "She's right here."

"Shall I—"

"It won't be necessary, I'll handle it from here."

"As you wish, sire," said the guard, before turning and leaving the room.

The prince handed her the object the guard had given him. "I believe this is yours," he said, smirking. "Miss Tee had shown it to me after I first found you."

Her mouth twisted in embarrassment as she examined the delicate piece of jewelry he'd dropped into her palm. It was her silver necklace that her mother had given her. She must've dropped it as she scurried to put the uniform on.

"Anyway, you were saying?" said the prince.

"I don't know how this got…"

She saw him fold his arms with a disappointed look on his face. She stopped as she clearly saw his distrust.

"Okay," she said. "Yes, I *was* in the castle. I wanted to see if my friends were right."

"Right?" he echoed. "About what, exactly?"

"They thought you might be behind the dark magic, and I needed to see for myself. It looks like I got my answer."

"And your answer is?"

"You're raising a three-headed dragon. A man lit up in flames under the supervision of your kingdom. It isn't hard to figure out. His body will be scarred for life, and—"

"He's dead, Ezstasia. The man died."

"He what!? He died!?" Ezstasia felt the sting of tears return, but she pushed them back as intently as she could. She refused to display any weakness in front of the prince. "His poor family. And to think I defended you against my friends. They almost died, too, you know. Wait. What am I saying? Of course, you didn't know. You didn't ask or care to hear their stories. They almost died from the magic in that forest. *Your* magic. I hope you know that his blood is on your hands!"

"How dare you!" said the prince, his face growing red. "He was one of the bravest knights I've ever met and a very dear friend! I've known his family for years. I'm appalled by your accusations!"

Ezstasia didn't know how to respond. She began to doubt her plan to speak with the prince, and even more, having brought her friends here in the first place.

"I'm sorry. I didn't mean... I mean, I know—"

"*What* do you know?" said the prince. "You know nothing." He paused and covered his eyes with his hand as he shook his head. Then he looked back up at her and sighed.

She saw his broken-hearted reaction and felt like her gut hit the floor. A wave of deep regret enveloped her.

"Come," he said, taking her arm, a bit too tight for her

liking.

As soon as he took her out into the corridor, two guards came running toward them.

"Sire, we'll take her to the dungeon for you," said one of the guards.

"Back away," he growled. They scattered to let him pass, with her in tow. She'd never seen him so agitated.

"You're hurting me," she said.

"You'll live."

The prince had never seemed frightening to her, but in this moment, she was afraid.

He led her down one hall after the other, not uttering a word the rest of the way. They passed through a massive room with paintings from floor to ceiling on all sides, and then through another long hallway. Eventually, they approached two enormous iron double doors.

The prince took a large skeleton key from his holster and placed it in the keyhole, turning the lock slowly. After a loud click echoed through the room, he pushed the doors open and ushered her into a cavernous stone hall. It was cool and damp, and its grey walls rose toward an arched ceiling. Thin tree branches and vines peeked out from the stone slabs on the walls from the floor all the way up to the ceiling, some of them even sprouting real, dark green leaves.

He led her to another thick stone door at the far end of the hall. The door was well hidden, behind the ancient vines. It was chained and locked, and even the chains blended in with the surroundings. The prince let go of her arm, giving her a bit of relief. He took out another skeleton key and placed it into the keyhole. She stood there in compliance and silently watched him turn the key.

"It looks like nobody's been here in ages," she said, observing some of the exposed dead roots on the floor.

He glanced at her. She wondered if he could sense the

sinking feeling she felt in the pit of her stomach. In that moment, she could only think of being lost forever, imprisoned in a hidden room.

"Is this where the rest of the dungeons are?" she said, a bead of sweat dripping down her forehead, despite the cool temperature.

The prince remained focused on the lock until it clicked. He pulled down the chain and with one big push, opened the large heavy door, causing some of the roots that had grown on it to crack off. He nodded and gave her a little nudge to indicate that she needed to go in.

At first everything was dark, but he pulled a lever by the door that set off a chain reaction of illuminated candles, revealing an enormous rectangular hall that went as far as the eye could see. An enormous red runner extended along the grey, stone floor. The walls to her left and right were covered from floor to ceiling in bookshelves, also extending as far and high as she could see. The books looked dusty and ancient.

A noise startled her. It was the prince closing the large heavy door behind them. Then he locked it.

"Are my friends in here?" she said.

Instead of answering, he looked into her eyes with a deep sadness. Not in anger, but more so in defeat, which made her feel horrible for the things she'd said earlier.

"I've already told you they're safe," he said. "Just follow me."

They walked down the long hall while she observed the tall wooden ladders that slid on tracks along both walls. This was the largest room she had ever laid eyes on. She felt like an insect in comparison.

The prince approached a bookshelf and slid a ladder aside that was in his way. She wondered how he even knew which bookshelf to stop at, but then noticed some odd markings carved into the floor, unusual shapes she'd never seen before.

The prince pulled several books halfway out of the shelf, then stepped a few feet to his left and pulled out two more. Then he removed another book completely and handed it to her. It was old and dusty, with no writing on the cover. She looked at it, not knowing what to make of it, but then watched as he reached his hand inside the bookshelf where the book had been. He appeared to be manipulating something with his hand. He startled her by grabbing her arm and pulling her next to him. Immediately, she heard a loud rumbling that sounded all too familiar. She dropped the book.

"There isn't a dragon here too, is there?" she said, as he turned her around to face the center of the room.

He smiled slightly, for the first time.

"No. Just be patient," he said. He picked up the book she had dropped and put it back in its place.

Several stone blocks on the other side of the red carpet began to rise slowly from the floor. As the stone blocks rose higher, she saw that they formed a pedestal. Resting on top of the pedestal was a single book, bigger than any book she had ever seen, with its cover peeling and faded and gold inscription on the spine. He stepped up to it, opened the book, and began rotating an iron crank that was inside of it. He turned the crank with great pressure and its noisy creaking echoed throughout the hall. He closed the book and stepped back. At once, the stone pedestal began to lower back into the ground, making even more noise than before.

The section of the wall behind her, where he'd pulled out the random books halfway earlier, began to slowly swing open. It revealed a light grey set of steps spiraling upward, accompanied by an ornate, silver bannister. Ezstasia realized that the pedestal was a key to open up this secret passageway.

The prince motioned for her to go through the doorway. "You're coming, too, right?" she said.

"I am."

Relieved to hear it, she entered and began to climb the spiral staircase. The prince entered behind her and closed the door.

Once at the top of the stairs, she saw an arched entrance to a large, square room ahead. The prince entered first and she followed him.

The room was extremely cluttered and dusty, with no adornments or tapestries that had been so prevalent in the other rooms in the castle. Its walls and tables were made of plain, dark wood. She could tell that they hadn't been touched up in centuries. Plain, wooden shelves haphazardly adorned the walls carrying a variety of oddities. A few shelves to her right contained oddly-shaped glass bottles filled with brightly colored liquids. She wondered if they were magic potions.

Ezstasia's eyes scanned the room. Some of the shelves held bulky, glass containers with lids, each filled with different colored powders. They also housed unusual iron gadgets, tin cups, and wooden bowls with faded inscriptions on the sides. Nearly all of the books around the room were dusty and covered in thick spider webs that she could barely see through. She shuddered remembering the sticky webs and furry creatures that lived among them in the Black Castle.

Three large tables had been arranged around the room, each one covered in books, metal gadgets, and a wide assortment of unusual objects. At the far end of the room lay a wooden chest with heavy, gold padlocks guarding whatever secrets it held. She spotted another chest in a small alcove in the back, all by itself, with even more padlocks guarding its contents.

She realized the prince had silently been analyzing her reaction and curiosity since they had first stepped inside the hidden room.

"So this is where you keep your magic?" said Ezstasia.

"There is indeed magic here," said the prince. "I inherited the items in this room when I became owner of the castle."

"I don't understand. Why show me this?"

"There's something I'd like you to see. Go look on that table," he said, nodding toward the table in the center of the room.

She walked to the table and examined it. All she could see were more artifacts and a bulky, old book. She picked up a few of the strange tools and tried to determine exactly what they were. One had a series of ancient dials on it. Then she opened the book and flipped through it as the dust rose to invade her senses. She waved the cloud of dust away so that she could breathe. All the pages included ancient mathematical calculations, accompanied by old script that she couldn't read.

As she closed the book with a thud, she noticed something glisten in the air, a colorful sparkle that looked all too familiar. She traced it downward and saw its source, partially hidden underneath the book. She'd recognize those feathers anywhere.

It was her arrow.

"Lady... Arrow," said the prince, with a touch of irony. "It seems I'm not the only one with a secret."

"You've known about our magic all this time?" she said, her head suddenly swirling with memories of her conversations with him.

"I did." He was expressionless.

"I hope you know we weren't using magic for evil," she said.

"Nor am I."

"But you have a dragon. *We* were only using it for a game."

"Funny, I don't seem to recall any game exclusion in the scrolls. I believe it said *all* magic was forbidden. Or perhaps I didn't look well enough."

"You know it's not the same," she said.

He paused and then smirked, which wasn't the reaction she expected. "Where did you get your magic from?" he said.

She hesitated, but knew she had to tell him something. Anything.

"One of my friends had it," she said. "I think he... or she... got it from an ancestor, but I don't ask questions. I—"

"But you do ask questions. Plenty of them. It's a peculiar habit."

The prince smiled again, which made her realize he was actually enjoying this.

"We didn't cause the magic in the forest," she said, firmly.

"I know that. I'm reasonably convinced that you and your friends are innocent."

"Reasonably?" She wasn't sure what he meant by that.

"Unless you convince me otherwise," he said, smiling. "You do tend to keep things to yourself, Lady Arrow."

"Me!? What about your dragon?"

"Ah yes, Trycernius. I suppose it's only fair I tell you, now that you've seen him. He's quite temperamental, and I have to admit he's getting more difficult to control."

"I could see that."

"When I was a boy exploring these grounds," he continued, "finding his egg was beyond my wildest dreams. It was a relic from the magic world that I had only heard about, and here it was in my possession. I'd found quite a few things but nothing as breathtaking as that. I turned the rest in, but the egg I kept for myself."

"Why did you keep it?"

The prince stared blankly.

"At first? Curiosity. I had a true fascination with the days of old. Of course, I never dreamt that it would hatch. But several years later, you can only imagine my surprise when it *did* hatch. Not only that, but the little creature had three heads! Why he waited until *then* to enter this world is still a mystery to me. I may never know. Anyway, I spent my teen years secretly tending to his needs in an abandoned barn and I watched him grow. But I knew even then that the writing was on the wall. It wouldn't be long before he grew too large to keep secret any longer, especially once I'd been crowned the Prince of Vynterra. It was clear I had no choice."

"So you had your knights hide him and keep him?"

"No, on the contrary. I sent him away. The scrolls command that for any magical creature. He couldn't fly yet and he was the size of a large hound. So I built a small craft out of wood. In the darkness of the night, I did exactly as the scrolls commanded and sent him off from the shores of the Forbidden Sea. They say those currents lead right to the Magiclands."

"But I suppose they didn't," she said.

"The truth is, I'll never know. Somewhere between the Vynterran Coast and the Magiclands, he must have learned how to fly, because several months later—I remember it was an autumn evening just like this—he appeared at my window in this very castle. I called for Sir Aldus immediately, who I knew I could trust with my life."

"Sir Aldus," she repeated. "I saw him in the Black Castle. He was one of those men in the black masks."

The prince nodded. "It was Sir Aldus who helped me reestablish the Valorian Order from among the most elite and trusted knights of the Vynterran Guard. In the old days, Valorian had created the Order for his most urgent and dangerous missions. In my case, I needed them to keep and care for Trycernius, which is a pretty dangerous mission in itself."

"So the men in the masks—they're the Valorian Order?"

The prince nodded. "They are. Unfortunately, things have become a bit more critical recently. So, we've begun training Trycernius for a possible war. Or at least trying to."

"A war!? With who?"

"I'm afraid that's the big question. I hope I'm wrong, but the signs are growing more severe."

He seemed distracted as he spoke. Ezstasia noticed he had been somberly staring at all the objects on the table with deep sadness in his eyes.

"If it makes you feel any better," he continued, "I haven't so much as touched anything in this room and I hope I never have to."

Ezstasia felt as if the weight of a thousand boulders had just been lifted off her shoulders. She should have trusted her instincts about his innocence from the beginning rather than making such horrible accusations. She just knew the prince had no part of the magic in the forest.

A thought occurred to her.

"Prince Alazar, can anyone else access this room?" she said. "Is it possible someone else is using any of this magic in the forest?"

He shook his head.

"You're standing in one of the best kept secrets in all the kingdoms, which leads me to what I need to say next. Please listen carefully."

"Of course," she said.

"I don't have to tell you the grave dangers that will come upon all of us if the wrong people find out about what's in this room. I need to know that I can trust you. You can't repeat a word about what you've seen here, not even to your sister."

"You have my word," she said.

"You've accused me of many things," he said. "Do I now have your confidence? Your *full* confidence?"

She nodded.

"I need to hear it from your lips, Ezstasia." He held a hand on her cheek, which sent shivers down her spine. She felt butterflies fluttering in her stomach as she looked into his eyes.

"You have my full confidence, my prince. Please trust that I won't mention a word of anything you've told me or shown me here today. This I promise you."

"Good." He smiled. "Then let's go get your friends."

₨ ₩ ₨ ₩

As Prince Alazar led her out of the room, he didn't return to the stairs, but took her through a hall on the left. As she followed, he led her through countless corridors and rooms that she didn't recognize.

"I don't remember any of this," she said.

"Neither do I." The prince grinned.

"Are we lost?"

"The entrance is always the same. The exit always changes. One of Valorian's great feats of design. In fact, you may never see this path again. But I can assure you we're going in the right direction."

"How do you know?"

"More of your questions, Lady Arrow. But this last one I'm going to keep a mystery."

Soon they came to a barred wooden door. As he lifted the bar and led her through the doorway, she heard the bar slam shut behind them. This part of the castle felt more like a dungeon. Even the air was dank and chilly.

They descended a set of steps into a narrow, exposed-brick hallway lined with guards. The guards stood at attention and tapped their swords on the floor as the prince passed. She realized she was walking on a slight decline just as she felt a rush of cool air hit her face. She wondered if they were beginning to walk underneath the castle.

She followed the prince through another arched hall that seemed more like a tunnel, and through a thick iron door, which a decorated knight politely opened for them.

Two guards instinctively followed them. It must've been an established practice.

The room they entered was dimly lit; the only light came from the sconces on the walls that had been strategically placed next to each dungeon cell. Groaning voices echoed throughout the room. They were coming from people in the dungeons.

"This is where you have my sister and friends!?" she said, horrified at the thought.

"Anyone who breaks into a royal domain gets placed in the lower dungeons by default," said the prince. "It's the law."

She couldn't believe the prince had allowed her friends and sister to be locked up in this place, but she had to remind herself they were here because of her.

As they passed by each cell, prisoners walked toward the bars and reached their arms out. Some prisoners held onto the bars and just stared at them eerily and intently. A few yelled profanities, which the prince ignored. The guards smacked weapons against their cells to knock them back.

Ezstasia covered her nose and mouth as they continued past more prisoners. The smell was awfully pungent and the curiosity of what they'd all done to get locked in here had piqued her interest.

They turned a corner and she noticed a disheveled woman with black, knotted hair standing in the cell just ahead to her right. The woman stared at her with wild eyes as they approached, smiling as if she knew something they didn't.

"The crumbling oak turns to ashes," said the woman, baring her crooked teeth, "and the chains no longer bind."

"Silence, woman," said one of the guards.

"In their almighty hands, the fate of man grows weaker still. You'll see. You'll all see."

"In whose hands?" said Ezstasia to the woman.

"*Eximum venirum sangamort*," said the woman, laughing. "*Eximum venirum sangamort!*" She kept repeating the same words as they passed her cell.

Ezstasia glanced over just in time to see the woman practically glide back to her small bed, repeating the same three words as rats scurried at her feet.

She couldn't stop looking back at the woman and nearly jumped out of her skin when the prince grabbed her arm.

"Don't worry about her," he said. "She's lost her mind. She's been in and out of the dungeons for years, spouting the same nonsense."

One guard went back and banged a sword against the woman's cell, though it didn't seem to faze her as she kept talking.

Ezstasia quickened her pace to keep up with the prince. They approached a much more illuminated area with an oversized cell up ahead.

"Your sister and friends are in there," said the prince. "I'm sorry they had to be detained, but I couldn't violate our own laws."

Ezstasia shoved right past the guards and the prince and ran straight towards the cell.

She saw Lanzzie sitting on the floor holding her ears. Fin, Randin, and Zander were crowded around her.

"What happened to her!?" yelled Ezstasia.

Fin jumped up first.

"Ezstasia!" he said. The others looked up, including Lanzzie, who jumped up and ran to the bars.

"You have to get us out of here, now!" said Lanzzie. Ezstasia didn't like the tone of her voice. She sounded panicked and afraid.

"She's been holding her ears because that crazy woman won't shut up," said Zander, walking up toward the bars.

"You don't understand," said Lanzzie, tears welling in her eyes. "I heard her yelling the same things that I heard in the forest!" She pointed in the direction of the woman's cell.

Prince Alazar and the guards approached the cell bars. "The forest? What are you talking about?"

Ezstasia had no idea what her sister was talking about either. And from the looks of the others, neither did they.

"When we were in the forest," said Lanzzie to the prince, "so many eerie things happened. But at one point, the ground lifted from below me and formed a pale, partially skeletal face of an old woman, bigger than my entire body. And that's not all, Prince Alazar. She spoke."

"And you didn't think to mention this before?" said Zander.

"I figured you'd think I was crazy."

"*All* our stories are crazy," said Zander. "Yours would've just added to the craziness."

"Hold on, hold on," said the prince. "What does the lady in the cell have to do with what you heard in the forest?"

Lanzzie looked back toward the prince. "I don't know how or why, but that lady in the cell is using the same words I heard in the forest!" said Lanzzie, terrified. "But the woman in the forest was old and decrepit—at least her face was. And she was made of roots and trees and dirt.

"What exactly did you hear in the forest?" said the prince. "Do you remember?"

"I won't ever forget it for as long as I live. She said: *As pure as light, as dark as night, the chaos is released.*" Then she looked down at me and said, *"The blood has already been spilled. The great battle begins.* She then said the same exact words that *that* lady's been repeating over and over. *Eximum venirum sangamort.* I'm sure of it."

"What do those words even mean?" said Ezstasia.

"I don't know," said the prince, "but I know who might. Meanwhile, I'll have my knights take the prisoner next door for questioning to see what we can discover about her."

Ezstasia felt her stomach move up into her throat at the thought of that creepy woman having anything to do with the forest.

"Now you, Miss Lanzzie," said the prince. "I need to know everything. Including what exactly you saw."

Lanzzie stood frozen, apparently still unsure of whether or not it was safe to trust the prince.

Ezstasia reached between the bars to pull her sister close to her as the guards yelled from behind her to stand back.

"It's okay," she whispered into her sister's ear. "He has nothing to do with the magic in the forest. I know that now. I can't explain, but trust me."

Just as Lanzzie nodded and accepted her advice, the prince blurted out, "Guards!"

The next thing Ezstasia knew, the guards were pulling her back away from her sister.

"Please escort Lady Arrow back to her room," he said. "And see that she stays there until further notice."

"What!?" said Ezstasia, as the guards forcefully led her away by her forearms. "What's happening? I don't understand."

The prince didn't respond.

She could hear Lanzzie calling for her as the guards led her past the other cells toward the exit. She tried fighting to get free, but the two large men had a tight grip on her arms.

"Let go of me!" she yelled. "Why are you doing this!?"

The guards remained silent and dragged her away. She felt like a criminal.

They led her out the heavy iron door. She realized that struggling wasn't any use; they weren't going to let her go. She let her arms go limp in defeat.

Ezstasia felt utterly alone and nobody offered any explanation. Who was that creepy woman in the cell that knew the same words Lanzzie had heard? Why hadn't Lanzzie told her about hearing something in the forest? They always told one another everything. What did those words mean? None of this was making any sense. Even worse, Ezstasia now wondered if the prince was, in fact, being duplicitous. She couldn't think of any valid reason he could give to explain what had just taken place.

CHAPTER TWELVE

Ezstasia paced around her chamber, deconstructing everything that had happened in the past several hours. As much as she tried to make sense of any of it, she couldn't. She was humiliated, and the prince's actions were every bit as confusing as the gibberish words the imprisoned woman spoke.

She stood at the window and stared out into the darkness. Soon, her confusion turned to anger. She could feel the blood rising to her face as she thought about the prince and his deceit toward her.

Time went by, and she wondered how long it would be before someone told her what was going on.

She spotted a silver tray with tea and scones on the table next to the bed. She picked it up with fury and threw the entire platter and all its contents to the floor. Maybe *that* would get their attention. Unfortunately, it only brought a moment's relief until she saw the broken teacups and scones strewn out all over the floor. It only took a minute until she began to feel guilty. Miss Tee had surely prepared it all for her enjoyment.

Just then, the bedroom door swung open.

To her surprise, it was Lanzzie.

"Looks like you dropped something," said Lanzzie, smirking, as she gingerly stepped over the upside-down tray, broken teacups, and crumbled scones on the wet floor.

"Lanz!" Ezstasia ran to her sister and wrapped her arms around her tightly with tears of relief pooling in her eyes.

"It's okay," said Lanzzie, patting her on the back. "He let us all go."

"I'm glad, but I still don't forgive him. In fact, I hate him." As soon as the words left her mouth, Ezstasia realized that she might have been just a little bit dramatic.

"Oh no you don't! In fact, we *all* know it's the exact opposite of that."

Lanzzie walked over to the bed and sat down on the soft blanket. She patted the spot next to her, so Ezstasia took the hint and sat by her sister.

"Think about it," said Lanzzie. "As soon as the prince began to pull information out of me, you whispered in my ear. How do you think that appeared to him?"

"It shouldn't have appeared to be anything. We're sisters. We whisper things."

"Be realistic. Think about the timing of that. It made it seem as if we were plotting to hide something from him."

"He should know me better than that by now."

"He just wanted to be certain he could trust us all."

"And does he? Trust us all? Because I thought we were past that already. Or maybe I was mistaken." She knew her tone sounded bitter, but she didn't care. She still wasn't convinced of the prince's motives behind sending her away, and it was obvious Lanzzie could read her anger.

"Ezstasia, he may be a prince, but if he really isn't behind it, then I'm sure he's just as scared and unsure as we are about that forest. With even the slightest inkling of uncertainty, he has the whole kingdom's safety to think about. And that means that he can't leave any stone unturned. It's what any prince worthy of his people would do."

"And how did you reassure him when apparently I couldn't?"

"You, my dear sister, were the main reason he was reassured."

"What? How?" She was confused again.

"He questioned us individually, just to make sure all of our stories added up. He asked me about Arrows and how we played it. He wanted to know about the powder and where it came from. I answered all his questions. You should have seen his face when I explained that the big flashing light in the forest sky came from Fin winning the game."

"Well, that's great and all, but what does any of that have to do with me?"

"That's what I'm getting to. He asked what you whispered in my ear. He said it was crucial that I tell him. He seemed more interested in that than anything else. So, I told him. I said you couldn't tell me why, but that you knew he wasn't behind the magic in the forest."

"What did he say?"

"I won't lie. His whole demeanor changed entirely. He looked happy and even a little surprised. He had the biggest grin, and then he released us!"

Ezstasia felt a lump in her throat, even as she tried to smile. Now she felt like a fool and was completely embarrassed, once again, for misjudging him.

She stood up to hide her blushing face from her sister and walked to the silver platter on the floor to turn it upright. She began picking up the broken teacup pieces and scones and put them on the tray.

"He wants us to come to dinner," said Lanzzie. "He

specifically asked me to come get you."

Ezstasia couldn't help but grin as she picked up the tray and turned around to face her sister.

"Then I suppose we shouldn't keep him waiting," she said, still smirking. She placed the tray back on the table, feeling sheepish for throwing it in the first place. Then something dawned on her.

"Oh wait, I'm a horrible sister," she added. "All this talk about the prince and I didn't ask about you. You were pretty traumatized, Lanz. Are you okay?"

Lanzzie looked at her with a soft smile, apparently trying to keep a brave face.

"I'm not sure any of us will ever be *okay* after all this. But the prince reassured me that he's on our side and is determined to get to the bottom of all this."

"I hope that means he's finally willing to hear about all your forest encounters," said Ezstasia. "After all, it may give him more knowledge about what's out there."

"Not only is he willing, our stories will be his entertainment for the evening. He wants to hear all of them, especially mine, since... well, you know, the voice and all. Aren't I the lucky one to have been singled out in that stupid forest?"

"I won't lie, that's weird that it only picked you to speak to. Maybe it spoke to me when I was knocked out and I just didn't hear it."

She grinned at the morbid thought and Lanzzie laughed.

"Seriously though," said Ezstasia, "I feel awful not knowing what happened to my own sister out there."

"Well, it's a story I prefer to tell just once, so you can hear it with everyone else. And I'm starved, so let's go before I start eating those soggy scones."

৪০ ৫৪ ৪০ ৫৪

Ezstasia arrived at the dining room with Lanzzie just as Fin showed up. They were the first to arrive.

"The others are on their way," said Fin. "Where's the prince?"

Ezstasia shrugged just as she heard running footsteps and an ear-piercing scream from behind her. It was one of the housekeepers.

"Guards!" she yelled, her face red with panic. "Guards!"

The two guards responded quickly and came running in.

"Quick!" she said, holding her chest. "Outside! It's horrible."

The guards ran to the hall and the woman followed them, nearly tripping over her own feet.

Ezstasia took one look at Lanzzie and Fin and they jumped up and followed.

By the time they got outside, the guards were already pushing their way through the gathering crowd. Screams were permeating the air. A few village women were running away with their children in tow, while others rushed toward the commotion. Ezstasia felt her heart pound as she struggled to get through the crowd to see what was going on.

Several guards physically picked people up to move them aside, making themselves a path. Ezstasia made her way through the same route, with Lanzzie and Fin right behind her. One mother was trying to cover her children's eyes. In the chaos, a man's elbow jabbed Ezstasia right in the mouth.

"Are you okay?" said Lanzzie in a panic. "You're bleeding."

"I'll be fine," she said, dabbing her lip with the back of her hand.

Fin whacked the guy in the back of the head as he disappeared into the crowd. It was so chaotic that the man didn't even seem to notice.

Ezstasia shook the pain off and pushed forward. She was finally able to see what everyone had been staring at.

In the center of the crowd, a teenage boy lay on a wooden board. His two friends, a redheaded boy and a blond-haired boy, wiped tears from their eyes as they observed. Ezstasia moved closer and got a better look at the injured boy's face. She was horrified.

The boy's eyes were wide open and his pupils were completely white. His shirt was torn open and his skin was a translucent gray, with black veins running down the right side of his face and down his chest and right arm. His left side had veins that were raised and spread through his skin like roots.

Lanzzie pushed Ezstasia aside and ran toward the boy.

"Fin, help me!" she yelled. "He needs help."

"He's dead," said one of the guards.

"He's not dead!" she said. "Trust me."

The guard put his hand on her shoulder. "He's dead, miss. We need you to move away."

"Let her tend to him!" said a male voice from behind them. The crowd began to part to make way for the man.

It was Prince Alazar.

The guards nodded and stepped aside, and Lanzzie knelt beside the boy.

"Can you help him?" said his redheaded friend.

"You have to fight this!" said Lanzzie to the injured teen. "Listen to me," she pleaded. "Think about the most beautiful memory you've ever had. I know you can hear me! Go to that place in your mind and stay there."

Fin was about to grab the teen's wrist to check his pulse, but Lanzzie slapped his hand away.

"Fight it!" she yelled at the teen. "If I survived it, so can you!"

"We were only playing," said the other boy, in tears. "He

asked us if we dared him to go into the forest at night. We didn't think anything bad would really happen."

In desperation, Lanzzie placed her hands on the injured teen's shoulders and began to shake him.

"Can you hear me?" she said to him. But seconds after she touched him, the black veins started to climb up her fingers and hands, too. Ezstasia grabbed her arm and tried to pull her away, but her own hands began to turn gray.

She jumped back, horrified, but as soon as she let go, her hands went back to normal. Lanzzie had pulled away from the boy too, and her hands and fingers immediately returned to normal as well.

"Can't you see that he's dead?" said a villager from the crowd.

"Does anyone have a mirror or a piece of glass?" said Fin.

A woman handed him a small mirror.

Ezstasia watched as Fin held the mirror to the boy's mouth without touching him.

Fin looked downhearted as he sighed.

"He's dead. He isn't breathing."

A gray-haired, frail man, who Ezstasia quickly determined was the village doctor, rushed forward after being summoned by a woman in the crowd. He confirmed the boy's death. The people were overwhelmed with grief. Ezstasia heard devastated sobs from every direction.

Prince Alazar stood tall and addressed the crowd.

"I need all of your attention," he said. A guard sounded a loud horn to get everyone to quiet down.

"Please remind all your friends, neighbors, children, and family members," said the prince, "of the decree that has already been put into place regarding the forest. Everyone must be aware of the seriousness of this. Make sure it's known, that until further notice, the forest shall be off limits to all villagers, lords, and ladies."

He looked around to make sure everyone was listening. The crowd was silent.

"It shall henceforth be posted throughout Vynterra that anyone trespassing on or near the forest grounds shall be imprisoned for a period of no less than sixty days. My knights will guard the forest perimeter, and, mark my words, we *will* explore every avenue to find out what has befallen this boy and ravaged our forest. For now, this boy's body shall be burned at sea in the morning with a proper ceremony in his honor. May I ask his family to step forward?"

The prince waited as everyone looked around.

"My lord," said the redheaded boy. "We know his family. We can alert them."

A guard approached the prince.

"With all due respect, sire, the burning of the body should not wait."

The prince was quiet for a moment as he gazed down at the boy's pale gray skin and raised black veins.

"Leave it to his family to decide," said the prince. "It's a bit of a journey to the sea. If they prefer to do it this evening, accommodate them in whatever means necessary. For now, see to it that the body is properly wrapped. And by all means, don't touch the skin directly." He looked at the two teens. "I will ask you to lead my knights to the boy's parents. My men will do the rest."

Ezstasia saw the boys nod. She held Lanzzie's hand and stood next to Fin. Three knights came to collect the boys.

The whole village seemed to go silent for a moment, until one person began humming a beautiful hymn that Ezstasia didn't recognize. Within minutes, everyone in the crowd was harmonizing with the sad, yet mesmerizing melody.

Ezstasia saw Meldon, Randin, and Zander come up beside her, but none of them said a word. They must've been watching from the back of the crowd. She looked over to the right and saw Ithron with his arm around Jezreel.

She glanced behind her and spotted Pallu with his newfound love. With all that had been happening over the last few days, she was grateful that her friends were all safe and well. She grieved for this poor boy whom she never knew, and for his parents, who would soon experience indescribable anguish.

The prince approached, elegant in his decorated uniform.

"We'll have to leave the boy to my guards," he said, looking at Ezstasia, her sister and her friends. "I'm afraid what we have to discuss can't wait any longer. This may be only the beginning."

CHAPTER THIRTEEN

Ezstasia felt her stomach flutter as she sat at the long, wooden dining table next to Lanzzie, observing the prince's reactions to each of their stories. The prince seemed especially shocked when Ithron had recited his horrifying near-death experience, and again at Zander's tale of the giant, wooden spider. He also seemed intrigued by Meldon's tale of the forest changing before his very eyes.

Finally, it was Lanzzie and Fin's turn to recount their experience. Ezstasia saw Lanzzie nudge Fin, indicating that he should go first.

"Well, at first, the forest looked like any other forest to me," said Fin. "But to Lanzzie, she kept seeing things appear and disappear. We realized pretty quickly that we each saw the forest very differently."

"It wasn't that quickly," said Lanzzie. "It took me a while to convince you."

"That's because you saw a giant bush with bright orange flowers, and I was looking at the very same bush that looked half dead with nothing but spiky gray branches. Not a trace of orange, or even a single flower. At first, I thought you were losing your mind. You could hardly blame me for thinking that."

"Go on," said the prince.

"We kept calling out for Ezstasia when we noticed the same blue fog in the distance that everyone else talked about. They were like warrior spirits or something, swaying back and forth and randomly disappearing and reappearing. It was strange. Then Lanzzie started talking about these huge jungle vines. I didn't see them, so I did a little experiment. I picked a random dead tree—there were plenty of those—and I asked her to describe it. Wouldn't you know, she started describing fancy flowers and colorful leaves. All I saw was a dead tree!"

"Knowing you two," said Zander, "you were probably acting like a bickering married couple out there."

"You have no idea," said Fin. "She even threatened to leave me so she could search alone. But anyway, what I saw next put an end to any bickering pretty quickly."

"What did you see?" said the prince.

"At first, it looked like Lanzzie and I were heading into an area with trees covered in black leaves, which I thought was odd enough. They were swaying back and forth, although there wasn't any wind. Then the trees started to sway harder. Before I could even say anything, black leaves started falling to the ground, hundreds, thousands of them all at once in some kind of coordinated way. It was bizarre."

The prince looked at Lanzzie. "Did you see the black leaves too?"

"No," she said. "I saw beautiful, green trees, with the occasional butterfly or insect fluttering around. There wasn't anything out of the ordinary. I didn't see what Fin described. No swaying trees. No black leaves. I didn't even see a single leaf fall."

"But you both saw the blue spirits in the distance, just like your other friends?"

"We did," said Lanzzie, "though dancing angels is a better description."

"Warriors, not angels," said Fin. "And they were swaying, not dancing."

"Please continue," said the prince, motioning to Fin. "You were talking about the black leaves falling."

"Yes, after they fell, they flew up again and this time they formed a pattern. That's when I realized that they weren't leaves at all. They were bats and they headed right toward me! I got on my rabbit and started riding away as fast as I could, and I yelled for Lanzzie to do the same. We tried to outrun them and—"

"I wasn't really outrunning anything," said Lanzzie to the prince. "I didn't even see one bat. I was just trying to keep up with Fin, to keep an eye on him, because he seemed to be hallucinating. And for my efforts, he pushed me off my rabbit." She smiled at Fin.

"I was trying to save you," he said. "I jumped off Zon, too. The little buggers flew up in the sky in a straight line and looked like they were going to dive-bomb us."

"A good excuse," she said, chuckling.

"Sorry, but who knew they were going to fly back up and circle us instead?"

"I'll take your word for it," she said.

Fin redirected his attention to the prince. "So anyway, they started circling around us like a tornado. All of a sudden, they shifted and began to gather right in front of me. They were forming a shape, similar to a large cloud."

"Well, what was it?" said Randin, after Fin paused. As brave as Fin was, Ezstasia could tell that he was slightly struggling to talk about this.

"It became a thirty-foot crow. Massive and horrifying and something I'll never be able to get out of my nightmares."

"What do you mean it became a crow?" said Pallu.

"I mean the bats flew together and formed the shape of a crow," said Fin. "Giant wings, big beak and all, with dark, crimson-red eyes. It even cawed and flapped its wings and moved its head like a crow. Except it was formed completely out of bats. It came toward me as if to swallow me whole, and I thought I was done for. I didn't think I'd ever see my friends or family again. Instead, it felt like he flew right into my body. I saw black particles surrounding me and covering the sky. Everything around me became as dark as a moonless night. I couldn't breathe. When my vision cleared, the crow was gone but I felt paralyzed. I could hear Lanzzie trying to talk to me, telling me to fight it, but it was like I was in a trance. The crow was taking over me."

"That's exactly how I felt," said Ithron. "When the skeleton came after me."

"Were you able to speak?" said the prince to Fin.

"Not then, no."

"I was trying to help him," said Lanzzie, "but it was like he couldn't hear me. I began to feel the ground moving right under my feet. At first, I thought I was imagining it, but then it shifted more strongly, the rocks, the trees, everything. That's when Fin fell to the ground. I could see that he was beginning to turn pale, and his skin started turning gray. I kept focusing on him, telling him to fight it and to focus on a lovely memory. He looked almost like that dead boy."

"Did you feel the ground shift, too?" said the prince to Fin.

"No, I couldn't see or feel any of that. I only remember losing my strength and falling. I could hear her talking to me, but I couldn't move. She kept talking about positive things like the cottages and my family and our friends and telling me to think about them. I don't know if it was that or what, but I started to get some of my senses back."

"I didn't see that he was getting better at first," said

Lanzzie, "because the ground started shifting and rumbling again, and it was much worse this time. It was so loud, I thought an earthquake was happening right before me. Pieces of trees and branches, and the ground itself, started to break apart, and then parts of the ground in front of me began to rise and fall. It felt as if the ground was breathing. I couldn't believe my eyes; the ground began to rise and form into something. With dust and dirt flying everywhere, it was hard to see what it was. Once the dirt particles settled, I saw it was a large head of an old woman. She was dead, partially skeletonized. The cracks in her skin were like the cracks in a desert and her scraggly hair was made up of dead trees and roots from the soil. Although her face was made up of elements from the ground, her eyes were black as night."

Ezstasia saw tears begin to form on Lanzzie's face. She put an arm around her and hugged her tightly.

Lanzzie took a deep breath and continued.

"That's when she spoke to me. With her loud, thundering voice, she said: *As pure as day, as dark as night, the chaos is released.* And every time she moved, large chunks of her face would fall crashing to the ground, exposing more of her rotting skull underneath. One almost hit me and I fell hard onto my back trying to avoid it. It knocked the air out of me."

"That's the creepiest thing I've ever heard," said Meldon.

"It gets worse. Her head turned toward me and she said, '*The blood has already been spilled. The great battle begins.*' I looked over at Fin, who was motionless on the ground and I knew he needed help, but I was afraid to move. I saw the blue angels in the distance, and they gave me hope."

"The fog silhouettes?" said Pallu.

"Dancing angels. They *must* be angels, because when I looked at them, I felt a sense of comfort. I forced myself to stand up but the old woman rumbled furiously and the ground lifted below my feet, knocking me over again. I got right back up and she faded away, or so I thought. But she came back with a vengeance. She reappeared and angrily said those three strange words, her voice sounding like rushing water. She was really angry."

"*Eximum, venirum, sangamort*," said the prince.

"Exactly. And she kept repeating it, while her giant face rumbled like an earthquake. I was shaking and I felt like I was going to black out. But I kept looking back at Fin and knew that he needed my help. I couldn't let go. Her mouth was made of cracked, hardened soil, and it opened wide as thousands of sand bees flew out and came right at me. Her entire face dissolved as her eyes, mouth, ears, and every part of her face turned into a swarm of bees. It was dreadful. They flew right through me and seemed to enter my body, just like Fin described with the bats. I felt weak and my body gave out as I fell right next to Fin. I couldn't find any strength inside of me to hold on. It was like all of my joy, hope, and purpose had been sucked out of me."

"Lanz!" said Ezstasia with a cracking in her voice. She felt broken-hearted, not only for her sister, but for all her friends. She couldn't believe that her disappearance had created so much pain and havoc for the people she loved the most. She grabbed her sister's hand and squeezed it tightly.

"I'd all but given up," said Lanzzie, "but then I thought of my sister and all the good things in my life that I wanted to get back to. I kept fighting it. I looked at Fin and told him to stay positive and think of only good things. I wasn't sure if he could hear me, but his eyes were open. I looked again at the dancing blue angels and they became even brighter. I felt like they were cheering me on, so I kept talking."

"I could hear her, and I actually started to feel better," said Fin. "Little by little, I could move my fingers and the rest of my body. Eventually, I was able to help Lanzzie up and we got on our rabbits. We were both exhausted, but we managed to ride off. We didn't get too far because we heard screams and that's when we found Ithron. Luckily, we were able to help him, and here we all are, alive to tell the tale. Thanks to Lanzzie."

Lanzzie took Fin's hand and held it.

"It's incredible that you both survived," said the prince. "It seems that somehow focusing every ounce of your energy on people and places you love helps form at least a partial resistance. It's also astounding that with all the dark magic in that forest, there's a positive force there, too, in the form of the blue spirits."

"It sure seems like it," said Fin.

"It gives me hope," said the prince, "but it also presents even more of a mystery about whatever it is that we're dealing with. Because, if this is truly a dark force at play, it's unlikely it would produce anything good."

"That's true," said Randin. "It makes absolutely no sense."

"That's the brilliance of it," said Meldon. "I admire it in a way."

"That's because you're strange," said Zander.

"It *is* brilliant in a sense," said the prince, "but we have quite a problem to solve." He turned back toward Fin and Lanzzie. "You should both be proud of the courage and perseverance you've shown. Lanzzie, you may not have been in time to help that young boy who we lost today, but you just may have saved many other lives by figuring out how to fight it."

Lanzzie looked up at the prince with reddened eyes. "I hope so, my lord."

"I must ask you all to excuse me. There's someone I need to speak with. Several of you have mentioned some incredibly dark creatures. I'm sure they felt terribly real. For all we know, they *were* real. The truth is, those creatures sound familiar to me. They're similar to the dark stories I read about as a child."

"What about the words?" said Meldon. "Do you know the meaning of them?"

"No, but I know someone who very well might. Please, all of you wait here. I'll return within the hour."

ᔕ ᘓ ᔕ ᘓ

After the prince was gone for some time, he returned to the room where Ezstasia and her friends had remained.

"Come," he said. "I'd like you all to follow me."

"Where?" said Pallu, wide-eyed.

The prince smiled. "To a part of the castle few have ever seen."

Ezstasia was wondering what part of the castle the prince was talking about, but once they'd ascended the spiral staircase and approached the massive doors, she recognized her surroundings immediately. The enormous wooden doors, exquisitely designed into the shape of an immense tree that reached the ceiling, were not a sight that could be easily forgotten. She had nearly opened them when the prince had caught her trying to leave the castle after her injury. Now she would finally get to see what was hidden behind them.

As the prince and his two servants stood in front of the towering doors, she could hear the chatter and whispers behind her. Her friends were, no doubt, in complete awe.

"Welcome to the room that Prince Valorian was most fond of in this castle," said the prince. He stood aside and motioned to the two servants standing by the ornate door handles. Together, they slowly opened both large doors outward, offering the first glimpse into what lie within.

Ezstasia walked in first, and after taking a few steps inside, stopped as she looked around in amazement. She was

221

standing in another enormous library, but this was no ordinary one. The immense, circular, two-level room had actual, giant trees built into the walls, with some of the branches extending up and across the high ceiling. If she didn't know better, and aside from the many books that lined the walls, she would've thought she was in a large clearing in the middle of a forest.

She continued walking further into the room with the rest of the group, marveling at the surroundings and the enormity of the trees around the perimeter of the hall. She noticed an especially wide tree on the far left with a hollowed out trunk. An entire sitting room had been set up inside of it. Jezreel squealed with delight at another hollowed out tree on the right, which housed an adorable tea table with two chairs.

Ezstasia was startled by someone clearing their throat from the other end of the room. She squinted her eyes and spotted an old man in a brown cloak standing behind a large, square, wooden table at the far end. The man closed a large book with a thud, which got everyone's attention.

"These glorious trees," said the man, his aged and weathered voice echoing throughout the room, "lived on the property long before this castle was built. But alas, they are no longer alive, merely restored to their former glory by the ingenious and passionate Prince Valorian."

This man, whose scraggly white hair and wrinkled skin made him look like one of the wise old sages from the scrolls, beckoned them all toward him. "Come," he said. "I have much to show you." Even from a distance, Ezstasia assumed that, although he was hunched over somewhat, he was likely quite tall when he was younger.

She and the others walked to the enormous table. Along the way, Ezstasia gazed around at the many hollowed out trunks around the room. One had a blanketed picnic area, another had a hammock, and the largest one even had cushioned chairs by a fireplace. They were all so inviting, each one its own canopy-covered oasis.

As they approached the old man, Ezstasia took notice of the ancient scroll he seemed to be poring over that was spread out on the table, as well as the old, dusty books, paintings, and numerous rolled-up scrolls that lay all around it, scattered in haphazard fashion.

"I'd like to introduce you all to my archminister, Eliezer," said the prince. "Eliezer's been with my family for many years."

"I'm sure my appearance looks to them as if I've been with your family for *centuries*, my lord."

The prince laughed. "If you could have, I know you would have been with us for generations, my dear, faithful friend. And every generation would have benefitted greatly from your wisdom."

"Ah, but the only true wisdom is knowing how little we actually know, is it not? Regarding the forest, I'm afraid our knowledge of it has decreased by the day. But thanks to your esteemed guests here, we may have fallen into a bit of good fortune."

"What did you find?" said the prince, with a touch of hope in his voice.

"Perhaps nothing," said Eliezer. "But from the words dear Lanzzie described hearing in the forest, we can make some educated presumptions, particularly regarding a few passages from the scrolls that make reference to the Great War."

"From the scrolls?" said Meldon, as he adjusted his eyeglasses. "So you believe what's happening could be tied to the past?"

Eliezer turned his attention to Meldon. "I believe it could be, yes. Might I inquire as to your familiarity with the ancient treaty?"

"I've read up on it a bit," said Meldon.

"Then you're a rarity indeed in today's times," said Eliezer. "For the rest of you, to understand the context of the treaty, it will be useful to understand the war that preceded it. Those were the days of Valorian, whose kingdom you now grace with your presence. He was said to have had a brilliant mind and a kind heart. He was next in line to be king following his father Izhar the First. This castle was an ode to all that Valorian held dear. He had a special fondness for all things of an arboreous nature. If I may be so bold, I would say that the only thing he loved as much as the trees were his books. It's been told that he would say, 'Books and forests are secret doors to escape through.' I would be foolish to disagree."

"With all these trees and books," said Pallu, "he must've needed a lot of escaping."

"Shhh," said Randin.

Eliezer held up his hand and smiled. "Escape is indeed the great reprieve," he said, "though one also has duties to attend to, and Prince Valorian was no exception."

He pointed to the large scroll that was laid out on the table that read *Lineagus Royalus* across the top. His shaky finger followed the generations until it stopped on Alazar. "You can see the full lineage here. Valorian's father was King Izhar the First. Prince Alazar's father, an equally wonderful man, is King Izhar the Great."

As Ezstasia strained her neck to peek at the parchment, Eliezer slowly reached toward the pile on the table and carefully pulled out another scroll that he gently unrolled. It was an etching of people and magical beings, all living in harmony in a lush, idyllic village full of farms and cottages.

"Here you can see the small mushroom-shaped huts of the *Mushrims* built right next to a villager's cottage, similar to one of yours I suppose. The magic and human worlds coexisted peacefully for generations. They shared the same land and even the same homes for particular occasions."

Squinting to look at the scroll, Eliezer slowly pointed to the faint outline of a figure standing next to an elaborate treehouse. "And here are the majestic *Unseen Wizards*."

"I don't see anything," said Pallu.

"Hence the name *Unseen Wizards*," said Zander, rolling his eyes.

"The Unseen Wizards are even more difficult to see in person, according to the scrolls," said Eliezer, "at least when they *choose* to be invisible. But in addition to their visual peculiarities, the Unseen Wizards serve atop the High Court of the magic world. But alas, we're not here simply to discuss magical creatures, as fascinating a topic as it is. We're looking for ties to our present situation. And yet, a bit of historical knowledge may indeed assist our efforts—particularly, the events leading up to, and immediately following, the treaty itself."

Eliezer carefully rolled up the scroll and rested his hands on the table.

"In those days, which were of a more harmonious nature, people made great use of magic. But as we know, any tool that can be put to great use can be put to great misuse. And that is exactly what happened."

"People began to use magic for achieving their evil schemes," said Meldon. "I read about that."

"You have passion for history, I see," said Eliezer. "Yes, quite so, and they used them to drive fear into the hearts of men. Horrific creatures, they produced. Some of them, I believe a few of you have seen. But I dare say, you haven't seen the worst."

Zander's face went pale.

"That must've been an awful time to live in," said Ezstasia.

"Oh, it was. But a resistance grew among the people, and a number of the benevolent kings supported those brave souls, including King Izhar the First. That, my friends, was the beginning of the Great War."

"A completely avoidable civil war, all because of greed," said Fin.

"Greed, power, and fear. All sides of the same coin," said Eliezer. "Many good people lost their lives, suffering at the hands of man and beast."

"But the magical beings helped the resistance, right?" said Meldon.

"Not at first. The magic world stayed out of the quarrel entirely in the beginning. But, on the verge of defeat, the depleted resistance appealed to the Court of Magic for help. Much of the magic world was suspicious of the violent and unpredictable nature of humans. And so, they were passionately divided on what their kind should do. It took the Unseen Wizards to finally break the impasse within the Magic Court by making the ultimate decision. They made the monumental ruling that all magical beings were to join the resistance for our cause. It came with great sacrifice, and by coming to our aid, the magic world lost many of their own."

"So how does all this relate to the treaty?" said Pallu. "This is too much for my head."

"Ah yes, the treaty. At the end of the war, which, thanks to the good graces of the magic world, we had won, a treaty was proposed so that no such conflict would ever happen again. The treaty declared that all magical beings were to immediately depart across the sea to the Eastern Isles. Those designated lands would henceforth be known as the Magiclands, and all forms of magic would forever be banned from all human lands."

"I'm surprised everyone agreed to that," said Fin.

"Far from it, I would say. There was a significant outcry from both the human and magic worlds. You must understand, people were asked to give up magic, which was inherent in their culture and in the very fiber of their being. And not only that, but magic was their most important form of protection. I ask you to also consider the perspective of the magic world. They had to leave their dwellings—the homes that they had lived in for the entirety of their lives—and go to a foreign land to start anew. All their cherished memories from the Human Lands would be lost to them forever."

"I'm surprised another war didn't begin," said Meldon.

"Bitterness endured, as it always does, but it's hard to deny that magic in the hands of humans had become far too hazardous. And so, the treaty was signed. It was swiftly followed by strict penalties for any violations that occurred, which was most famously demonstrated in Valorian's dreadful fate—death by hanging for the unlawful possession of magic. A terrible tragedy for such a beloved prince. In any case, I believe this takes us to our current predicament."

"How so?" said Meldon.

"Let's look, shall we?" said Eliezer.

With his shaky, wrinkled hands, Eliezer slowly unrolled another large scroll that was resting on the table.

"Miss, Lanzzie," he said, looking up, "can you kindly repeat what you heard in the forest? One bit at a time, if you will."

Lanzzie took a deep breath. "The first thing it said was, *'As pure as light, as dark as night, the chaos is released.'*"

"Thank you," said Eliezer. "Now, I want you all to think. Does that have any relation to what any of you experienced in the forest?"

"Strange," said Meldon, "but it actually does. The phrase, *'as pure as light and dark as night'* seems to refer to something that possesses both good and evil. The fact is that some of us saw some very beautiful things, while others saw horrific things."

"Precisely," said Eliezer. "And what of the second part of the phrase?"

"*The chaos is released*," said Fin. "I think we've all seen the chaos in that forest. Whoever or whatever is behind it may have just released it. But why release good magic along with the bad?"

"Why indeed," said Eliezer. "*That* is part of our mystery. Miss Lanzzie, please continue."

"It said, '*The blood has already been spilled. The great battle begins.*'"

"'*The blood has already been spilled*,'" echoed Eliezer. "We must wonder. Whose blood? Is the voice referring to the blood of our ancestors during the Great War or something more recent? Yet even so, I would say the most striking turn of phrase is '*the great battle*.'"

"That's odd," said Ezstasia. "Even the lady in the prison said that the greatest battle was yet to come."

Eliezer pointed to a section on the scroll.

"This verse is of particular interest," he said. "Because the same words were uttered at the conclusion of the Great War, when the forces of darkness suffered their final defeat. One of the brutal creatures created by humans using dark magic uttered these dying words to none other than King Izhar the First, who had just pierced the beast's heart with a silver sword: *Vo Pensi fini?* Which translates to 'You think it's finished?' Then the beast said, '*La Mesabellum ete venire*,' which means 'The great battle is yet to come.' Izhar himself documented it in the scrolls shortly before his death years later."

"This is getting really scary," said Pallu.

"Ah, but it gets even more interesting. In the creature's final breath, it said, '*Ne levitorum eximum de terrason*,' which means, 'We shall rise again from the depths of the earth.' This saying is then repeated throughout the scrolls in its shorter and more widely known form: *From the depths cometh bloodshed*, which in the old tongue happens to be the very words Miss Lanzzie heard in the forest, '*Eximum Venirum Sangamort*.'"

"Those were the words!" said Lanzzie.

"Indeed," said Eliezer. "*From the depths cometh bloodshed*."

Ezstasia felt the fine hairs on her arms stand up.

"So what does all of this mean?" said Fin. "Are you insinuating that the darkness in the forest is because of an old curse?"

"Not so fast," said Eliezer. "We would be foolish to presume. But we do know that there seems to be intent behind the darkness, with a potential direct tie to the Great War."

The room grew alarmingly silent.

"So, in a nutshell," said Zander, "someone wants us all dead."

"What do we do now?" said Fin.

"It appears that I must journey to Rhyceton in the morning," said Prince Alazar from behind the group. "I must alert my father of the threat." He looked at the group. "Since you've all made such an impact on our findings, you're welcome to join me on the trip, but only if you wish to do so. You might find Rhyceton interesting. Besides, your personal experience and accounts may be useful."

"I've always wanted to see Rhyceton," said Meldon. "The Great Library alone would be a sight to see."

"Count me in, too," said Fin. "Who else is up for the trip?"

"I think we should all go," said Ezstasia. Everyone agreed.

"I can just see my hero painting now," said Pallu, "gloriously positioned over the fireplace."

"This is no time for joking," said Zander. "You do realize we could all die."

"You know, you're right," said Pallu. "Can you imagine how much *more* my painting would be worth after my heroic death?" Pallu laughed and gave Zander a push. "I know what you're really thinking, so relax Zander. We're not going into the forest. But if we do, I'll bring my spider-squasher."

"Do we have to bring him?" said Zander, rolling his eyes.

"The greatest virtue of all," said Eliezer, as he let out a slight chuckle, "is to bring love, joy, laughter, and inspiration to others. Master Pallu, I advise you to stay *just* who you are. You're a tremendous asset to your friends."

"See?" said Pallu. "I'm an asset!"

"You're half right," said Zander under his breath, smirking.

The prince bid farewell to Eliezer, and Ezstasia and the group followed him out of the room. She'd read about Rhyceton and its beautiful mountaintop kingdom surrounded by a dense forest, but never dreamed she'd actually get to go there. She definitely didn't feel ready to pass through another forest any time soon, and she still felt a knot in her stomach as she thought about the implications of dark magic returning on a larger scale. It made her long for the simple days at the Cottages.

As she began the walk down the long hall to her room, she observed everyone quietly dispersing in different directions. She noticed Pallu yawning, which made her realize how exhausted she was herself. She looked forward to a good night's sleep. The last few days had been eventful to say the least. She was almost afraid to think about what awaited them next.

CHAPTER FOURTEEN

"Is that Pallu?" said Ezstasia, squinting to see the two figures approaching the entrance to the stables.

"That's him," said Zander. "Late as always. Except this time, he's with the village girl that he's been stalking."

"Her name's Ellie," said Ezstasia.

"I think she likes that he stalks her," said Randin. "But what's she carrying?"

"I think it's Pallu's food basket," said Zander.

"That's a big basket," said Fin. "How long is he expecting this journey to take?"

As Pallu and Ellie came in from the glaring morning sun, their faces were beaming. Ezstasia had never seen him so happy.

"Good morning, ladies and gents!" said Pallu.

"Did you rob a bakery?" said Randin.

"It might be a long trip," said Pallu. "You'll be thanking me later when you're all hungry."

"Aw, that's so sweet of you," said Ellie, hugging Pallu. "Thinking of all your friends. You're definitely the sweetest peach in my basket."

"How many *peaches* does she have?" said Zander.

Pallu smiled as he proceeded to his rabbit while holding

231

his satchel.

Prince Alazar rode in on a striking black horse. Several horsemen followed behind him, wearing silver breastplates and chainmail. They must've all been coming from the Royal Stables, which Ezstasia had learned from Miss Tee were separate and to the eastern side of the castle.

"Is everyone packed and ready?" he said.

Ezstasia was tying the last of her supplies onto Tia's saddle while Fin took count of everyone.

"We're all set, sire," said Fin.

"Good. I want you all to be aware that this is difficult terrain we'll be crossing. Rhyceton is over a day's journey south from here and we'll be traveling through mountains and crossing the Galoran River. I see you all have the supplies and rations we provided. Please be sure to stay together. My knights will do their best to protect you."

"Protect us?" said Pallu. "From what?"

"From anything and everything."

"Don't worry, Pallu," said Zander, patting him on the shoulder. "If anything attacks us, you can beat it with one of your loaves."

"Even big spiders?" said Pallu, grinning.

"Not funny," said Zander, getting on his rabbit. "Not one bit funny."

The prince and his horsemen trotted out of the stables and Ezstasia and the group followed. She was surprised to see how many villagers had gathered outside to see them off. Word must've spread about their journey.

As they rode off, she saw Pallu blow a kiss to Ellie, who was standing in the crowd, carrying the large empty basket and waving a white, dainty cloth.

"Be careful!" yelled Ellie, as she dabbed the cloth below her eyes.

"Wow, I've never felt so proud in my life," said Pallu.

"But you haven't done anything yet," said Zander.

"A hero in the making, my friend."

They followed the prince out the Western Village Gate and then south through the same road that led to the Cottages. After about an hour, he led them toward the sea and then south again, through wide areas of green grass that extended on all sides, as far as the eye could see. They stopped for a short break, but then continued riding for a few more hours until the landscape began to change. Small yellow and white wildflowers dotted the land around them and the road grew rockier and narrower. In the distance, the faint outline of mountains could be seen on both sides, and after a while, the largest of all the mountains began to emerge on the horizon.

They finally paused for another break to give the rabbits some rest. Ezstasia was exhausted already from the sun, so she could only imagine how the rabbits felt. She tied up Tia and placed some greens and berries in front of her and walked over to the prince.

"Down past that valley is the Galoran River," said the prince, wiping his forehead with a cloth. "That'll be our first challenge. We'll be crossing at low tide, but the currents can be tricky."

"Do you travel to Rhyceton often?" she said.

"Not often enough, if you ask my father," he said, filling a small water bucket for his horse. "But too often, if you ask Torrance," he added, patting the beautiful, black steed. "He's made this trip more times than a poor charger should be asked to do. Isn't that right, Torrance?" The horse whinnied and seemed to nod his head.

Before long, they were back on the journey and descended the hill toward the dense forests of the valley.

"Are we really going through that forest?" Zander called out to Prince Alazar.

"No other choice," said the prince. "Just stay close."

Ezstasia rode up beside Zander. "Don't worry, it's not the forest we were in," she said. "This one should be fine." She hoped she was right. But if she wasn't, at least they'd all be together.

They entered into the woods and Ezstasia was relieved to see that these trees, while old, didn't look nearly as unusual as the ones in the forest near Old Vynterra. She still couldn't help but feel nervous riding through the thick woodland, and from the looks of the others, they were apprehensive, too.

After a while, they emerged from the forest to the banks of a large river, just as the prince had mentioned. This must be the Galoran River, Ezstasia thought to herself. The river was wider than she expected, and the land on the other side was surprisingly barren from what she could see. There wasn't a touch of green, just rocks, boulders, and pebbly sand.

"We'll cross here," said the prince, turning Torrance around to face the group. "Even at low tide, there can be a bit of a current and sudden drop-offs, so please be careful."

He motioned for several of his knights to go first -and he followed suit. Three other horsemen stayed behind on the prince's orders to make sure the group made it across safely.

Ezstasia watched carefully as the prince and his guards crossed the river. It didn't look to be too deep, it may have reached up to their horses' knees at most, but even so, the horses seemed hesitant to walk further in. Little by little, their riders coaxed them through the flowing waters. About halfway across, she noticed that the horses were swimming, so they must have been passing one of the drop-offs that the prince had spoken of. She looked down at Tia's webbed feet and hoped she'd do okay. The giant rabbits were accustomed to streams and creeks, but if the water became too rough, she wasn't sure how she'd react.

"Lads," said Fin, "who's going to tag behind the ladies to make sure they're safe? The rest can go in front with me."

"I will," said Zander.

"Me too," said Pallu. "Not that I'm afraid to go in first or anything, but I want to make sure the ladies are safe."

"And *we'll* make sure you two are safe," said one of the horsemen, laughing.

Fin and Ithron entered the water first, followed by Meldon. Once Ezstasia saw them reach the halfway point and saw the rabbits swimming, she sighed with relief.

"Ready?" she said to Lanzzie and Jezreel, peeling off her shoes like the others before her. They nodded and did the same, riding beside her to the riverbank. Pallu and Zander lined up behind them.

"We'll catch you if you fall in," said Pallu.

Ezstasia proceeded into the river with the others, and it wasn't bad at all. Her feet were cold from dipping into the water, but if that was the only discomfort, she could live with it. The problem was that the water was murky so she wasn't able to see where the drop-off point might be. As they approached what appeared to be the halfway point, she gripped Tia's reins tightly. Within a minute, the rabbit dipped lower into the water and was unmistakably swimming.

"Good girl, Tia!" She held the reins as Tia made her way across.

"Hey lady," said Zander, smiling as he approached her on his rabbit. He and Pallu had just caught up to her, while Lanzzie and Jezreel were just ahead. She turned around to see the horsemen lagging slightly behind to bring up the rear.

"Oh no!" yelled Pallu, behind her to her left.

Ezstasia turned her head just in time to see one of Pallu's loaves floating downriver. Pallu started to slide off his rabbit's saddle as he reached for the runaway bread that was quickly drifting toward the sea.

"Pallu, don't even think about it," said Zander. "Some things, like soggy bread, aren't worth dying for."

"That was freshly baked!" he yelled, reaching with his left hand until it looked like he was about to fall into the water.

"Pallu, you have twenty more," yelled Ezstasia as she put her arm out, just in case she needed to grab him. "Please. Get back up before you slide off."

"Pallu, you're crazy," said Zander. "It's gone."

As Pallu pulled himself back onto his rabbit, they watched as it floated further down the river and out of sight.

"Goodbye, bread," said Pallu. "And thank you both for saving my life," he added, jokingly.

Just then, Tia bucked slightly as her legs touched the river bed, and then she returned to her usual gait.

They finally emerged from the river and dismounted their rabbits on the once-dry riverbank that was now splattered with mud from the animals. Pallu and Zander walked to the river's edge, so Ezstasia joined them.

"Are you all okay?" said the prince as he approached.

"We're all good, except for Pallu's bread," said Ezstasia, smiling. "Should we hold a memorial service for it, Pallu?"

"Ha! Actually, the death of my bread on these travels has made me curious," said Pallu. "Is the river the hardest part of our journey?" He looked toward the prince.

"If you're afraid of water, yes," said the prince. "If you're afraid of heights, no."

"Heights? Um… we don't have to climb *that*, do we?" Pallu pointed to the large, rocky mountain in the distance straight ahead.

"I'm afraid we do. The kingdom is at the top," said the prince, as he turned to go to his men.

They all began to travel again and progressed through a wide, dirt path lined on both sides by high rocks with a smattering of trees atop of them. Before long, they emerged from the path and came to a pebble-covered hill that was more challenging to ascend than it looked. Once on higher ground, they traversed through slightly uphill rocky terrain for what felt like forever, though they stopped for occasional breaks. The sun was beginning to go down and Ezstasia felt a chill in the air. Eventually, they reached a plateau at the foot of the mountain. It was dark by now; the only illumination was coming from the guards' torches and the glowing moonlight. She could see that everyone looked just as exhausted as she was. The prince stopped and addressed everyone.

"We're going to camp here," said the prince. "You will all need your strength to get up that mountain in the morning."

"Thank the wizards!" said Pallu, as he dismounted his rabbit. "Thumps couldn't have made it another foot."

"Neither could his rider," said Zander.

"Do you know where that expression comes from?" said Meldon.

"What expression?" said Zander.

"'Thank the wizards,'" said Meldon. "It originated in the old scrolls when the Unseen Wizards decided that all magical beings had to enter the war and help our ancestors."

"That's great, Meldon," said Pallu, as Fin approached. "Anyway, do you know what I've been thinking, Fin?"

"How would I know what you're thinking?" said Fin.

"Good question," said Pallu. "Well, I'll tell you. I've been thinking that the mountain may be too much for Thumps."

"What are you saying?" said Fin.

"I'm just saying this looks like a nice, comfortable place to stay awhile. It's nice and open. I have plenty of food. I think Thumps and I will wait here while everyone—"

"Pallu!" said Fin. "We're not leaving you here."

"Fin, hear me out. I already saw, firsthand, how that tiny, little river ripped a loaf of bread out of its perfectly secured spot in my sack and carried it away to its soggy death. I can't even imagine what that gigantic mountain—"

A wolf howled in the distance, stopping him in mid-thought. The long, soulful wail echoed all round them. Another wolf joined in, and then one or two others, their song filling the air.

"On second thought, I think we should stay together," said Pallu. "Strength in numbers and all that."

Fin looked at him blankly and then laughed as Pallu walked away toward his rabbit.

"Well, that helped change his mind," said Ezstasia. "But do you think we need to worry about those wolves?"

"No, they sounded far away," said Fin. "I'm sure the prince would let us know if they were a concern. We should be fine."

"*We should be fine*," said Zander. "Famous last words."

🐲 ℞ 🐲 ℞

While everyone was busy setting up their tents, a few of the horsemen worked on building a fire. Ezstasia left her tent only partially set up and walked over to address the prince. He was conversing with one of his knights, the one she'd seen him riding next to for most of the trip.

"Lady Arrow," said the prince. "This is Sir Kyrian. He is one of my bravest and most loyal knights."

The knight bowed his head. "Pleasure, my lady." His voice was deep and strong, fitting for a tall man with a face and torso that appeared to be chiseled out of stone.

Ezstasia curtsied. "Thank you for your protection."

"It is my duty to serve."

"My lord," she said, addressing the prince, "are you certain that staying here is the best decision? We do need to get word to Rhyceton as soon as we can, do we not?" She wasn't even all that concerned about the wolves, but she *did* feel like they were running out of time against whatever evil forces may be returning.

"My lady, do my ears deceive me?" said Kyrian. "Did you question the prince's decision?"

Ezstasia was silent for a moment as she tried to digest the knight's response. She felt her face redden once she realized what she had done.

"I… I'm sorry," she said. "It was just a question."

"A question is never just a question to a royal, especially in the presence of others. Not unless they seek your counsel." The knight spoke more in an advisory tone than a harsh one, but it didn't make it any less embarrassing.

The prince looked at Ezstasia with bright blue eyes that she couldn't help but stare into, though she wasn't sure if they conveyed disappointment or empathy. He was a master at keeping his emotions in check.

Ezstasia knelt down, feeling horrible. "I apologize, my lord. I didn't mean to challenge your decision."

"I forgive your question, Lady Arrow," he said with a slight smile.

As she rose, she looked around and realized everyone was staring at her, which made her feel even more humiliated. She felt the blood rush to her face as anger began to slowly boil underneath her skin. She suspected the prince probably felt as uncomfortable as she did, though it was hard to tell based on his calm demeanor.

"You can all go back to your duties," said the prince.

Feeling numb, she returned to set up her tent. Despite her emotions, she couldn't help it and found herself looking toward the prince on occasion. There was no doubt that he was a good man and a humble prince, but he also had the ability to make her feel nervous. It made her realize how out of place she felt in his company—a mere cottage girl, not worthy of any royal respect or attention.

"You look troubled," said the prince, behind her. She jumped, not realizing he was there. "You weren't entirely wrong, you know. But I couldn't envision your friends making it safely across that mountain in the dark of night."

"No, it isn't that," she said, unsure how much she should say.

"What is it then?"

"My lord, I don't belong here."

"What do you mean you don't belong here?"

"I mean… you call me Lady Arrow, which is nice. It really is. But I'm just a girl from the Cottages who doesn't even know when to quiet her tongue when necessary. My friends at least had to battle evil forces in the forest and overcome them, so I could see why you'd want them. But me? I'm just a clumsy girl who fell off her rabbit and blacked out."

"If you hadn't fallen off your rabbit, none of us would be here. Your friends wouldn't have come looking for you and we'd probably know very little about what we're dealing with until it was too late. Ezstasia, falling off your rabbit gave us a fighting chance."

Ezstasia looked at the ground as she pondered his words.

"It doesn't make me feel any more worthy. It was dumb luck."

Prince Alazar gently put his fingers under her chin and redirected her gaze toward him.

"Was it dumb luck that you brought your friends all the way back to the castle to tell their stories? That you risked everything to find out the truth? Don't underestimate yourself. I'll tell you the same thing Eliezer told me when I was a boy and I doubted my abilities to be a prince. He said 'Wherever you are, you're exactly where you need to be.' Ezstasia, you could find a great treasure and have it lead you to an even greater disaster. Or you can fall off your rabbit and… well, you get the idea. The truth is, you're brave, you're strong-willed, and you don't give up on people, and that's why you're more worthy than anyone I know of to be called Lady Arrow."

Ezstasia felt a lump in her throat as a wave of emotions overtook her.

"Do you really believe that?" she said, wiping a tear from her cheek.

He smiled. "I wouldn't say it if I didn't."

"Thank you, my lord," she said, trying to gather herself as he walked away.

For the first time, she felt like she belonged—like she could really make a difference, no matter what happened from this moment on or what mistakes she'd most assuredly make. She held her head high and felt the anger and humiliation lift from her body. With a new sense of purpose, she finished her tent and then joined her sister and friends, who were already sitting around the campfire telling stories. It would be a relaxing night for a change.

ಐ ಇ ಐ ಇ

"Ezstasia, wake up! Wake up now!"

Ezstasia thought she was dreaming, but as her head cleared, she realized Lanzzie was peering down at her.

She wiped her eyes. "Is it morning already?"

"Never mind that," said Lanzzie. "You have to get up. Wolves attacked the camp!"

She was still groggy and her thinking wasn't clear.

"Wolves? What are you talking about?"

She sat up and tried to open her eyes, squinting as the sun shone through the opening in the tent. She could see people busily running back and forth.

"What's going on!?" she said, growing alarmed.

241

"I told you," said Lanzzie. "Wolves attacked the camp last night. Someone was killed and another man was hurt."

"Killed! Who?"

"One of the horsemen. The prince is sending some of his men back to the castle with the man who was hurt. We have to pack our things immediately. We're leaving for Rhyceton. Hurry."

"Why didn't I hear anything?" she said, still in a daze.

"None of us did. Get up. I'll help you pack. I'm sure we'll find out more from the prince."

Ezstasia rose from her makeshift bed and began to stuff the blankets that Miss Tee had given her into her canvas sack. Lanzzie helped pack up the rest of her belongings. Once everything was packed, she followed Lanzzie out of the tent and gazed around at the chaos. She noticed in the distance, the prince was talking to Sir Kyrian and another knight as they stood on a high rock scouting the area. The prince and his knights remained there for a few minutes and then stepped down and headed back toward the camp where the rest of the group was packing up.

"What's going on?" said Fin. "How did this happen?"

The prince gestured to Kyrian, who then stepped forward.

"His Royal Highness the Prince needs everyone's attention," Kyrian announced with his booming voice.

Those who were packing in their tents came out and gathered around to listen.

"As some of you know," said the prince, "there was a wolf attack before sunrise. Sir Borak here, came to alert me." The prince motioned to the knight who was standing next to him, a stocky, bald man with a red face.

"Sir Borak," said the prince, "please share with the group what you saw."

"Of course, my lord."

Borak stepped forward and cleared his throat.

"I was on watch," he said, "an' I heard noises just outside the camp, where Sir Ulric and Sir Brom set up their tents. They liked to be near trees I s'pose. Anyway, at first, it just sounded like trees rustling. But then I heard a yell—a little nip of a yell that sounded like it was horribly cut short. You best believe I ran there as quick as I could, and that's when I saw it—or him or her. It was a big, white wolf an' it was draggin' Sir Brom away into the trees. It was at least twice as big as any wolf should ever be. I'd have to say Brom was already dead, given what I saw of him. I froze, but the beast stopped to stare right at me before carryin' the rest of poor Brom off. I knew that he was no ordinary wolf. Those creepy eyes were shining—and even in the night I could see they were clear as crystal—like big, pure diamonds."

"It can't be," said Meldon.

"Aye, that's what I told my eyes," said Borak. "But that was a Diamondwolf I saw, mark my words, lad."

"But they haven't existed in centuries," said Fin. "They're extinct."

"Not any more, they're not," said Borak. "Come back from the dead, they have."

"What about Sir Ulric?" said Ezstasia. "What happened to him?"

"He's lucky to be alive. When the creature ran off, I heard a groan just above my head. I readied my sword, because who knew what was up there? Well, wouldn't you know, Sir Ulric, who's one of the strongest men I know, managed to get 'imself up a tree, even after that horrible thing took a chomp at him. He dropped out of that tree like a rock right in front of me, so I brought him back to camp."

"Two of our horsemen took him back home this morning to be treated," said the prince. "We're hoping he survives the trip."

"What do we do now?" said Meldon. "If that really is a

Diamondwolf, what if he comes back for us?"

"It's a bigger problem than that," said the prince. "We scouted the area at sunrise, and we believe there's more of them. We could see the movement in the shadows up ahead."

"How will we get to Rhyceton?" said Fin.

"I don't know how many of you know your history," said the prince, "but these Diamondwolves were created for one purpose and one purpose only. To kill humans. We don't know why they're back or how or who's leading them, but if the scrolls are any indication, they should have one huge weakness that we may be able to exploit."

"The sunlight," said Meldon.

"That's right," said Kyrian.

"I can't emphasize enough how important it is to stay out of the shadows and move quickly," said the prince. "Direct sunlight burns their eyes and coats, so they hunt at night and in the shade."

"There are shady spots all over that mountain," said Fin. "How will we stay in the sunlight all the way to Rhyceton?"

"You're not going to Rhyceton," said the prince.

"What do you mean? We're not?"

"I've decided to send you all back to Old Vynterra, accompanied by Sir Kyrian and Sir Layton. It's become far too dangerous."

"Can't the wolves attack us on our way back?" said Ezstasia. At the same moment, a young, fit knight—most likely, Sir Layton—stepped next to Kyrian.

"They can. Still, that journey seems safer than going to Rhyceton. The path is mostly open, and even the pass through the rocks and trees is pretty wide. Just be sure to stay out of the shadows. Besides, you only need to make it to the Galoran River before sundown. They won't cross the water."

"Why not?" said Fin.

The prince looked at Sir Kyrian and gave him a nod.

"The Diamondwolves in the scrolls didn't like water," said Kyrian. "We don't know why, but some people think their creators inflicted them with certain weaknesses on purpose. Nobody really knows for sure."

"I have to ask," said Meldon, adjusting his glasses. "What if these wolves aren't like the ones in the scrolls?"

"For all our sake, let's hope they are," said Kyrian. "For now, the mission's clear. We head to the river as fast as we can. Follow the sunlight. Stay out of the shadows."

"I want to go to Rhyceton," said Ezstasia, stepping forward. Kyrian looked shocked and, as she looked around, so did most everyone else. She turned to address the prince. "My lord, if you'll excuse me, if it's safe enough for Your Highness, then I assume I'll be just as safe. I know the danger, and I take full responsibility for my decision. I want to be a part of stopping this horrible magic, whatever it is. I don't want to stay back and feel helpless."

"What are you doing?" whispered Lanzzie.

The prince stared back with a blank expression for a moment, then nodded.

"Very well," he said. "I won't stop you."

"If my sister's going, I'd like to go, too," said Lanzzie.

"You don't have to do this," said Ezstasia.

"Yes," said Lanzzie. "I do."

"You've all been made aware of the dangers," said the prince. "Still, whoever wishes to join me to Rhyceton, I'll allow it. But make your decision quickly, and don't make it lightly."

"I'd like to go, too," said Fin.

"And me," said Meldon. "The learning opportunity is too great to pass up."

"Anyone else?" said the prince.

Ezstasia looked around and everyone else looked too frightened to make any kind of decision.

"Very well," said the prince. "Ezstasia, Lanzzie, Fin, Meldon—I'll need you all to come with me. The others will follow Sir Kyrian and Sir Layton. And remember, stay out of the shadows. These wolves are as white as snow and twice the size of normal wolves, but they know how to stay hidden and can pounce on you before you even see them. Stay in the sunlight and you'll be safe."

Just as the prince started to turn around, Randin stepped forward.

"I'm going, too," he said.

"What!?" said Zander. "No you're not!"

"I have to, little brother."

"You can't," said Zander. "Because I can't do it. Not after that spider. And now having to face those wolves in the mountain? You know I can't."

"I'm not asking you to, and I wouldn't let you if you tried."

"Why?" said Zander, tears welling in his eyes. "Why are you doing this to me?"

"I'm not doing it to you. I'm doing it *for* you. After I saw what happened to you—after you almost died—I'm not going to sit and watch while some evil magical force, or whatever it is, kills you or any of us without a fight. I need to do this."

Zander broke down sobbing and fell to his knees. Randin went to comfort him.

"It's decided then," said the prince. "Say your goodbyes quickly. I'm afraid time is not in our favor."

Ezstasia hugged Pallu, Jezreel and Ithron, and offered additional comfort to Zander. After everyone said their goodbyes, they all got on their rabbits and went their separate ways.

The prince motioned for his assigned knights to join him. Ezstasia followed, along with Lanzzie, Fin, Meldon, and Randin, who kept glancing back sadly at his brother.

As she rode off with the group, she could hear Zander's sobs in the distance. She couldn't help but feel responsible for tearing the brothers apart. After all, she was the first to insist on going to Rhyceton. She felt awful for the two of them. She especially understood how Randin felt, because she felt the same way after what happened to her sister. But, in spite of it all, this was something she just had to do. She needed to be a part of this.

As they pushed forward onto the mountain path, the sun shone in her eyes as a wolf howled in the distance.

ꝏ ಐ ꝏ ಐ

Pallu rode beside Zander on the way to Old Vynterra and Ithron and Jezreel tailed behind them. Sir Kyrian and Sir Layton led the way. The group had already stopped several times, and Zander had been quiet for the entirety of the journey.

Pallu breathed a sigh of relief. The Galoran River was still a ways ahead, but it seemed likely they'd get there before nightfall. They were already approaching the pebbly hill Pallu remembered from the day before.

"Hey, at least it's downhill this time," said Pallu, trying to cheer up Zander.

"Not for my brother."

Zander kept his head down, as he had for most of the trip.

"He'll be okay. He'll be back, you'll see. Meanwhile, let's go find him a pretty little wife. We should find one for you, too."

Zander just shrugged his shoulders and kept riding.

"Hey, let's sing a song," said Pallu. "It'll cheer up Ithron and Jez, too."

Zander barely shook his head and ignored him.

Pallu wasn't sure what to do for him, so he let him be for a while and just rode beside him quietly. Meanwhile, his own guilt was nagging at him for not joining the others on the way to Rhyceton. He had to admit, the wolves terrified him to his core. But also, he and Thumps would've just slowed them down. He would have ended up making them all wolf bait. He confirmed to himself that this was the better option. Plus, he needed to be here for Zander.

He rode further and felt another wave of guilt as he realized that getting back to Ellie had been a motivating factor for him as well. It made him feel even worse to acknowledge that, because he felt that his real concern should be for his friends who could possibly face danger on their way to Rhyceton. He began to worry.

"Relax, Pallu," he said out loud to himself. "They'll all be okay."

"What?" said Zander.

"*Now* you answer me, when I'm talking to *myself?*" said Pallu.

"Why did you say they'd be okay? Do you think maybe they won't?"

"I'm just feeling guilty, Zan, just like you. But we shouldn't. They wouldn't want us to. Besides, either one of us could've slowed them down if we panicked. Then we'd be feeling guilty about that."

"I suppose you're right," said Zander.

"I make sense sometimes." Pallu smiled, happy with the small victory of helping Zander's mood.

They descended the hill, which was harder than Pallu had expected, and before long they were heading into the long pass, lined by high, forest-covered rocks. The tall rocks and trees cast shadows along the dirt path ahead. He remembered the prince's warning to stay out of the shadows, though the knights up ahead didn't seem to take any notice. He glanced up above and thought he saw movement in the trees overhead, but it could've been his imagination.

"Do you think we could go a little faster?" Pallu yelled to the knights.

Pallu watched as the two knights continued at the same pace. They must not have heard him.

"Why?" said Jezreel, riding up beside him. "Did you see something?"

"No, but just because I don't see something doesn't mean it's not there. Those shadows could be hiding things… like wolves."

"Take it easy," said Ithron, catching up to them. "There's no wolves out here. They're more likely chasing the other group for dinner."

"Are you serious!?" yelled Zander, his face red. "Did you really just say that? Maybe you should be the wolves' din—"

"Whoa, everyone calm down," said Pallu.

"Ithron, seriously," said Jezreel. "That was wrong on so many levels."

"Okay, I'm sorry," said Ithron, although he didn't sound terribly sorry.

"I think I just saw something," said Pallu. "We should really speed this up."

"Relax, Pallu, you're just on edge," said Ithron.

"Wait," said Jezreel. "I just saw something, too. Up there in the trees." She pointed to a row of trees up ahead to their right, atop the high rocks they were about to ride through.

"I don't see anything," said Ithron.

Pallu searched up in the trees where Jezreel was pointing. He spotted something big and white moving swiftly through the forest above. Then he saw a second one. They were Diamondwolves. And they were following them.

"We need to go faster, now!" he yelled to the knights. He felt his blood rush through his veins as he gripped Thumps's reins tighter.

Layton pointed to the trees above. Kyrian glanced up at the trees and turned his head back toward the group.

"Can your rabbits run at full speed until we get to the river?" he yelled.

Pallu looked down at Thumps, who was already looking tired. The rabbits would also need to expend all their energy in order to cross the river.

"I'm sorry, Thumps," he said, petting the rabbit's soft ear, "we're gonna have to try."

He glanced over to Jezreel and she nodded.

"We can make it," shouted Pallu to the knights.

The two knights increased their speed to a steady gallop, and Pallu and the group tried to keep up. Layton pulled his horse to the side, letting the group pass, and then brought up the rear. Pallu was thankful that Layton was there to help keep the group safe and ensure that nobody fell behind.

Pallu was starting to perspire from the blazing sun, but he was never so glad to have the sunlight beating down on him. He glanced up and now spotted three wolves keeping pace with them, then a fourth.

"The light is our friend, our shield and our sword!" Pallu shouted. He figured if he spoke like a warrior, then maybe he'd believe it. But, it wasn't really working. All he could think about was how quickly he wanted to get to that river.

As they raced ahead in the sun, the only sound they could hear was the rabbits' breath. Pallu noticed that Zander looked like he was really struggling emotionally. His face was red with tears.

"Zander, don't worry," he said. "You know why your brother's gonna be okay? Because we have the wolves distracted and those sun-wimpy things can't touch us in the sunlight. The river's just ahead. Everything will be fine." He wasn't sure if he was trying to convince Zander or himself.

Zander's face changed from fear to determination as he sped up his rabbit.

"That's it, my friend," said Pallu. "We're warriors!"

They rode quickly along the path, and Pallu kept looking up to see where the wolves were. The beasts were still following them in the shadows of the trees.

"Do you hear that?" said Jezreel from behind.

"Hear what?" said Pallu.

"It's the river! Just ahead!"

Over the sound of Thumps's huffing and puffing, he could make out the rushing waters.

"I hear it too!" said Pallu, laughing with relief. "Zander, what'd I tell you. There's the river!"

Glancing over at Zander's beaming face, Pallu could see that even he seemed happy.

As Pallu tuned in to the beautiful sound of the river, Jezreel rode up beside him.

"Do you remember the river sounding like this?" she yelled. "The water sounds louder than before."

At that moment, Layton rode quickly past them to catch up to Kyrian.

"That water's way too loud," yelled Layton.

The knights didn't seem to be paying any attention to the wolves. They seemed more worried about the river. Pallu looked ahead and recognized the green and yellow bushes that lined the path to the river.

"I can't believe how deafening it is," said Zander. "It sounds like a waterfall."

They followed the knights down the wide, rocky path that wound around to the riverfront. They continued around the path until they finally approached the river.

Pallu couldn't believe what he was seeing. The knights

dismounted their horses and walked toward the river's edge. Pallu did the same and everyone followed. The once calm river was flowing violently like wild rapids and the water level was up to the high bank.

"Is it a high tide?" said Ithron.

"That's no tide," said Layton. "Not at this time of day."

"Is this normal?" said Pallu.

Kyrian shook his head. "I've never seen anything like this. It doesn't make any sense. We observed the clouds and they departed to the east three nights ago. The weather's been nothing but calm ever since. This is not a natural occurrence, I can tell you that much."

"Do you think it's dark magic?" said Ithron.

Kyrian just looked at him and shook his head. "I don't know what it is. Anything's possible I suppose."

Pallu looked up at the trees above them and didn't see anything. Ithron joined him.

"I don't see the wolves," said Ithron.

"That's a relief," said Jezreel.

"How does not knowing where the wolves are bring you relief?" said Zander. "It brings me fear."

"Let's not worry about where the wolves are right now," said Ithron. "Because if we can solve *that* problem," he said, pointing to the river, "then we can solve *that* problem," he added, pointing to the shadows in the high rocks to their right.

"Okay, so then how do we get across?" said Zander.

"We don't," said Kyrian. "Not here, anyway."

"Sir Kyrian," said Jezreel, "how long do we have before sundown?"

Kyrian remained silent as he stared at the current. He appeared to be scrutinizing the raging waters. He and Layton walked further upriver and gazed out east. The two knights had a brief discussion, but Pallu couldn't hear what they were saying. Shortly after, Kyrian returned to the group.

"Sir Layton and I are going to ride upriver to see if we can find a spot to cross. If we don't see anything, we'll check downriver, but it's likely to be worse toward the sea. You should all be safe here until we return."

"*Should* be safe?" said Zander, with angst in his voice.

"We still have some sunlight left and you'll be in the open. Whatever you do, don't go anywhere. Stay in the sun."

"It'll be dark before long," said Jezreel.

"Exactly why we must be on our way," said Layton. "Time is not on our side."

The two knights mounted their horses and began to ride off.

"Wait!" yelled Pallu.

"Wait for what?" said Sir Kyrian.

Pallu was almost too frozen with fear to speak.

"They're… here," he muttered.

He turned and pointed upward to the terrifying creatures.

Everyone was silent as they looked up in the direction where Pallu was pointing.

"What if you two aren't back by the time the sun sets?" said Ithron, without turning around. "They look like they're ready to eat us." He kept his gaze fixed on the wolves. They were waiting patiently for the moment that they could attack.

"We will be," said Layton, tapping the tip of his sword against his hand.

"Is there anything at all we can do?" said Jezreel. "Anything?"

"Yes," said Kyrian. "Pray that we find a crossing."

The two knights that had brought Pallu a feeling of safety and comfort, rode off. The fear that entered his body was almost unbearable. He shifted his gaze back to the shadows.

The Diamondwolves were staring down at them from the high rocks, growling and salivating. He felt a chill down his spine as he saw how aware and intelligent they appeared to be. The towering beasts moved in unison and shifted their heads quickly, attentively responding to every single sound. Their eyes glistened like glass and they were enormous with beautiful white coats. It was hard to believe they were so ferocious. They exposed their jagged, razor sharp teeth as they growled and clamped down their strong jaws with sheer ferocity.

Pallu noticed the lowering sun briefly shone on one of them and it immediately backed off from the edge of the cliff. Their sunlight was their only advantage in this moment, but Pallu knew that as soon as the sun set, they would be utterly helpless against the wolves' brutality.

CHAPTER FIFTEEN

After some passing of time from Kyrian and Layton's departure, Pallu realized that he needed to distract his mind from all the negative thoughts. He walked to his sack and pulled out some greens and a water tin for Thumps. He headed to the edge of the river to fill the canister, careful not to fall in. If possible, the rapids were even more violent than when they had first arrived, only moments ago. He glanced back up at the wolves, and they looked as hungry as ever.

Jezreel was slightly upriver, scouting out the area.

"Don't go too far," Ithron yelled to her.

"You could help me," she said. "I'm trying to see how deep it is."

"It doesn't matter how deep it is," said Ithron. "We'll never get across in that current."

"Hey," said Zander, "I have an idea. What if we tried to build a bridge?"

"Are you serious?" said Ithron. "Why don't we just flap our wings and fly over while we're at it? We couldn't build a bridge if our lives depended on it."

"Our lives do depend on it," said Zander. "I'm just talking about knocking a tree over or something. It beats just sitting here and waiting to be eaten alive."

"Does it?" said Ithron.

"How about a boat?" said Jezreel. "We could tie up a bunch of branches with vines."

"I like that idea!" said Pallu.

"The closest trees," said Ithron, pointing toward the wolves, "are up there. Does anyone feel like going up there to cut some branches? Because I don't. Bridges, boats—all of those ideas are useless. If there were any possible way of crossing here, the knights would've considered it before they left."

"Well, if they're not back when the sun sets, we may not have a choice," said Pallu. He was dreading the thought of that.

"I can't believe this is happening," said Jezreel. "I'm completely and utterly terrified."

"Jez, we'll be okay," said Ithron. "We'll be on the other side by nightfall, I promise you. They'll be back."

"Yes, that's it," said Pallu. "Think positive."

"You know, Pallu," said Zander, "what you said to me earlier has made me feel a little better."

"What did I say again?"

"That we were distracting the wolves. You're right. It really may be saving my brother's life. And our friends' lives."

"That's one way to look at it," said Ithron.

"It's the only way to look at it," said Pallu, though he had to admit to himself he was as frightened as Jezreel.

"They look hungry," said Zander, glancing up nervously toward the wolves. Their shining, menacing eyes remained targeted as they paced back and forth. They snarled and snapped at one another.

"Seeing them hungry is making *me* hungry," said Pallu. "I'm going to join Thumps for a little nourishment. Does anyone want anything?"

"Food is the last thing on my mind," said Jezreel. "But I'll feed Buttons."

"How can you even eat at a time like this?" said Zander.

"It's easy to eat when I'm hungry," said Pallu.

Pallu walked back to his rabbit's saddle and took out some bread and aged cheeses, which he had found great for long journeys. He also grabbed pieces of bread for Jezreel, Zander, and Ithron, who all gladly accepted once he took it to them.

Pallu smiled when he saw everyone taking more food from their rations and then feeding their rabbits. It was like they all just came to life, their spirits lifted. He liked to think he had a little something to do with that.

As time passed, their conversations began to dissipate and they took turns pacing back and forth from their camp to the river, which was only a few feet away. Pallu caught himself and the others glancing up at the setting sun with increased frequency, and then anxiously toward the waiting beasts.

"Do you think Kyrian and Layton are okay?" said Jezreel.

"I hope so," said Pallu. "I hope they didn't run into more wolves."

"I hope they didn't decide to abandon us and cross upriver on their own," said Zander.

"They wouldn't do that," said Pallu.

"How do you know?" said Zander. "I'm not sure I'd race back to complete strangers if I found a clear path to safety."

"You'd be surprised what people will do for the ones they love and respect," said Pallu. "Just look at what your brother did for you."

"That's different. These people don't even know us."

"I wasn't talking about us. I was talking about the prince. That's who they serve, and he asked them to protect us."

Zander offered up a slight smile of relief.

"Hey," said Ithron. Pallu looked to see Ithron pointing up

to the cliff where the wolves were.

"The wolves," said Ithron. "They're gone."

Pallu scanned the area, but he couldn't see any sign of them.

"Well, that's worrisome," said Zander.

Pallu and the others stayed in a tight circle as they looked around in all directions for the wolves.

"Guys," said Jezreel, "the sun is setting."

Shadows began to gather on the ground ahead, creeping ever so slowly toward them. Pallu glanced toward the river.

"We may have to cross," he said.

"That river hasn't let up," said Ithron. "If anything, it looks even stronger than before."

"Where are those wolves?" said Jezreel.

"Where are those knights!?" said Zander.

Pallu gazed up at the darkening sky.

"Guys, I think we're about out of time," he said.

Just then, Jezreel gasped, her face white with terror. She pointed straight ahead between the high rocks. The wolves were standing at alert, nearly obscured by the shadows. They had made their way down from the cliff. They snarled with viciousness and stared at Pallu and his friends head-on, their glistening eyes piercing through the dusk.

"They know," said Ithron.

"Know what?" said Zander.

"That it's dinnertime."

❧ ☙ ❧ ☙

With the wolves waiting to attack, Pallu sprang into action, hastily packing his belongings.

"Pallu, what are you doing?" said Jezreel.

"Not something I want to do," said Pallu, glancing up and down the river as he fastened his supplies back onto his saddle and mounted his rabbit.

"That's your plan?" said Ithron. "Crossing that?" He pointed to the wild current.

"Not getting eaten is my plan. The knights aren't back yet, so what else can we do?"

"Pallu, remember your soggy bread," said Zander. "You don't want to end up like that, do you?"

"No, Zander, I don't. But I only see two choices here and that one definitely seems like the better one."

"Only two?"

"Yes. We can be pulled apart alive by wolves or we can take the same plunge my soggy loaf of bread took. I vote soggy bread, and I'm pretty sure Thumps agrees."

"What about trying to outrun them?" said Zander. "Our rabbits are fast."

"So are they," said Pallu. "And run to where? You'd have to outrun them until morning."

"What do you think Ithron?" said Jezreel.

"I hate to say it, but he's right," said Ithron. "We all need to try to get across that river."

Ithron and the others began quickly packing up the few tins and canisters that were left out, and then mounted their rabbits.

"Let's go closer to the river," yelled Pallu over the raging waters.

None of them said a word as they delicately steered their rabbits toward the water. As loud as the river was, Pallu could hear his heart beating out of his chest. He glanced back to see the large, white wolves moving forward with the shadows, growling louder and louder, saliva dripping from their mouths. He shifted his gaze to the sky, wishing he could somehow will the sun to stay.

They arrived at the river's edge just as he watched the sun slowly sink into the dark orange and purple horizon.

"Get ready!" he yelled. "When the sun is gone, I'll yell, and we can all go in at once!"

He wondered how he and Thumps were going to avoid being overtaken by the raging rapids and thrown against the rocks.

Pallu glanced nervously at the rabbits' large feet just inches from the rushing water. He could feel the cold spray from the water against his face, as if daring him to enter. He gripped his rabbit's reins tightly, afraid to make the move, but even more afraid not to. As chilly as he felt near the water, his hands were sweating profusely. He could see the others looked as terrified as he was.

He gazed up, as the sun was disappearing into the purple oblivion.

"On my mark," yelled Pallu. "One…"

The wolves howled, nearly startling him off his rabbit.

"Two…"

The light from the sun vanished and the second Pallu looked back, he saw that the wolves had already begun their lightning-fast sprint directly toward them.

He was about to yell 'three' but he was interrupted by a faint yell that came from upriver. He glanced quickly and spotted Kyrian and Layton wildly motioning for the group to come their way.

"Guys, follow me, now!" yelled Pallu to the others, as he led his rabbit toward the knights as quickly as he could.

"Run, Thumps, run!" he yelled, struggling to hold on as the rabbit sprinted forward, as if Thumps knew they were in life-threatening danger. He glanced back to see the others racing for their lives, but the wolves were rapidly gaining ground.

"Faster, Thumps!"

The two knights were heading back upriver as Pallu tried his best to help Thumps catch up.

They rode through brush and trees, navigating over rocks and through tall grass, and avoided any obstacles that were in their path. Pallu nearly panicked when he felt something come up beside him, but it was Zander rushing past on his rabbit. Ithron and Jezreel raced past him on his left, leaving him and Thumps last—not a place he relished being at the moment. He glanced back to see the wolves almost upon him.

"Thumps, you have to go faster!"

As the group got farther and farther ahead of him, he contemplated steering Thumps into the river, but he got distracted when he spotted Kyrian and Layton arguing about something up ahead.

To his surprise, Kyrian turned his horse around and began racing back toward him as Layton continued to protest even more wildly. Kyrian drew his sword as he charged forward past the others, each of them turning their heads in horror as he passed them.

The wolves were snapping at Thumps's tail, and Pallu could almost feel their hot breath behind him as they growled with hunger. He wasn't ready to die.

Pallu leaned forward, hoping it would help Thumps gain speed, but he lost his balance and held onto the reins for dear life. The wolves came up beside him and chomped at Thumps. They barely missed him. Thumps continued running as fast as he ever had before and Pallu steered him in zigzag movements to deter the wolves. He struggled to hold on as he saw Kyrian getting closer, his horse kicking up dirt as it galloped like lightning.

"Keep going!" yelled Kyrian as he approached, raising his sword to strike. "See you on the other side!"

Pallu kept charging ahead, horrified at the thought of Sir Kyrian facing the wolves alone. As he headed quickly toward the others, he glanced back to see the knight slashing wildly with his sword at the vicious beasts as they all attacked at once. Pallu continued riding Thumps through rocks and dirt and over a large fallen tree branch.

Just as he straightened his balance on Thumps, he heard a horrifying scream behind him that rattled him to the bone. His stomach rose to his throat as he realized what had happened. He could see the others up ahead looking back in terror. He was afraid to look back, but felt he had to.

As Thumps soared over a large rock, Pallu turned his head just in time to see the wolves overtake Kyrian and his horse. They leapt on him, one after the other and tore him and his horse apart. Pallu's heart sunk. One of the bravest men he'd ever met had sacrificed his life for him and his friends.

He returned his attention forward, glancing back on occasion through his watery eyes at the horrific scene. He was determined not to let Sir Kyrian's death be in vain. Just as he caught up to the others, he turned around to see three of the wolves racing forward once again, while the other wolves continued to eat the remaining flesh.

"They're coming back!" he yelled to the others.

The group picked up speed as the wolves got closer, until they came to an enormous fallen tree that blocked their path and extended into the river, partially submerged. Layton's steed bucked when the knight slowed him to a halt. The others were forced to stop as well, in spite of the approaching wolves.

"What do we do?!" yelled Zander. "We're trapped!"

"No, get in the river!" yelled Layton. "This is the crossing! The trunk has blocked the current at least halfway across the river. Go now. Quickly!"

Pallu watched nervously as Ithron and Jezreel rode their rabbits into the evening water, the luminescent moon rising over the horizon. They seemed to be doing okay as long as they remained alongside the trunk.

Layton waved for Zander to hurry in next, and then Pallu.

As he led Thumps to the water, Pallu glanced over to see the wolves approaching. Layton drew his sword.

"No!" yelled Pallu.

"You just go!" said Layton. "Quickly! Get across that river!"

Pallu tried to hold on to Thumps as the rabbit swam along the fallen trunk. He could see the others ahead in the moonlit river. All he could do was hold on to Thumps and hope.

He glanced back to see Layton slashing his sword at one of the wolves, slicing its nose. That wolf backed away but, another leapt forward. Layton's horse bucked wildly, kicking the white beast back. Their white fur shimmered, glowing in the darkness. Layton quickly turned his horse around and led it into the river, the wolf nipping at its tail.

Pallu nearly fell into the water as he looked back in terror to see Layton on his horse entering the water, while the three wolves climbed onto the trunk one by one, following him. They walked a few paces, but two wolves stopped and turned around, frightened by the rapids crashing against the trunk. The third wolf continued forward, snapping at Layton from above. The knight jabbed at the wolf with his sword but he couldn't reach it.

Pallu returned his focus forward, relieved that Sir Layton had made it into the water. Though it was dark, the moon was full and he could see his friends up ahead passing the end of the trunk and entering the wild part of the river. They seemed to be struggling and were forced downriver by the strong current.

"Pallu, look out!" yelled Layton from behind.

Pallu looked back to his left just in time to see the wolf racing toward him on the partially submerged trunk.

"Swim faster, Thumps!" yelled Pallu.

The large, white creature thrashed toward Pallu with

intensity. Holding tightly to the reins, he fought to make it past the trunk as the wolf stood at the very edge of it. He passed the trunk and the force of the water immediately threw Thumps to the right. Pallu attempted to paddle with one of his hands, but it was to no avail.

"You're almost there!" yelled Layton from behind. "Keep going! Don't go against the current!"

Pallu held on for dear life, but he lost his balance and fell into the violent river. Swimming became a losing battle. He just wasn't strong enough and the water was much too powerful. He thrashed around intensely with every goal of saving himself, but his muscles began to cramp and wear out. He realized and determined in his mind that he wouldn't have the ability to beat the current.

Pallu decided to at least try to get Thumps to safety. He mustered every ounce of energy and strength that he had left in him. He brought his knees up to his chest and made a huge push with his legs toward the rear end of his rabbit, pushing Thumps closer to the safety of the riverbank. Exhausted, he let his arms go limp as the water flowed and furiously raged around him, and with a last breath, Pallu succumbed to the force of the rapids and allowed the cherished memories of his life to replace the fear in his mind. He closed his eyes tightly and allowed himself to sink and be taken with the river's current.

ꟷ ꟷ ꟷ ꟷ

The next thing Pallu knew, he was lying on his side, spitting up water on the riverbed.

He looked up to see Zander, Ithron, and Jezreel sitting around him with their rabbits. Both fear and relief were plastered on their faces. He was told that in an act of unequivocal courage, Layton had gotten off his horse midstream and fought with the current while he swam toward Pallu. Layton was able to successfully grab him and pull him across the river.

Pallu rolled onto his back, thankful to be on solid, muddy ground and grateful to be alive. It was all, thanks to the courage of two knights whom he had barely just met. He especially thought of Sir Kyrian, whose tremendous, gut-wrenching sacrifice would not be forgotten.

CHAPTER SIXTEEN

Pallu opened his eyes to find that he was still lying on the ground. He must've dozed off, though it couldn't have been for long because his hair was still wet and his clothes were drenched. He vaguely recalled Zander looking down at him, encouraging him to rest while they all set up camp. He sat up to look around. Thumps was half asleep next to him and the friends were nowhere to be found. He spotted some canvas tents set up back by the trees and figured the others must be there. As he slowly rose, he noticed Sir Layton kneeling by the river with his head down; he was mourning his lost friend.

Pallu wondered how long the two knights had been friends. He wanted to thank Sir Layton for saving him, but he didn't want to disturb him quite yet. For now, he quietly led Thumps back toward the trees so he could set up camp and find a good spot for a camp fire. On his way, he heard a wolf howl and the hairs on his arms stood up. He stopped to hear where it was coming from, afraid to even breathe in case they could sense him. Then he heard it again. Wherever it was, it sounded far away. He turned and realized it was coming from across the Galoran River. He exhaled and continued on toward the trees.

Once Pallu found a good spot by a tall tree, he set up his tent and unpacked his belongings. Still soaked, he peeled off his wet shirt and trousers, leaving his undershorts on, and stepped back out to hang the wet clothes over some branches to dry. Just as he began to set out tinder and kindling among the logs for his fire, he heard footsteps behind him. He turned to see Zander approaching. He had a confused look on this face.

"Pallu, what in Izhar's ghost are you doing!? There's a lady out here!"

"I know there's a lady here," said Pallu. "That's why I'm still wearing these soaking wet undershorts, so be thankful for her presence, my friend." He smiled, glad to see Zander's face.

"This is too much for my eyes," said Zander. "This can't be unseen."

"What can't be unseen?" said Jezreel, arriving with Ithron. "Oh!" she added, spotting Pallu. She immediately averted her eyes and stifled a laugh.

"Pallu, what are you doing half-naked?" said Ithron.

"What does it look like I'm doing?" said Pallu. "I'm building a fire and drying my clothes," he said, pointing to the tree branches and the fire that he finally got started. "Wet clothes make me itch and give me rashes. You can all do the same and join me if you like, unless you'd rather swash around in yours."

"That's not a bad idea, actually," said Ithron, who began peeling off his clothes as well.

"Actually, it's a good idea," said Jezreel. "It beats getting sick." She walked into her tent to undress in privacy.

Zander rolled his eyes and shyly started peeling off his wet shirt and trousers. Once undressed, he covered his bare skin with his arms in embarrassment. "At least there are no ladies present now," he said.

Just as he said that, Jezreel came back out, wrapped in a small blanket that had somehow remained partially dry in her sack through the river crossing. Pallu and Ithron couldn't help but laugh at Zander.

Pallu laughed so much that his stomach hurt. Giving it a rest, and with a large smile, he stared into the dancing fire when he heard a noise coming from the direction of the river. It was Layton. They watched as he tied his horse up by the rabbits and approached the campfire.

Everyone was silent, no doubt unsure what to say, but Pallu felt he should at least say something.

"You must be freezing in those clothes," said Pallu. "We're all getting warm by the fire."

Layton offered a weak smile. "So, I see," he said.

"We're terribly sorry about Sir Kyrian," said Jezreel. "He was a brave man to do what he did. We're eternally grateful for his sacrifice."

Layton appeared on the verge of tears, but held his composure. "There were none more brave," he said. "Someone will wish that they'd never been born once I find out who's behind this."

"If it weren't for the two of you, we'd all be dead," said Pallu. "You risked everything for us, and for me. Thank you for saving my life."

"We did our duty," said Layton. "Nothing more and nothing less. I'm glad you're all alive."

Layton patted him on the back, smiled, and walked over to the trees, where he stripped down to his undershorts. As he turned toward the group, Pallu was dumbfounded at how muscular the man was.

"Wow, you're like a perfect specimen," said Pallu. "You're buff!"

"Pallu!" said Zander. "What does that even mean? Buff?"

"You've never heard of buff?" said Pallu. "You know, it's

the opposite of puff and fluff." He patted his belly causing it to wobble around. "I'm puff, and maybe a little fluff, but he's definitely buff."

"Maybe this 'stripping down' stuff wasn't such a good idea," said Ithron, covering Jezreel's eyes while she giggled and slapped his hand away.

"Yeah, on second thought," said Zander staring at Layton, "I'd rather look at Pallu's naked body. I'm beginning to feel inferior."

"I think maybe he should put his clothes back on," said Ithron.

"All I know," said Pallu, taking a large piece of bread out of his sack, "is that I want to look like that one day." He pointed at Layton with the piece of bread and took a large bite.

"Well it's not going to happen by eating *that*, my friend," said Layton.

"I know," said Pallu with his mouth full. "That's why I said *one day*. Today is not that day. Tomorrow probably won't be either, now that I think of it."

Layton smirked and glanced back and forth between Pallu's stomach and the enormous loaf of bread he was about to take another large bite from.

"Don't do it," said Zander.

Just as Pallu stopped mid-bite, everyone began laughing, even Layton. Pallu joined in the laughter, too, satisfied that he managed to lift their spirits.

ꕥ ꕥ ꕥ ꕥ

After a deep, restful sleep, Pallu awoke bright and early. He knew the smell of his cooking would fill the air and rouse anyone who might still be sleeping. He wanted to surprise everyone with a hearty breakfast after the horrific ordeal and tragic loss from the day before. At the very least, it would fuel their bodies for the journey back to Old Vynterra.

"Pallu, are you using magic?" said Zander, just emerging from his tent.

"Magic?" said Pallu, wondering what he was getting at.

"How else can you explain the fact that you never run out of food? Those food sacks must be endless!"

"I just like to be prepared, my friend."

Zander grabbed a piece of bacon from a stone next to the fire and watched as Pallu cooked the last of his flat bread.

Soon after, Ithron approached and tossed his packed-up belongings on the ground.

"Did you kill a wild boar this morning?" he said, grabbing a piece of bacon before going to his now dry clothes and putting them on.

Jezreel came out of her tent already dressed and began packing up. Pallu noticed she looked really down, no doubt from yesterday's devastation.

"Jez are you okay?" said Pallu. "Are you hungry?"

"Thanks Pallu. It smells amazing, but I just don't have an appetite right now."

Ithron walked to her and gently rubbed her back as she wiped away a few tears.

"You okay?" said Ithron.

"I'm okay. Or maybe I'm not. It's like I woke up from the most horrible nightmare and it turns out to be true. I can't imagine what poor Layton is going through."

They both looked around the camp.

"Where is he?" said Jezreel. "Have any of you seen him?"

"I'm not sure, but his horse is here," said Zander. "Pallu, have you seen him?"

Pallu signaled to them with his finger to hold on, while he finished the large piece of bacon that he'd just taken a bite of.

"No," said Pallu, gulping down his food. "He's not inside his tent?"

"His tent's all packed up," said Ithron.

"I'm sure he'll be back," said Pallu.

"Oh. There he is," said Zander, pointing in the distance.

Layton was walking toward them from the river. He was holding a long, silver object in his hand that glistened in the sun as he walked.

"Did he take his sword with him?" said Ithron. "I guess that's wise. You never know what could be out there during these dark times."

Pallu began to clean up, but then turned his attention toward Layton, who was now approaching with the large sword in his hand. He looked upset and his eyes were red.

"Are you okay?" said Pallu. "That was smart to take your sword."

"It's Kyrian's," said Layton, holding the sword up, its razor-sharp tip pointing toward the sky. "He would've wanted me to have it."

Pallu's mouth dropped in disbelief.

"Wait a minute," said Zander. "How did you get his sword? You didn't—"

"I did," he said, lowering the shiny weapon. "I went back downriver to say my final farewell, and—"

"But that's impossible," said Jezreel. "The river—"

"Come look at the river," said Layton. "All of you."

Pallu and the others followed the knight to the river. When they got there, Pallu couldn't believe his eyes. The once raging waters were now calm and only inches high.

"How is it so low?" said Pallu.

"I don't know," said Layton. "I could see the sword from this side of the river, shining in the water. I was able to walk right across."

"Did you see his... um, I mean... was he..." Jezreel was

stumbling over the right words.

"This sword was the only thing left of him," said Layton, sparing her the awkwardness.

"I'm sorry to ask this," said Pallu. "I hope it's not insensitive or anything. But, how long have you known Sir Kyrian?"

"Known him?" said Layton, taken aback. "All my life," he added. "He was my brother."

Pallu's heart sank, and a chill ran through his entire body. He intuitively glanced over at Zander, whose eyes were watering as he undoubtedly thought about his own brother.

"I'm sorry," said Pallu. "I didn't know."

"None of us did," said Jezreel.

"I saw the two of you arguing before he turned his horse around," said Pallu.

The knight took a deep breath. "I wanted to be the one to go against those beasts, not him. It should have been me. I pleaded with him to let me face them. But he rode off before I could do anything. I don't even remember what his last words were."

"I do," said Pallu.

Layton looked surprised and immediately curious as he turned toward Pallu.

"First, he told me to keep going," said Pallu. "But then, the last thing he said as I rode away was, 'See you on the other side.' I'm so sorry he didn't make it like he hoped."

Layton smiled. "The other side," he echoed. "Brave to the end, that was my brother. He wasn't talking about the other side of the river. He knew he'd meet his end with those wolves. He was talking about the great beyond."

Layton held up the sword again. "See you on the other side, brother!" he yelled to the skies, sword in the air. He lowered the sword back down and touched the edge with his finger as he observed it intensely. "But not until I've used this to avenge your death."

Pallu looked at Layton's determined face, which was illuminated by the morning sun. Layton's spirit must've been catching, because even Pallu felt a little of the knight's courage enter his body. As he looked around at the others, it may have been his imagination, but they, too, seemed to be standing just a little bit taller. It appeared they were all ready to battle against this mysterious, rising evil.

ಶಿ ಛ ಶಿ ಛ

It hadn't taken long for Pallu to pack up the rest of his belongings, or so he thought. Still, the others were on their rabbits and waiting for him when he finished loading everything onto Thump's saddlebag for the journey.

As soon as he was ready, they headed off on the long trail that led back to Old Vynterra. They traveled north for a while, first through the tree-lined valley and then down a narrow, rocky path that led to a spacious expanse of green hills Pallu had remembered from the way up. The majestic mountain ranges could once again be seen in the distance on both sides, leading him to wonder what deep mysteries may lie hidden in them.

After a break, Sir Layton led them west, bypassing the Cottages, and, more importantly, the forest. All the while, Pallu kept looking out for Diamondwolves—or any other unexpected creatures, for that matter. As the trip went on and they finally made their way onto the north road to Old Vynterra, he became less and less concerned—though his mind kept returning to the others who were headed to Rhyceton. He wondered how they were faring.

Before long, the Western Gates of Old Vynterra were at last within their sights. As he squinted to see the ancient kingdom that somehow felt like home, Pallu noticed something peculiar. Hundreds—perhaps thousands—of knights were surrounding the entire kingdom, holding their bows. The army of knights extended out along the path leading toward the entrance to the gates.

He quickly rode up to Sir Layton.

"Is that normal?" he asked.

Layton shook his head. "They're on high alert. I've never seen it like that."

"It's a little intimidating," said Zander. "They're not going to mistake us and shoot their arrows at us, are they?"

"I hope not," said Layton.

"You hope not!?" said Zander. "That doesn't make me feel any safer."

They continued over a steep hill and then through the tree-lined tunnel formed by the upper branches on both sides. As the road curved, the path ahead was also filled with knights, bows in hand.

Pallu felt his stomach tighten with the thought of hundreds of arrows coming their way.

Just as Pallu and the group approached, the knights made a path for the arriving party. Slowly, the enormous iron gates opened and a decorated knight stepped forward from inside.

"Eliezer is on his way," he said to Sir Layton. "He has been notified of your return."

Sir Layton led the group further in and just as they got near the Black Castle, an old wooden carriage arrived. Two knights exited the carriage and helped Eliezer step out.

"We were expecting more of you," said Eliezer as he approached the group. "Have you any news of the prince?"

"We believe he and the others are in Rhyceton," said Layton as he dismounted, a servant rushing to grab the horse's reins. "But their path is a dangerous one, as was ours. My brother is dead."

"Oh, Sir Layton, I am so terribly sorry," said Eliezer. A

look of deep pain lingered on his face. "Was his life taken by the wolves?"

"It was," said Layton.

"I have always respected and admired your brother," said Eliezer. "I'll light a candle for him this evening. It was Sir Ulric who told us of the dreadful attack on your camp."

"He's alive?"

"Yes, yes. A bit worse for wear, but he'll recover. As you can see, we've engaged the entire Vynterran Guard to protect the kingdom."

"A wise move."

"Tell me, Sir Layton. Is it true that these may be the Diamondwolves of old, as Sir Ulric and his companions have reported?"

"I can assure you it is, Archminister. But my brother's sword shall put an end to whoever is behind this barbarism once and for all." He raised the sword's black leather hilt slightly from its scabbard to show Eliezer.

"A worthy and justifiable quest," said Eliezer. "But I fear this is a far different enemy than we've faced before. The wolves are just the beginning." He nodded for the carriage to leave and waved for the group to join him on the path that would take them to Valorian's Castle. "Come," he said. "We have much to discuss."

Pallu and the others dismounted their rabbits and handed their reins to a waiting stable keeper. They followed Eliezer and the two knights on the path toward the prince's castle. It wasn't long before villagers gathered around them, shouting questions from both sides.

"Where is the prince?" said a bearded man on their right.

"Is everyone else dead?!" shouted an old lady.

"Why isn't the prince with you?" said a man standing next to her.

Within seconds, the guards rushed in and pushed all the

villagers back.

"The prince is in Rhyceton!" shouted Sir Layton. "Now, please, go back to your homes."

During their walk along the path and through the Western Village, Layton relayed the story of their misadventures to Eliezer. Pallu and the others followed closely behind. Most of the villagers were now respectfully keeping their distance, except for a small group of young children who were following behind them, giggling.

"With all due respect, Archminister," said Layton, "I think we need to send a party to Rhyceton to escort the prince home. He'll need all the help he can get if he's to make it back safely."

"First and foremost," said Eliezer, "we are duty bound to guard our kingdom against great threat, as written in the archives and signed by the prince himself. He is a man who looks out for his people before his own well-being. The threats from our neighboring forest are not ones to be ignored, but therein lies our dilemma. If we send a small party, they'll fare no better against the Diamondwolves than you did."

"Then let's send a large party," said Layton. "There will still be more than enough men to guard the kingdom. Fifty men are all I ask for. I'll lead them myself."

"Make that fifty-one," said Pallu, loud enough for Layton and Eliezer to hear. "I want to go, too."

Zander elbowed him. "Are you crazy?" he whispered.

"We'll have fifty other knights around us," Pallu whispered back. "They'll keep us safe."

"I think this is just your leftover guilt speaking," whispered Zander to Pallu. "You know, for not going to Rhyceton."

Layton turned his head and smiled. "I admire your spirit, my friend, but I meant fifty *trained* men."

They descended the hill that marked the end of the Western Village, and the group of children following behind them ran off after shouting and waving goodbye.

"The thought of sending our precious knights into harm's way against an unknown enemy gives me pause," said Eliezer. "There is no historic precedent that favors a clear decision. But your point is noted, Sir Layton. The prince is indeed in need of our help."

Eliezer paused in thought as they proceeded through the Road of Sorrow. After they were about halfway through, he stopped and looked at Layton. "I'll grant you your fifty men, but I have one stipulation," he said.

"Of course. What is it?"

Eliezer rested his hand on Layton's shoulder. "You must wait till morning."

"Morning!? But time is of the essence."

"Oh yes, time *is* of the essence," said Eliezer, agreeing. "But so is the safety of our men. I won't have all of you wandering in the dark at the mercy of those beasts."

"We'll have enough to fight them."

"I admire your spirit, my friend," said Eliezer, echoing Layton's own words to Pallu, "but you must be careful that the anger from your brother's death is not clouding the wiser decision. The prince may already be in Rhyceton, perfectly safe within the kingdom's walls and under the protection of his father's knights. I cannot risk a slaughter of fifty men. You'll leave in the morning. As regent in the prince's absence, that is my decision."

Layton averted his eyes, clearly unhappy, but conceded to Eliezer's authority. "As you wish, Archminister," he said.

The two men resumed walking while Pallu and the others followed quietly.

"One other thing," said Eliezer as they approached the Eastern Village. "There are different paths to Rhyceton. One is lesser-known and far more rugged, but it will save you time, which I know is of great concern to all of us. Perhaps a bit more relevant, you will not find any trees along that path."

"Fewer shadows," said Layton. "I'll take it."

"Good. If you will be so gracious as to join me this evening at dinner, I will have a map prepared; drawn and ready."

Layton smiled. "Excellent. I'll gather the knights immediately and tell them the plan."

With that, Layton departed the group as Pallu, Jezreel, Ithron, and Zander followed Eliezer to the castle.

ಐ ಛ ಐ ಛ

After a comfortable night's sleep in the castle, Pallu was up bright and early. On one hand, he was excited to see Sir Layton and the fifty knights ride off to Rhyceton, even though it looked like a stormy day. But on the other, he was worried to death about how Ezstasia and the others were doing. He wanted to be a part of their rescue, but he knew there was no way he could go without getting in the way. Still, as he walked down the palace corridor, he couldn't help but dream. He turned around and headed into the armory, attempting to be quiet so as not to attract anyone's attention.

He picked up a large sword that had a white dragon's head on the pommel and branches with leaves carved into the black wooden handle. He realized that it was much heavier than it looked as he carefully waved it around. He tried on an armor breastplate, but he couldn't fit the straps around his large waist. Frustrated, he hung it back on the wall. Next to it, he noticed a collection of dark gray masked helmets. They were all lined up on a mahogany shelf, each with different designs. He selected one of them and put it over his head, lowering the mask with a squeaky thud. It restricted his peripheral vision to the point where he could only see straight ahead. How could knights even fight like this?

Just as he turned to fetch the sword, he bumped into something to his right. He panicked and moved backward, hitting an even larger object. Within seconds, a deafening crash made him nearly jump out of his skin. His stomach in knots, Pallu turned to see what kind of damage he had done. He lifted the metal eye cover and gasped when he saw that he had knocked over an entire suit of armor that had been on display. The pieces were scattered across the entire floor. He quickly went to pull the helmet off his head, but it was stuck.

Before he could even think, the sound of footsteps echoed in the hall. Just then, Zander came skidding into the doorway.

"Zander, I'm so glad it's you!"

"Pallu?" said Zander. "What in Izhar's ghost are you doing? I heard a—"

Zander stopped mid-sentence when he saw the suit of armor sprawled out on the floor. "Oh!"

"Never mind that," said Pallu. "Help me get this helmet off my head."

"Are you serious!?" said Zander. "Is it really stuck? Or is it your brain that's stuck?" he added, laughing at his own cheesy joke.

"Hurry up and help me!" said Pallu. "Stop fooling around."

"Uh… with the looks of this room and your stuck head, I'd say *you* were the one fooling around."

Zander grabbed the helmet with both hands and tried to help Pallu get it off, but it was hurting too much.

"It's not budging!" said Zander.

"Maybe go get some butter," said Pallu.

"You're thinking of food at this moment?"

"Yes, it will help it slide off."

They heard a loud horn blaring from one of the open, arched windows.

"What's that?" said Pallu.

"It came from outside. I think the knights are leaving."

Before he could respond, Zander was off and running toward a large window in an alcove opposite the armory. Pallu followed him. He was still wearing the clunky helmet and trying to pull it off his head as he ran; the metal mask clinking with each step.

Pallu couldn't believe how beautiful the view was, even though storm clouds threatened in the distance and a thick fog was setting in—not to mention he also had to turn his head in all directions to see anything through the helmet. Beyond the gardens, throngs of people crowded around as the double row of fifty knights on horseback followed Sir Layton. The rider next to him was carrying a gold and blue flag with the symbol of a tree stitched into it. As Layton rode to the front gates and stopped, the knights on the outside perimeter parted to clear a path.

"Hey, what's that?" said Zander.

"What's what?" said Pallu, lifting the metal face cover again on his helmet.

"Way out there in the distance."

Pallu turned his head toward where Zander was pointing just as the helmet's face cover dropped shut again. Frustrated, he tried to pull the helmet off his head again, but to no avail. Zander pointed him in the right direction. Through the eye slits, he could see what looked like thousands of figures coming toward the castle on the winding road in the distance.

"Is that an army?" he said, trying to make out what they looked like in the fog.

"I can't tell," said Zander.

They continued to watch as the horde came closer.

"Are those even people?" said Zander.

Pallu stared intently through the helmet's opening. It was difficult to see them through the dense mist, staggering as they marched forward. The line seemed to go on forever. Further past the horde, in the distant sky, came flashes of lightning, rumblings and peals of thunder.

"Could this get any creepier?" said Zander.

"Zander, I don't know *what* that is," said Pallu. "There are thousands upon thousands of them. Do you think the knights even know they're approaching?"

Zander held his head against the large window and looked down.

"It doesn't look like they do," he said. "People aren't even looking in that direction."

"We have to go warn them," said Pallu. "Now!"

Just as they were about to run out of the alcove, Miss Tee entered.

"What was that loud ruckus I hea… oh dear," she said, noticing Pallu's helmet.

"We have to go warn the knights," said Pallu. "There's something coming."

"*Something?*" said Miss Tee, alarmed. "Well, you should take that helmet off or you won't see a thing."

"Um… about that," he said. "I can't."

She reached over and flipped a lever on the right side of his helmet, loosening the helmet's front and back halves as she removed them both from his head.

"I'll return this to its rightful spot," she said.

"Thanks, Miss Tee. Oh, and somebody also knocked over a suit of armor."

"*Something* is coming," she said, still dwelling on that. "And *somebody* knocked over the armor? You're a bit of an ambiguous fellow, aren't you?"

"Please tell Eliezer about the something that's coming!" he yelled as he ran past her and into the hall with Zander.

As soon as they got outside in the threatening skies, Pallu and Zander were forced to pummel through hundreds of villagers.

"Pallu!" yelled Jezreel. She was standing in the crowd with Ithron just where he and Zander were passing.

"There's an army or something, coming," said Pallu. "We're headed to warn Sir Layton."

Jezreel's eyes widened as she tugged at Ithron's arm.

"Ithron, we need to get inside the castle," she said, frantically pulling him. "I don't want to be out here."

As Jezreel dragged a confused Ithron back toward the castle, Pallu raced forward though the crowd, Zander at his side. Finally, they had the knights in their sight.

"They haven't left yet," said Pallu, half out of breath.

He approached the two rows of knights, running between the horses, just as they started moving forward.

"Wait!" he yelled. "Don't go yet!"

Sir Layton stopped his horse and turned it around.

"Pallu?" said Layton, looking slightly annoyed. "I thought I told you we can only use trained knights."

"No, it... isn't... that," said Pallu, trying to catch his breath. "There's something coming toward us. We saw it from the castle."

"What is it?"

"That's the thing," said Zander. "We aren't sure. But there are thousands of them."

"What are you talking about?" said Layton. "Thousands of *them*?"

"I'm telling you," said Zander. "It was at least fifty times the men you have."

"I saw it, too," said Pallu, stepping outside the castle's

open gates. "Coming from that direction." He pointed northeast.

Layton addressed his men. "Knights, advance behind me!"

Pallu and Zander walked between the horses as the knights slowly pushed forward past the gates.

"Shouldn't we be leaving this to them?" said Zander, looking worried.

"Definitely," said Pallu. "I don't want to be anywhere near whatever's coming."

"So, let's get out of here," said Zander.

"Wait, I just want to see if anyone needs our help," said Pallu.

"You confuse me. One minute you're a chicken and the next you want to be a knight."

"What's wrong with that?" said Pallu.

As the oncoming horde rounded a curve that came from the east, Layton stopped and held his hand up, signaling the knights to halt. Pallu instantly knew that Layton had seen them. He could hear his own pounding heartbeat as they watched to see exactly *what* was coming from the distance.

"Can you see anything yet?" Pallu asked Zander, whose eyes were wide as he shook his head.

"Bows ready!" yelled Layton, and they all drew their arrows toward the air.

Pallu watched and waited, holding his breath. When he saw the horde start to appear on the horizon through the dense mist, he began to back up. Zander inched backward as soon as he noticed Pallu was no longer next to him.

Little by little, the enormous throng of uninvited visitors began to appear.

Layton kept his hand up waiting to give the signal to fire the arrows.

Pallu saw that someone at the front of the horde was waving a large flag back and forth. He squinted to see it through the fog. It appeared to be red and black with a sigil in the center.

"The twin ravens!" said Layton. "It's the Rhyceton flag. That's the prince!"

"Prince Alazar has returned!" yelled one of the knights behind Layton. The knights lowered their bows and began to cheer.

"That must be all of Rhyceton with him," said another knight.

"Wait," yelled Layton, lifting his hand to quiet the cheering. "Something isn't right."

Pallu looked back toward the crowd of people; they were emerging out of the thick fog. Many of them were limping and dirty and others appeared to be bloody and lacking strength. It wasn't long until he spotted Ezstasia and a little girl both sitting on Tia. They were about ten people deep into the crowd. Her rabbit wasn't hard to miss among the people, horses, and carts.

"Look Zander, it's Ezstasia!" he said, more than a little relieved. "And I bet that's Lanzzie behind her!"

Zander gazed out intently at the huge swarm of people as the skies rumbled again with thunder.

"Where's my brother?" said Zander. "I don't see my brother."

CHAPTER SEVENTEEN

As she rode with the massive caravan, Ezstasia was exhausted, but she counted her blessings knowing that the people of Rhyceton had to face a horrific nightmare back at their kingdom. She couldn't imagine having to fend off those wolves. She felt especially bad for the sweet little girl that she had ridden with for the entire journey. The poor girl hadn't uttered a word to Ezstasia; she didn't respond to any of her questions either. Ezstasia wondered what exactly the girl had witnessed or where her family was. She tried once again to get her talking.

"Can you tell me your name, sweetie?" she said.

The girl was silent, though she'd occasionally twirl her curly hair with her small finger. She looked about four or five.

The thunder rumbled again, just as it had been doing on and off for the last hour. As she patted the little girl's shoulder to encourage her not to worry, the skies opened up and the rain began to fall. She lifted the child's hood from her dark brown robe and gently placed it over her head to keep her from getting wet.

Ezstasia looked ahead to the front of the group and spotted an army of knights in the distance slowly coming toward them. They appeared to be holding a flag, which she assumed to be the flag of Old Vynterra. It was a sight for sore eyes and she couldn't help but smile with the thought of seeing her friends again.

She looked forward to being back in the prince's castle and couldn't wait to finally rest and take a long, warm bath. She recalled the lush aromas of lavender and lemon oil that had arisen like a flowery mist from the inviting bathwater. It felt like a lifetime ago.

"We're nearly there," she said to the little girl, holding her arm around her for comfort as the rain continued to fall steadily.

The girl turned her head toward her for the first time.

"Will my sister be there?" she said, small tears forming in her large brown eyes.

"Were you with your sister back home?" said Ezstasia.

"Yes, but we were separated when our auntie..." Her voice trailed off.

"What about your auntie?" said Ezstasia. "Were you with her? Do you have a mum and dad?"

"Just our auntie," said the girl. "I don't know where she is. Or my sister."

"Well, I'll help you find them both when we get to Old Vynterra. I promise. My name is Ezstasia. I'd love to know yours."

The little girl faced forward and was silent for a moment.

"Aurelia," she said. "But my sister calls me Pickles."

"Pickles!? That's a cute name. Let me guess. You like pickles?"

"Yes. How did you know?" said Aurelia, looking back at Ezstasia with wide eyes.

"Lucky guess, I suppose." She couldn't help but chuckle. "Well, shall I call you Pickles or Aurelia?"

"Either is fine," said the girl, returning her gaze forward.

Ezstasia prayed she'd be able to reconnect the girl with her family. So many people had been separated in the chaos, and some lost family members to the wolves.

"I like your bunny," said Aurelia, finally starting to open up.

"Her name's Tia," said Ezstasia. "And I can tell she likes you, too."

The girl looked up at Ezstasia and smiled as the rain washed the last few remnants of tears from her precious face.

Ezstasia looked up to see the knights racing forward in the distance as a loud clap of thunder echoed through the skies. The noise startled her, as well as many of the horses. They whinnied and bucked while their riders did their best to calm them. Tia was completely oblivious.

Ezstasia held Aurelia tightly and then noticed Lanzzie ride up on her right.

"Why are there so many knights?" said Lanzzie. "Do you think something happened?"

"I don't know," she said.

The king held up his hand and the horsemen stopped. One by one, the horses and wagons came to a halt, and the large group followed suit. The Vynterran knights were rapidly approaching.

Ezstasia held onto Aurelia as she watched nervously with Lanzzie.

"I'm sure everything's fine," said Fin, riding up beside Lanzzie. "The knights aren't drawing their bows or pulling out their swords."

"I hope my brother made it back okay," said Randin, just arriving as the rain finally let up.

"I'm sure he's fine," said Lanzzie, "oh… wait! There's Pallu! He's running behind those knights. And Zander is right next to him!"

As the king, the prince, and their knights greeted their

compatriots in an emotional reunion, the prince motioned for the rest of the caravan to resume moving forward.

Ezstasia and the others rode their rabbits toward Pallu and Zander. Randin leapt off his rabbit and ran as fast as he could toward his brother. It warmed her heart to see the twins embrace one another with such joy and relief.

Ezstasia dismounted and helped Aurelia off of Tia. Before she could even say anything, Pallu approached with a big grin on his face.

"My best friend!" he said as he gave her a bear hug that practically took her breath away.

"And who do we have here?" he said, looking down at the little girl.

"This is Aurelia," said Ezstasia, "but her sister calls her Pickles. She's looking for her sister and auntie. We have to help her."

Pallu bent down to face the little girl. She looked alarmed and hid behind Ezstasia.

"I can show you where to get the best pickles in the world," he said.

"You can?" said Aurelia, peeking at Pallu from behind Ezstasia's right leg.

"You bet I can! You happened to have come across the best pickle finder ever. In fact, I—"

"Pickles!" Ezstasia heard a girl yell from a few meters away. She was about ten or eleven years old and waved frantically toward them. She was standing next to a smiling redheaded woman.

"Aurelia! Over here!" said the woman.

"My sister! My auntie! There they are!" she said to Ezstasia. She gave Ezstasia a big hug and ran off toward them.

Ezstasia felt her eyes tear up as she saw the two young girls embracing. Their aunt bent down and hugged them both with a motherly affection.

Relieved to see Aurelia reunited with her family, she looked around for the rest of her friends.

"Pallu," she said. "Where are Jez and Ithron?"

"They're fine," he said. "They're in the castle. Jez dragged him in like a little puppy."

"And he followed?" said Fin, approaching.

"And... he followed. He does that a lot now. But anyway, she was kind of scared."

"Of what?" said Fin.

"Of you," said Pallu. "All of you. We saw so many of you and it was foggy and we didn't know who you were. Come to think of it, I'm still not sure. Is this really the *entire* kingdom of Rhyceton?"

Ezstasia looked around at the knights and saw that they were helping the new visitors place their belongings on horses and donkeys. Some were helping the tired, injured, and weak climb onto empty wagons that had just been brought in from Old Vynterra.

"It was terrible," she said, addressing her friends. "When we arrived in Rhyceton, we found total chaos. People were missing. There was damage everywhere. All the people were barricaded inside of their homes. There must've been a few thousand housed in the king's castle alone."

"What happened?" said Pallu.

"It was the Diamondwolves. They attacked the kingdom the day before we got there. The people were afraid they'd return, so the prince convinced the king to bring his entire kingdom to Old Vynterra."

"That was pretty daring," said Pallu. "Especially knowing those wolves are wandering around out there."

"You're not kidding! Luckily, Eliezer gave the prince a map with multiple routes. The prince selected one in particular. He thought it would be the safest way to get us back here."

"Did you see any of the wolves?"

"Thankfully, no. None of us did. They were gone when we got there. And it's a complete mystery as to where they went."

"I know where they went," said Pallu, with a tone of deep sadness. "They attacked our group on our way back. In fact, we'd all be dead if it weren't for Sir Kyrian and Sir Layton."

"What!?" Ezstasia felt her stomach drop.

"Trust me, you don't want to be anywhere near those wolves."

"This really happened!?" she said as she looked at Pallu. His eyes were becoming red and he looked away. "They really came for you... I can't believe it! I'm so relieved you're all okay; I don't know what I would—" Ezstasia couldn't finish what she was saying; she felt she might cry at any moment. She couldn't imagine the thought of losing her friends, especially Pallu.

"Well, not all of us are okay," said Pallu. "Sir Kyrian gave his life to save us. His brother Layton is pretty torn up about it."

"Wait," said Fin. "Sir Layton is his brother?"

Pallu nodded. "We were all surprised, too."

"Prince Alazar will be devastated," said Ezstasia. "They were close." With all that she was hearing, she couldn't hold her emotions in any longer. Tears were welling up in her eyes.

"He already is," said Fin. He pointed up ahead to the prince.

They all looked up and saw that the prince was speaking to Sir Layton. Prince Alazar had lowered himself onto one knee, in honor of Sir Kyrian. His heartbreak was evident. The prince wiped the tears from his face with the back of his hand, which crushed Ezstasia more than she would've expected it to. She couldn't imagine what the prince was feeling—or how Layton felt, for that matter.

She felt devastated for the two of them. She remembered how highly the prince spoke of Sir Kyrian when he introduced her to him. She looked over at Pallu, who bowed his head in sadness, and then glanced back over at the prince.

The whole world seemed to go silent for a moment. Sir Layton held his composure and pulled out the sword that had belonged to his brother only a short time ago.

"Let's get back," said Pallu, turning his gaze toward the people of Rhyceton. "The new visitors may need our help."

The crowd proceeded toward the castle gates. As they walked, Ezstasia considered what Pallu had said. Many of the people from Rhyceton would need help finding loved ones and many others would need their injuries nursed. The prince's servants might need help finding rooms to get everyone settled in. There was much to do.

As they made their way toward the castle, the most important issue of all stayed on her mind: What exactly was causing the Diamondwolves and dark magic to reappear after so many centuries? And what would be the plan to protect themselves against this threat that has already taken many innocent lives?

ဆ os ဆ os

Finally back in her room at the castle, Ezstasia remained busy moving her belongings around to make space for Lanzzie and Jezreel. Because of the arrival of the refugees from Rhyceton, everyone had been required to open up their chambers to make room for the new guests.

On the way to the castle, Pallu and Zander had recounted the details of their awful experience, and shared about how two of the bravest knights they'd ever known had risked their own lives to save theirs. Ezstasia made a mental note to offer her condolences and her gratitude to Sir Layton.

As Ezstasia placed some of her things in the small, wooden box on the desk, her mind drifted between the mysterious forest, the vicious wolves, and the changing river. She couldn't help but wonder what could be next.

Her thoughts were interrupted by a loud knock on the door.

She closed the box and walked to the door to open it. It was Lanzzie and Jezreel, holding piles of clothing and other belongings in their arms. Ezstasia greeted them and grabbed some of the clothes off the top of Lanzzie's pile and placed them on the bed. Lanzzie and Jezreel set the rest of their items down on the bed as well.

"You should see it outside," said Jezreel, her face beaming. "Now that the rain stopped, the village is full of life. The shops and the bakeries are open and they're all giving things away to the people from Rhyceton. People are even singing songs at the Crazy Root. It's wonderful!"

"But before we go out there," said Lanzzie, "the prince wants to see us all in his study."

"Do you know why?" said Ezstasia.

"No, but Miss Tee was the one who told us, and she said it was important. We told her we'd come and get you. The others are heading there now. Are you ready to go?"

"I suppose I am," she said. She took a mental note of all the items that she wanted to organize once she returned to her room.

‮   ‰ ‱

Ezstasia felt her stomach flutter as they entered the hall that led to the prince's study. The last time she was in this hall, she was returning from the Black Castle to confront the prince. The situation was now entirely different. She wondered what news he might have for them. She hoped it was not to inform them that they were all going to be sent home without any explanation of what had been happening in the Human Lands.

As she, Lanzzie, and Jezreel approached the three, large mahogany doors, two knights stood guard. The unusually tall one on the right tapped on the rightmost door and the other knight opened the center door.

"The prince will receive you now," said the tall knight, with a deep voice.

Lanzzie stepped into the room first and Ezstasia and Jezreel followed her. She was startled when the knight shut the door behind them. She looked around the room and noticed that the rest of her friends had already arrived and were quietly observing various objects in the study—all except for Pallu, who was nowhere to be seen. She rolled her eyes at the thought of him being late to something so important. She'd always known him as the tardy one for everything since their youth, but she thought he would make sure to be on time for this.

The prince sat at his desk signing parchments. He finished the last one and glanced up. Ezstasia, Lanzzie, and Jezreel bowed awkwardly. She wasn't quite sure what the proper etiquette was, even after all this time. There were a few open chairs placed strategically around the study, but she decided to stand just as the others were doing.

"Welcome," he said, as he rose from his chair. "Gather around. This will only take a few minutes." He looked around and then added, "Are we missing someone?"

"Pallu should be here soon," said Fin.

"Splendid," said the prince.

They waited in awkward silence and Ezstasia nervously glanced around the study. She'd forgotten how large the room was, with books from floor to ceiling along the wall behind the prince's desk. She noticed for the first time that the desk had a three-headed dragon motif carved into the legs. She wondered if it represented Trycernius. On the opposite side of the vast room stood several rows of tall bookcases and an octagon-shaped, oak map table; a thick tree trunk supported the table, which had been specifically created for drawing out maps. Intricate carvings of vines and leaves adorned the dark, wooden walls. It was fascinating to see the interior designs that were inspired by the tastes and peculiarities of Valorian. She spotted a winding stairway that led to an upper level, which looked like it housed even more books.

The door opened and Pallu walked in, out of breath.

"Sorry I'm late, Your Highness," he said. "I was... well... I fell asleep."

"Glad you could join us," said the prince, stepping around to the front of his desk to address the group.

"I've asked you all here for an important reason," he said, sounding serious as he leaned back against the edge his desk. "As I'm sure you all realize, the problem we face is far bigger and more powerful than all of us."

Everyone nodded while he looked around making direct eye contact with each of them.

"In a fortnight," the prince continued, "five kings and one queen—the heads of all six kingdoms, representing all the Human Lands—will hold court in this very castle. My father has already sent couriers to summon the other five. I've been asked to present our current predicament to the court and I'd like you all to join me."

Ezstasia breathed a sigh of relief.

"We'd be honored," said Fin.

"The answer is a definite yes," said Pallu.

"I don't really think it was a question," whispered Zander.

"Will the king be okay with having us there?" said Ezstasia, suddenly remembering Kyrian's advice to never question the prince in front of others. "I'm sorry," she added, "I didn't mean to ques—"

"Why don't you ask him yourself?" said the prince, smiling. She heard footsteps coming from the winding staircase.

Just as she turned toward it, her whole body tensed up. King Izhar the Great was descending the spiral, wooden staircase and coming right toward them. She wasn't sure what to do, so she curtseyed. Though he was known for his wisdom and compassion, the king had a very imposing presence, tall with broad shoulders, long, greying hair and beard, and piercing blue eyes like the prince.

"The king," said Izhar, speaking in the third person, "is more than okay with your presence." He smiled a surprisingly gentle smile for a man with such power as he stepped into the room in front of them.

"The truth is, I owe a great debt of gratitude to all of you for your dedication in surfacing this dreadful problem that we now face. In fact, I insist you join us." His authoritative voice was clear and true—at once, cordial and confident. Even though Ezstasia had traveled to Rhyceton, the chaos had prevented her from having the chance to meet the king personally. She'd only seen him from a distance, and even that was a surreal moment for her. *This* was beyond belief, actually standing in the same room as the legendary Izhar the Great.

"There is, however, one other matter we must address," said the king. "My son tells me your discoveries in the forest began with a little touch of magic of your own—a game you call *Arrows*."

Ezstasia wasn't sure how to respond, and it seemed the others weren't either as they looked around at one another in silence. She wondered whether acknowledging it would be an admission of guilt. After a few seconds of awkward silence, she decided to answer truthfully, just as the king himself would likely do.

"It's true, Your Highness," she said.

"And you are?" said the king.

Ezstasia felt her skin tingle with the sudden realization that maybe she shouldn't have spoken up.

"I'm Ezstasia, sire," she said curtseying again, though she wasn't sure why.

"Ah, the one and only Lady Arrow. Well, Lady Arrow, it is an offense, however minor, to use magic in the Human Lands. Of that, I'm sure you are aware."

"We are, sire," she said, torn between the fear of what he was going to say next and the excitement that he actually knew who she was. "Your Highness, we're—"

King Izhar held up his hand to stop her from continuing. He smiled again and looked around at the group, observing their reactions. They all remained quiet.

"That being said," he added, "the prince and I have agreed that your indiscretion shall be overlooked."

The king paused and she noticed her friends glancing at one another in relief.

"Lady Arrow," the king continued, "you and your friends have shown remarkable persistence in making us aware of the dangers that began in the Forest of Arrows."

Ezstasia gasped and looked toward the prince. He looked down and stared at the wooden floor. This was an unusual reaction from him, considering that he was generally very well composed and didn't shy away from direct eye contact.

"The Forest of what?" said Zander. "Arrows?"

The prince looked back up and took a deep breath. "It seemed a suitable name, considering that your Arrows game is what began all this."

"So, you're saying we have an evil forest named after our game?" said Ithron. Pallu elbowed him on his side.

"I appreciate your candor," said the prince as he laughed. "Let's just say if you *hadn't* played that game, it's anybody's guess as to how long it might've taken before we figured out what was happening within those trees and throughout our kingdoms. One boy is already dead. There could've easily been many more."

He looked directly at Ezstasia and smiled. "It's to all of our benefit that you *did* play that game and so gracefully fall off your rabbit." Redirecting his attention to the whole group, he added, "And all of your courage has helped us greatly, which is why we are pardoning your wrongdoing."

"It is our aspiration," said the king, "that by pardoning all of you, it will show you our deep appreciation for your efforts."

"Yes my lord," said Ezstasia. "We are more grateful than you know. Thank you, Your Highness, and *Your* Highness," she said while blushing toward the prince. He smiled fondly at her and redirected his attention to the floor.

She couldn't believe it. She had battled in her mind if the feelings were mutual or not, but after witnessing his mannerisms during this meeting, she knew she had to be right in thinking that he must feel *something* for her.

"Thank you from all of us, sire," said Fin.

The group all bowed in respect to the king and the prince.

"Of course, with that being said, we will ask that you share your stories with the court," said the prince. "They'll need to hear every detail firsthand, so they have a clear idea of what we're up against. Between the forest, the Diamondwolves, the Galoran River, and the attack on Rhyceton, we're hopeful that they'll accept my solution."

"My son will recommend a solution that is both daring and dangerous," said the king. "But he has convinced me that it is also entirely necessary. It's quite possible that we may require your assistance in this endeavor."

"Of course, sire," said Fin. "Whatever you may need of us."

"Good," said the king. "Then all is settled. Meanwhile, for the next two weeks, I wish you all good fortune during your stay here."

As the group thanked the king once again, the prince rang a bell for the guards. Within seconds, the two knights came in to escort the group out.

On the way out, Ezstasia overheard Prince Alazar talking quietly to his father.

"The court will have to get over their fears," said the prince. "There is no other way through this that I can see."

"My son, what you desire is for a court of rulers to challenge their own beliefs. To support something that was, up until now, unthinkable."

"Yes, but even they can't deny it's our only option. The evidence is clear."

"Evidence or not, I'm afraid their response is out of our hands."

CHAPTER EIGHTEEN

"There's no need to be nervous, dear," said Miss Tee, as Ezstasia finished putting on the same emerald gown she'd worn the very first time she met the prince.

"I'm trying not to be," said Ezstasia, as Miss Tee helped her tie the gold, braided rope around her waist.

The last two weeks had gone by quickly. She and Lanzzie kept themselves busy as they helped the prince's staff in the castle. The others had primarily helped out in the village, where the king had many of his people assisting those in need. Pallu got to spend plenty of time with Ellie, working in the bakery together to help accommodate all of the extra visitors.

But now, the day Ezstasia had been anticipating had come. Her mind was flooded with a mix of excitement and dread, thinking of the moment when she and the others would have to speak in front of a room full of powerful monarchs.

"Just remember," said Miss Tee. "They're just ordinary people who eat, dress, and breathe. Just like you and I."

"Well, not *exactly* like you and I," she said, smiling.

The door opened and her sister entered.

"Wow, don't you look stunning!" said Lanzzie, looking beautiful herself in the powder blue and white gown Miss

Tee had laid out for her. "We're all out in the hall waiting. Pallu is even ready, if you can believe it."

Ezstasia gently put her necklace on and thanked Miss Tee before heading out the door with her sister.

Ezstasia couldn't believe how nice everyone looked in their formal clothing. Fin had a sheepish grin that she recognized as his usual way of showing discomfort. She knew he felt silly all dressed up.

Two of the prince's servants escorted them through the hall and down the main spiral staircase. They proceeded toward the dining room, but turned left toward the front of the castle. Two knights stood guard in front of an enormous, arched wooden door with the same insignia that she'd noticed on the Old Vynterran flag.

The servants led the group to the door, which the knights promptly opened.

Fortunately, Prince Alazar was standing just inside and escorted them in. Ezstasia felt a tinge of intimidation at the sight of the many illustrious people in the room. Eliezer had described them all so well to her and her friends that she felt like she knew them already.

Queen Elenor of Maldora was easy to spot, as she was the only woman of royalty in the room. She was a short, hefty woman with long, wavy, auburn hair and a very direct manner. At least, that's what Ezstasia gathered, from the way she was lecturing the man opposite her. He was a dark-skinned, kindly-looking man and his striking grey hair stood out against the deep purple of his elegant surcoat. That must've been King Amnon, ruler of the western island of Nali.

Along the wall to the right of the room was a long, narrow, silver table, upon which rested an incredible banquet of food. Near it, an enormously overweight man with unkempt hair and an unruly beard and mustache—no doubt

King Baldar of Laderia, based on Eliezer's accurate description—was chomping on a turkey leg while he chatted with another king. Judging by the other man's hawk-like features, solid build, and long scar down the side of his face, she knew he had to be King Zaros of Valta. Eliezer had described him as a brilliant strategist, but also quite demanding. The Valtan army was said to be the largest and most feared in all the Human Lands, and all the kingdoms coveted their flawless Valtan weaponry.

On the far left side, beyond the giant meeting table stood King Izhar, who was in deep conversation with a tall, rugged man with long, golden blond hair. By process of elimination, she assumed that the blond man must have been King Aramor of Dragos. She'd heard tales of the fishing kingdom to the north and its famous Tower of Dragos, but never thought she'd see its king in person.

As she marveled at all the rulers, it dawned on her how silly she and her friends must've appeared, standing with their mouths open, awkwardly staring at everyone. Just then, a man in a lavish, burgundy uniform entered the room and rang a bell.

"That's my father's scribe," Prince Alazar whispered to her.

King Izhar motioned for everyone to take a seat. He sat at the head of the large, oval table, while the monarchs took the other seats. Ezstasia and the others took their seats in the outer rows. The width of the meeting table alone exceeded the length of any dining table she'd ever seen, making it feel as if everyone was greatly separated.

She felt her palms begin to sweat as she anticipated how the monarchs might react to her friends' stories. Most of all, she was curious about what the prince's risky solution would be.

"I appreciate you all coming on such short notice," said

Izhar, as he brought the session to order. "I've asked my son, Prince Alazar, to lead our meeting. Not only does he have firsthand knowledge of the imminent threat that you read about in my letter, but he will graciously share his plan for addressing the problem. After all, this situation may affect your kingdoms sooner than you think."

He nodded to the prince. Prince Alazar stood and bowed before taking his seat again.

"Moreover," said the king, his crisp voice echoing throughout the room, "we have taken the liberty of inviting nine young men and women from the Cottages. They have shown remarkable fortitude in bringing this problem to our attention. I don't mind saying their stories are remarkable and may alarm you. I must caution you that their accounts include a direct warning from the one whom we believe to be our enemy."

He nodded toward Ezstasia and the group and they all rose and bowed as the prince did earlier.

"And so," said the king, after they sat again. "Let us begin."

ಖಾ ಆ ಖಾ ಆ

The opening sessions had gone better than Ezstasia had expected. The king had vividly recounted the Diamondwolf attack on Rhyceton. He then allowed the group to stand together to share their stories. The prince had instructed them beforehand to omit the information about their own use of magic. He was worried that it would deter from the original purpose of the meeting.

The monarchs listened attentively as the friends told of Zander's encounter with the giant spider, Ithron's near-death experience with the black smoke, and Fin's confrontation with shape-forming bats. Pallu, Zander, Ithron, and Jezreel had taken turns sharing their stories about their narrow escape from the wolves, the treacherous river, and the death of Sir Kyrian.

All the while, King Amnon of Nali asked pointed, yet sincere, questions about each scenario, and seemed most curious. Queen Elenor was initially skeptical, but even she became more inquisitive as they continued.

Lanzzie had shared her story last, and there was an audible gasp in the room when she relayed the message she heard in the forest of a great battle that was coming. Clearly, the monarchs had understood that whatever force had emerged from the forest was not one to be reckoned with.

Now, it was the prince's opportunity to share his strategy. Ezstasia took a deep breath as the prince rose and, slowly and deliberately, walked around the room as he spoke.

"You have all now heard the stories," he said. "And I understand that you may feel shocked or fearful. We're hopeful that these chilling accounts, as well as my father's urgent plea to you will propel you to consider embracing what I'm about to share. As we've described in detail in our letter to you, we have already lost two brave knights along with an innocent boy who ventured into the forest on a simple dare. Between these deaths, the wolves, and the river, we're sure that the danger is spreading and will only continue to worsen. The message from the voice in the forest is clear: *Eximum Venirum Sangamort.* From the depths cometh bloodshed. That voice, though the source is still unknown, told us that the blood has already been spilled and that the chaos is unleashed. I can assure you that this chaos has begun. And we need to stop it before it grows."

"Yes, yes, we're all aware that you have a problem in the southeast," said Elenor indignantly. "You've bashed us over the heads with it for the last hour. Not to say that it wasn't intriguing, because it very much so, was. But now what do you propose to do about it?"

"Yes, Your Majesty, it *is* in the southeast at the moment," said the prince, "but I assure you that you're also in imminent danger of this evil. It *will* enter your territory soon enough, just as it has ours, if it isn't stopped. This enemy cannot be fought with armies alone."

"Well, what can it be fought with?" barked the gruff, unsophisticated King Baldar. "Fairy dust?" He laughed alone.

"It's clearly evident that this is dark magic," said the prince, ignoring King Baldar's flippancy. "And in order to fight magic, we need magic."

"Have you gone mad?" said King Zaros. "Have you forgotten the treaty?"

"I'm not talking about using magic left in the Human Lands," said the prince. "I am proposing a voyage to the Magiclands to seek the advice of the Unseen Wizards."

Ezstasia was shocked. She heard the gasps and saw all the wide eyes and knew instantly that every other individual in this room was every bit as shocked as she was. It was to be expected for such a bold, and formerly unheard of, suggestion. All of the monarchs began protesting at once.

"Silence!" yelled King Izhar, banging his fist on the table.

Once everyone quieted down, the prince said, "Can anyone deny that some remnant of the days of magic have returned? Is it not obvious?"

"Even if that's true," said Zaros, "if the magic world is, in fact, waging war upon us, why would you undertake a fool's errand by voyaging directly into the belly of the beast? The very thought is ludicrous."

The prince looked directly at Zaros. "If the magic world were going to wage war against us, they would've done it long ago, and not like this. This is something far more insidious." He turned his attention to the other monarchs.

"Do any of you have a better idea?" he added. "Any of

you? This is why we've called you all here. We wished to warn you of the danger and to receive any suggestions that hadn't previously been considered. We hoped you might even want to send a delegate or two in support of the journey."

The room remained quiet.

"None of you had to see a young boy die in a way you couldn't imagine in your worst nightmares. I witnessed that evil with my own eyes. You didn't see the wolves either. They're as monstrous and vicious as the scrolls describe."

"I'll kill the Diamondwolves myself," said Zaros, puffing his chest out. "I can return with my army in a fortnight."

"Did you not hear me!?" said the prince, becoming visibly outraged. "Killing the wolves will do nothing, even with your elaborate weapons. More wolves will come, and so will other dangers that no human army can fight."

"You don't know that," said Queen Elenor. "It could simply be some lost magic that was recently unearthed, and some naïve soul is experimenting with it. It could die out just as fast as it arrived."

"The magic that we witnessed is too powerful and widespread to simply dissolve into thin air," said the prince.

"Then let me give you my suggestion," said King Zaros. "We can burn the entire forest down to eradicate the problem once and for all."

"Nobody will be burning anything down in my territory," said King Izhar. "Who knows what demons and devastation that might unleash?"

"And what about the river?" said the prince. "Are you going to try to burn that down too? We don't even know the origin of the magic. We'd be fools to act before finding that out. And what about the horrors we haven't even discovered yet?"

"Well, when you discover them, let us know," said Elenor.

"I've made my offer," said Zaros. "I can help you fight the wolves and contain the forest. We'll then have less to contend with and we can make a more informed decision. If you don't want that help, then you may deal with this situation as you wish. However, I will not condone a voyage to the Magiclands. It would break the treaty that has been in place for hundreds of years."

"Prince Alazar," said King Amnon, "with all due respect, there is a reason no man has ever attempted such a journey. Once you cross the sacred border, the sea is guarded by the ancient beasts. And if by some miracle you were to survive that, it's written that the River of Blood surrounds the Magiclands as a reminder of the treaty. They say there are dead souls floating within it, waiting to grab anyone who crosses. And these are but a few of the threats we're aware of. What about the ones we're *not* aware of?"

"The treaty was put in place for a reason, Alazar," said Zaros. "You'd be wise to remember it was the cost of preserving our very existence." He looked at Izhar. "You cannot let your son go on this impulsive journey. Not only will it put his life at stake, it could place all our kingdoms in jeopardy. I will not let that happen."

The prince threw up his arms in frustration.

"It seems to me," said Izhar, "that some of you are willing to open your mouths, but not your ears. Have you not listened to what my son has been saying? I assure you, this situation will not dissipate, nor will it succumb to traditional battle."

"Couldn't the very magic that threatens us now be seen by the magic world as a breach of the treaty?" said the prince. "We could easily be blamed for it."

"Is it not more likely," said Amnon, looking at Alazar, "that someone in your village has unleashed this magic and must be caught?"

"No human would dare," said Alazar.

"Or so you think," said Elenor. "Evidence seems to prove otherwise."

"I still insist we find a way to contain this problem ourselves and find the culprit," said Zaros. "Valta will support that approach entirely."

"And I'll send my Laderian armies," said Baldar, banging on the table. "Those wolves won't stand a chance against both our armies."

"Oh hush, Baldar!" said Elenor. "You're a pompous fool and you'll go with whichever side you think will win. You're Zaros's puppet. We all know that."

"It's a battle we *can't* win," said the prince. "Do you all not see it?" He looked around the room, searching for any sign of agreement.

"You want to journey to the Magiclands," said Elenor. Then she looked at Zaros "And *you* want to attack the wolves and burn the forest. Well, I'll light a candle for the both of you when you're dead, along with all your men."

"And what do you propose?" said Zaros. "Because you must be implying you have a better idea?"

"Dear, unless it comes north, I don't propose anything," said Elenor.

"I am of like mind with Queen Elenor," said King Amnon of Nali. "My island is in the western sea. What is happening here is not happening there. The cause of this havoc may very well be one of your own conspiring. You have a regional problem here and you have the option to fight it however you choose."

"King Aramor," said Izhar. "You've been quiet. What say you to all this?"

All eyes were on Aramor as he remained silent for a few seconds. Then he spoke.

"I've been listening to all sides," he said. "King Izhar,

we've been friends for many years and I respect your judgment. But you've put me in a difficult position. I must think first of the kingdom of Dragos. We're a seafaring people. We have a decent army and a formidable fleet. But even though our island is far north, none of that will mean a thing if the magic world doesn't take kindly to Alazar's journey."

"And if I don't take the journey," said the prince, "any dark magic that currently threatens us could rapidly spread north. You must all understand that I'm taking every precaution. I intend to take the witnesses from the Cottages, if they would agree to join me." He glanced back at Ezstasia and the group. "There are said to be magical beings with the ability of second sight in the Magiclands," he added. "They'll be able to sense from the witnesses that we speak the truth and come in peace."

"That is, *if* the old tales of 'second sight' are even correct," said Aramor. "It could be merely a rumor, or even a parable."

Ezstasia's spine tingled with fear at the thought of going on the journey, but she was also excited to be a part of something so significant. She was thrilled to experience it with her friends and especially the prince. She heard several of her friends gasp. Lanzzie grasped her hand and squeezed it tightly.

"You'd risk all of their lives for nothing but a sprinkle of false hope," said Zaros. "You're a bigger fool than I took you for. I therefore *oppose* your journey. I've explained my reasons."

"I haven't been offered any superior ideas," said the prince. And so, my plan will remain. We set sail in the morning."

"How dare you!" said Zaros. "What's the meaning of this? Why did you waste our time if you were going to follow your own whim?!"

"I must do what's best for my kingdom," said Alazar. "I was open to hearing better solutions and thus far have received none. I'm aware of the dangers of this plan, but I was positive that you'd all see the importance of making this journey, and the futility of not doing so."

"If you think I'll bury my head while you cause a war that we'll likely never recover from," said Zaros, "you're wrong."

"You have a right to protect your kingdom," said Alazar. "And I have a right to protect mine. If what you said is a threat, we both know that your armies are in Valta. By the time you return, I'll be far across the sea. I only hope I can make it back with help before this evil worsens and spreads to your lands."

The prince looked around at the shocked faces of the monarchs. Zaros stood and glanced back at several of the men behind him and nodded. They rose.

"My input on this matter is done," said Zaros. "I've said my peace." He turned toward Izhar. "And you stand behind this suicide mission? I thought you far wiser."

"And I thought you a strategist," said Izhar.

Zaros sneered and began to leave the room with his men. On his way out the door, he turned and added, "You'll be hearing from me, my friend."

After Zaros left, the prince turned to the rest of the rulers.

"I know this voyage will be tremendously difficult," he said. "I'm not under any illusion to the contrary. That is why I'll be enlisting two thousand of my finest men to help in whatever means necessary. I have three ships ready to sail, including the Valorian."

"The Valorian!?" said King Aramor. "That ship hasn't sailed in hundreds of years. I didn't know it still existed."

The prince smiled. "That's what everyone said about this castle, and all of Old Vynterra for that matter. We've restored most of it."

"It's still a fool's errand," said Elenor. "No matter how many men and ships you have."

"You would prefer to bury your head in your Maldoran pottery and pray to your gods that this simply goes away," said the prince. "I can tell you, it will not. What Miss Lanzzie heard gave us a warning and we'd be fools to not listen. If this does tie back to the Great War, then we won't be able to fight any of it without help from the magic world."

"And if they refuse?" said King Amnon.

"If they refuse," said King Izhar, "then we are already dead." The great king sighed. "From what I've gathered based on your responses, it seems none of you support this decision. Is that assessment incorrect?"

Ezstasia looked around at the blank faces in the room. The silence was deafening.

"You're putting us all in danger," said Baldar, looking at Izhar. "I make no promises."

"I won't fight you," said Elenor. "But neither can I support you."

Izhar looked at Amnon, who remained silent for a moment. Then the Nalian leader said, "I have no comment."

Finally, he turned to King Aramor of Dragos. "Can I rely on you, *my friend?*"

Aramor lowered his head, then glanced back up. "The risks are great, but I have no doubt that you arrived at your decision with the best intentions. I will consult with my advisors," he said. "It's the best I can offer you at the moment."

"Very well, then," said Izhar. "Then our time here has come to an end. We all have a duty to protect our kingdoms, but we must also consider all of humankind. We have not been at a greater risk since the Great War. May the stars guide my son in his journey, and may the magic world find favor in our cause."

CHAPTER NINETEEN

Back in her room, Ezstasia closed up the wooden box and placed it back in the desk drawer. She decided to store away anything precious, like her mom's necklace, while away on the journey. She'd already lost it once.

She still couldn't believe they'd actually be going to the Magiclands. She surely didn't like the idea of confronting giant sea creatures or a river made of blood, but she and Lanzzie had agreed that accompanying the prince was the right thing to do. All of humanity depended on it.

She looked over at Lanzzie, who was sitting on the floor beside the bed folding some of her clothes to pack into her sack. Ezstasia didn't mind the silence at a time like this, and it seemed Lanzzie was in deep thought, too.

She walked to the bed, grabbed her sack, and began taking clothes from the pile and stuffing them into the sack.

"Ezstasia, are you going to take—"

A firm knock on the door startled them both.

"Lady Arrow," said a female voice. It was Miss Tee.

She put her sack down and opened the door.

"I'm so sorry to disturb you," said Miss Tee, "but your presence and Lanzzie's has been requested in the prince's study. I've already notified your friends and I believe they're on their way. Would you like me to take you there?"

"That won't be necessary, Miss Tee. I remember where it is, but thank you. We'll head there now."

"Very well, then," said Miss Tee as she left to continue her work.

"I wonder what it's about," said Lanzzie.

Ezstasia turned to her and shrugged. "Maybe something about the journey?"

„ ‘ „ ‘

When they arrived in the prince's study, everyone was there, even Pallu. There was only one person missing: the prince.

Ezstasia and the others looked around the room while they waited for what felt like an eternity, but was likely only a few minutes.

"What do you think he'll tell us?" said Pallu.

"Obviously he'll share details of our trip," said Meldon. "These types of things take extreme planning. We'll probably get instructions on what to pack and how to keep ourselves safe."

"Do you think we'll have a choice whether we want to go or not?" said Zander. "Because I'm not so sure I want to go."

"I know I don't," said Pallu.

"The prince needs our help," said Ezstasia. "All of the kingdoms do, whether they realize it or not. We're the reason the Unseen Wizards will even believe him. They will be able to see that our stories are true."

Just then, the door opened and Eliezer stepped in.

"I do apologize for my tardiness," he said.

"No worries, my lord," said Fin. "The prince still hasn't arrived."

"Oh, I'm afraid Miss Tee wasn't precise in her message,"

said Eliezer. "It was I who requested your presence here. The prince is busy preparing for the long voyage. I'm sure you can imagine how much planning is involved."

Eliezer stepped into the room and motioned for them to take a seat. He sat at the prince's desk.

Once everyone was seated, he picked up an old, copper, balance scale that was sitting on the desk and placed it in front of himself. He lifted a golden coin off the right side, causing the two sides of the scale to even out.

"You can also imagine," he said, "that the prince must weigh many options as the ruler of Old Vynterra, and some of these options are quite delicate. For example, there are tremendous threats here at home as well. We must remember that the threats do not only lie across the sea. Both must be considered."

Ezstasia wasn't sure what he was getting at.

"Three ships set sail in the morning to a land that hasn't been seen or ventured upon since the days of old. The Valorian, the Willow, and the Arboran. Half the Vynterran Guard will make the journey. The other half will stay behind to protect our dear kingdom. The Valorian, we hope, will make it all the way to the Magiclands."

Eliezer looked around at everyone to make sure they were all following.

"What about the other two ships?" said Meldon. "Won't they be going to the Magiclands?"

"The Willow and the Arboran will assist with getting the Valorian to its destination. That is to say, beyond whatever dangers are lurking in the seas. According to the scrolls, there are many. It shall take every spear and arrow we can spare, but we will still need help here in Old Vynterra. So, as you now understand, we can't send everyone. Oh, I suppose I'm rambling. My point is that everyone has a role to play. Which brings me to all of you."

"We were told our role in the meeting, sir," said Fin. "We've all discussed it and we're more than honored to be a part of this. Well, most of us." He looked at Zander, who appeared frightened beyond his wits.

"From what I understood," said Ezstasia, "the prince said he needed us as witnesses."

"Ah yes, but not *all* of you are witnesses," said Eliezer. "The witnesses are those of you with direct exposure to the worst offenses from this unspeakable magic: Miss Lanzzie and Masters Fin, Zander, Meldon, and Ithron." He paused and looked at each of them.

"That's all the prince is taking?" said Ezstasia, feeling panicked. "I don't understand. We've all had some kind of interaction with it."

"Not really," said Randin. "What interaction did you have, or did I have for that matter?"

"You watched with your own eyes what happened to your brother," she said, feeling blood rush to her face.

"He's talking about firsthand experience," said Ithron.

"It's a matter of precaution," said Eliezer, as everyone quieted down. "Those five are the only ones the prince is willing to risk taking to the Magiclands. The rest of you will have important roles back here in Old Vynterra."

Ezstasia couldn't even process what she just heard. Her breathing grew tight and she thought she might explode with a thousand different emotions at any moment. She couldn't fathom being separated from her friends while they were risking their lives, and especially her sister. She'd also looked forward to taking this incredibly important voyage alongside the prince. This was the worst of all possible outcomes for her, and one that she hadn't expected. Lanzzie grasped her hand to comfort her.

"Can I switch with Ezstasia?" said Zander. "Because she really wants to go, and I'd just as soon... well, my brother is—"

"I'm afraid the lines have been drawn," said Eliezer. "The prince was quite clear." He turned to the rest of them. "I understand some of you are not happy with this decision. I hope you'll come to the realization that this issue is beyond all of us. It is sometimes useful in these situations to remember, as they say, the 'bigger picture.'"

"You said fighting those sea creatures will take every arrow you can spare," said Lanzzie. "My sister is the best archer of all of us, except maybe for Fin."

"She's far better than me," said Fin, no doubt being modest.

"Seriously," said Pallu. "I once saw her shoot an apple off the head of Mr. Codsworth's lawn statue from across the gardens."

"I remember that," said Randin. "I still can't believe she made that shot."

"I understand that every one of you wants your group of friends to remain intact," said Eliezer. "Please realize the prince has his reasons. He has given this much thought. He was well aware that some of you would be quite upset. Brothers leaving brothers. Sisters leaving sisters. These decisions were far from easy for him to make. However, the very future of our kind depends upon these rulings. If you'll excuse my presumptuousness, there's a small, but wise bit of advice I've shared with knights and princes and even kings over the decades." He rose from his chair and looked at each of them. "Whatever situation you find yourself in," he said, "you are precisely where you are intended to be."

Ezstasia remembered the prince telling her these very words. And at the time, she believed them. She even remembered feeling inspired by them. But hearing them now just felt empty.

"I have a hard time accepting that," she said. "I thought I

found my purpose. Now I'm not so sure."

Eliezer offered a gentle smile as he clasped his hands together. "I'm afraid you have it backward, my dear," he said. "Your purpose finds *you*."

ॐ ॐ ॐ ॐ

Ezstasia was back in her room. She had rushed there while everyone remained talking after the meeting with Eliezer. Her friends were overwhelming her with their overly sympathetic responses to her situation and she had just wanted some peace and quiet. As their conversation shifted to speculation about the journey, she had managed to slip away without anyone noticing. No matter how much she tried to hide her feelings and pretend that she was okay with the prince's decision, she still couldn't fathom not being on that ship with Lanzzie.

She'd thought about going to find the prince, but knew that it wouldn't be of any use. Even if she could find him, he already had enough on his mind. She didn't want to become a burden to him. Besides, it was clear that he didn't want to risk someone being there who didn't absolutely need to be. She understood it. But that still didn't make it any easier.

After the emotional highs and lows of the day, she just wanted to clear her head. She needed to spend a few hours in the outdoors alone with nature to digest everything that was happening. Most of all, she needed to blow off some steam; her frustration had reached a boiling point. She'd get to say her tearful goodbyes later.

It would soon be dusk, and the nights had been chilly as of late, so she thought it wise to bring some warmer clothes along with her and grabbed her half-filled sack. She looked through her additional garments on the bed for something that might be suitable.

Ezstasia didn't want to be confronted with more well-meaning, yet annoying comments, so she began to rush. She scooped the clothes into her bag, grabbed her cloak from the rack and headed out the door before anyone could see her.

As soon as she got outside, she put her cloak on and headed toward the village stables where Tia was kept.

The village was busy, not only because of the visiting monarchs and their entourages, but also because of all the Rhyceton refugees. People seemed to be running to and fro with everything from food carts to firewood to bundles of clothing. Between the fear of the unknown horrors that had been threatening the kingdoms and the excitement of all the visitors, people were out in the streets en masse, conversing with one another.

When she finally got to the stables, she saw to her relief that the stable keepers were busy, so she had no trouble taking Tia out. She saddled up the rabbit and rode out of the Western Gate without any questions from the guards. After all, leaving wasn't a problem. Coming in was a different story.

As she rode south in the direction of the Cottages, she took in the sights and smells of the mountains and trees. After about an hour or so of riding, the sun had nearly set as she began looking for a place to stop and give Tia a chance to rest. On her right was a wide open meadow with high grass and an occasional bush or tree. To her left she saw the dense forest she remembered passing in her prior trips to and from the Cottages. Beyond the forest, she could see the enormous, beautiful mountain range she recalled from her prior trips. In the growing darkness, she could barely make out the tops of the majestic hills.

She slowed Tia down and gazed into the mysterious forest. As darkness fell and the crescent moon rose in the deep purple sky, her heart began to pound with the realization that it might not be as safe of a ride as she had presumed. With all the emotional upheaval, she'd almost forgotten about the Diamondwolves. While they hadn't yet been reported on this side of the river, there was nothing to say they couldn't appear anywhere at any time, especially in the obscurity of the evening shadows.

"Tia, I'm thinking we better head back," she said. "We can rest when we're closer."

Just then, she heard movement in the trees. It could've been the rustling of leaves from the wind. She halted Tia and listened closely. The wind blew against the trees again, causing a loud crackling. She was convinced it had to be a natural occurrence, but with the recent events, nothing would surprise her.

"It's just the wind," she said out loud to the rabbit, more so for her own reassurance. She continued listening intently for any sudden sounds.

She felt butterflies in her stomach as she began to pull the rightmost rein to turn Tia around. Just as her rabbit started to turn, she spotted something else up ahead to the right. It was a glimmering light in the meadow.

She stopped Tia again and stared. It was yellow and flickering, like a fallen star that had flattened in the dark field, just to the right of the road.

"What is that, Tia?"

Curious, she led Tia ahead to get a closer look. The rabbit seemed hesitant.

"I know, girl," she said. "You're not as curious as I am. Maybe that's a good thing."

When she got closer to it, she decided to tie Tia up by the left side of the road. She dismounted the rabbit and tied her to a tall tree, putting some berries she'd brought from the stables on the ground for her. She crossed the dirt road and trudged through the tall grass in the blackness of night, using the lights ahead as a guide.

Quietly, she made her way through the field, gazing at the flickering light. It almost looked like a campfire. In fact, the closer she got, she realized it *was* a campfire. Someone was out there. But who? And why?

Though every fiber of her being told her to go back to Tia and return to the castle, she wanted to see who could be out here. She knelt down in the tall grass and moved slowly forward until she could make out the camp.

It was a small camp, with about ten to fifteen tents, each glowing with the illumination of the candles inside. In many of them, she could see the silhouettes of their inhabitants moving around. At the center of the camp, a huge fire was lit, with people standing and sitting around it, conversing.

She moved even closer, and at this point, she was nearly crawling. She prayed that nobody would spot her. She noticed a couple of bushes up ahead and darted behind them.

Hiding behind the bushes, she could now see that they were knights. She overheard two men arguing. They were walking from the campfire toward the back of one of the tents. She recognized one of them. It was King Zaros from the meeting with the monarchs. She wondered if he and his men were camping on the way back to their kingdom. Then she remembered something Eliezer had said during his briefing about the monarchs. Zaros's kingdom, Valta, was in the far northwest of the continent, so they would've been entirely in the opposite direction. Besides, Eliezer had also said the monarchs had all sailed to Old Vynterra, except King Baldar, whose walled kingdom of Laderia was situated in the central region. They definitely weren't near any ports to reach their ships.

She remembered the heated debate between Zaros and the prince, which piqued her curiosity. She tried to remain hidden in the tall, dry grass and crawled toward another bush closer to where the two men were walking. Her feet rustled against the brush, and she froze as she saw Zaros turn his head right in her direction. Thankfully, he resumed his debate with the other man.

After the men parted, she spotted another bush with more coverage and she quickly rushed to hide behind it. The camp was bigger than she thought; the tents were several rows deep.

She could see a knight behind one of the rear tents, pacing back and forth in the dim, yellow light of a nearby torch. He was the one Zaros had been arguing with. But where was Zaros? She'd lost track of him. The man stopped and stared up into the stars before walking toward the campfire.

Ezstasia felt nervous. She crouched on all fours and began making her way back in the direction of the road, passing several tents as quietly as she could, while trying her best to stay hidden. She heard whinnying up ahead that came from the road. She looked up to realize that all of the knights' horses were tied up by the road, not more than ten yards from where Tia was. She hoped none of the knights would need to go back to their horses until she had left.

As she passed another tent, she heard voices coming from inside. She could see the silhouettes of two men through the tent as their hands waved around in an agitated manner. They were arguing about something. She got closer to listen.

"It's our duty," said the taller man with a deep voice. "We have no choice."

"We always have a choice," said the other one, who sounded like an older man. "These are difficult times. But this? This is wrong."

"We have our orders."

"We also have consciences," said the older man. "Can you live with such a decision?"

"None of us will live at all if we disobey orders. You'd be wise in your old age to remember that. I have a family to care for. *That's* what matters to me."

Just then another shadow entered the tent.

"Is there a problem here?" said the third man. It was King Zaros.

"No sire," said the tall man with the deep voice. "We're just gather—"

"Leave us," said Zaros.

"Of course, sire," said the tall man as he left.

Ezstasia held her breath as the man walked only a foot from where she was hiding.

"You don't approve of our mission, Sir Karek?" said Zaros to the older man.

"Whether I approve of it is of little consequence, my lord. But I understand the importance of the mission, if that's what you're asking."

"You've been by my side for many years," said Zaros. "What we are about to do cannot bear even the slightest hesitation. It would pain me to have to issue… consequences."

"I'm at your service, my lord," said Karek.

"Good," said Zaros. "These are difficult times, but we must remain firm in our resolve. I'll see you in the camp."

As Zaros left the tent, Ezstasia began to panic. She wasn't sure when they were all leaving, but if it was any time soon, they'd surely see Tia when they went to their horses. She crawled as fast as she could until she heard someone walking behind her, headed in her direction. Quickly, she rolled to the side and looked back. The knight was carrying several large swords toward the horses. He would've walked right over her if she hadn't moved.

Just then, Zaros came back and approached him. She had nothing to cover her except the shadow of night and hoped they wouldn't spot her.

"Sir Blake," said Zaros, holding out a small sack. "Take this with you."

"Ah yes, the gold," said Blake in a deep voice as he took the sack from the king. She realized he was the same tall man who'd been arguing in the tent with the older man, Karek.

"Remember, when you ride east, you'll see the village. Ask for Goram. The Vorokians may be savages, but for the right price they'll serve us well. I've dealt with him in the past. Be sure to tell him you represent King Zaros."

"I will, my lord. Is there anything else?"

"Yes. Hurry back with them as quickly as you can. Time is already running out."

As Zaros left and the imposing Sir Blake continued toward the horses, Ezstasia held her breath. She watched as the knight walked to one of the horses and loaded the sack of gold and his weapons onto the saddlebag, before untying and mounting the steed. He prepared to leave, but suddenly halted the horse. He seemed to be looking in Tia's direction, as if he'd heard something. She could feel her heart pound in her throat and hoped he couldn't hear her rapid breath. She stayed perfectly still watching him. After a few seconds, Sir Blake shook the reins and then galloped off.

She crawled toward Tia, and just as she approached the road, she heard two more knights walking toward her. She remained still as she watched Tia across the street, hoping the oblivious rabbit wouldn't make a noise.

"Did he take my horse?" said the one knight, who was quite stocky and bald.

"Now why would he do that?" said the other, a light-haired man with a gravelly voice. "He has his own."

"Mine's faster. He asked me if he could take her."

"Well at least he asked," said the fair-haired knight as they approached the horses. "Blake never asks."

"I told him he couldn't!"

From across the road, Ezstasia heard Tia make a noise that came from pulling back against her tie. The men must've startled her.

"What was that!?" said the light-haired knight.

"Probably a squirrel."

"It sounded bigger than a squirrel."

"You're just hearin' things."

Tia moved again and a branch cracked.

"I told you I heard something!"

Ezstasia froze as the two men rushed toward Tia. She spotted a wagon by the road and dove toward it in the darkness, quietly squeezing herself under it.

"It's a saddled rabbit!" said the stocky, bald knight. "Go warn the others. There's a spy in the camp. I'll wait here."

The blond knight ran toward the campfire as Ezstasia looked around for a better place to hide. She crawled out from underneath the wagon and felt something pointy jab against her back before she could even get up.

"Found you," said a voice behind her. It was the bald knight. She could tell by his voice.

She thought her heart was going to beat out of her chest.

"Stay put," he said.

She felt the last bit of hope she had left exit her body as she laid her head on the ground in defeat. She didn't even look up at him.

"I have the spy!" he yelled. A bunch of knights ran toward them from the camp.

She glanced up to see multiple sets of legs coming toward her. One walked steadily closer and stopped just in front of her.

"Stand up," said the familiar voice. It was King Zaros.

Slowly, she rose until she was standing face to face with him.

He looked taken aback when he saw her face. "I know you," he said. "You were at the meeting today. I didn't take you for a spy."

"I'm not a spy," she said.

"Said every spy I've ever met. Why are you here, *not-a-spy?*"

"I'm on my way home to the Cottages."

"And you just happened upon our camp? Quite convenient. Tell, me, Miss…"

"My name's Ezstasia, Your Highness."

"Tell me, Miss Ezstasia." He put his face uncomfortably close to hers. "Why were you sent here? And by whom?"

"Nobody sent me here," she said. "I'm telling you the truth. I was on my way and I saw the lights. I was curious to see who was here."

"Curiosity killed the cat," he said, backing up slightly. "And a great many of my enemies. Answer my question. Why are you really here?"

"I told you," she said. "I just want to go home."

"What did you hear during the time that your… curiosity overtook you?"

"Nothing," she said. "I swear I didn't hear anything. You don't have to worry about me."

"Do I look worried?" he said. He looked around at the other knights, who began to chuckle.

"She's lying, sire," said the blond, gravelly-voiced knight. "We found her rabbit tied up near our horses. She was snooping around the camp."

Zaros looked at her and smiled. "My guard says you're lying," he said. "What do you have to say to that?" Everything about his sing-songy, mocking manner and tone made her skin crawl.

"I was walking around the camp," she said, lying. "Not snooping."

"Walking around my camp for an evening stroll," he said.

"I hope you enjoyed it, because you'll get to see plenty more."

He looked to the stocky, bald knight and then the blond one. "Tie her up," he said.

"You can't do this!" she said, as the knight took a rope from one of the other men. He grabbed her tightly with his grimy, unwashed hands. "I didn't do anything wrong!"

The knights brought her to one of the few trees in the camp, while some of the other men pulled Tia toward her. Ezstasia squirmed as they held her against the tree. They fastened her arms behind the tree with the rope, and then tied her legs together. They left her there, completely alone, and they walked back toward the camp.

For the next hour or so, she fought endlessly to free herself from the ties around her ankles and wrists as she watched the drunk knights parading around by the campfire. It was of no use. Her skin was raw against the rope and it hadn't budged an inch.

After a while, her shoulders began to ache and her legs felt even worse. The pain grew unbearable and she could barely remain conscious. To make matters worse, the smoke from the campfire had drifted her way, burning her eyes. But she couldn't give up. She had absolutely no idea what these men were capable of.

As time went on, she became more and more exhausted from the ordeal. She couldn't help but to worry about the prince and the plan that Zaros had in store for him. She felt weak and entirely helpless.

After more pushing and pulling, her head grew heavy and she could no longer stay awake. She found herself drifting off into a nightmare of enormous sea creatures and a terrible storm in the ocean's raging waters.

ಬ ಚ ಬ ಚ

Pallu was watching Lanzzie pace back and forth in the bedroom that she shared with Ezstasia and Jezreel. He wasn't sure what to do to help her. She was beside herself. He had to admit, he was getting a bit worried too. It wasn't like Ezstasia to abandon her friends, let alone her sister. This was like the forest situation all over again.

"Should we go find her?" said Lanzzie.

"Where would you even look? You never know with her. She visits dragons and hides with spiders and ends up in faraway kingdoms with princes."

"You're not helping."

Pallu walked to a small armchair in the corner of the room and sat on it, barely fitting between the arms. "Lanz, you saw how upset she was when she heard she couldn't go with you. Being separated from you and her friends and even the prince, for an unknown length of time, I'm sure it tore her up inside. Her whole life was turned upside down in one quick moment. I'd be upset, too."

"But to leave and not say goodbye? That's even beyond *her.*"

"Exactly," said Pallu. "That's why I know she'll be back."

"She took all of her clothes. I wouldn't be so sure."

"It doesn't make sense. She must've left something here. Look around for her stuff. Maybe it's under the bed."

"It's not. I looked."

"Then look somewhere else."

Lanzzie walked to the tall cabinet where they kept some of their clothes, but remembered that she had already checked there. She went to the opposite end of the room to the desk and opened the drawers. In the top drawer was a small wooden box. She took it out and opened it.

"Her necklace is here!" said Lanzzie. "The one my mom gave her. She'd never leave that."

"I told you," said Pallu. "Trust me, she'll be back."

He watched Lanzzie put the necklace back into the box and close it before placing it back into the drawer.

"I hope you're right," she said, "because if she's not back, I can't go on this trip."

"What do you mean you can't go? You have to go. The whole world's survival could depend on you and the others getting to the Magiclands. They need you. Ezstasia would be the first one to tell you that."

"I wouldn't even be of any use. I'd be totally consumed wondering what happened to my sister. I'm really worried. You never know with the way things are going around here. Something bad may have happened."

"Nothing bad has happened, Lanz. She's just upset. Get some rest, I'm sure you'll see her in the morning, if not tonight. Now please get some sleep and let your sister cool off. Don't make me sleep in the hall, either, to check up on you. You have to stay in your room. Seriously Lanz."

"Okay, I'll try. But if she isn't here by morning, I can't promise I'll be on that ship."

"She'll be here," he said.

Lanzzie walked to the side of the bed and stared at it. Pallu rose from the chair and made his way to the candelabra that stood on a small stand on the other side of the bed. He grabbed a candle from it to guide his way back across the hall.

He gave Lanzzie a hug before leaving the room and gently closed the door. He was doing his best to make her feel better, but he was just as concerned as she was. Things weren't adding up.

As he made his way to his bedroom, he paused to make sure Lanzzie wasn't going anywhere. Satisfied that he didn't hear any footsteps, he continued to his room.

༄ ༄ ༄ ༄

Ezstasia awoke to the sound of running, banging, and loud talking. She'd almost forgotten where she was, but the pain quickly returned to her arms and legs reminding her that she was helplessly tied to a tree.

She opened her eyes and watched hundreds of men run back and forth carrying items. There were far more people than the tents could've possibly held that she had remembered the previous night. And most of these men weren't knights; she actually wasn't sure what they were. They wore furs, leather skins, and sandals, and carried axes and other rudimentary weapons. Most of the men were huge, with long, braided hair and thick, unkempt beards. Even some of their facial hair had braided strands with ties. Several of the men hit one another just for fun and laughed boisterously. They must've been the Vorokians that Zaros had been talking about. No wonder he called them savages.

She looked at Tia as she continued to fidget with the ropes, though the pain quickly put an end to any notion of escaping. Tia was relaxing and looking around as if she hadn't a care in the world.

"Tia," she whispered loudly. "Chew my ropes, will you?" She was kidding, of course, although slightly hopeful, and the rabbit just looked at her. She nibbled on some grass and went back to resting.

Just then, one of the Vorokian men looked her way. He was skinny and filthy, with scraggly hair that was either brown or blond; it was hard to tell through all of the dirt. He began to approach her.

"Who do we 'ave here?" he said. "Aren't you lovely?" He smiled a half-toothless smile.

"Leave 'er be!" yelled one of the other tribesmen. "It's time to go!"

She started squirming again trying to loosen the ropes, wishing this creepy man would go away.

"Hey, can I have 'er!?" he yelled to the others.

Several of the king's knights came forward.

"What do we do with her?" said one of the knights.

"She's injured," said an older knight with grey hair. "She needs treatment." She recognized his voice as Sir Karek, the conflicted man she had seen through the tent the previous night.

"We should ask the king," said another knight.

"I think you should give 'er to me," said the scraggly Vorokian.

Just then, she looked up to see the knights parting to make way for King Zaros, who was arriving alongside a stocky, bald knight.

The king stepped up to her and studied her face.

"I had almost forgotten that we needed to tie up a few loose ends. So what shall we do with you?" he said, lifting her chin.

"I just want to go home," she said, her voice weak from thirst.

"To the Cottages?" said Zaros. "I suppose you can't do us any harm now, whether or not that's your true destination."

"Sire," yelled a short knight who was running from the area where the camp had been set up. "The men are ready to go. We have to get to the docks before those ships sail."

Her eyes widened with the sudden realization of their plan. They weren't just planning to attack Old Vynterra. They were going to do something to the ships before they could even take off!

The king must've noticed the look of shock on her face.

"You really didn't know?" he said. Then he smiled crookedly. "Well, now you do."

He turned to leave and the appalling Vorokian man inched

closer toward her.

"Please, King Zaros!" she yelled. "You must let them sail!"

"Your Cottages will thank me," he said loudly as he walked away.

"What do we do with her, sire?" one of the knights called out.

Zaros threw up his hands from up ahead. "Whatever you wish," he said. "She's of no consequence now."

"Leave 'er to me," growled the Vorokian.

She watched in horror as the knights all ran to their horses to catch up to the rest of their army that had already ridden away.

The savage got right up in her face, his reeking breath invading her senses.

"We know how to handle criminals," he said, grinning.

He removed a knife from the side of his fur vest and Ezstasia, sickened with fear, felt herself losing consciousness again.

Just then, the man let out a deafening yell. A look of sheer horror crossed his face. His eyes bulged and his mouth opened grotesquely. Blood spots began forming all across his chest. He fell to the ground and Ezstasia looked over to see the grey-haired knight, Sir Karek, standing behind him. He held a large, bloody dagger in his right hand.

"I'm sorry, Miss," he said, holding the dagger up to her body, as she cringed.

To her utter relief and surprise, he cut the ropes loose from around her waist and from her legs. He then walked behind her to free her arms from behind the tree.

She let out a moan and brought her arms toward her to let them rest for a moment. She watched the knight walk toward Tia. He untied her and handed Ezstasia the reins.

"I won't forget your kindness," she said.

"These are scary times we live in," said Sir Karek. He

looked toward the last remaining knights who were preparing to leave. "But we can't forget what makes us human or none of it would be worth fighting for. Neither Zaros nor I nor anyone else knows the right path to take. We don't know what will truly save us." He bowed to her. "Now you make it home safely, Miss."

In the distance, a knight rode toward them.

"You must go, now!" said Sir Karek, helping her up to her feet. He held her arm as she walked to Tia and lifted her atop the saddle. "Hurry!"

She felt a new sensation of adrenaline and swiftly grabbed the reins and rode off. She had to get back to the castle and gather any knights she could before Zaros and his men could stop the ships—or worse."

ₒ ₓ ₒ ₓ

Ezstasia was finally approaching the castle's front gates, having taken as direct a route as she could. Although relieved to finally be at the castle, she was worried about Tia who was limping. She had injured her leg while jumping over a boulder on the way back. The large rock had blocked the only shortcut to the castle.

Ezstasia was exhausted herself and still in pain from the tightly wound ropes that held her all night. Her wounds ached and she desperately needed water. Weakly, she hunched over her rabbit, unable to stay upright. A group of knights in the distance saw her condition and quickly rushed toward her.

"It's Lady Arrow," said one of the knights. "She needs tending to."

"No!" she shouted. "Please take me to Eliezer, quickly! The prince's life depends on it!"

As the knights helped her off Tia, she said, "My rabbit.

She's hurt. Please get her to the stables."

An elderly woman came forward and took Tia's reins. "I'll see to it that she's taken care of, Lady Arrow."

Just then, she spotted Eliezer coming from the castle toward her. Despite the pain in her legs, she ran to him. The knights followed.

"What happened?" he said. "Your sister and friends—."

"I'll explain later," she said. "The prince is in danger. His whole voyage is at risk. I was captured by King Zaros and his men. He's on his way to stop the prince from sailing to the Magiclands, but I don't know what they plan to do."

"He won't get far," said a knight with a deep voice. "He doesn't have a full battalion."

"He has other men with him," she said. "Thousands of them. They're savages. He called them Vorokians."

"Vorokians!" said Eliezer. He turned to the knight with the deep voice. "Sir Ulric," he said, "please go tell Sir Aldus that we will need the Valorian Order immediately. Gather the Vynterran Guard, too. You must get to the docks at once." He turned to Ezstasia. "You, dear, come with me."

"I need to go with them!" she said. She wasn't about to be denied the chance to help save her sister and friends.

"Of course you're going with them! But for now, come with me. Quickly! We haven't much time."

She followed Eliezer to the castle, surprised at how quickly a man his age could move.

They hurriedly went through the castle as people stared at them from all directions. He grabbed a large torch from the wall and he led her through corridors that she hadn't seen before. They opened secret doors and walked through the hidden hallways. Eventually, they arrived inside a torchlit room with tiled floors and mirrored walls with gold trim and pearl inlays separating each panel. Along the wall, large golden shelves held a variety of weapons. Eliezer led her to a large, bronze bow that was so luminous and reflective, it almost looked like it was glowing from a furnace fire. It was like nothing she'd ever seen before.

He picked up the bow and handed it to her.

"This belonged to Valorian himself," he said. "It was rumored to bring him abundant luck during the Great War. Some even said it may have had a touch of magic." He winked. "At any rate, nobody can deny its workmanship. I thought that it may bring us good fortune in the hands of the girl who once shot an apple off a statue's head from a great distance."

Ezstasia was in complete awe as he handed her the bow.

He grabbed a medium-sized, golden chest with the Vynterran sigil design inscribed on the top of it. He unlocked it and pulled out a pearl-lined, canvas quiver full of elegant arrows that had a touch of real gold glistening in their feathers.

"Come. We must hurry," he said, placing the bag on her shoulders.

"I hope I'm worthy of it," she said. "Is there anything specific I need to know about shooting this?"

"When you aim," he said, "don't miss!"

He led her quickly out the door and through a completely different route than they took to get here. They exited through the side door of the castle, where hundreds of knights stood lined up outside. At the head of the army were knights in black armor, which Ezstasia knew to be part of the Valorian Order. She recognized Sir Aldus in the center.

Eliezer approached Sir Aldus alongside Ezstasia. She could sense that he was surprised to see her carrying Valorian's bow.

"Bring her with you," said Eliezer. "She's seen the Vorokians and observed their ways. She's also, I might add, a distinguished archer."

"With quite the distinguished bow," said Sir Aldus. "As you wish, Archminister."

The same village woman who had taken Tia was now bringing forward a majestic, black Friesian horse. It was truly one of the most beautiful animals Ezstasia had ever seen.

"Your steed, Lady Arrow," said the woman.

Ezstasia mounted the horse and made sure the quiver of arrows was secured tightly on her back.

"Get to the shore as quickly as possible," said Eliezer, looking at Sir Aldus. "For the sake of every kingdom in the Human Lands, those ships must sail!"

CHAPTER TWENTY

Lanzzie was beside herself as she rode with Fin on the sandy path that led to the lower docks. Old Vynterra had several docks, as explained by Sir Layton en route. The monarch's ships were located at the upper and middle docks, just north of here, though most of them, had likely set sail back to their kingdoms earlier that day.

As harrowing as this journey would surely be, the only thing Lanzzie could think about was Ezstasia. She prayed that her sister would be at the docks to say goodbye, but she was losing hope by the minute.

"She'll be here," said Fin.

"Why do I feel like she won't?" she said. She wasn't trying to be negative. She just knew her sister wouldn't disappear all night only to show up at the docks. She knew something was wrong.

"We'll find out soon enough," he said. "Look."

She looked up ahead where he was pointing. Through a break in the trees, she could see part of a ship's mast in the distance. Her legs trembled with dread; the anticipation of getting on the ship without knowing whether Ezstasia was okay was more than she could bear. She knew it wasn't really a choice, though. Between Pallu and Fin, they'd beat it into her head this morning that Ezstasia would want her to make the journey, no matter what. Besides, as Fin had explained, she was the most important witness of all.

They continued following Sir Layton along the sandy path and through the trees, accompanied by a number of villagers and knights. She wasn't sure where the rest of her friends were in the large group—they had gotten separated during the walk—but she took comfort in knowing that they were close by. As they emerged from the trees and onto the massive, white sand beach, Lanzzie felt an overwhelming feeling of reverence wash over her.

Three of the largest and tallest ships she'd ever seen were tied to the docks in the sparkling, turquoise waters. Their grandeur was astonishing. Long gangplanks led up to each of the ships and hundreds of knights and crewmen, were carrying cargo and leading animals and horses up to board the ships. Throngs of people crowded the beach to observe the most historic departure any of them would likely ever see in their lifetime.

"Sweet carrot sticks!" said Meldon, riding up beside her.

"The big ship in the center is the Valorian," said Sir Layton. "We'll be boarding that one with the prince."

"Incredible," said Fin. "I would've been thrilled just to be on one of the smaller ones."

"I don't see her, Fin," said Lanzzie, looking at the massive crowd.

"It won't be easy to spot her in this crowd." She could tell Fin was doing his best to reassure her.

She noticed that he was also scanning the crowd in all directions. She turned around and spotted Ellie and Pallu quickly walking toward them. They were holding hands as they wove through the people.

She shifted her gaze toward the three enormous vessels waiting by the shore, each with several colossal masts that essentially took up the entire skyline. The Valorian was the most majestic of all, with its deep cherry wood and a carved, painted figurehead of a beautiful woman on the extended bow. Her ravishing golden hair was cascading down the ship's prow on both sides. Toward the rear of the ship, the raised deck at the stern looked like it housed special cabins for people like the prince and his staff.

"That's Princess Allura," said Sir Layton, pointing to the ship. He came up beside Lanzzie on his horse and dismounted as he spoke. "She was Valorian's wife. That's the original figurehead, fully restored."

Lanzzie was captivated by its magnificence and couldn't believe she was face to face with the historic carved out image of the stunning Allura. She glanced over at Fin, Pallu, and Ellie, who seemed to be in awe, just as she was.

The other two ships had been constructed with a light maple wood and were smaller ships, but they were still overwhelmingly impressive. Lanzzie noticed a group of men pulling the gangplank away that led to the Willow, so that ship must have been fully loaded. The only gangplanks still in place led up to the Valorian and the Arboran.

She resumed searching the crowd for Ezstasia but an older man startled her by grabbing Jewel's reins. She looked up and realized she was the only one still sitting on her rabbit. She saw Randin and Zander run up to some of her friends who were staring at the ships. She dismounted and handed the reins over, watching as a group of men led their rabbits through the crowd toward the Arboran.

Lanzzie walked toward her friends and heard them begin to say goodbye to one another. She hurried to catch up and do the same. Once she approached them, Randin was hugging Zander tearfully. She looked around once more for Ezstasia. She felt heartbroken when she realized that there still wasn't any sign of her. She didn't want to give up.

"Excuse me, Miss Lanzzie," said Ellie, as she meekly tapped Lanzzie on the shoulder. Lanzzie turned toward her and Pallu.

"I want to promise you," said Ellie, "that Pallu and I won't give up until we find your sister. We'll look everywhere if we have to."

"That's right, Lanz," said Pallu. "Ellie and I will find her."

Lanzzie felt grateful for the two of them and hugged them both. Even though she was worried sick, their dedication had surprisingly brought her a small amount of comfort.

"I can't tell you how proud I am that my friends are going to the actual Magiclands," said Pallu. He looked out again at the docks. "Can you believe those ships!? They're massive! You know, you may even be able to spot Ezstasia from the ship."

Just as Pallu finished his sentence, a loud horn sounded. It had come from the trees behind the beach. A group of knights parted the crowd to make room as King Izhar emerged on a white horse with his men alongside. One of his horsemen carried the red and black twin-raven flag of Rhyceton.

As she watched the pageantry of the king and his guard marching through the cheering crowds, another horn sounded. Toward her right, the prince arrived with his horsemen. Two riders behind the prince held the blue and gold flag of Old Vynterra. The thunderous roar of the crowd was deafening as the two sets of knights rode toward the docks.

Lanzzie looked around and watched as several couples shared a final embrace and fathers said goodbye to their sons and daughters. And yet, Ezstasia wasn't anywhere to be seen.

"Remember," said Pallu. "We won't stop looking. Meanwhile, you go and save the world."

Lanzzie nodded and hugged Pallu and Ellie again.

Meanwhile, she noticed that Jezreel and Ithron were walking toward them. By the looks of Jezreel, with her reddened eyes and persistent sniffles, she wasn't taking Ithron's pending departure well. She also noticed that Randin and Zander were busy encouraging one another.

"It's time," said Sir Layton. Lanzzie turned to see the prince and his men standing up ahead waiting for them. The king was beside the prince on his horse and Izhar's men stood to the side in formation. She noticed a group of men beginning to pull the gangplank away from the Arboran. She took one last look around to try to grab a glimpse of Ezstasia, and then reluctantly followed the rest of her friends behind Sir Layton up onto the Valorian.

She looked back with tears and sorrow at Pallu and Ellie, Randin, and Jezreel. She couldn't help but wonder if she'd ever see them again. Hoping that only good fortune lay ahead for all of them, she prayed the stars would guide their journey and that Pallu and the others would find her sister alive and well.

She turned her head toward the ships and walked with Fin and Meldon. Ithron and Zander were already up ahead with Layton. On the way, she spotted an old man in the crowd, standing straight and proud with an infectious smile, bowing as they passed. As sad as she might have been, his face had given her a sense of pride and a necessary reminder of how important this mission was. It offered her a sense of purpose. And in an odd way, she felt like it was Ezstasia sending her a message: to keep going, and that it's okay to be scared, but also that some things in life are just bigger than all of them.

As they approached the prince and the king, she took one final look back. In the distance she saw another army of knights walking out from the trees.

"I think that other army is late," she said to the prince.

"What other army?" he said.

She pointed back toward the trees. "*That* other army."

The prince looked into the distance. His eyes widened with a fear that she had never seen in him before.

"Zaros!" said the prince. "Who's that with him?"

"Vorokians!" yelled Sir Layton.

"Get to the ships now!" yelled King Izhar. "Go!"

"You'll never defeat them," said the prince. "There are too many."

"Who said anything about defeating them?" said the king. "Now go!"

The prince hesitated, but obeyed, and rushed Lanzzie and the others past him.

"Take them!" he yelled to Sir Layton. "I'll be right behind you."

Layton quickly led them onto the gangplank. Lanzzie ran as fast as she could up the flimsy board after the others, glancing back to see the prince and his men following behind her.

"Cut the lines!" yelled the prince. She watched as a group of men by the docks heeded his orders and ran with their axes toward the Willow.

She climbed onto the Valorian behind Meldon, Fin, Zander, and Ithron, and craned her neck to see the knights swinging their axes by the Willow's lines. They broke its thick ropes and the smaller ship slowly, yet eagerly, inched away from the dock.

Once the Willow was set free, Lanzzie watched nervously as the men ran to the Arboran's lines and cut them one by one. Her heart in her throat, she watched as the ships began to part from the dock. The Valorian was the last remaining ship. She looked back toward the oncoming army and watched countless men continue to run out of the trees and head straight for them. Some were knights, but most of them were Vorokian savages. There must've been hundreds of them.

"Hoist the sails!" yelled one of the crewmen.

She climbed a wooden ladder to the upper deck and was nearly knocked over when knights rushed past her. She saw that they had unsheathed their swords in preparation for battle and exited the ship. She continued to the deck and ran to the edge to look down at the beach. Fin and the others ran up beside her.

She heard a loud noise behind her and gazed up to see multiple layers of massive, square sails rising up on three separate masts, while dozens of crewmen desperately pulled the lines. The sails all began to expand and catch the wind.

"What's taking so long!" yelled one knight from the deck below.

Lanzzie looked down at the docks and watched in horror as a group of knights drew their swords to defend the ship against the Vorokians. King Izhar and his men bravely rushed toward the oncoming army, grossly outnumbered. Within seconds, the two armies clashed, and Zaros's men completely engulfed Izhar and his knights.

Izhar fought bravely; he battled three to four men at a time, engaging and killing one man after the other. The Vorokian men fought like savages, using shields, clubs and other barbaric weapons that Lanzzie had never even seen before. There were just too many of them. She looked over at the prince whose eyes expressed deep defeat and sorrow. She knew that the outcome was going to be devastating.

The people in the crowd were running toward the trees and to the sides of the docks in a panic, tripping over one another and over themselves. Children screamed and cried loudly as their mothers scooped them up and ran toward the trees. Lanzzie frantically looked around for Pallu, Randin, and Jezreel, but she couldn't spot them anywhere.

"Get the weapons!" yelled someone behind her.

Fin and the others ran back to help some of the knights lift several heavy crates and she watched as they attempted to pry them open.

Just then, Lanzzie spotted Pallu and Ellie on the beach. They were pulling Jezreel toward some large rocks by the coast. Randin was running to catch up to them. Relieved they were safe for the moment, she continued looking for her sister among the chaos as the Vorokians and King Zaros's men tried to forcefully get through to the ships.

She looked down to see whether the lines of the Valorian had been fully cut yet, and was devastated to see the men who were cutting them had both been struck down with spears. Another group of men rushed toward the lines and picked up the axes near the fallen men, only to be speared themselves. Two knights jumped off the ship and made their way to the axes, picked them up, and began to cut at the remaining rope that held the ship to the dock. They finally cut the lines of the Valorian loose. Flying spears struck down the brave men, just as the ship began to pull away from the dock.

Lanzzie couldn't believe what she was seeing on the docks and on the beach. Men ran toward one another with axes in hand, dodging one another and fighting for their lives. The clinking of the swords, shields, and other weapons could be heard from every direction. One knight grabbed a sword from the scabbard of one of Zaros's men and killed the man with his own sword. Another fought valiantly, using three weapons at a time to fend off one oncoming Vorokian after another, until one of Zaros's men killed him from behind. By now, most of those on the side of Rhyceton and Old Vynterra were struggling desperately, and they began falling one by one.

As she looked around, brave male villagers picked up the weapons of the dead to help keep King Zaros's men from breaking through to the ships. The piercing screams of men felled by swords and axes could be heard alongside the panicked whinnying of injured horses. Innocent villagers struggled to flee from the battlefield, frantically screaming and running out of the way. She watched in horror as a few of them were senselessly killed when they had the misfortune to cross paths with one of the brutal Vorokians.

Lanzzie had never witnessed anything so gruesome in her entire life. The whole scene was horrifying, with countless knights slaughtered along the beach. She couldn't find King Izhar to determine whether or not he was still alive. It was becoming dreadfully clear that Zaros's army had won the battle and was about to invade the ship.

Zaros led his men past the defeated army toward the Valorian. When he reached the end of the dock, he held up his hand and halted his men after realizing that the ship had already been cut loose from the dock. He yelled something to his men—she couldn't make out his words—and they all turned and retreated north up the coast. They must have been pleased by the damage they had done, as few of Izhar's and Alazar's men were left standing.

She shielded her eyes from the sun and looked hastily for the prince. She spotted him up at the helm with several guards, working tirelessly to steer the ship out of port. The devastating agony from having lost so many men and possibly his own father, was evident on his face. With a knot in her stomach, Lanzzie returned her gaze to the beach.

She looked up the coast and spotted a single knight from Zaros's army riding quickly back down toward the ship. He was alone and appeared determined, racing with a vengeance in the ship's direction. As he got closer, she determined by his wavy braids and fur garments that he was one of the Vorokians. He was holding a large bow as he rode. Near the ship, he halted his horse and drew the bow. Her heart sunk as she realized exactly where he was aiming.

"Prince Alazar!" she yelled. With all the noise on the ship and knights running back and forth, the prince couldn't hear her. She turned to run toward Fin, who was closer to the prince, but a large crate blocked her way, with smaller crates next to it alongside two wooden barrels. She screamed louder to get the attention of the knights, or anyone that could hear her for that matter.

"Prince Alazar!"

She turned back toward the beach and watched with painstaking dread as the Vorokian released his arrow at its intended target.

"Prince Alazar!" she screamed at the top of her lungs.

She watched the arrow fly across the sky directly at the prince who was still unaware. The inevitable future of a decimated Old Vynterra and the destruction of her very own Cottages flashed before her eyes.

As Lanzzie helplessly tracked the velocity of the arrow, she saw another bright object dart across the sky from the opposite direction. It was another arrow and it was moving even faster than the Vorokian's.

To her amazement, the incoming arrow knocked the Vorokian's arrow right off its path with a deafening bang. The savage's arrow shattered before it hit the prince, and its remnants fell to the sea.

That got the prince's attention; he and the other knights on board rushed to the outer deck to see what had caused the loud explosion.

Lanzzie was bewildered, and she saw that the Vorokian was, too.

She searched the beach to see where it came from and saw an army of knights—mostly in black armor—rushing toward the docks from the south with a single knight leading the way. The prince and his men began to cheer with a frenzied excitement.

"Who are *they*?" said Fin, as he pushed one of the heavy crates out of the way and stood beside Lanzzie.

She squinted her eyes as the leader of the army drew an arrow mid-gallop, remaining upright on the majestic, black horse. A large group of black-armored knights followed closely behind.

Then she realized. This was no ordinary knight.

"It's Ezstasia!" yelled Fin. "What is she doing!?"

Lanzzie gasped and held her breath. The Vorokian kicked his horse into full gallop. He grabbed an arrow from his quiver and reloaded his bow while racing toward her sister. They headed straight toward one other, both of them with determined ferocity and without the slightest hint of fear.

"No!" shouted Lanzzie.

She watched helplessly as Ezstasia barreled forward on her horse from the opposite direction of the Vorokian, bow drawn. Before she knew it, Ezstasia had released her arrow with such lightning speed that she could barely see the flaming streak darting across the beach and straight into the Vorokian's chest. He instantly dropped from his horse. The man never even had a chance to fire his own arrow.

The ship erupted in bittersweet cheers and the crowds that had scurried to the trees from the beach came out from hiding. Lanzzie could barely breathe. Tears welled up in her eyes with the realization that her sister really was still alive.

"Ezstasia!" she shouted. But the ship had sailed so far from the port already that she knew her sister couldn't hear her.

Still on her horse, Ezstasia turned her head and looked directly at Lanzzie. She lifted her bow and waved it at the ship while she trotted on her majestic steed toward the injured knights and villagers strewn out across the docks and beach. Lanzzie knew that her sister was waving at her. With a flood of emotion, she smiled through her tears and waved back. She didn't know what bizarre twist of fate had brought her sister to lead the most powerful army in Old Vynterra, but she was glad it did.

Just then, the prince came up beside her, along with Meldon, Zander and Ithron.

She glanced sideways at the prince's melancholy expression as he stared out at the disappearing Vynterran coast. She thought of his father, King Izhar, and hoped that he had survived, though it was impossible to tell amongst the piles of bodies left scattered on the beach. The king fought gloriously in that overmatched battle. There was no question as to why he was known as Izhar the Great.

"Do you think he's alive?" she said. "Your father?"

"I don't know," said the prince solemnly.

She held her head down, not quite sure what to say.

"I'm sorry," she said.

He looked at her and smiled faintly. "Your sister is quite the inspiration," he said. "You all are. I would be dead right now if it wasn't for her. And our mission would have ended before it even began. That relentlessly determined girl from the Cottages saved us all."

"If there's one thing she is," said Ithron, "it's determined."

"And she sure is great with a bow," said Zander. "I think this beats her apple shot."

"Apple shot?" said the prince.

Lanzzie and the others laughed.

"I was actually going to eat that apple," said Meldon. "But nobody remembers that part of the story."

Lanzzie smiled and gazed back toward the shore. She watched as the people got smaller and smaller while the wind carried the Valorian and the other two ships into the great unknown. It wasn't lost on her that all of those people's lives could well depend upon the adventures that she would now be undertaking alongside the Prince of Vynterra and the greatest friends anyone could imagine. Now, more than ever, she wanted this mission to succeed. What she saw Ezstasia do had awakened an intense desire inside of her—a desire to fight for mankind. This journey *had* to succeed. She had a sister to get back to.

„€„€„€„€

Looking out among the hundreds of dead and injured, Ezstasia was filled with a potpourri of emotion. She was eternally grateful to be alive, and more than anything else, relieved that Lanzzie, her friends, and the prince were safe and sailing to the Magiclands. She was hopeful that their journey would bear fruit. She only wished she'd had a chance to explain to Lanzzie what had happened, and couldn't imagine the worry that she must have put her through. She was grateful to have had one last look at her, even if it had been from a distance. She couldn't help but worry about what horrors they might face on their voyage. The thought that she might never see any of them again was unbearable.

As people approached her to thank her for her courage, she realized that she didn't feel like much of a hero. There weren't any victors in this battle. Only survivors. It would be a rough road ahead.

She stepped carefully through the fallen knights and horses, looking for anyone still alive and in need of help. People began to come out from behind the trees to survey the damage. In the distance, she saw a familiar face in the crowd. Pallu was coming toward her, holding Ellie's hand. She ran toward him.

"Thank the stars you're alive!" she said. "Both of you."

"Thank the stars *you* are alive!" said Pallu. "You had everyone worried sick."

She hugged Pallu and was overcome with emotion. She was thankful to be reunited with him. She glanced around at the other people walking aimlessly in a daze.

"Where are Jez and Randin?" she said, concerned.

"Back by the trees," said Pallu. "You know Jez. She didn't think it was safe to come out here yet. But tell me about you! How did you do that!? And who were those men wearing furry things anyway?"

"It's a long story," she said. "They're Vorokians. I'll tell you more on the way back."

"Well whoever they were, one of them came right up to us holding a giant axe."

"How did you get away?"

"I used my speed, of course," said Pallu smirking. "With great precision, I reached into Ellie's bag and offered him a lemon cake."

"Our kingdom for a pastry," said Ellie, smiling.

Just then Ezstasia heard a groan coming from under a pile of men.

"I'm sorry," she said, "we have to try to help these people. Even if there's little we can do."

"Come, Pallu," said Ellie. "Let's try to help."

Ezstasia made her way to the injured knight and called others over to help him.

"Lady Arrow," said a voice from behind her. It was Sir Aldus. "I don't think I've seen anyone do what you did. That was truly remarkable. You're one of us, now."

"Thank you, Sir Aldus," she said, humbled that he'd think so. "I still have a lot to learn."

"Yes," he said, "you do. But if you're willing, we will offer you the best instructors in the kingdom. I'll see to that myself."

She smiled at the thought of it. Just then she heard another agonizing groan. She looked around to see where it was coming from.

"Over here," said Aldus.

She ran to see Aldus trying to lift a fallen white horse that had several bodies lying underneath it. She and some of the knights helped him drag the horse away and an arm slowly rose from underneath the bodies. Ezstasia and Sir Aldus removed the dead bodies and saw the injured man who lay underneath them.

It was King Izhar, covered in sand and blood.

"Sire!" said Sir Aldus.

"You're alive!" said Ezstasia.

Izhar coughed. "For the moment it seems," he said.

"I'll get help, Your Majesty," said Aldus.

Izhar held up a hand to stop him and shook his head.

"Tell me," said the king, weakly. "Did my son make it? Did the ships leave?"

"Yes, Your Highness," said Aldus. "Thanks to Lady Arrow."

King Izhar sighed with relief and grabbed Ezstasia's hand. "And Zaros?" he said.

"He took his army and left," said Ezstasia. "We don't know where he went."

"I know where he went," said the king, holding a large wound on his ribs. "He's gone to his ship." He coughed and then looked at her and Sir Aldus. "But he won't find it."

"I don't understand," said Aldus.

"I had my men burn that Valtan monstrosity to ashes last night. I knew he was planning to intercept our ships at sea. This mission was far too important to risk it. I just didn't count on him coming here with the bloody Vorokians."

He tried to sit up, so Ezstasia helped him.

"He's a formidable foe," said the king. "Pity. He could've been a powerful ally. Now, I fear you'll have your hands full keeping the peace."

"He'll declare war on us now," said Aldus.

"We were already at war," said the king. "From the moment we announced this journey, he was ready to attack. It's better to have a clear enemy than a duplicitous friend."

King Izhar groaned again and held his ribs. Ezstasia put her arm around the back of his neck for support.

"My son left this land as a prince," said Izhar. "And he'll return as a king." He grabbed Sir Aldus and pulled him closer. "Until then, you must form a resistance. Zaros will declare martial law as the dark magic spreads. Gather all of the villages. You *must* not give up. I know Zaros will not." The king paused to catch his breath. "Tell my son when he returns, that I believe in him and that I know he will be a great and powerful king."

Izhar turned his head toward Ezstasia. "Lady Arrow," he said. "I believe in you, too. You're more essential to us than even *you* know."

His head lay back against her palm.

"Long… live… King… Alazar," he muttered with a long, painful breath.

That breath would be his last. King Izhar the Great had passed to the great beyond.

Ezstasia watched as Sir Aldus was overcome with great emotion, tears rolling down the sides of his cheeks.

"He's gone," he said quietly to Ezstasia. "Eliezer is regent now. He'll need our help. I'll head to Old Vynterra and inform the others. We'll need help placing these bodies on the wagons to take for burial."

"I'll catch up," said Ezstasia as they both stood. "I need a moment," she said, as her lips quivered and her eyes welled up with tears.

Sir Aldus bowed his head and returned to his horse.

Ezstasia took one long look at the fallen king, the man that she had heard so much about, and yet had only just met.

It had only taken a short encounter with him, a man of such preeminence and strength, yet great humility, to make a lasting and powerful impact on her. As she took a deep breath, his last words to her, 'I believe in you,' filled her heart with strength. It infused her with a renewed commitment to help sustain the kingdom until the new king returns.

She walked toward the shore, stepping over the masses of fallen bodies as villagers and knights alike wandered around tending to the injured.

She stepped onto the wet sand and felt the water wash over her feet. Just then she heard footsteps in the sand walking toward her. She turned to see little Aurelia, the girl she'd carried on her rabbit from the town of Rhyceton. Her auntie and sister stood a ways back.

"You didn't tell me you were Lady Arrow," said Aurelia.

Ezstasia smiled and picked her up.

"You're right," she said. "That wasn't fair, was it? You told me your nickname was Pickles, and I should've told you mine was Lady Arrow."

"It's okay," said the adorable girl. "I do feel a little scared though." She looked toward the war-ravaged beach with wide eyes. "Do you have any stories you can tell me?"

Ezstasia held her tightly and redirected the girl's attention seaward, pointing out to the horizon.

"Do you see those ships way out there?" she said. "On those ships are the bravest warriors I've ever known. One of them is my sister. And another is our future king. One day, they'll return. And their stories will be the greatest stories of all."

ABOUT THE AUTHOR

As a celebrity hair stylist who has worked on many films and major motion pictures, V.F. Sharp is no stranger to entertainment. But in recent years, she's decided to follow her passion for the storytelling side of the business, a passion  she's had since she was a young girl telling ghost stories to her family and friends.

The Forest of Arrows: The Prince of Old Vynterra is her debut novel and is the first in the Forest of Arrows trilogy. The concept for the entire trilogy came to her in a dream, and she hopes to inspire readers of all ages through this mystical tale of epic fantasy, infused with a touch of wonder, horror and suspense.

To stay up to date on Ms. Sharp's work or to be the first to know when the next book in the trilogy is released, please visit her website at www.vfsharp.com, where you can sign up to receive email updates, as well as read other news about her writing and appearances.

CPSIA information can be obtained
at www.ICGtesting.com
Printed in the USA
LVHW011224130520
655436LV00003B/30